THE CRYSTAL PAWN

THE KEYRALITHIAN CHRONICLES

BOOK ONE

DEBORAH JARVIS

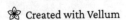 Created with Vellum

This book has taken a long time to come to fruition and would have been impossible without the dedicated work of so many people including my husband Robert Nolan, daughter Rosalynde Jarvis, and son William Jarvis for their patience and support. A huge round of thanks goes to my friends Jennifer Goodwin, Cathie McWhinnie, and Kevin Gavel for the amazing themed dinner/editing parties. Yes, I know that cashews and crescent rolls are comma shaped. You'll notice I've gotten much better over the years, which is good, as I now teach kids how to use them!

A thank you also goes out to Serenity Colley for designing the original cover art for the first year of release. The new cover art has been created by Kayla Drakehart, another former student who is now a graphic artist. Both ladies deserve a round of applause for their amazing work.

Finally, a very special thanks goes to Sophia Kelly Shultz for helping me beat this book into shape (sometimes with a sledgehammer!) and find the errant misplaced modifiers that escaped my notice. Curse those waving balconies, Sophia!

INTRODUCTION

A long time ago, I read a book titled *The Last Unicorn* by Peter S. Beagle, and from that time until the present day, I have been a huge fan of the genre of fantasy novels and movies. I grew up in the 1980s, a time when some of the best books and films in the genre were made, and my experiences as a teenager were formed by what I read and saw.

For as long as I can remember, I have been writing stories, and this book is one of the best efforts of all of the adventures and dreams I have worked on over the years. It has been a labor of love (and anxiety) that brings it to this format.

Why publish it myself? Well, first of all, I am a teacher, and as such, have to carefully allocate what time I have. The search for an agent who might be willing to take a chance on an unknown writer has thus far been fruitless, and I have come to believe that more people may get a chance to see this story by publishing it myself. This has been a hard decision, but one that I firmly believe to be true.

Secondly, the self-publishing market has been a growing business for a while now, and I feel that it is the best place to be seen and possibly discovered by readers looking for something new.

Third, I really want people to read this book and enjoy it. This way will ensure that my words reach an audience and maybe in that way, I can influence those minds the way that Peter S. Beagle once influenced me. It is not a vain hope. It is the best chance for this book to do what it was intended to do - educate, illuminate, and entertain.

After all, what is literature for if not to provide escape from the real world between the covers of a novel, even if only for a little while.

---Deborah Jarvis

September 8, 2020.

1

"Who ever thought that it would come to this?" asked Count Nerfal Ettar, shaking his graying head in wonder as he guided his horse down the long-neglected garden path. He could remember a time when roses rambled over the now-dilapidated archways, the air filled with their cloying fragrance, and crimson phlox had edged the walkways like the sun's last light. All gone now; all dead. He shook off the memories, focusing ahead on their goal. "Who would have thought that my foolish youthful dalliances would one day prove to be our salvation and not the fanciful blunderings my father once thought them to be?"

The white wolf trotting beside the stallion glanced up at him and gave a barking laugh.

"Would that your father were here to hear your admittance of their foolishness!" she said, her voice like a bronze bell with rumbled undertones.

The lightness of her words did not conceal the sadness that underlay them, and Nerfal glanced down at his companion with growing concern. The stresses of the last few months were showing on the old wolf, and Lady Nersh, who had always appeared ageless, now looked like the elder she was. Her soft white coat appeared scruffy, and he noted that she shuffled her feet a little as she trotted along. Nerfal frowned slightly. Six months earlier, she would have been bounding beside his horse, leaping at butterflies and laughing at the way he groaned when he dismounted. Darlena's brutal death had affected all of the members of his house to varying degrees. Lady Nersh had been hit in a way that sapped the vitality from her carriage, and Nerfal did not know if it would ever come back.

The path that they were on wound through an overgrown part of Nerfal's vast estate that had been, in his youth, a part of the cultivated gardens. His father had given the order to let it grow wild after finding that Nerfal was using the ancient portal, thought to be safely closed, to visit his sweetheart on another plane. Knowing the instability of such portals and fearing that he might lose his eldest son, the old count had forbidden Nerfal to go near it again, reinforcing his order by using magic to lock the gate.

Nerfal had been furious with his father but had agreed, in the end, that perhaps it was just too dangerous to be traipsing back and forth between worlds. After a long enough time, he had managed to almost forget about the gate and hadn't thought about it in years. That was, of course, until last week. Last week, he had despaired that there was no one of the Ettar blood to safeguard against the gathering armies to the west. Then, with no warning, a stranger had appeared on his doorstep with news of a hitherto unknown daughter and, overnight, everything had changed.

The revelation had hit him hard, throwing off all of his normal reserves about non-Kin showing up at his home unannounced. The very thought that he had a daughter by his long-lost-love had distracted his mind from dwelling on the mysterious stranger, and it wasn't until after his perplexing guest was hours gone that he had thought to wonder exactly who his visitor might have been. The man, if he had indeed been a man, with his unreadable blue eyes and unusual spiral mark in the center of his forehead, had managed to make it all the way to the Keep without alerting any of the Talking Folk that patrolled the forests. Nerfal had made inquiries, but no sign of his arrival or departure could be found.

He sighed. There were no easy answers to any of his questions as of late. The death of his daughter Darlena had made him feel as if his whole life was unraveling around him, and he realized how much of his world had involved his child. The stranger had slipped past all of his defenses and had arrived without any warning at all, and it had taken Nerfal almost an entire day to realize that there was something odd about this.

Lady Nersh glanced up at him, noting the frown that played across his features.

"Is he bothering you again, our enigmatic visitor?"

"Yes," said Nerfal, patting the damp neck of his stallion. "Who could he have been? The only answer that I can come up with is too preposterous to consider."

"And that is?" she prompted.

Nerfal shook his head, not even wanting to give voice to his supposition.

They turned a corner, and an ornate gate loomed before them, a huge wrought iron monstrosity that arched over their heads in ivy-wrapped splendor. The gate led into a thick tangle of woods and heavy underbrush that showed no evidence of ever having been tamed. Nerfal halted his horse and dismounted stiffly. Lady Nersh stood panting, looking first at the gate, then at Nerfal.

"This is it?"

"This is it," he confirmed.

His attention was drawn to the dirt in front of the gate. The soft earth bore the impression of hoof prints that could only be a day or two old, made since the last rainfall. There were two sets, one entering the gate, one returning. Both were cloven with a distinctive heel print the likes of which belonged to only one creature of their realm.

Lady Nersh looked at Nerfal, her countenance unreadable.

"I take it that this answers my previous question," she said.

Nerfal didn't answer her. Instead, he stepped carefully over the footprints and placed his hand on the top of the gate. He felt the tingle that he associated with magic, and his eyes widened. Whoever had opened this gate had not *undone* the locking spell his father had placed on it many years ago, he had *broken* it, and with enough power to leave an unsubtle trace of very powerful magics behind.

"No more doubts," said Lady Nersh, suddenly looking up at him. Her eyes were more alive than they had been in days. "Whatever there is about this girl, Nerfal, she has something that warrants some very special attention."

Nerfal nodded and gave the gate a gentle push, speaking the keying phrase that triggered the portal. It swung open on hinges that showed no evidence of the many years of neglect, and Nerfal led his horse through with Lady Nersh at his side.

The only sign that anything was happening was an instant of complete sensory loss. One brief second of no light, no heat, no sense of touch at all, and they were through to find themselves on a pine needle-carpeted path that wound its way through the woods and along the edge of a sparkling lake. The spicy smell of the pines washed over them in a wave of heat and resin. Lady Nersh shook herself, the silver chain of office that she wore about her neck chiming softly, and the stallion whickered, pulling against the reins. All else was still, save for the water lapping against the shore, and the occasional bird call in the distance.

Nerfal felt a rush of nostalgia and excitement as he looked on a scene he had never thought to see again. There were so many memories that he had tried to repress, and they were all coming back to him now as he stood on the path. He turned and looked at the gate. On this side, it looked like a section of dilapidated picket fence, complete with peeling white paint and weathered gray boards. It was set off the side of the main track between two sections of an old stone wall that Nerfal had noted crisscrossed the woods at regular intervals. No one would be tempted to try to open the rickety-looking gate that appeared to be rotting where it stood, and perhaps that was how the portal protected itself.

"Now what?" asked Lady Nersh.

Nerfal nodded at the leaf-strewn path.

"That way a short distance," he said. "That is where the cottage is."

Lady Nersh moved to join him as he led the stallion down the trail.

"Just what kind of reception do you expect we will receive?" she said.

"Well..." Nerfal began.

He fell silent. The hoof prints by the gate told him that there was a good chance that someone knew that they were coming and that they would be expected, if not welcomed. He shook his head, recalling the words of his mysterious visitor.

"Nerfal Ettar, Lord of the Mountain Reaches, Shaper, and chosen of Rathal to rule the Talking Folk still in these lands, hear me. All is not lost to thee. On another world, whose doorway thou dost know, lives a daughter of thy blood with all of the required magicks and more. Go to her. Ask for her help. The way will be prepared."

Nerfal broke out of his reverie to find Lady Nersh still looking at him askance. Taking a deep breath, he summoned up a smile and ruffled the fur atop the wolf's head.

"I think that we will be well-received," he said with more confidence than he felt.

Lady Nersh nodded more to herself than in acknowledgement of Nerfal's answer, and together they walked on in silence, accompanied by the gentle rhythm of the waves hitting the sandy shore. The wolf's paws made little noise upon the leaf-litter, and both of the companions kept to their thoughts as they walked along.

The morning air was warm but bore a slight spicing of ginger and lemon, the scent of fresh fallen leaves. The path they followed was carpeted with red and gold, and the light that filtered down through the trees was tinged with crimson. The final vestiges of insect life still buzzed in the air, and the last fluttering flights of butterflies made their dancing way through the woods, heading south in their attempt to outrun the first frost. Dragonflies and damselflies hovered in the air like tiny bright jewels and reflected sunlight in flashes of ruby, amber, and sapphire.

Nerfal and Lady Nersh both walked on, lost in their own thoughts. Nerfal wondered if his newly-discovered daughter would even believe half of what he had to tell her, and if she did, well, what real reason would she have for going anywhere with a tall, strange, middle-aged man whose existence was probably just as new to her and made even more alien by an inborn ability to change shape? Never mind the fact, he mused as he ran his hand through his curly mop of hair, that he bore proof of his abilities in the form of two tiny goat horns that made him resemble a satyr more than anything else. An old satyr, he amended after a moment as he caught sight of the proliferation of grey hairs amid the shrinking tangle of black.

The path suddenly curved to the right, and there, across a clearing, stood a small wooden house. Nerfal stopped to study it. It had always seemed curiously built, with half of its lower level below ground and its upper level accessible via a flight of stairs to a wooden platform raised-up on posts. He had seen the house years before, and at that time, there had only been a stair leading to the door. He wondered at the change.

"We are expected, I think," said Lady Nersh, softly.

Nerfal looked at the platform to see a man sitting in a reclining wooden chair with a book in one hand and a glass of bright yellow liquid in the other. He appeared to be in his late sixties with well-recessed silver hair and a lean build, clothed in a red plaid shirt and indigo pants. A pair of double-glassed spectacles perched precariously on his thin beak of a nose, and Nerfal thought that he looked for all the world like a serious little twig owl contemplating a snack.

The stallion, impatient to get to the cool shallows for his drink, neighed, shattering the peace that had surrounded them. The noise caused Nerfal to start and Lady Nersh's hackles to rise. The wolf automatically dropped into a crouch, but when she realized the source of the sudden noise, she stood up straight and licked her lips in embarrassment.

The man on the porch had put his book and glass down on a small table and was studying the newcomers. His posture was relaxed, but Nerfal noticed the wary glint in his eyes as he peered at them from behind his glasses. The man stood, waiting for Nerfal to make the next move.

Dropping the reins of the stallion, Nerfal walked towards the house; out of the corner of his eye, he saw Nersh leading the horse towards the water and was grateful for the wolf's thoughtfulness. Reaching the foot of the stairs, Nerfal stopped and raised his hand in greeting.

"I am Count Nerfal Ettar, Lord of the Mountain Reaches," he began, and stopped, unsure of how to go on. Then, as the bright blue eyes watching him narrowed a bit, he added, "I loved your daughter in my youth. I never knew that there was a child. My own father saw to that."

The man moved to the top of the stairs in two swift strides that belied his age, and his owl-like features spread into a slight smile.

"Randolph Hawes," he said, his voice a strong middle bass. "Yes, I know a little of what happened."

He reached out his hand, and Nerfal stepped up onto the porch to grasp it. Randolph's grip was strong and firm, and Nerfal could tell that the man was taking a measure of him through his handshake.

"Sit, please," said Randolph, gesturing to another chair near the small table. Nerfal seated himself. "Yes, I had a visitor a couple of days ago. Deirdre was here when he arrived and also heard the story. Neither of us blames you for your absence. You didn't know. I only wish that Julia had known the reason why you never came back to her."

"Where are Julia and Deirdre?" asked Nerfal, sitting on the edge of his chair, surprised at the surge of excitement that ran electrically through him at the thought of meeting his old lover and their daughter.

"Deirdre drove into town to get some supplies we needed," said Randolph, "She didn't want to go, but I knew that she would pace a hole in the floor if I didn't find her something to do."

"And Julia?"

"Julia...died. She contracted pneumonia the winter that Dee turned four," Randolph reached up and settled his glasses more firmly on his nose. "I'm sorry to have to tell you this. It still affects me pretty hard too. Not an easy burden to carry, and not easy on Deirdre to have only an old man to raise her all these years."

"What of your wife?" asked Nerfal, recalling the stiff woman that Julia had pointed out to him once from a distance.

"Sarah would not admit that any child of hers could conceive and bear a child out of wedlock. When I told Julia that she was more than welcome to stay and have her baby here, Sarah packed her bags and moved back to live with her family in Georgia. I received the divorce papers in the mail."

Randolph trailed off and reached for his drink. Lady Nersh returned with the stallion and walked up the stairs, dropping the reins over a post on her way up. She reached the top and sat down next to Nerfal.

"This is the Lady Nersh," said Nerfal. "She is one of the ambassadors from the Talking Folk, and one of my oldest friends and advisors. Lady, this is Randolph Hawes, Julia's father."

Lady Nersh bowed her head to Randolph and spoke in her low bell-like voice.

"I am very glad to meet you," she said and grinned to see his eyes widen as she spoke.

"I met your daughter once," she continued. "Count Nerfal wanted me to see what Otherworlders looked like. I told him later that she looked funny with no horns. I was a pup then and had never been outside the Reaches. Most of the members of the Ettar clan have small horns to mark their association with the land and their agreement with Rathal."

"Who is Rathal?" asked Randolph.

"He is the Unicorn King, the immortal half of the Double Kings," said Nerfal. "He once ruled side by side with the tsavon, Tali, the mortal side of the partnership. Rathal ruled over the magical beasts and peoples, while Tali ruled over the Talking Folk. When humans came to Keyralithsmus, our last stronghold, Tali sacrificed himself for his peoples, and Rathal left, appointing my ancestors as caretakers of both the magical beasts and the Talking Folk. Most of the magical creatures have gone south to several valleys below our borders, but the Talking Folk have stayed, and they remain mostly autonomous. Many of them feel that someday Tali and Rathal will return to reclaim their realm."

"They may not have long to wait," said Lady Nersh, looking at Nerfal in a knowing way.

Nerfal nodded, glancing up at Randolph.

"Your visitor the other day was either Rathal or one of his messengers. Due to the arrogance he displayed to me when he showed up at my doorstep yesterday..."

"Yes, I got a dose of that attitude myself," chuckled Randolph. "You believe that it is the king himself, correct? What does it mean?"

A crunching sound of stone grating on stone caught their attention, and a strange contraption Nerfal had seen once or twice on previous visits rolled into view, rumbling down the gravel driveway. Lady Nersh pricked up her ears and peered at the vehicle with undisguised curiosity. The horse shied and laid its ears back at the sound.

"It's a car," said Randolph. "A horseless carriage, it used to be called."

"What happened to your horses that you had to invent a machine to do their work?" asked Nersh.

"Well, nothing," admitted Randolph as they watched the car roll to a stop. "People just invented something stronger and faster. Of course, they break down and pollute the environment, but in many ways, they are a good invention."

"What of the horses?" asked Lady Nersh, looking at Randolph wide-eyed.

"People still ride them, but it is more for pleasure than necessity," said Randolph. He turned to Nerfal. "I don't mean to alarm you, but Deirdre can't ride."

"What do you mean?" asked Nerfal, turning to look at Randolph. "She does not ride horses?"

Randolph shook his head.

"It came down to a choice between riding or art lessons. She chose art, like her mother."

Nerfal groaned softly and turned his attention back to the vehicle as the door of the car opened. A young woman got out, holding bags in both hands, and raised a sandaled foot to kick the car door solidly shut. She walked towards the house, and when she got to the foot of the stairs, she paused and looked up.

For Nerfal, it was like seeing Julia again for the first time. With the exception of her darker hair, Deirdre was the spitting image of her mother. It was as if he had gone back in time twenty-odd years and found himself faced with Julia the last time he had seen her.

Deirdre's hair was a glory, spilling in tumbled chocolate waves to about halfway down her back. Her eyes were a soft blue with tiny smile wrinkles already present at the corners. She was fairly slim, and about her shone a strength of soul that he had not anticipated finding. He watched as she gathered herself and slowly walked up the stairs to meet them. He rose from his chair and bowed to her.

She looked at him for a moment and set the bags down next to the table.

"You must be Nerfal," she said softly.

"I am Count Nerfal Ettar, Lord of the Mountain Reaches. You may call me Nerfal if you like."

"But not Father?" she asked with a raised eyebrow and a small quirk to the corner of her mouth. "No. I can see that neither of us is ready for that just yet. "

She offered him her hand, and he took it, bemused to find that her handshake was as firm as her grandfather's.

"I am glad to meet you, I think," she said. "Let's just say it all comes as a bit of a shock to see you."

"It has been a surprise for us all," said Nerfal. "May I also introduce you to Lady Nersh of the Talking Folk."

Deirdre turned to where the wolf stood, and Lady Nersh bowed her head, saying, "I am most honored to meet you, Deirdre."

Deirdre's mouth fell open for a long moment before she was able to close it again and she stared at the wolf.

"You can speak?" she asked incredulously.

"Yes," said Lady Nersh, grinning broadly and showing a great number of teeth. "We of the Talking Folk clans have had that ability for a very long time."

Randolph chose that moment to clear his throat, and Deirdre glanced over at him.

"Please put the groceries away and bring out the pitcher of lemonade from the fridge. I need a refill, and I am sure that you and Nerfal are both going to need a drink before you are through."

Deirdre nodded and collected the bags again.

"Be right back," she said.

They watched as she slipped inside the house. When the door had closed behind her, Randolph turned to Nerfal, his gaze sharp.

"Tell me the real reason that you are here. Why would a unicorn king find it necessary to involve himself in a country that had run itself for…"

"Three hundred years," supplied Nersh.

"Three hundred years," continued Randolph. "Why now? Is it normal for this sort of…divine intervention…to take place like this?"

Nerfal sighed.

"When my daughter Darlena was murdered, she was preparing for an ordeal that might possibly have saved all of the land of Keyralithsmus, including our home in the Mountain Reaches. Rathal originally chose my family because somewhere back in its lineage, one of our family members had relations with a dragon while it was in human form. Our blood carries the potential to shapeshift into a dragon, but it can only be realized in our women.

"Darlena was in training because our old enemy to the west is on the move, expanding its holdings and trying to reach the coast so as to have access to the sea and shipping. It is our fear that they would wipe out the magic beasts and the Talking Folk completely. Rumor has it that magic is frowned upon as being unnatural and that talking beasts like Lady Nersh are really demons. All the usual nonsense held to by those who do not understand."

"Why is it important to shapeshift into a dragon?" asked Randolph, finishing his lemonade, and swirling the ice cubes in his glass thoughtfully. "One dragon can't stop an army, can it?"

"No, but one dragon can call the other dragons to help. When the humans moved into Keyralithsmus, the dragons, the centaurs, and a few other magical creatures moved south. The unicorns left the continent altogether. In Rathal's case, he had lost his queen, and had no interest in staying to rule what was to him a place of ghosts and haunted memories."

"So that's all that really has to be done, right? Become a dragon and call them to fight at the right time?" Randolph set his glass down with a thunk. The ice clinked. "That doesn't seem to be a very big ordeal."

Nerfal noted the other man's sarcasm and smiled ruefully.

"There is that challenge, compounded by the fact that no one remembers how it is done. The last few tries met with failure. Books hint at magic mountains and miracle valleys, but we have no clear idea as to where they are or how this was accomplished."

"You are forgetting something else," said Nersh. "Darlena was murdered in the Carathusin Castle, right on the grounds, by a minotaur, of all things. Someone with very good connections does not want us to succeed."

"Makes it kind of hard to do what you are asking of me, doesn't it?" asked Deirdre, coming up to stand behind her grandfather with a pitcher in one hand and two glasses in the other. "Fill me in please."

As Deirdre poured the lemonade, Nerfal recounted everything he and Randolph had discussed up to her arrival and the first part of their more recent conversation. For most of it, she sat listening, but once, after Nersh spoke, she jumped up and ran into the house, returning seconds later with a bowl into which she poured a small amount of lemonade. Nersh tried it, found it to her liking, and greedily drank a full bowl when Deirdre poured it for her.

When they were finished, Deirdre looked thoughtfully at Nerfal.

"Why a minotaur?" she asked. "Why not a human assassin?"

"Minotaurs have long been viewed as the most savage of the woodland races. Much worse than trolls or goblins. Minotaurs may not be the smartest creatures, but they are cunning and have no fear. Using a minotaur is a good way to strike terror into someone's heart."

Nerfal paused, not sure what else he should say.

"No one will place themselves between a minotaur and its intended victim," added Lady Nersh, "To do so is death for a man and worse for a woman. It was ordered only to murder Darlena. We got that much from it before it killed itself. Minotaurs have strict codes of honor that does not allow a captured one to live, except at Coliseum where they are compelled by magic not to kill themselves. Better to get slaughtered by the young lords who go to fight them."

Nerfal nodded. "What she says is true. Even still, I must ask you, even knowing the danger, will you help us?"

Deirdre sighed, exchanging glances with Randolph before responding.

"Seems like a lot to give a country I've never seen for a father I've never known," she said. "You are asking me to risk death for you. I can't ride, I have no real belief in magic, so no matter how much you tell me that it runs in my blood, I am going to have problems with it." She laughed, "I don't even have horns! Will the others in your country believe that I am your daughter without some sort of proof?"

Her last words were tinged with a touch of hysteria, and Randolph stood up.

"I am going to start supper," he said. "Nerfal, how soon do you need an answer?"

"By tomorrow morning," said Nerfal

Randolph nodded and turned to go into the house. Upon reaching the door, he paused and looked back.

"I was wondering, Lady Nersh, if you would assist me in the

kitchen. I don't know what you prefer to eat, and rather than insult you by offering the wrong thing, I thought that you might add your input so you could tell me what would be appropriate."

Nersh laughed and rose to her feet.

"Such a courteous speech from one who just this day met his first talking beast," she exclaimed, still laughing. "Of course! I accept your invitation *most* gratefully!"

She trotted over to the door,. and as she went inside, Nerfal heard her say,

"Such a change! You would not believe what most humans try to feed me!"

The screen door bumped closed behind them, and Nerfal turned back to Deirdre who was standing at the edge of the porch, staring out at the water. They remained in an awkward silence for a moment, listening to the wind coming off the lake rustle the red and yellow leaves and watching the water sparkle in the afternoon sun. Finally, Deirdre turned back to Nerfal.

"What is to prevent what happened to Darlena from happening to me?" she asked.

"Truthfully, there is nothing to prevent it. We can try to be prepared for the possibility. We can train you as quickly as possible to be ready to call the dragons and keep a guard on you, but honestly, if the rulers of Perstalia or this hidden spy really want you, only a great deal of luck and training will stop them. That is why speed is so important."

"What do you have in mind?" she asked.

"What I want to do is take you back with me and spend a couple of weeks getting you ready to go to the capital. Queen Brena has been apprised of the situation and has granted us a little time so that you can learn some of the etiquette and skills of our country. Only the Queen; the Captain of the Royal Guard, Marshall Rialain; and Lord Tomille, the Royal Magician will know of your origins. The members of my immediate household will be told as well. Others will simply be told that you are the daughter of an old love of mine with whom I dallied in my youth."

"Your bastard daughter, you mean," said Deirdre, a tinge of anger in her voice. "Won't that make them look down on me?"

"Some may not be overly happy about it, but once the Queen accepts you and makes it clear that you are welcome, others will do so as well. My family is already excited that you are coming. My wife, Elaina, has been readying things for you ever since our visitor told us of your existence. I am glad to see her doing it. The loss of Darlena struck her very hard, and you have given her something else to think about. We have no other children. After Darlena, Elaina could not have any more, and I think that she is looking forward to having someone to teach and nurture."

"I would have thought that she would resent me," said Deirdre. "All things considered."

"No," said Nerfal. "No, Elaina has not a single cruel bone in her body. She looks after my cousin's children so often that she has become a second mother to them. Children and animals love her."

"Yes, but I am not a child anymore."

"No," agreed Nerfal, "you are not."

Silence fell on them again, and not long after, Nersh came out to call them in for dinner.

———

Deirdre sat at the water's edge, looking out at the setting sun as it reflected red on the lake. A light breeze blew the water in ripples across the surface and the leaves of the maples on the far shore looked as if they were on fire.

A strange feeling of peace had stolen over her after she had come out to the shore, and she had given up any pretense of thinking about her dilemma. Instead, she simply let the beauty of the autumn sunset wash over her.

To her left, in the shallow marshy section of the lake, a great blue heron spread its wings and pranced two graceful, gangly steps before swinging powerfully skyward. Deirdre followed its slow flight over the lake and watched until it vanished beyond the fiery maple trees, swallowed by the sun.

The breeze blew stronger, lifting the hair from her forehead, sending a chill down her back. Even within her warm leather jacket, she could feel the bite of the winter to come. She shivered and let the sun bronze her cheeks as she raised her face to the sky.

"It is not an easy choice you have been presented with," came a low, resonant voice.

Somehow not surprised to find the wolf suddenly sitting next to her, Deirdre nodded.

"Tell me something," said Nersh. "How is it that you can hear us talk of dragons and minotaurs and not be incredulous? I thought that there were no magical beasts on this world."

Deirdre laughed and turned to look at the wolf.

"Confused you, haven't I?" she said. She shook her head and looked back out over the lake. "Thus bears the fruits of a classical education! Randolph read fairy tales to me all the time when I was young. When I was ten, we graduated to Bullfinch's Mythology, and then it was only natural that I should read C. S. Lewis and Tolkien. I have been immersed in classical myth and modern folklore for as long as I can remember. In college, I played a game called Dungeons and Dragons, where you get to pretend that you are in a medieval realm, fighting ogres, trolls, dragons, and just about anything else you can imagine. After a while, talking about them seems normal."

She sighed and looked back at the wolf.

"Somehow, it really doesn't prepare me for this, though. Not when the risk is real and my life could be in danger. Still, going to another world is somewhat appealing. I never really felt that I fit in this world. There's not a lot here for me to miss, really. Just Randolph."

The wolf looked into Deirdre's eyes, sharp yellow meeting deep, muted blue.

"There has been much sorrow in our country of late. Two years ago, a group of raiders from Perstalia crossed our borders, skirting around the Bearuegna Mountains that borders us to the west and coming down through the Northern Passage. They killed the old King and Queen, then disappeared back into the mountains, leaving the two adult children to rule. The raiders had with them a scouting pack of minotaurs and snowbulls, great huge cousins of the minotaurs with shaggy white fur and blood red eyes. The new Queen's brother, Prince Benjamin, led the royal forces out to find them and, with Captain Marshall Rialain's help, had them on the retreat. During the last push, a minotaur burst through and ran the prince through with a sword. Marshall, who was Benjamin's best and closest companion for more years than I care remember, rushed to aid him. By the time he arrived, both the monster and Benjamin had disappeared. The prince's body was found the next day, mutilated and hanging from a tree by his feet. His throat had been slashed open, and the snow beneath was red with his blood."

The wolf closed her eyes and continued.

"Six months ago, an advance party from Perstalia came through the same passage and slaughtered the guards posted there. We fought them back again, and they retreated. Then, two months ago, Darlena was walking alone in the gardens of the Carathusin Castle when she was attacked. Again, a minotaur was involved. She was dead within minutes, the minotaur within hours. We have no idea how it got into the castle. It must have had help from within.

"We are out of options," said Nersh, turning back to Deirdre. "The advance group that came through the Northern Passage was not many but was so ferocious that it dealt the garrison a huge blow. We have only about two thousand troops available, and our intelligence has it that the main body of their army is much larger than that. We have two choices: either abandon the land or ask for your help. If the dragons can be called to our aid, we have a good chance of beating them back. No one alive can face a dragon in full flame and fury."

"There really is no choice then, is there?" said Deirdre, skipping a stone out across the surface of the water. It bounced four times and sank from view into the dark lake.

"There is always a choice," said Nersh gently. "You should know that Nerfal is a good man and, had he known of your existence, he would have come to you long before now. He loved your mother very much, and it pained him greatly to have to part from her without even a goodbye."

Deirdre stared out at the lake, taking in the dark blue-black clouds that lay scattered across the sky, each tinged with a hint of scarlet, and listened to the last sad crickets of the year. The trees along the far shore were black now, crepe paper silhouettes that stood out starkly against a backdrop of sky and cloud. Beyond, the first evening stars glimmered, shining bravely and growing brighter as the bowl of the sky dimmed, and the theater of night began.

An owl cried from a tree behind the cabin, and a flight of bats shimmered overhead as Deirdre slowly rose to her feet.

"I'll sleep on it," she said, shoving her hands into the pockets of her jacket, the leather creaking in protest as she moved.

They started back up the trail to the house.

"Where is Nerfal, anyway?" she asked the wolf.

"Oh, your grandfather was showing him that box contraption with the glass front, the one that shows pictures."

"Oh, no," groaned Deirdre. "Poor Nerfal!"

"Why? It looked fascinating," said Nersh.

"Yeah, that's the problem."

2

Nerfal woke the next morning just before dawn and lay on the unfamiliar bed, staring out the window at the brightening world for a while, marveling at a land that could produce such flawless glass for windows. Even the best craftsmen in the kingdom still made glass with at least the occasional wrinkle or course of bubbles through it. These simple windows, which Randolph had assured him were so ubiquitous in this world, would be highly prized in Keyralithsmus.

He finally made himself get up when it became clear that he was not going to get back to sleep. Picking up his tunic and jerkin from where he had left them on an overstuffed chair, he slid them on. After grabbing his stiff riding boots from where they stood by the door, he walked downstairs, his unshod feet making little sound on the carpeted steps.

The downstairs was still dim, but the small light in the hallway shed just enough illumination that he was able to avoid bumping into any of the shadowy furnishings. He swiftly crossed the kitchen, paused to pull on his boots, and opened the door, stepping out into the cool air of the fall morning.

The deck was still mostly in shadow, and a fine layer of dew coated the table and chairs with tiny beads of moisture. Nerfal breathed in a deep draught of the chill air and walked over to the edge of the deck. Glancing down, he saw his blanketed horse moving restlessly about at the end of his short tether. Nerfal felt a flash of guilt at having to tie the stallion so close all night, but there had been no other solution.

He stood another moment in quiet contemplation of the morning and then moved, descending the steps now slippery with a fine film of dew. He untied the horse and led it down to the lake for a drink. The animal pranced and frisked on the sandy path, glad for the freedom of motion, and it tossed its head, causing Nerfal to shorten his grip on the rope. Reaching the shore, he let out the rope again, and the stallion lowered its head to drink greedily from the clear, dark water.

The sun was just beginning to come up from behind the low hills, its pace reminding Nerfal of his own sluggish rising. Tall trees across the lake were in silhouette with pinions of light lancing through them as the sun struggled to gain the sky. Brilliant rays suddenly brushed across the water, setting the surface afire, and Nerfal had to squint in the reflected brightness. Light danced like burnished copper on the ripples that chased their way across the lake, stirred into life by the slight but steady breeze that had begun to blow low across the water.

Crouching down, Nerfal glanced into the lake, trying to catch sight of his reflection in the dim, tea-colored liquid. His aquiline features jumped out at him as always: arching eyebrows, clear brown eyes, and a hooked nose that was neither too big or too small for his rounded visage. He thought it was an open and honest face, and he wondered if Deirdre felt the same.

The sounds of a resident flock of geese echoed across the still lake, and Nerfal rose in time to see them climb into the air on sleep-fettered wings. The sunlight blazed beneath them, bronzing their wings and turning their white bellies a salmon pink. They flew out across the lake and disappeared beyond the trees. The horse raised his head to follow their flight and whickered softly before returning to its drink. The scene was peaceful, and it seemed strange to Nerfal that at such a critical time, a place of such tranquility could still exist.

He was so caught up in the beauty and the stillness that he didn't catch the slight scuff of leaves on the path behind him. It wasn't until he sensed another presence at his elbow that he turned and, still lulled by the quiet, accepted Deirdre's sudden appearance by his side. He turned to face her, noticing the circles under her eyes and the vague puffiness surrounding them. She had been crying, and her face was pale and splotchy from lack of sleep.

The horse snorted, done now with its drink, and pulled toward the patches of tall grass along the shore. Nerfal let out the lead rope, and the animal began munching with a solid determination.

"I...had no sleep last night, as you can see," she said, looking him in the eye, "and spent a long time staring at the ceiling, my thoughts going around and round and getting nowhere."

She sighed and turned to look out over the lake. Nerfal watched as the sun caught the highlights in her hair and turned them crimson. Her eyes grew moist as she looked at the water, and Nerfal felt the enormity of what he was asking her to do. To leave her home, to walk alone among strangers, to try to complete a daunting task that if successful, would repel a large invading army. To risk her life in doing so for people she had never met.

"I'll go," she said at last, "but if I do, I want your word that I will be able to come back when I want. If I decide tomorrow that I want to come home, you will bring me. Not that I will, but I want to know that the way home is open to me."

"I will promise you that, but with a condition of my own. I want your word that you will not insist on coming home at the first hint of trouble. That you will stay for as long as possible before asking that of me."

"Agreed," said Deirdre. "That's fair."

"Then it is settled. I will bring you back when you wish, if you are having trouble coping, and you will try your best before asking me," said Nerfal. "How long before you are ready to go?"

"Well," said Deirdre, gathering herself and blinking back her tears, "what do I need to pack?"

"A few changes of clothing to hold you until we can have some made to fit. Any small treasures that you cannot bear to part with for long. Other than that, not much else I can think of. Most things here would give your origins away to others, and there are those that we cannot trust with that information."

Deirdre nodded and began to lead the way back up to the house.

"Give me an hour," she said, making her way carefully up the stone-strewn path. Nerfal glanced down to see that her feet were bare, and he smiled to himself as he recalled how often Deirdre's mother had walked the woods the same way. He took up the slack in the horse's lead and followed her towards the house.

By the time they reached the deck, Randolph was waiting for them at the table. The moist table and chairs had been wiped down, and there was a glass pot of something dark, steaming hot and smelling fragrantly of a rich, sweet scent. There were three mugs, containers of fine white sugar and cream, and next to them, a plate of hot berry muffins that were dripping with butter.

Randolph beamed at the pair as they approached and waited for them to join him before helping himself to the muffins. Nerfal took one and bit into it, savoring the tender bite of the berries and the richness of the butter. Deirdre poured herself a cup of the hot liquid and added generous quantities of both sugar and cream to it. She sipped the brew and smiled with contentment.

"It's coffee," said Randolph, noting Nerfal's inquisitive glance. "It is an addictive stimulant that many, many people here drink on a daily basis. Try some."

"Addictive?" asked Nerfal, alarmed.

"Not in a bad way," laughed Randolph, "though it does help wake one up in the morning, and some claim they can't get up without it. I meant you get to like having it."

"Here, try mine," said Deirdre, handing Nerfal her cup, and watching him sip it hesitantly. His face broke into a delighted grin, and Deirdre took one of the other mugs and made herself another cup.

"Where's Nersh?" she asked her grandfather, biting into one of the muffins.

"She's already been and gone," said Randolph. "She said that she would be back in a while."

"Did she say where she was going?" asked Nerfal.

"Nersh said that she was a wise wolf and was going back for a horse for Deirdre," said Randolph, turning to look at his granddaughter. "I take it that you have decided to go?"

Deirdre patted the sides of her mouth with a corner of her napkin and nodded.

"How did she know?" she asked Nerfal.

"What I would like to know is how she memorized the keying phrase," said Nerfal, looking perplexed. "It took me weeks to learn it. As to how Nersh knew that you would go, she sometimes gets feelings about things."

Deirdre grinned and set down her empty coffee mug.

"Or maybe I was transparent enough last night, and she could tell that I had more or less made up my mind that I was going, even if I wasn't ready to admit it to myself." Deirdre sobered and looked at Nerfal, "She *is* a wise wolf."

"She is indeed," nodded Nerfal. "I have known her for most of her life, and even though she was young when I met her, Nersh is in many ways my senior and certainly wiser in ways of the heart than I. Darlena's death hit her hard, however, and she has not recovered. I would give almost anything to see her leaping at butterflies again. It was always her favorite game when we travelled."

He took a bite of his muffin and felt Deirdre's eyes on him. Looking up, he smiled, and said, "I have no regrets in finding out I had another daughter, I promise you."

She nodded and refilled her coffee cup, sipping at it and looking at him thoughtfully over the rim.

From the cool recesses of the woods came a jingling sound, and they all turned to see Nersh trotting down the path in the company of a large black horse who seemed to literally float over the ground as it moved. Its black leather tack was accented with silver inlay. Deirdre could see small shining bells that chimed merrily with the animal's movement sewn to the triangular points of the green barding and along the fancy reins. The horse lowered its head as if to say something to Nersh, and the wolf laughed heartily.

"Now how did she accomplish that, I wonder?" said Nerfal to himself.

"What do you mean?" asked Deirdre.

"Hmm? Oh, that is Vexanious. He was Prince Benjamin's mount until the boy's death several years ago. Vexanious returned to the Mountain Reaches and swore that he would never bear another rider."

"He swore? He's a talking horse?"

"Indeed he is. The Talking Folk do not often serve humans, but the bachelor stallions of the horse tribes will, on occasion, volunteer to carry members of the royal family. Vexanious was with Prince Benjamin for over ten years, and they were truly friends as well as working partners."

Nersh gave a barking yip and trotted up the stairs. Nerfal also noticed that she looked inordinately pleased with herself, and her eyes were narrowed in the brightening sun as she smiled.

The stallion also mounted the steps, albeit a little slower. He stood, glistening with a slight sheen of sweat, but otherwise showed no signs of his exertions. He regarded them soberly, and Deirdre noticed that there was no bit on the bridle that he wore about his massive head.

"My Lord Nerfal," he said, his voice low and resonant, "the Lady Nersh has told me of what has transpired, and that our new Lady has had no riding experience. I wish offer my services to your daughter. My Lady," and here he turned to Deirdre, "I am Vexanious of the Talking Folk."

He bowed his head and made a leg to Deirdre. For a moment, Deirdre had no idea what to say to the shiny raven-black stallion that stood bowing to her, his head so low that his mane brushed the deck.

Hearing a wolf talk had seemed almost normal, or at the very least, not quite so unbelievable, but a horse was another matter. In the role-playing games that she had enjoyed in college, while wolves did occasionally talk to one, horses spent most of their time being monster fodder. One did not talk to them; one merely hoped they might be there for the hasty retreat from a dungeon. Talking to a horse just seemed odd.

She shook off her stray thoughts and regained her composure enough to speak to the animal.

"Thank you very much," she said.

The horse drew itself upright and looked at her.

"It is only because of the need to keep you safe that I am aiding you. Once you have the basics of riding down, I will be returning to my quiet herd life," said the horse. His posture relaxed a little, and his voice softened, "If I can teach a block-headed young prince to ride, certainly I can teach a girl. Providing, that is, that you will act sensibly and listen to what I say, not just sit on my back giggling and braiding flowers into my mane!"

He snorted indignantly, and Nerfal leaned closer to Randolph and Deirdre, saying in a heavy whisper, "My niece, Jenna, asked Benjamin to give her riding lessons. She really is not the horse-riding type, and I don't think her focus was on the lessons. Thankfully she is the only one of my nieces that is like that. She and her sister Castra live in the Carathusin Palace in Remembrance, the capital city of Keyralithsmus. You will meet both of them soon enough, along with Queen Brena."

"Ah," said Deirdre and turned to the horse. "No fear of that. I don't giggle!"

Randolph made a harrumphing noise, and Vexanious gave her a sideways look before excusing himself to get a drink. Deirdre stood up and looked at her grandfather as the horse clomped his way down the stairs.

"I'd better go get packed. Where'd you put my knapsack when we got back from camping?"

"I hung it up down cellar by the tool rack," said Randolph, "It needed to air after that bottle of bug spray spilled in it."

Deirdre rolled her eyes.

"I'd almost managed to forget about that," she said, ruefully. "Be back in a few."

She walked into the house, letting the screen door slam behind her, and Randolph turned to look at Nerfal.

"I know that she's made up her mind, and I believe it to be a very mature, sensible decision. However, she's still my granddaughter and as much my little girl as Julia was." Randolph sighed, "Take care of her, Nerfal. Keep her as safe as you can."

Nerfal nodded. Lady Nersh rose from where she lay by his chair and stretched, her white coat glistening in the sun.

"We have already lost too much, and the war has not even begun," she said. "We will do everything in our power to protect her."

Vexanious trotted back up from the lake and came to a stop next to Nerfal's stallion. The bay snuffled at him in greeting before the black horse walked up the steps to rejoin the group at the table. He sniffed the muffins and daintily accepted one when Randolph peeled off the paper and set it before him.

A few minutes later, the screen door creaked open, and they all turned to see Deirdre walking out of the house with a battered khaki colored knapsack slung over her shoulder. She still wore her earlier outfit of blue jeans and cream-colored top, but in place of her leather coat, she wore a lightweight dark blue cloak made of wool with a fur-trimmed hood, and her feet were shod with heavy black leather hi-tops.

At Nerfal's raised eyebrow, Deirdre smiled and fingered her cloak.

"Shades of my misspent youth," she said. "The essential in L.A.R.P.ing basics. Live Action Role Playing, Nerfal. We pretended to fight monsters and go on quests."

She turned to Randolph and gave him a hug, which he returned strongly, smoothing her hair and kissing the top of her head.

"Be safe," he said to her, stepping back and looking at her. "Your mother would be proud."

Deirdre nodded, tears glinting in her eyes.

"It won't be forever," she said. She stood up tall, but her voice quavered just the tiniest bit on the last word. "I *will* be back."

Vexanious had walked down the deck stairs and stood waiting at the bottom near the bay stallion. Deirdre walked to the top of the stairs and looked down at the large black horse standing below. Nerfal descended the steps past her and went over to the tack he had left on a stump the night before. Unwrapping it from the oiled cloth he had put it in to keep it dry, he set about saddling the bay.

Deirdre watched him for a moment, then turned to Randolph who stood unmoving by his chair. His face was sad, but his eyes glinted proudly.

"I have the book with me," she said to him softly. Nersh glanced up at her curiously, and Deirdre smiled at the wolf.

"Later," she said, nodding at Nerfal. "I think that he'll want to be sitting down when he sees it."

Nersh nodded and trotted down the stairs to take the reins of Nerfal's horse. Vexanious stood, stamping one hind foot impatiently.

Deirdre smiled once more at her grandfather, then walked down the steps to where Nerfal stood by Vexanious's left side. Lacing his fingers together, he made a step for Deirdre.

"Put your left foot in the stirrup, and I will boost you up," he said.

Deirdre did as she was instructed and found herself sitting astride the broad back of the stallion, leather saddle creaking as she shifted her weight into a more comfortable position. Vexanious grunted and muttered unintelligibly under his breath.

"Find the other stirrup," the horse said as Nerfal took the bay's reins from Nersh and swung up into the saddle. "Now place the bar behind the balls of your feet."

Feeling around until she found the iron bar, Deirdre slid her foot into it and shifted until the fleshy part of her feet rested just beyond the bars.

"Good," said the horse. "Now, push your heels down and grip with your lower legs."

Deirdre complied and sat holding the reins loosely in one hand. She looked at Randolph, and for one brief moment wondered if it was too late to back out. Randolph smiled reassuringly.

"You'll be fine," he said. "Take care of yourself. I love you."

Nerfal swung the bay's head around and started the horse off down the path. Nersh trotted ahead of him, and Vexanious turned to follow at a walk. Deirdre grabbed at the high crest of the saddle and managed to stay seated as the horse moved out. She gave a small glance and wave to Randolph before turning to grip the saddle again.

Vexanious snorted and flicked an ear back at Deirdre.

"Relax," he said. "If I were a normal horse, I would be standing at a complete stop. Sit back a little, square your shoulders, and just ride with the rhythm of my stride. I will not let you fall. Do not forget to keep your heels down."

Deirdre tried to follow the stallion's instructions, and she let herself slowly relax enough to sway a bit. Looking ahead, she saw Nerfal riding easily, talking with Lady Nersh. The wolf seemed much more alert than the previous day, as if a weight had been removed from her soul. Deirdre hoped that she was the cause and that they wouldn't be too disappointed if she failed.

The fallen leaves gave off a sharp ginger snap smell that she inhaled deeply, taking in the smells of horse and leather as well. The day promised to warm up a good bit, and she wondered what the weather would be like in her father's realm.

Nerfal turned in his saddle and smiled back at her, "We will be at the gate in a few minutes, and then it is a short ride to the Keep after that."

"Keep?" chuckled Deirdre. "Sounds ominous!"

"Well, truth be told, it is more like a glorified stone mansion. It is tiny compared with the Carathusin Palace in Remembrance, but our family is content with what we are able to produce on our lands. We never wanted anything on a grander scale,"

"True," said Lady Nersh, "Most of our food comes from farms run by members of the Ettar family, and the servants we require are related for the most part. Younger boys serve as pages and servers at meal times, girls usually as cooks and Ladies-in-Waiting. Elaina herself does a great deal of the baking and has one of the finest apiaries in the Mountain Reaches."

Deirdre shivered at the thought of all those bees. Nersh noticed her reaction and grinned.

"Elaina has a great fondness for bees," she said. "You will find that honey is a staple and beeswax candles are common in every room. She also manages to incorporate bees into almost every motif, so be forewarned."

"Several of my nieces share your prejudices," chuckled Nerfal. "They have either gone to Remembrance or have married into one of the farming families that do not keep bees. For a while, every farm had an apiary of some sort. Now, only about half of them supplement our candle and honey supplies. Mountain Reaches honey is in great demand in Remembrance. All of our surplus goes to the city in return for various fish oils and sea products that we ourselves enjoy."

Nerfal stopped his horse, and Vexanious walked forward to come even with the bay. Nerfal pointed to a rickety wooden gate set into an old rock wall that lay slightly off of the path. The paint was peeling from the grey weathered boards, and the rusty hinges looked to be on the verge of self-destruction.

"That's it?" asked Deirdre, incredulously. "I have been by this thing a thousand times and never gave it a second thought. I've even gone *through* it a few times. How is it a portal?"

"One has to know the proper phrase to key it. As to its appearance, would you not question a brand new gate out in the middle of the woods? I believe that it was the intention of its creator that it be left alone."

"Who made it?" asked Deirdre.

"Legend has it that it was the Unicorn King himself, as a way to keep in touch with his kin on this world. There are several gates like it in our world, but this is the only one for which the keying phrase is still known," Nerfal said as he dismounted his horse and took a tight hold on the reins. "Now, I am going to lead old stubborn here through as he has no love of gates, and I do not wish to be thrown in the middle of nowhere. You can stay on Vexanious; he knows what all of this is about. Just hang on as we go through, and we will be out the other side in a few moments."

Nerfal led his horse up to the gate and spoke a few words that melted like a snow crystal from Deirdre's mind as soon as she heard them. The rusty hinges were oddly silent as the gate opened of its own accord, the air inside it shimmering. Nerfal tugged on the reins and led his recalcitrant animal through, with Nersh close on his heels. Vexanious followed behind the wolf, giving Deirdre no more than a second to think about what was happening before they were through. She glanced back at the gate and saw that on this side, it was a towering ivy-wrapped edifice of wrought iron. The archway she beheld bore no resemblance at all to the decrepit, old wooden gate through which they had just come.

Nerfal remounted the bay and led the way through a maze of overgrown hedges that looked like no species of plant Deirdre had ever seen before. Not, she added to herself, that she was in any way an expert. The leaves of the bushes had an odd shape, something of a cross between serrations and lobes, and the flowers were shaped like dogwood blossoms, but were a light sky blue, shading to cream in the center.

Sunset-colored butterflies danced amid the blossoms and lit coral bursts amidst the blue. Nersh trotted along stiffly, but with joy and snapped her jaws at the fiery insects when they flew too low.

"Autumn-blooming starfire flowers and kettlefire butterflies," said Nerfal. "You are lucky to see the butterflies. In a normal year, they would have migrated south by now, but our weather has been mild, and they have stayed far longer than they do most years. A warm wind that the Talking Folk call 'Contra's Breath' is responsible. It only happens about once every twenty years, and it is supposed to mean a lucky year and a warm winter. Let us hope that the former is true and not the latter. A warm winter will mean an early spring start for Perstalia."

The bay stumbled on an exposed root and grunted noisily. Nerfal patted the stallion on the neck and promised him his rest soon. Vexanious snorted and tossed his head in what Deirdre assumed to be amusement, but he said nothing.

The hedges gave way to tall sculptured trees that stood pillar-like along the paths. Deirdre caught glimpses of cultured flowerbeds beyond the trees, but the rest of the land was obscured by a series of dark green hedges. Nerfal led them through the maze of paths, and soon they left the gardens behind, eventually coming face-to-face with a grand stone mansion that stood a good four stories high.

Nerfal stopped and waited for Vexanious to come abreast of the bay. Deirdre looked at her father quizzically, and he turned to her, smiling.

"This is it," he said. "Certainly not as impressive as the palace in Remembrance, but large enough as you can see."

"Not exactly cozy, either," chuckled Nersh, interpreting Deirdre's slight frown correctly.

"No, but parts of it are homey enough." Nerfal spurred the stallion into a trot, "Come on; let us go."

Lady Nersh bounded away after him, and Vexanious began to walk after them, becoming outdistanced.

"Do you think that you can handle a trot?" he asked.

"I can try," she said, and the horse broke into a ground-eating pace that, smooth as it was, still jounced her around.

"Try to move with my gait," he called. "Use your legs and move with me."

Deirdre tried to comply, but felt more and more uncomfortable until she suddenly remembered watching riders on TV and how they 'posted' with the horse's stride. She tried it, caught the rhythm, lost it, and caught it again. Looking up, she was surprised to see how much they were gaining on her father, and it wasn't until Vexanious praised her on her quickness that she realized that she had actually done it.

She faltered briefly, caught the rhythm again, and held it, discovering in the process that the trot wasn't all that bad. Nerfal glanced back and waved, slowing the bay so that they could catch up at the gate. Vexanious slowed to a walk as he reached them, and they proceeded to enter the keep.

A narrow, decorative moat surrounded the grey stone keep, and they crossed the small bridge that spanned it, entered through the two huge doors that were flung wide, and came to a stop inside the tiny courtyard. Deirdre took in the kitchen garden and the large mews that housed only a couple of hawks and a petite kestrel. An elegant water fountain chuckled against the wall overlooking the gardens, sending a spray of water into the air and creating rainbows where the sun caught the droplets.

Two boys in their early teens ran up to where Deirdre and her father sat, their curly hair mussed and tangled. Both wore blue tunics and knit woolen hose of a burgundy color. At their belts hung nearly identical knives with handles of carved bone. The main difference between the boys was their hair color; one had hair of a sandy hue while the other was a dark brunette.

Nerfal dismounted and handed the reins to the darker haired of the boys. The youth grinned, and as Deirdre accepted Nerfal's help in getting down, she had to resist the urge to ruffle the boy's mop of hair.

The other boy took Vexanious's reins and slid the hackamore bridle off of the horse's head. The stallion bowed his head in thanks, and the boy's green eyes twinkled mischievously.

"Boys, this is my daughter, Deirdre," said Nerfal. "Deirdre, these are your cousins Dorin and Brede. Dorin will one day be Lord of the Mountain Reaches as he is closest in blood to me. Brede will get his father's farm and, if he chooses, will have the position of head councilor. Take care of the horses now and meet us inside."

The boys bowed and led the horses away as Nersh came trotting up to Nerfal from inside the castle proper and smiled a toothy grin.

"All is in readiness," she said.

"Good," said Nerfal. "Take off your shoes, Deirdre. In order for the Land to recognize you quickly, you must be in constant contact with it. Wear your shoes during riding or, once Arvid starts you in swordplay, during practice, but try to go barefoot at all other times."

Deirdre bent down, unlaced her shoes, and removed them, pulling off her socks and placing both inside her knapsack. Nerfal nodded to her, and they followed the old wolf inside.

"What exactly do you mean by recognize?" asked Deirdre as they walked through the grey stone corridors.

"Well, although your blood is tied to the land, they have never really come into contact with each other. The magic in your blood needs waking, and the best way to do that would be to do a complete awakening ritual. However, as we only have about three weeks before we have to start for the capital, that is not practical. We can only let you go barefoot as much as possible and, when you are ready, take you through the formal introduction to the Land."

"What does that entail?" she asked.

"I will tell you when the time comes," said Nerfal. "None of it is painful, though some of it may seem alarming. Darlena went through it and, next year on their thirteenth birthdays, Dorin and Brede will as well."

"Sort of a rite of passage?" Deirdre hazarded.

"Yes. It is the time when the magic, if it is present, will manifest and also means that the ability to shapeshift will emerge," Nerfal smiled. "Dorin hopes to have a stag as one of his forms, like his uncle."

They rounded a corner and found themselves facing a pair of round-topped doors set into a double arch. Stained glass windows portrayed a white creature that looked like the cross between a bear and a great spotted cat in the left door and a gleaming unicorn in the right. They were both rampant, rearing up in a display of defiance, but unlike the similar beasts on royal crests in her world, Deirdre noted that they both wore crowns, and unlike the one used on British crests, the unicorn bore no chains.

"So we remember," said Nerfal. "The unicorn is Rathal, and the other creature is the tsavon, Tali. They were the creators of Keyralithsmus."

He pushed open the door bearing the image of the unicorn and led the way inside to a large stone-floored room with tall rough-hewn beams curving up to support a high slate roof. Multi-tiered chandeliers hung on long chains and held thick candles that burned fiercely and cast many shadows around the room. The air was thick with the smell of beeswax and sharp-scented herbs that crunched underfoot amidst the clean rushes. Deirdre recalled that similar pungent herbs were often used to help drive off vermin.

Tall oval windows set in ornately-carved stone frames faced in towards the courtyard, and the window glass itself was thick and chased through with lines of bubbles. Morning light filtered brightly through and lit the room with a hazy brilliance.

At the far end of the room, a huge fireplace sat deeply recessed within the wall, and the fire that burned merrily on the long grate threw off a great amount of heat into the chill stone room. The logs themselves sat upon black metal andirons shaped like oak trees and there was no screen to keep the sparks from falling on the stone hearth.

On the side opposite of the windows was an alcove in which stood an extensive table set with all manner of food and drink, most of it fruit or grain in origin, though what appeared to be a baked fish sat proudly in the center of the meal.

About the table sat three women, all of whom were clothed in medieval style dresses, dyed bright autumn colors of russet and citron. Their hair was pulled back into simple braids, and the oldest bore a coronet on her brow. All three also had horns, and as they looked at her, Deirdre felt oddly naked and had to resist an urge to touch her own brow.

The oldest of the three, though her crowned beauty was hardly lessened by her age, rose and held out her hands to Deirdre.

"My dear, do not look so alarmed. You are among friends here, and you have nothing to fear at all. I am Elaina, your father's wife and the mistress of this keep. You are most welcome here."

Looking up a Nerfal, she mock sighed and shook her head.

"Has he told you nothing of your heritage? No, I see he has. I only jest. And who knows? Once the Land accepts you, you may grow your own horns in time."

Elaina drew her over to a chair, followed by an amused Nerfal. He bowed to his wife and turned to leave.

"I will deposit Deirdre's pack in the Ivory Suite and leave you to talk," he said.

"It is ready," said Elaina, her voice taut, "although I do not see why the Sapphire would not suffice..."

"Elaina, we must preserve the illusion for any who might watch," said Nerfal softly. "We do not know who let slip word of the dragon trials, but we do know that someone here is responsible. If I do not put her there, they will think that she was rejected by the Land or, worse, that she was an imposter. She already has one strike against her; no Ettar has ever had the power without the horns. I hope that they will appear before we reach Remembrance. I do not know for sure that they will, and there is no precedent for this thing happening before. Please, for these three weeks..."

Elaina nodded stiffly, and Nerfal bowed before leaving through an opposite set of doors. Deirdre watched him go, and then looked apprehensively around to Nersh where she lay by the hearth. The wolf glanced up at Deirdre and gave her a reassuring lupine grin.

Elaina resettled herself at the table and, smiling at Deirdre, motioned for her to be seated.

"I have forgotten my hospitality and my manners. May I introduce you to your cousins, Deluce and Merinda. Both of these ladies live on outlying farms, but occasionally join me for a few days to discuss hive production and honey. Do you like bees, Deirdre?"

"Not particularly," said Deirdre. "To be truthful, they scare the dickens out of me."

"They scare the what?" asked Merinda, brushing a stray strand of light brown hair out of her eyes.

"It's a saying where I come from. It means that they scare me a lot," said Deirdre.

"Ah," said Merinda. "You are going to have to mind what you say around here. If you sound too foreign, people are going to start asking questions."

"Too true," Elaina agreed. "Be very careful in choosing your words."

Deirdre nodded and accepted a plate heaped high with strange fruit and fish from Deluce. She took a tentative bite of the fish and found it delicious.

"Is it true, what Nerfal said about me actually growing horns?" she asked between bites.

"We hope so," said Elaina. "It is a sign that your blood will be accepted by the Land. Only then will you be able to shapeshift."

"What can you become?" asked Deirdre, picking at the unfamiliar fruit and finding them palatable.

"A broad winged cloud goose," said Elaina proudly. "One of the most powerful flyers known to our kind."

"I thought that you all had three forms," said Deirdre.

"Only those of Ettar descent," said Merinda. "Deluce and I also have only one form as Elaina is our blood aunt. Our cousin Therin, however, can become a bear, a hummingbird, and a turtle. He is Dorin's father, and *his* father, Brachin, was Nerfal's younger brother. He was lost in the war, fighting alongside Prince Benjamin."

"It is a pity about the prince," said Deluce, her soft voice floating above the table like smoke. "He was one of the nicest of the Kin."

"True," said Merinda, "Kin being those without horns, Deirdre. We are all related by blood, though some of it is thinner than the rest."

"Still, he had the most beautiful eyes," said Deluce, dreamily.

"And those eyes only watched Darlena, as you well know. No manner of fawning or sighing could change that!"

"Ladies, do not speak so of the dead," said Elaina, pain flaring in her eyes. "The past is the past...Excuse me."

Elaina rose and ran from the room. Merinda glared at Deluce.

"Wonderful timing!" she chided.

"I only spoke the truth," said Deluce, tears threatening. "It was not I who mentioned Darlena!"

Deluce rose from her seat, dabbing at the corners of her mouth with her napkin, and swept out of the room, following her aunt.

Merinda sighed, looking after her cousin.

"For all she has two children of her own, sometimes you would think that she was one herself," said the woman, shaking her head. "I am nearly as bad, bringing up Darlena. Deluce had her heart set on marrying the prince, but her blood was not strong enough. Tradition requires a tri-formed shaper to sit in the throne of the Ivory Castle. That is something she could never have been, no matter how much she desired it."

"Can you tell me about the Ivory Castle?" asked Deirdre, toying with her fork on the now- empty plate.

"It is the Mountain Reaches' seat of influence in Keyralithsmus. It is where Benjamin and Darlena would have lived once they were married. By blood, it now belongs to you and whomever you pick as your consort. There are several at Carathusin with the right qualifications, you know."

"Consort!" Deirdre exclaimed, her fork paused halfway to her mouth. "You mean to say that I must marry someone, too?"

"Traditionally, the Ivory Lady marries the monarch's closest male relative. To be the Ivory Lady is to hold an immensely powerful position, one with great access to the queen. After Benjamin's death, the honor fell to Marshall Rialain, cousin to the queen and Captain of the Royal Guard."

"Are you saying I have to marry him?" asked Deirdre, staring across the table in disbelief.

"Technically you should, but no, you do not have to. No one will force you to do that for which you have no desire, but...it will no doubt be strongly... encouraged." Merinda sighed and gave Deirdre a half smile, "It is not such a bad choice. Marshall is charming and generous with his affections. He is also not bad looking."

Deirdre snorted a laugh.

"I am not planning to stay that long," she said. "As soon as I call these dragons, I am going to go home. I am not going to marry anyone."

Merinda stood and looked at Deirdre with utter disdain.

"You may think that this all sounds very easy, but history proves that attempting the transformation does nothing but bring about one's death. Do not be so quick to assume that you have the strength to perform this. Those brought up in our family could not do it. What makes you think that you can?"

She turned and stalked out of the room. Nersh watched her go and, rising stiffly, walked over to where Deirdre sat.

"Well," said the wolf, licking her lips, "that went smoothly."

"I am glad you think so," said Deirdre. "I didn't mean it to sound that way."

"I know," said Nersh. "Give them some time to adjust. Come; allow me to play the proper hostess and show you to your rooms."

Deirdre rose from her chair and followed the wolf through the same set of doors Merinda had used.

"You will have to forgive Merinda," said Nersh, leading the way into a wide torch-lit corridor. "She has had her hands full trying to keep Elaina's spirits up and has seen very little of her own home these past few months. She thinks that your comments meant that you are overconfident and foolish. *I* know that you meant to say if instead of when, and that your confusion over the idea of marrying someone was muddling your speech."

"Exactly," said Deirdre, "Will you...?"

"I will speak to her, if you like, but I suspect that Merinda will be at your door within an hour without my aid," Nersh said as she led the way up a white marble staircase. "The women of the Reaches tend to speak their minds, then leave to calm down. It is common here."

Deirdre followed the wolf up the stairs, stopping to examine an oil painting of a glowing castle perched on a great cliff looking over the sea. The color was intriguing and as rich and vibrant as anything she had ever seen. There was something very odd about the stone that the castle was built of, though just what it was, Deirdre could not put her finger on. She stared at the painting for a few long minutes, but nothing came clear to her mind.

"Come on," called Nersh, who had paused to wait for her halfway up the second riser, "I suspect that you would like to rest a little and take some time to put your mind at ease."

Deirdre followed her the rest of the way up the stairs and into another long corridor, this one paneled in dark wood and hung with many paintings of men and women, all of whom sported a variety of horns upon their brows.

"Your ancestors," commented Nersh. "About three hundred years of them. Some of them lived at the time of the Conquest, when humans first came to this land."

"It all seems so unreal," said Deirdre, gazing at the portraits as they walked down the hall. "A whole other family on a world I never knew existed, a plane where magic exists and is used on a daily basis..."

Nersh laughed.

"I suspect that such powers exist on your world as well. I just think that you have all forgotten how to use it!"

She stopped in front of a large pair of white doors on the left hand side of the corridor and looked up at Deirdre.

"These are your rooms. Nothing so grand as the suite at Carathusin nor as private as the rooms at the Ivory Castle, but I think that you will like them."

Deirdre pushed open the right hand door and was struck dumb by the sight that met her eyes. The room was dazzlingly bright after the dim, torchlit corridor. A white marble fireplace dominated the right half of the chamber, and on all of the walls were hung tapestries of white flowers. By the fireplace, a settee and two wide deep chairs of dark brown wood stood and were softened by matching white needle-

point cushions and throws. Against the far wall between two doorways stood a small table of the same dark wood on which sat a crystal
decanter of what looked to be a golden-hued wine. Two beautifully
etched goblets sat next to the decanter, both displaying a delicate floral
design.

Deirdre stepped onto the dark floor and a sweet, musky fragrance
rose into the air. Her steps crackled, and she glanced down to see that
the floor was strewn with more grasses. She then looked up to see a
high ceiling, its rough-hewn beams held in place by large wooden
pegs. She stopped midway into the room and looked about herself in
total wonder.

Behind her, Nersh laughed as she watched Deirdre examine the
marble fireplace and the matching candlesticks atop the mantle
holding the ubiquitous beeswax candles. Between them stood a delicate ivory statuette of a rearing unicorn, and Deirdre ran her fingers
over the carved surface as if afraid that it might break.

"Do you have nothing to match this in your own world?" Nersh
asked, as Deirdre moved to touch the decanter's deeply cut surface.

"Yes, but never any place I have lived. I mean, Randolph and I did
okay, but only the wealthy had embroidered tapestries and ivory
statues."

Nersh smiled.

"If you think that this is impressive, wait until you see the suite at
the Carathusin Palace. They make these seem like pauper's quarters in
comparison."

Deirdre sat down on the settee and placed her elbows on her knees,
her head in her hands.

"Truthfully, Nersh, how much chance do I have to succeed?"

The wolf sighed and stared at the statue on the mantle for a long
moment before answering.

"If it was not for our visitor, I would say that you had little or no
chance at all," she said, "but the fact that the Unicorn King took an
interest in you and decided to seek you out...well, that vastly improves
the odds."

"Do you really think that it was him?" asked Deirdre, sitting up straight.

"I have no doubts," said Nersh. "The wolves are the oral lore keepers of the Talking Folk, and it is rumored that a long time ago, there was a prophecy that alluded to this very event. The story was lost ages ago, and only the basic concept, that a lady recognized by Rathal would come to save us, remains in our memories."

"Does Nerfal know this?"

"He may guess," said the wolf. "The Shapers were once the custodians of a scroll on which this was written, but during the Conquest, his people divided, and the part of the clan that carried the scroll vanished. There is no record of it now."

Deirdre laughed, "Sounds like the plot in one of my books or games. 'Find the scroll that unlocks the key to all things.' Odd to think that it might be true in this case."

"It just may be," said Nersh, a thoughtful expression on her face. "Do your games explain how to find lost tribes?"

"Sometimes, though I doubt that it will help in this case. Our games always had someone to help us to get back on track, like some kind of game master. I don't think that we have that luxury here."

"Who is to say?" said Nersh, stretching her long legs before her. "Maybe Rathal himself will take that role, nudging you back on to the right path when you stray from it. I would not count on it, mind, but he does have some interest in these matters; otherwise, you would not be here."

Deirdre nodded, and Nersh rose, turning towards one of the unexplored doorways.

"In the meantime, may I suggest that we complete our tour? If you think that this sitting room is nice, you will love the bedroom."

———

They had just finished their inspection of the heavily tapestried bedchamber when a knock came at the outer door. Nersh gave Deirdre a knowing look, and they went to answer it.

In accordance with Nersh's prediction, Merinda stood in the doorway, her arms full of clothes.

"I thought that these might fit you," she said. "Elaina and I chose some of Darlena's gowns for you to wear until the tailor has a chance to make you some of your own."

Deirdre stepped aside to allow her to pass. Merinda walked straight into the bedroom and began to hang the dresses in one of the two enormous wardrobes that took up all of one wall. Deirdre and Nersh watched her in silence.

"There you are," she said, hanging up all but one of the gowns and laying it on the bed. The dress was a russet color with gold trim and had a very long skirt. Merinda turned and looked at Deirdre.

"I am sorry for what I said earlier. I realize that our customs are not your own and that you must feel out of place. I apologize if I caused you distress."

Deirdre ventured a smile.

"I am sorry if it seemed like I was treating your problems as if they were simple issues. I'll do the best I can, and I understand how serious this is. I just haven't thought much past the part about the dragons. If I do succeed, I was under the impression that I would be going home again."

"Ah, that explains your reaction to marriage! No harm done. Now, would you like to try on the gown here for size? You are a lady of the Northern Reaches now and will soon be to all the realm. Oh yes," laughed Merinda, grinning at the dumbstruck look on Deirdre's face, "once you are confirmed by the Queen, you become a Lady of Keyralithsmus in full standing, and ladies almost always wear gowns."

Deirdre nodded and, once she had stripped her own clothes, let Merinda help her into the dress. The fabric was warm and soft, yet unfinished, reminding Deirdre of raw silk, and the skirts hung in heavy folds from the dropped waistline. The bodice was of a modest cut with decorative lacing that made it seem as if the neckline continued lower than it actually did. The sleeves were a bit long, but several braided strands of thin pink ribbon helped to tie up the excess and keep it out of her way.

"Very nice, if a trifle tight in the chest," said Merinda. "We will visit the tailor tomorrow and get your measurements taken. You need some better fitting gowns made for you."

She moved toward the main door and turned to glance back.

"I am glad that you have come, and I hope that things will get easier for all of us. The noon meal will be in an hour. I will come to get you then."

———

Deirdre walked into the room a bit self-consciously, not sure what kind of figure she cut in the bright russet dress, but Nersh nudged her along with her long muzzle. Deirdre smiled down at the wolf, feeling more at ease with her solid presence.

The great hall seemed much brighter than it had that morning as the sun now streamed through some of the high windows. Elaina, Deluce, Brede, and Dorin were already seated, and as Deirdre approached the table in Merinda's wake, Nerfal entered from the door on the opposite side of the room.

"Well," he said, looking around, "I trust that this morning's chaos has been straightened out? My ladies, let us remember that however unfamiliar and new we are to each other, we are all a family here. There are doubtless going to be problems, but let us try to deal with them as best as we can."

He smiled at his wife and at Deirdre, then sat himself down at the head of the table. Deirdre and Merinda also sat down as several servants appeared to spread the table with all manner of fish and fowl. The boys ate large portions of everything and between mouthfuls, asked Deirdre as many questions as they could think of about her world. Did animals talk there? Could anyone shape change? What was the magic box with moving pictures that Nerfal had told them about? The list was endless. She answered them as best she could, managing only a scant occasional mouthful before being beset by another barrage of questions.

Elaina and Merinda would sometimes manage to interject one of their own questions, and the meal passed quickly in that manner. Afterwards, they retired to an adjacent room to sit in a group of deeply cushioned chairs and couches and relax with large goblets of wine.

"You know, you actually look a great deal like Darlena," commented Elaina. "I can see your father in you."

"And a lot like Judeth too," said Nerfal. "I can see myself in you, but I can see your mother more."

Merinda smiled, "She has your hair, Uncle. Aside from that...well, it does not matter. When you go to Remembrance, just tell them that she looks like her dam."

Nersh chuckled, looking up from where she lay by the fire.

"Merinda spends too much time with her horses, Deirdre. If Vexanious would not have agreed to teach you, I was going to ask Merinda. Sometimes, I think she is a horse!"

"You have a lot to learn in three weeks," Nerfal continued, tapping the stem of his wine glass. "Names, history, riding, maybe some swordplay..."

"But I *can* swordfight," said Deirdre. The others looked up in surprise, and she continued, "I was vice-president of my college fencing team for two semesters and was on the team for about three years total. That and the six years I spent in the SCA, a year in NERO, and a year in Realms gave me a lot of practice. Granted, most of those were dealing with wooden or padded weapons, but the theory was sound. I scored more hits than I had scored on me."

Everyone gave her puzzled looks and glanced at Nerfal to see if he had any notion as to what she was talking about. He gave them a perplexed shrug, and they looked back to Deirdre.

"I have no idea to what you are referring, aside from the fencing," said Nerfal, laughing, "but it sounds like you have had some teaching.

Was this the game you told me about? This is a benefit I had not counted on. I am sure we have a light rapier or thin sword that you would be comfortable with. I will have Arved begin your instruction this afternoon. Tonight, we will start on the history of Keyralithsmus. Have you been taught any threadcraft?"

Deirdre shook her head, and Nerfal looked at the ladies.

"Well, we will start you learning that too," he said. "All women do a little embroidery or sewing. You can practice while I go over our history. Merinda, please call for the tailor in the morning. I want three formal dresses, three day-to-day dresses, and a riding habit for her. You will also need to work with Vexanious as much as possible. We have to have your skills perfected by the time we get to Remembrance, or we will not stand a chance at fooling the council. There are some advisors who are trying to get the queen to dissolve the alliance between the shapers and the humans altogether. Others want to put a member of the non-Kin on the throne. With any luck, you will grow your horns before we leave."

He paused for breath and looked at his daughter, "I do not know if you will grow them, Deirdre, if they would be permanent, or if they would fade when you return home. Worse comes to worse, I could create an illusion that they are there."

He set his glass on a low, round table and, after a long moment, rose from his chair.

"Come," he said, "let us go meet Arved."

3

Time went by quickly, and Deirdre learned faster than she ever thought she could. Mornings were spent on horseback, learning to balance and to use only her knees to grip instead of relying on the stirrups. Vexanious had met her the second morning wearing no tack at all and had taught her how to get onto his back and how to stay there. By the end of the second week, she could stay on him at a trot, using only her leg muscles and a tight grip on his mane. She was so sore at the end of each lesson that she could barely move without wincing but, as the days went by, her skill began to improve. She remarked to Nerfal that she didn't feel quite so much like she was being subjected to slow torture anymore.

Likewise, her sword fighting practice was going well. Arved had found a long, thin practice sword that had a good heft and perfect balance for her. Her afternoons were spent sparring with Arved and Dorin. Her cousin had a good sense of the blade, but Deirdre's previous training sometimes let her win their matches. Arved noted more than once how rare it was for a girl of no recognized background to have any experience. Dorin had been taking lessons since his fifth birthday. Deirdre's three-year's of competitive fencing, combined with four-odd years of play-fighting should not have been enough to allow her to beat Dorin as often as she did. Arved shook his head, but Dorin simply glowered good-naturedly and commented that she needed to have some kind of advantage.

Evenings were spent learning needlepoint and listening to Nerfal tell stories of her family. Several times, she had caught herself nodding off, but Merinda would give her a light jab in the ribs that brought her back to awareness. The topics of magic and mystical beasts were not boring – far from it – but Deirdre was so exhausted by that time of the day, she could barely keep her eyes open.

In between lessons, there were hot baths, visits to the tailor, trips around the land, and lengthy discussions on who she was likely to meet at the castle, who they were allied to, and what castle lord or lady watched over what sections of the kingdom. Meals were the only time she could actually relax and even her baths were too short to really help her unwind. Each night found her falling asleep as soon as her head reached the pillow.

The beginning of the third week marked a change in Vexanious's training schedule. He met her as usual in the courtyard but led her into the barn instead of out into the grassy fields. The air had grown cold and had a bitter snap to it; their breath misted for the first time since Deirdre had been there, and a glistening of frost coated the ground.

"The time has come for you to learn about tack," said Vexanious, entering the long walkway that led between the stalls. "The tack room is down here. Follow me."

He led her through the row of stalls into a large room at the end. Looking in, Deirdre saw brushes, combs, saddles, bridles, halters, whips, and all manner of equipment set neatly about on pegs or on shelves. Vexanious proceeded to lecture her on the proper use of the various brushes, having Deirdre try out each one on his shining hide. After a while, he nosed his tack and had her bring it outside. He also had her fetch a second bridle, this one with a straight bit to practice the use of a full bridle, not just the bitless headstall he usually wore.

They entered the courtyard and, for the next hour, Deirdre learned more than she ever wanted to know about tack.

"Good," said the horse, finally, "Now, slip this bridle off, and we will try the full one. Remember what I told you about the bit. Do not pull!"

Deirdre slipped the bit into the stallion's mouth, watching him chomp on it a little until it warmed up. Then she slid the headgear over his ears, tightening the throat latch and adjusting the cheek pieces while he supervised.

"Good," said Vexanious, muffled a little by the bit. "Ready?"

Deirdre nodded and climbed into the saddle. It felt odd not to have contact with the stallion's back after two weeks of bareback riding, and she adjusted the stirrups to where they wouldn't hinder the use of her knees.

"Now," said the horse, mouthing the bit, "use the reins and gently... gently... pull to the right."

Deirdre did so, and Vexanious turned his head with the pressure.

"Good, now the left...good! Remember to use the opposite knee, too; it aids the pull. Okay. Pretend I am a normal horse. What do you do?"

Deirdre nudged Vexanious's side, and he began to walk.

"With a normal horse, you would need more of a kick. How about a trot?"

Deirdre kicked harder and found herself bounced around in the saddle as his gait sped up.

"Do you remember moving with my gait that first day? We did not do it while we rode bareback because my stride is smooth enough. Try it now."

Deirdre did and almost fell out of the saddle.

"Wait a beat! Use your knees to grip. It is possible without stirrups, but it takes longer than we have to learn. There you go! Good. Try to keep it."

Catching the rhythm, Deirdre managed to maintain it as they trotted around the courtyard. Vexanious's hooves drummed a double beat that echoed off of the walls of the keep and slowly, Deirdre began to feel comfortable with the motion.

"Use the reins!" called the horse. "You have to guide me. Now, outside!"

They rode out through the gate and into the sparkling fields glowing white with frost.

"We are going to try cantering today," called the horse. "Sit and use leg pressure to signal a change of pace."

At Deirdre's signal, the horse broke into a graceful canter, and Deirdre gripped with her legs as hard as she could. For a minute, they simply ran, and then Vexanious called, "Use the reins! Any normal horse would have no idea what you wanted. Watch out for the branches; we are headed for the orchards."

Deirdre grabbed up the reins and pulled Vexanious's head to the left, away from the trees. They cantered along for a while longer.

"Head back," said the stallion at last. "That is enough for today."

They cantered back to the castle, slowing as they entered the gates. Vexanious stopped of his own accord outside the stables and waited for Deirdre to dismount.

"Get this thing out of my mouth," he commanded, and Deirdre swiftly complied.

"Ack! Ick, that is awful! I hate the taste of metal! Pleah! The last time I had a bit in my mouth was when I taught the prince about ten years ago. I think I was three at the time. Slip my halter on, Deirdre, over my ears. Now, lead me around. You have to be sure to cool horses out completely, or they will sicken. Do not let them drink too much, either, or they will get colic. Feel my chest, between my forelegs. You can tell if a horse is too hot that way."

Dorin came running over, and Vexanious stopped.

"Good. Let the boy take me now. You have done enough for today.

"Yeah," said Deirdre, "I really want a bath. My forehead is itchy"

The horse looked at her, and Dorin laughed.

"Well-a-day!" exclaimed the horse. "I do not wonder at your fore-head itching!"

Deirdre reached up and felt two hard bumps just under the surface of the skin near her hairline. A shock of adrenaline ran through her, and she felt sick and excited all at once.

"The Land has accepted you," said Dorin with a grin.

"Oh," said Deirdre, with a tremble in her voice. She dropped the lead rope and ran inside.

———

Merinda knocked on Deirdre's door and took the lack of reply for an invitation. Deirdre looked up from where she lay crying on the bed to see the older woman entering the room. Merinda sat down next to her on the bed and smiled reassuringly.

"It is not easy, is it?" she asked.

"No," said Deirdre, sniffing. "Just when I think I've gotten everything sorted out, poof, something else happens! Talking animals, sure, no problem. New world...got it. But now this...I'm not sure I am ready for this."

Merinda smiled, "The Land obviously felt that you were. Otherwise, this would not have happened. I am glad it did. Nerfal was going to risk putting a spell on you that might be seen through or broken. It also means that you have the power needed to carry this through. I had my doubts for a while, but now..."

"Thanks. Vexanious seemed a bit surprised as well."

"He thinks very highly of you, you know," said Merinda. "I think he will offer to serve you as he did Benjamin. Herd life never suited that stallion. He has been getting fat and lazy. This will do him good."

Deirdre propped her head up on one hand and looked at Merinda.

"Tell me about Benjamin," she said. "Everyone has spoken well of him."

"He was kind," said Merinda, turning to stare out the window. "Everyone loved him. He inspired trust and faithfulness in people by being honest. His death hurt us all, especially Darlena and Marshall. They spent a lot of time together after Ben died. They had gotten very close, and many were conjecturing that a wedding might be in the near future. I honestly think that she still was not over Benjamin, no matter what the court gossips said. She had loved him deeply. And then she was killed."

Merinda looked down at Deirdre.

"I know it sounds petty, but I was prepared to dislike you. Darlena and I were close, even though we were separated by more than ten years of age. I was angry at Nerfal for bringing in someone to take her place."

"And now?" asked Deirdre, sitting up.

"I think you have your own place to fill," said Merinda. "I would like it if you were to be my friend."

"I think I can do that," said Deirdre, smiling.

————

At the meal that noontime, Nerfal congratulated Deirdre with a glad embrace and a look of relief. The other family members hugged her and fussed over her. The two boys gave her sidelong glances and nibbled at their food. At last, Dorin blurted out,

"Does this mean that Deirdre gets to go through the ceremony before me? She has only been here two weeks!"

"Dorin, she is much older than you," said Nerfal, "The magic is hurrying in her to catch up, and she needs to go through the ritual before she goes south to Remembrance. Otherwise, she may never be able to become a dragon or anything else. Your time will come, boy. Patience!"

Brede laughed, and Dorin hunched his shoulders a little. He managed a half smile in Deirdre's direction, which she returned nervously.

"Sorry," he said, "Just a little jealous, I guess."

"Waiting is hard," said Deirdre. "You're anxious for things to come about. I would gladly trade places with you. This is happening way too fast for me!"

Dorin grinned, and after they had finished eating, Deirdre followed her father up to his chambers on the second floor. The sitting room that they entered was paneled in a rich, dark amber wood the color of aged honey, and the floors were laid with wide boards that were worn smooth with use and age. Several plush chairs and couches had been placed near each other, and a brace of comfortable settees were arranged close to the fireplace.

Nerfal closed the door behind them and guided Deirdre to one of the settees covered in brocaded brown velvet. He took a seat in an armchair opposite her and clasped his hands together, bowing his head. He stayed that way a moment, and then looked up into Deirdre's eyes.

"This afternoon, we will tack up the horses and ride into the mountains," he said, his voice tense. "We will travel to a certain cave in the mountains and once there, I will instruct you further. You must believe me when I tell you that no harm will come to you. Please trust me in this. You must ally yourself with the Land, or you have no hope of succeeding. Go get a cloak from your room. I will meet you in the stables."

Deirdre swallowed hard and left her father, his jaw tight, packing his saddle bags in the room behind her.

4

The horses trotted at speed up the steep incline, picking their way up the narrow grassy expanse that ran between the last of the foothills and the first real mountain. Both Vexanious and Clonder, Nerfal's bay, were blowing hard as they paced up the hill. Deirdre stared about her at the sparsely forested expanse that marked the true beginnings of height. It was nearing dark, and she couldn't help shivering in spite of her warm wool cloak.

The sun was setting behind them, tinting the rock face a shiny crimson that reminded Deirdre of drying blood. Unbidden, an image of Fiver's vision from the beginning of *Watership Down* came to mind. This was not a comforting image, she decided, and pushed it aside quickly. They rode into a passage between tall rocks that curved slightly to the right for a way, and Deirdre began to feel claustrophobic with the narrow walls around her.

The first stars of evening were beginning to show now as well. Nerfal had said nothing the entire trip and had ridden so stiffly that she was surprised that he stayed atop his mount. She could tell that he wasn't thrilled with what he was doing but apparently found it a necessity, though not an enjoyable one.

The narrow track suddenly disappeared, and Nerfal reined in his stallion. Dismounting, he led the bay to the left of the seeming dead end and between two huge slabs of rock that had appeared to be a solid cliff face. Behind these monstrous rocks was a small clearing and beyond that, the enormous black mouth of a cave.

Nerfal stopped his horse by a soot-blackened fire pit, and Vexanious halted there as well. Her father motioned to Deirdre to dismount, and he turned to remove the tack from his stallion. Deirdre climbed stiffly from Vexanious's saddle and followed suit.

"Help me gather some wood," said Nerfal, tersely.

Deirdre looked around her and located a few small branches that she broke up and set by the fire pit. While she did this, Nerfal set about building a fire with the first batch she brought and placed over it a small tripod and kettle that he had retrieved from his saddlebags. He filled the kettle from his water skin and crushed up the contents of a small bag. The earthy smell of mushrooms filled the air as Nerfal tossed them into the kettle.

As he crouched by the fire, stirring the concoction that boiled and bubbled, giving off evil-smelling fumes, Deirdre watched him, noticing how alien he looked with his horns glistening redly in the light. The shadows grew darker behind him as the sun disappeared, and the fire cast eerie shadows and flickers of light upon the stone walls of the hollow, causing Deirdre to shiver.

After a short silence, Nerfal removed the mixture and set it on a rock to cool. Night had come completely, and stars twinkled brightly overhead. He turned to the mountain, raised his arms, and called out a long string of foreign, guttural words. The air seemed to shimmer in response, and he turned back to where Deirdre stood by the fire.

"You must remove your clothing," he said. "What happens in that cave is between you and the Land. There must be nothing to interfere."

Deirdre looked at her father for a moment, seeing man's sanity and magic's madness warring within him. She nodded and awkwardly began to undress, nervously folding her clothing neatly beside her. The cold air caressed her skin, causing her skin to stipple with goose flesh.

She removed her undergarments last, setting them by the pile of clothes, and stood trembling under the stars. Nerfal walked to the iron pot, picked it up, and crossed to where Deirdre stood barefoot on the stony ground. He dipped two fingers into the pot and proceeded to streak the mixture along the sides of her neck, on the insides of her wrists and ankles, and along the insides of her thighs. He touched between them once briefly in a ritualistic fashion that sent shivers up her spine.

"Close your eyes," he said, and she felt him rub a little across each eyelid. He then placed a finger on her lips, and when she opened her mouth she felt him place a smear of the foul tasting paste on her tongue. She swallowed with a shudder.

She watched him as he reached into the saddlebag again and pulled out two strips of black cloth. Her trust in her father wavered for a second when she realized what he meant to do, but she said nothing. She gathered her courage and steadfastly fought down her fear.

Nerfal tied the first piece across her eyes, making sure that she couldn't see. He then took her wrists and bound them firmly behind her back. Her senses were beginning to fade from the mixture he had given her and when he led her, presumably, into the cave, she was no longer able to feel the cold.

On they walked, and down, each step bringing a further cessation of touch and taste. Even her hearing seemed to be gaining a tunnel-like echoing quality, and her mind reeled at the dimming of the world. She even lost her sense of direction for a time, her mind blanking out for whole minutes.

She was vaguely aware of being helped into a boat and of the vessel moving across a body of liquid that didn't sound like water. A gritty crunch told her that they landed sometime later, and she was helped from the boat onto a solid shore. Nerfal gently guided her onto something cold that sank slightly as she stepped onto it. There was a dull clanking sound of chains, and she felt, as if from very far away, two metal cuffs lock closed around her ankles. The echo of the boat pushing off from the shore came distantly to her ears, and the drop clack of oars slowly faded in the distance. A short time later, there was a dull, hollow boom, and silence fell deeply around her.

Her senses stopped retreating and began to return, much to Deirdre's relief, but now a new effect of the drug began to take hold. She began to see things, tiny slivers of dreams. They grew as the darkness faded, and she found herself standing in a field of tall golden grass. The sun was shining in the bright blue sky, and there was a light wind blowing, rippling the grass in waves. Far away on the horizon, Deirdre could just see the beginnings of a forest.

She turned around to see another forest at her back and beyond that, tall mountains like those beyond Nerfal's keep. She looked back at the grassy expanse and saw a tall rangy black and white pinto mare with one blue eye and one brown walking towards her through the grass. The mare inclined its head in greeting and veered off to the left. Deirdre followed, and the mare led her across the field and to the top of a small hillock where she stood, looking at Deirdre expectantly. Deirdre looked down, and there below her she saw thousands of men wandering in and out of a small city of canvas tents. She wondered why she hadn't seen them when she had arrived, for that many tents would have easily been visible from beyond so small a mound.

Deirdre looked at the mare and found the horse looking back at her, their reflections in each other's eyes. Above them, the clouds began to sail by faster and faster, the bright blue darkening to a vibrant purple. The sun set in a last instant, and with the coming of the dark night came also the darkness of the cave, and Deirdre found herself back within its echoing blackness.

Shifting her balance, she heard the muffled sound of the chains at her ankles. Her arms were growing stiff behind her, and she strained to hear any sound. It was like listening through earmuffs. She could feel the cold now, and she remembered dimly from her ecology class in college how most caves stayed a constant forty degrees year round. Her bare flesh prickled, and she shivered in the cold.

Oddly, though, her feet weren't cold, and she glanced down fruitlessly into the darkness. Something tickled her ankle, and the feeling of warmth crept up an inch, accompanied by a new feeling of wetness. She remembered the damp splashes as they crossed the lake and the little click as she stepped onto the platform. She tested the chain on one foot, careful not to lose her balance, and heard a gritty sound as the links rubbed together. She wiggled her toes and felt something like wet sand between them and under her feet. The room was beginning to flood.

As her heart began to race, the drug took effect again, and she found herself in an evening forest, perched on a low branch of a tree. A path ran beneath her, rutted and well-traveled, covered with a carpet of dead autumn leaves. There was a chill in the air, and yet, she wasn't cold.

A caravan was approaching from the west, a full complement of people and horses. As they neared, she saw both men and women in the party, all riding gaily-bedecked horses and chatting cheerfully. One man looked up as they rode beneath the branches, and Deirdre was horrified to see that he had no face.

A soft rustling of feathers above her caused her to look up. Perched on a branch not a foot from the top of her head was a large peregrine falcon staring at her with its bright golden-brown eyes. Its breast feathers were cream colored with black splotches, and it clacked its hooked beak twice in greeting. Even in the dim light, she could see herself clearly in the pools of its eyes, and it nodded silently at the path below.

Deirdre looked back to see that the group had almost completely passed beneath her tree when suddenly black shapes flung themselves at the party from all sides. Horses reared, and wagons rattled off the path as the teams pulling them panicked. Screams issuing from non-existent mouths echoed through the night, and the men drew their swords, steel flashing in the fading light. The shapes were no more than black smudges with no form and no substance, yet they attacked, and they killed.

Looking up at the falcon, Deirdre saw the reflection of a bright blue blaze in its eyes, and suddenly all was dark again. She was back in the cave.

The air was becoming warmer, and she found that while she had been wherever the drug had taken her, the warm sand had ascended past her knees and was now creeping between her thighs. She tried to shift her feet, but the weight of the sand prevented any movement.

She tried to comfort herself with the idea that Nerfal had no intention of harming her and that others before had been through this type of ceremony, exiting unscathed when it was complete. These thoughts helped, but as the sand crept higher along her legs, she could not help but wonder if this wasn't some unique ploy to do away with her.

As the sand touched her mid-thigh, she was again plunged into the dreamtime, brought once again into bright daylight. The sun was filtered this time between the green light of overhanging leaves and branches. A stream rippled noisily somewhere nearby, and Deirdre walked towards it. The air was steamy and moist, and the trees looked like those she had seen in pictures of rainforests, all moss-covered and drooping with vines.

The stream hove into view as she approached it, and she found herself walking along its bank, stepping over huge roots and occasionally long lines of insects. Sunlight patterned the forest floor in a crazy patchwork of gold and green, while in the branches above, huge birds decked in bright scarlet and sapphire feathers called to one another loudly.

She tripped over a root and fell flat on the ground, her chin coming to rest on the bank of the stream. For a moment, she lay sprawled among the roots with her eyes closed, and when she opened them and lifted her head, she found herself face to face with a large river otter. Deirdre saw her face reflected clearly in its eyes, and it chittered amiably and flicked its whiskers with a flippant twitch of its nose. It then tilted its head downstream and led the way along the bank. After what felt like hours, they came to the edge of an overgrown path that had been crudely cleared at some point in the past, and which was slowly being reclaimed.

The otter shuffled softly and backed slightly into the foliage. Deirdre did likewise, and as she sat amid the verdant growth, she heard something approaching. The brush parted and out walked a group of travelers. Like the people in the former vision, none of them had faces, and they trudged along silently through the brush. They passed through the leafy undergrowth and were gone, swallowed again by the jungle.

"What does it mean?" whispered Deirdre to the otter.

The otter only held up one paw and looked back down the path. Deirdre followed its gaze and a few moments later, a white blur of light came down the path, following the others. It moved without sound, stirring not one leaf and making no mark on the ground. As it passed where she and the otter crouched, it paused and seemed to focus on them. For that brief instant, Deirdre had a clear image of a pearl colored horn and two bright blue eyes. It rippled then, sending out a shiver of multicolored starbursts that dazzled Deirdre's eyes. When she could see again, the vision had passed, and she saw nothing but the blackness of the cave.

The sand had reached her breasts and was rising slowly to cover them. Breathing wasn't difficult yet, but she could feel how heavy it was around her legs and knew that it would soon be much harder. The sand now encased her hips, and she could no longer move either of her legs. Her fingers and hands were similarly trapped and although she could flex her elbows, it wasn't easy.

The air was much warmer, too, and the sand that now covered her body to the collarbones had become almost hot to the touch. Deirdre wondered if it was an effect of the drug. Her hearing seemed to be fading again, so it seemed likely. The air was very hard to breathe, and sweat beaded on her forehead.

Still the sand rose, and when it tickled the base of her throat, she felt a tremor of fear. It hadn't stopped at her chest as she had thought that it might. Breathing was now difficult and sweat was running off of her forehead and onto the blindfold still tied tightly about her eyes. The sand was still rising, and she realized then that it might not stop and panicked, screaming for help. Her hearing faded completely, and by the time she had exhausted herself, she felt the sand touch her chin.

That was enough to almost set her off again, and she tilted her head back until it rested on the sand, trying to keep her face free as long as possible. It crept slowly up her cheeks, filling her ears with warmth, and slowly slid over her tightly closed mouth and over her eyes. As she felt it slide into her nose, closing off her air, the drug rose up again and took her away.

It was dark here too, and warm, but she was free to move around and cautiously slid one foot in front of another, not sure what she would find. A warm glow seemed to come into view ahead of her, and she moved towards it, grateful to find that it began to brighten enough to see by. She walked forward with greater confidence and soon found herself in a huge cavern glittering with jewels of all colors, piles of brassy gold, and gleaming silver. She stared at it in amazement, having never seen such a vast array of wealth simply strewn about before her. It was everything she had ever read about a dragon's lair, and when she looked up, she saw the beast.

It sat, glistening white, upon the uppermost platform of gold, and it turned its long-snouted head upon its sinuous neck to look straight at her. Its green slit-pupiled eyes watched her unblinking in the low firelight of the tree-sized torches that lit its abode.

Neither of them moved for what felt like a long time as the dragon half opened its wings and stretched out its long neck until its face came within inches of Deirdre's own. It stared at her, no reflection in its huge elliptical eyes, and its warm breath stirred Deirdre's hair and blew it back from her face in a wave.

The great beast drew back its head and reared up on its haunches, letting forth a huge roar, loud and trumpeting. Deirdre clapped her hands over her ears and closed her eyes. The ground shook beneath her, and she cried out in fear. All became still and silent, and Deirdre opened her eyes to find herself once more eye to eye with the great beast. It opened its mouth and spoke softly,

"Not-dragon fears the flame,

"Not-dragon knows not its name."

The dragon backed up a step and inhaled deeply. With a loud grating sound, it spat fire at Deirdre, and just before the vision vanished, Deirdre saw the face of a young man looking back at her. Then all went black.

————

She stood alone, free from drug, bond, and sand, with no trace of any of them upon her body. It was still dark in the cave, but she had a sense of completion and of regret, for she felt that although she had been accepted by the other animals she had met, the dragon had rejected her. Her heart sank, and she lowered her head.

From the darkness came a low sound, half hum and half breath, of barely audible song. The noise grew until it was clearly music, and a wind rose around her, seeming almost visible to the eye as it lifted her hair from her brow.

"Little sister, the Land accepts you and welcomes you into its embrace. You are truly a member of the Ettars, and the Land has recognized you by the horns upon your brow."

"But I failed the final test. The dragon refused me!" cried Deirdre.

The air whirled around her, sighing and moaning in disharmonious chords.

"It did not fully accept you, that is true," sang the wind, "but it gave you a hint as to how you may attain it. You must follow this clue in order to prove yourself worthy of the dragon's aid. Do not tell anyone yet of what the beast has told you. Nerfal is a true and honest servant of the Land, but his love for you may blind him to the need."

"Did he try to stop Darlena? Is that why she was never able to become the dragon?"

The wind's whistling became very low and very still for a few moments before whispering, "Darlena never saw the dragon."

The air stilled, its music vanished, and Deirdre stood staring into the darkness, her head reeling with the last bit of information. How could it be? Darlena had been born in this land. Wasn't that enough? Or was it the vision of the dragon that gave one the power to become it? She pondered over the bit of rhyme it had quoted her but was unable to make much sense of it.

As she stood on the platform contemplating the events that had transpired during her experience, a dull boom sounded in the distance and torchlight flooded the cavern. Deirdre saw Nerfal step into a small boat and row across what she could now see to be a lake of watery sand to where she stood. She waited patiently, her mind still reeling.

He landed the craft and leapt to the shore, hugging her fiercely as he laughed with relief. He released her and wrapped her cloak around her shoulders, guiding her swiftly into the boat and rowing back across. From there, he led her from the cave and back out to their campsite.

Outside, Deirdre was amazed to see the sun rising low from behind the mountains and feel the chill of the early fall morning. It was dawn, and that meant that she had spent the whole night in the cave. Nerfal handed her clothes to her, and she dressed quickly, accepting the cup of semi-sweet hot cocoa-like sweetling that Nerfal proffered and sitting down by the fire.

Vexanious walked over to her and wuffled her hair in greeting. Silently, he lay down behind her, providing her with a backrest and his warmth. She settled up against his smooth side gratefully and warmed her hands around the rough clay mug. She felt raw and newborn in the chilly new day.

"So," said Nerfal, his tone light, but taut with worry, "how did it go?"

Deirdre sighed and closed her eyes, leaning further against Vexanious's side and letting the warmth of the new sun revive her.

"It was probably the most...I don't know how to properly describe it, Nerfal. Tense, thrilling, exciting...terrifying, definitely terrifying, experience I have ever had. The drug you gave me, a hallucinatory plant mixture of some kind, right?" At his nod, she continued, "It both dimmed and enhanced my perception, forcing me more inside myself. The sand–was that real?"

"Yes, it is the Land's way of testing your mental abilities and of cleansing you. It is not easy to deal with, especially under the influence of the drug. You do not seem horribly upset by that part. Why?"

"Faith," smiled Deirdre, looking at Nerfal. "I mean, it would be really silly of you to bring me all this way just to kill me, right? There are much easier ways. That, and I trusted you."

"Thank you for that. It puts me at ease to hear you say that. I had fears that trust would not be enough." Nerfal sipped his own cup of sweetling and said, "So, what did you see?"

"I saw a horse first," said Deirdre. "It met me in a wide field that looked to be below your lands. I saw these mountains, but from a greater distance than from your keep and beyond some woodland. The horse led me to a hill, and over it lay a vast army."

Nerfal frowned and nodded.

"The horse is one of your animal forms. What you saw is what you will become once you master the ability to shapeshift. The event...that may well be the mustering of armies when the Perstalians make their attack come spring. Or it may be only a possible outcome of things in the future. It is too early to say. What else did you see?"

Deirdre described first her encounters with the falcon and then the otter to Nerfal, including her impressions of blue lights and spiral horns. Nerfal had no thoughts on the first, and nodded to himself on the second. He stressed that neither event was set in stone. When she was finished, he sighed and shook his head.

"There was nothing more?" he asked.

"I did have a fourth vision," she said.

His eyes lit up, and he looked at her expectantly.

"I saw a dragon," she said.

Nerfal sat up straight and fixed her with an intent stare.

"What did it do?" he asked.

"It looked at me for a moment, then it spat fire at me."

"It said nothing to you?" he asked. Deirdre shook her head, remembering what the wind had said about her father holding her back, and Nerfal sighed, "All is not lost. At least you saw the dragon. Most people never do, so there is still hope for us. The jungle scene you described may be down below the Southern Mountains. That is where the dragons are said to have gone, back when they left Keyralithsmus. The Queen may order an expedition to go and find them. It is a dangerous place to go alone and far too dangerous a place for you."

Deirdre said nothing and finished her chocolate without comment. Nerfal smiled at her reassuringly, thinking her silence to be acquiescence rather than reticence.

"In any event," he said, standing and stretching, "you have gone through your initiation and are now officially an Ettar in looks as well as in blood. Feel your forehead, Deirdre."

He turned and began to pack up their belongings, casually watching her reaction. Deirdre touched her brow to find two tiny pronged horns growing there. She felt a thrill run through her as she rubbed the smooth double-tined horns and shivered with fear and delight.

"Did they suddenly just grow there while I was in the cave?" she asked, looking up at Nerfal. "Yesterday they were just little bumps."

"Nobody knows for sure how it happens, but the ritual somehow completes their growth. That is as big as they will get, by the way, and you will get used to them in time."

Vexanious made to stand, and Deirdre moved from his side, rising to her feet to make room for him to do likewise. Nerfal tacked up both of the horses and helped Deirdre into her saddle.

"You look like limp straw," said Nerfal. "We will take it easy on the way home. Nothing fancy. Just sit."

He mounted his own horse, and they headed back on the road to the keep. Deirdre reveled in the warmth of the sun on her back and the songs of the birds, but she still felt a deep unease at her failure to be accepted by the dragon. She tried to keep it from her face, however, and focused to Nerfal's stories of his own childhood on the long ride back to the keep.

5

Deirdre sat in her room, warm in a heavy wool robe, as close to the big fireplace as she could get and still stand the heat. Night was gathering in and around the big house, and there was a definite chill in the air. Nerfal had mentioned that this was the true harbinger of winter and that the cold would be soon setting in with a vengeance. There might be a couple more warm days, but winter was truly on its way.

It had been, in all ways, an exhausting day. They had arrived back at the keep in early afternoon and, by then, Deirdre had been all but asleep on Vexanious's back, lulled by the gentle sway of his walk. The entire family had gathered to greet them; most came from the outlying farms that Deirdre had seen maybe once in passing. Elaina had rushed her to the great hall and plied her with food and wine until Deirdre felt fit to burst. Other family members milled about the hall, eating, talking, congratulating her, and asking her more questions than she felt she could ever answer. The boys, Darin and Brede were the most persistent, for they soon would be making their own allegiance to the Land. Deirdre told them very little outside of her visions as Nerfal had cautioned that the cave and its secrets should not be discussed with those not already initiated.

To her surprise, very few of the other residents had been through the cave ritual, and a word to Nerfal confirmed her suspicions. Not every member of the family went through the initiation. It was experienced only by Nerfal's family, or by the next in line for the position of the Ivory Lady. Some women had been through two rituals in their lifetimes and had gained their other two forms in the cave some years after originally growing their horns.

The rest of the evening was spent at the tailors; her wardrobe was mostly finished and needed only a final fitting and the selections of trims and, on the two more formal gowns, jeweled beads and gold threads to be patterned and sewn. Deirdre tried not to laugh as the tailor chalked lines for golden threads and placed dots for small faceted garnets to be stitched. It seemed overdone to her and, in light of her earlier experiences that afternoon, of very little importance.

Dinner was a quiet affair with only the central family members and Nersh. They talked in hushed tones, but each of them bore a look of pride and hope that they had carried since she and Nerfal returned that afternoon.

After eating, Deirdre had retired to her rooms and been pleasantly surprised to find a hot bath drawn and waiting for her. She had soaked until the water had cooled, wrapped herself in her robe, and curled up on the settee by the fire in the sitting room. She stared into the flames, deep in drowsy thoughts, and the worries that had plagued her since she first arrived seemed dim and not so important. Her mind wandered, thinking about the dragon's riddles and the Ivory Seat, so when the gentle tap came at her door, she at first did not respond to it. Only when it came a second time did she rise and walk over to the door, shearling slippers scuffing softly against the wood.

Nerfal glanced up from where he stood seeming transfixed by the brass knob on the door. He also looked tired and drawn, and Deirdre realized then that her father had not slept the night before during the vigil outside of the cave.

"Come in," she said, opening the door wider for him, and he stepped slowly inside. He was still fully dressed, and, like her, he was wearing soft slippers on his feet. He nodded at her and walked over to a chair by the fire. Deirdre closed the door, returning to the settee.

"I wanted to thank you," he said, slowly. "Thank you for trying so hard and going through so much. I realize that much of what you have undergone was not in the original agreement we had. I just did not want to tell you everything in the beginning. I was not sure that the Land would accept you as thoroughly as it has."

"And now that it has?" she asked.

"We will be leaving for Remembrance in three days. Vexanious wants to spend as much time in practice with you as he can before we get there, so you will be riding more than anything for the next couple of days."

"Won't he be coming with us?" asked Deirdre trying to hide her disappointment at the thought of losing the stallion's company and tucking her hands into her sleeves to warm them.

"Oh, yes, he certainly will be coming, but it will not do for him to be calling out instructions to you once we get into the city. You need to appear as if you have ridden all your life. No one must guess you are not from here."

Nerfal sighed and clasped his hands together, resting his chin on them and looking at his daughter.

"I wonder sometimes if you have any regrets or worries about what you have done," he said. "I think that you must feel very out of place here."

"Only sometimes," said Deirdre. She stared at the fire for a moment. "Most of the time it all seems...I dunno...normal. It's hard to describe. Hold on a second."

She stood up and walked into the bedroom, returning a moment later carrying a large, green hardbound book. She handed this to Nerfal and leaned over the back of his chair, watching as he opened it.

"This was my mother's," she said. "She drew them before I was born."

She peered into Nerfal's face as he opened the book and began to slowly turn pages. About a third of the way through, he stopped, his eyes growing wide and round with surprise.

"Randolph gave it to me after I entered into art school about five years ago," she said. Nerfal glanced up at her, and she nodded. "Good likeness, don't you think?"

"So you knew?" asked Nerfal.

"That you were my father? No. I had no idea that her drawings were anything but pure fancy. When I saw you, though, I remembered the book and decided to bring it with me."

Nerfal continued to flip pages and stopped again a little further on.

"This one," he said, glancing up at Deirdre again. "The style is different. This is of Nersh and me by the lake. Did you do this?"

She nodded.

"I found that I could draw at a really young age. Randolph arranged for me to take lessons from a local artist friend of his. Won a few contests, made a little money on the side. Went to college for art and came out with a piece of paper that simply confirmed that I could draw and paint." Deirdre laughed and moved to sit back down by the fire. "But I'm good at it. I was going to turn professional and had dreams of earning quite a bit of money."

"Was?" prompted Nerfal gently.

"Well," she said, chuckling, "first, there's the little matter of these horns upon my head. Even though they are only about two inches tops, people are going to look at me a little funny. Second, well, who's to say? I like it here, Nerfal. Aside from Randolph, there is no one back there I'd really miss. A bunch of wannabe artist friends who never call unless they want to borrow money and who are about as deep as mirrors, a few credit card companies who have more of my money than I ever spent in the first place, and a couple of ex-boyfriends I'd rather forget. Providing I can visit Randolph, I see no reason to return permanently once this is all over."

"Yes," said Nerfal, "once this is all over. If it ever *is* all over. It may be that you will not want to stay should Perstalia conquer us. If we cannot call the dragons, there is very little hope of us defeating the invaders. We will try, of course, but they outnumber us greatly."

He rose, handing the notebook back to Deirdre. She took it without a word and hugged it to her chest.

"Get some sleep now," he said. "Only three days left. Things are going to be hectic."

Deirdre watched him as he let himself out, shutting the door behind him. She then rose, banked the fire, and went to bed, still clutching the sketchbook, the last page of which bore, unseen by her father, the words the dragon had given her.

6

"It is days like this that I wish I had never become a diplomat," said Nersh, glancing up at the sky and shaking herself as a cold gust of wind mussed her fur yet again. "I could be curled up by a warm fire, asleep, if I had been a wiser wolf in my youth."

Count Nerfal laughed and patted his stallion on its shaggy neck. The bay's winter coat was beginning to come in rapidly, and the horse was somewhat irritable with its itchy growth, lashing his tail across his haunches. Vexanious sported a similar coat, though the talking horse had seemed almost gleeful in the past day and a half since they had started out for the city. Nerfal wondered absently what Vexanious thought of the whole affair but said nothing to the stallion. He was enjoying the journey too much to question the big horse's jubilant mood.

Deirdre smiled at Nersh's grousing. It was now afternoon. They had only been on the road for an hour earlier today, their second morning out from the Keep, when they had come to the spot Deirdre had seen in her vision. It was as she remembered, directly below the tree line, on the very edge of the plains. Grasses gilded a golden autumn brown rippled like waves on the sea and covered the gentle hillocks and rises in a constantly undulating mantle of sun and shadow. They had turned to see the mountains above the Keep rising purple and black above the trees, their tops already capped with snow.

Now, later in the day, the mountains became more distant as they rode down among the foothills and began to reach gently rises with fewer trees. The horses ambled along drowsily in the crisp air that smelled of dried grass and ginger, Nersh grumbling a little to herself as she trotted off ahead of the horses. Her gait was stiff, but she seemed to have more energy than she had in the several weeks previous, and the old wolf acted much happier in many ways. Grinning, Nerfal turned to look at his daughter where she rode next to him.

Deirdre rode easily in her saddle, her head held high, and she looked around with intense curiosity. All of these sights were new to her, he reminded himself, and he watched her take in the landscape with his own renewed sense of wonder. She made a striking figure as she sat on the black horse dressed as she was in an ivory-hued riding habit with dark blue velvet diamonds sewn across the bodice and a matching pattern around the base of her skirt. Sunlight picked out the red highlights in her hair and lit up her whole face.

Noting his glance, she looked towards him, eyes quizzical.

"What is it?" she asked.

"You certainly look nothing like the Otherworld woman who crossed over with me three weeks ago," he said. "You sit a horse as well as any of the ladies in my court, you carry yourself with a certain flair... what have we done to you?"

Deirdre laughed and looked off into the distance for a moment. She smiled, shaking her head.

"I think," she said, "That you unearthed the person I was always meant to become."

When he said nothing, she glanced over at him to see him looking at her with a puzzled look. She smiled and continued.

"People," she went on, "spend all their lives trying to get to a point where they become the best they can be. A lot of them never succeed, due to fate or poor judgment, or just lack of trying. I think that I am now where I have been trying to get for most of my life. I still have plenty to learn, I'll still grow, but I am on the path, my path, and that makes me feel really good."

Nerfal nodded and looked ahead as the road continued over the ever-decreasing hills with their occasional trees and the bright grass between. In the distance ahead, a small wood was visible, and he smiled, knowing that, if all went well, their trip would be over by nightfall.

"There are very few people," he said, "who could have such faith in a stranger as you have displayed. I think that it was not so much my unearthing yourself as it was you being willing to take the steps and risk everything that you had to in order to get where you needed to be."

Deirdre stared ahead into the distance, absently patting Vexanious on the neck.

"You may be right," she said, "but the journey's only just begun."

She grinned at him, noticing that he'd caught her pun.

He snorted his amusement and nodded at the trees in the distance.

"Well, this part of the journey is very close to its conclusion," he said. "Once we pass those trees, we will be able to see the coast, and I would guess that we will be at the castle by dinner."

"So soon?" she asked, almost wistfully.

"You sound like you want to spend another night on the road," said Nerfal.

"Last night wasn't so bad," smiled Deirdre, thinking of the family they had stayed with. "I guess that I am just nervous about meeting the Queen and having to watch myself so closely in everything I do and say."

"It will not be easy, no, but Brena knows about you and will support your position. You may well hear mutterings about your right to the Ivory Castle seat, but I assure you, the horns on your brow and your visions in the cave are more than enough proof for the Queen."

"Speaking of which, when do you plan on teaching me how to shapeshift?" asked Deirdre. "We haven't had very much time to talk about it."

"I know," said Nerfal, "I planned to wait until we were on the road again to the Ivory Castle. We can go straight there from Carathusin, if you like, though there is one detour I feel might be worth making. Before we left, I received a notice that Lady Judeth of Garey Manor will be holding a ball in your honor."

"A ball? Isn't that a little...well...foolhardy, given the situation?"

"Not really," said Nerfal. "It is a reassuring gesture on her part. She likes to do that. She tends to take care of people. We do not have to attend it, but it would be a good way for you to meet some of the other lords and ladies from various parts of the country. It had completely slipped my mind until now. Some of the other castle folk will be going as well, lesser nobles who wish to get out of the city one last time before the snow flies. It promises to be a large event, one that you might want to attend."

"Ah," nodded Deirdre, swaying to Vexanious's gentle stride, "Sort of an 'everything's ok' gesture. Does she know that she is doing it that way, or is she just not grasping the full implications of the pending war?"

"Judeth knows all too well," said Nerfal, glancing sharply at his daughter. "She lost her father in the last incursion and has made it her mission to keep everyone on a level keel. Brena has told me that she wants to make you visible to prove to any doubting nobles that you are real."

"Oh, great!" said Deirdre. "I thought that you said I didn't have to go!"

"We do not *have* to go," said Nerfal. "Let us just say that it is strongly encouraged."

"Funny," said Deirdre, "very funny. Only there's one little problem."

"What would that be?"

"In all of your lesson plans, you left out one small, significant thing. I don't know how to dance."

Nerfal turned and looked at her, his expression stunned. He then looked skyward and clasped his hand over his eyes, shaking his head in disbelief. Nersh glanced back and slowed a little to let them catch up.

"What is it?" said the wolf.

"Would you believe that I missed something so elementary?" he laughed. "You do not *dance* in your world?"

"Well, we do, but I tend to trip over my feet a lot."

Nersh chuckled.

"You should have seen Nerfal when he learned to dance. His father hired him four different teachers before he found one who could teach this man to place his feet correctly."

"I can teach you some simple steps that are used in most of the dances," said Nerfal, glaring at the wolf, as she trotted away laughing. "Sometimes I really think she likes to tease me too much."

The horses ambled along through the mid-afternoon sunlight that forced its way through the gathering clouds. The air cooled even further as the sunlight was slowly diminished, and a chill crept into the air.

"It occurs to me," said Nerfal as they finally drew close to the trees sometime later, "that your world is a wonderful mass of contradictions. Ladies learning to sword fight rather than dance, horses being ridden only for pleasure..."

"Which seems odd, even from my perspective," said Vexanious.

"But that's the way it is," sighed Deirdre, "odd as it may seem. Some women can't sew either, did you know that? Others can't cook or clean. Often they do things even better than the men, and some men cook very well. I am sure that it happens here too, just less often."

"I suppose that you are right. The women I know do have odd talents, come to think of it...but at least," said Nerfal, with a twinkle of laughter in his eyes, "*they* can dance!"

———

It was full dark when they finally passed through the woods and came, at last, to the headlands. The land rose up steeply, a segment of the rocky coast that reared to a great stretch of land above the sea, and the strong smell of the ocean air came to her. It was on top of this plateau that the city of Remembrance and the shining edifice that was the Carathusin Palace stood, perched far above the sea and glowing from within as if carved from magical light. Deirdre recognized it at once as the castle in the picture that had captured her attention so strongly the first day she was at the Keep.

"Each block was hewn from crystal deposits in mines far away," said Nerfal as they paused to admire the glowing castle. "They were brought down by dragons in homage to Tali in his days as king. It became the central castle of Keyralithsmus when the humans came to live in this realm, and one of our own bloodline has resided on the throne since the pact with Rathal was made. The hornless Kin often come here as they feel accepted, yet are among family."

"I'm sure that the politics are in full swing here," said Deirdre.

"Oh yes, there is a great vying for the Queen's attention." They rode on, and Nerfal continued, "Most of the posturing is done to attract someone's notice. It is like this in any court where power is involved, is it not?"

"True," said Deirdre. Vexanious began to labor up the steeply twisting road that led to the city. "It's the same in our world. I hope I am not expected to play that game. Fawning is not in my nature."

Nerfal laughed.

"You will certainly be a mystery to them," he said. Just then, his horse stumbled, and he patted it on its glossy neck. "Not long now," he said fondly. "Hot mash and a warm stall for you tonight, my friend."

"Warm hearth and a belly full of supper for me, I hope," said Nersh. "I am going to be some sore come morning. All this traveling, at my age!"

Nerfal laughed, and they continued to weave their way up the switchback road as it wound its way to the top. It was a very wide road and well-maintained, with strong fencing at the edge, so it was not as unnerving as it could have been. As they continued to climb, and the tops of the trees were suddenly below them, it occurred to Deirdre that this road was not particularly comforting either. She longed to be somewhere that she didn't feel as if they might potentially float off into space.

About halfway up, the road curved once more and brought them face-to-face with a guard post cleverly hidden within the rocks. Two guards in white uniforms wearing grey sashes barred the way with crossed spears.

"State your names and business in the capital, if you please," said one, peering at the wolf and the two horned riders.

"Count Nerfal Ettar and Lady Nersh d'Wulvra escorting the newly proclaimed Ivory Lady, Deirdre Ettar, to her first audience with Her Royal Highness, Queen Brena Tanols," said Nerfal formally. "We are expected, gentlemen."

The guards lowered their spears and bowed to them.

"Her Majesty sent word that you would be arriving, and that you would be expected before sunset," said one. "Just a moment, and I will see to your escort."

He disappeared into the outpost and returned moments later with two men and their horses.

"How do you fit all of that into the cave?" asked Deirdre

"Caves actually, my Lady," said the first guard. "This set of caves goes all the way to the guard station in the castle. The whole hill is connected in some fashion. They say it was done by dragons before they went south."

"Dragons!" the second guard snorted. "I have never seen any, have you? They exist only in legends, if at all."

"Ah, my young warrior, there you are wrong," said Nerfal, "but look sharp. We wish a warm bed and a good meal. I assume that Queen Brena will be alerted of our arrival?"

"Already done, my Lord," said the first guard. "One of the other officers has been sent through the caves to take word to the castle." He pointed to the two other men, who were mounting their horses. "These two will lead you now, if you like."

"Yes," said Nerfal. "Do lead on. The hour grows late, and we are cold."

The mounted guards led as they continued the rest of the way up the road. Once at the top, Deirdre got a much better look at the Carathusin Castle. It was a sight that took her breath away. The castle glowed softly from within and lit the night. The plateau it rested on was only steep on the side they had come up and to the north where it met the mountains that bordered the sea. The other two sides sloped gently down to meet the fields and shore, and managed to host a complex, brightly lit city, one larger than she could ever have imagined existing there.

The castle was at the topmost level, surrounded to either side by the homes of the wealthy. As they drew closer to the castle, they passed shops and hostels, taverns and temples, all arranged precariously on ledges of land above the sea. By the pale light of a partially clouded crescent moon, she could see the sails of ships in the harbor below, gleaming softly white in the moonlight, the illumination from their lanterns dancing on the waves near the shore.

A few more turns of the road, and they were passing huge mansions sheltering behind imposing stone walls, many guarded by armed men at their front gates. Behind some, the sounds of laughter and gaiety rang out while others lay dark and eerie. These latter had guards who stood back in the shadow, nodding sullenly to the escorts as they rode by.

Their path turned abruptly, and suddenly the towering castle stood directly in front of them, torchlit and seeming as bright as the moon itself. They were led up to a great set of arched wooden doors that opened out to the sides of the portal, like wings. The bottom of a raised iron portcullis was visible just beyond the doors, and two more liveried guards clad much like their escorts flanked the entrance. Past them, a passage led into the castle grounds beyond, and the whole party came to a halt while the mounted guards spoke to those at the gate.

Deirdre sat momentarily unable to do anything but stare at the huge castle in disbelief. The whole thing looked like it belonged in a Disney theme park. Huge blocks carved from milky translucent quartz made up the main body of the castle. The walls arched gracefully upwards, and the corner towers were topped with mosque-like bell caps. Flags fluttered from every pinnacle, lit brightly from below, all a deep red color with the Keyralithian heraldry emblazoned on them: a stone tower flanked by stag horns between which lay a hoof print unlike any Deirdre had ever seen. Nerfal had shown it to her some days before and informed her that it was the print of a unicorn – two cloven halves and a triangular piece behind.

The leader of their escort bade them follow him into the bright corridor. Deirdre noticed that the castle had been built for defense as well as beauty. Arrow slits lined the passage on both sides, and several 'murder holes" opened in the ceiling, providing easy access to pour deadly liquids into the somewhat narrow passageway.

They rode beneath another portcullis at the far end of the passage and out into a huge open courtyard. The area was planted with flower beds and fruit trees, now bare of leaves and all but the most shriveled of fruits. Small two-person benches were tucked in secluded corners of the hedges, and graceful wrought-iron gazebos stood amongst the roses, fragrant with the last dying blooms. The smell of the sea was fainter here, but still was pervasive behind odor of the flowers.

Near a central gazebo, two domed cages held white doves cooing softly as they settled down for the night, and a white peacock strutted vainly in the light of the torches, shrieking hideously as the company slowly rode past. Its matching mate preened nearby, and ran from the horses as they approached.

They passed through a low gate set on one of the man-high walls that surrounded the gardens and came into the courtyard proper where men, horses, and servants meshed together in chaotic splendor. Deirdre caught a brief glimpse of a kennel full of barking, milling hounds eagerly watching their keeper approach with a tray full of meats. In another corner stood a huge mews filled with hawks and falcons of all kinds, each in its own section; huge gyrfalcons, noble red-tails, and swift peregrines. Magnificent horses were being led in and out of the stabling area, each one groomed to a glossy sheen. It looked like absolute chaos to her, but she sensed an underlying rhythm to the activities, and she laughed to herself, picturing the people she saw suddenly confronted with rush hour traffic in Boston. They would most likely feel very much as she did now, and she gripped Vexanious's reins even tighter, sobering as she realized where she was.

"Gently!" he whispered through clenched teeth, and she relaxed her grip.

They arrived at last at a large paddock that occupied a full quarter of the courtyard, giving the horses an acre or so to run in. It made Deirdre even more aware of the span of the castle itself to realize the size of the interior. Their own horses splashed across the muddy ground, coming to a stop near the entrance to the stables, a large building that seemed to grow out of the castle itself.

The guards dismounted, and one walked inside the stable. Minutes slowly passed, and Deirdre shivered, pulling up the cloak's hood to ward off the fine mist that had started to fall. Nersh moved to stand under Vexanious as the mist changed to a steady rain, and all of the horses were snorting and shifting uneasily.

"This is absurd," said Nerfal, finally.

He dismounted the bay and led the horse over to where the other guard stood. He thrust the reins at the man and helped Deirdre to dismount. Leading Vexanious, Nerfal motioned Deirdre to follow him, retrieving the reins of the bay from the startled guard and walking into the barn.

The inside of the building was blessedly warm and dry, well-lit by lanterns and protected sconces. Deirdre, following behind the steaming horses, saw the first guard down at the end of the hall arguing with a tall, burly man dressed in worn brown leathers and wrapped in a scarlet cloak.

"Bartholomew!" hailed Nerfal. "Is this the way you treat royal guests now? Leave them sitting out in the rain and the cold?"

The man turned, his jaw dropping momentarily. He spun back to the guard and placed his gigantic hands on his hips, scowling.

"Why did ye not tell me that the horses still had riders, ye daft bastard!" he said in an angry tone, his accent sounding almost Scottish. "Ye let the Lord and Lady sit out in the cold while y'tried to argue me for my bet on tomorrow's race? I will be telling yer captain about this and no foolin! Get back to yer post!"

The man stormed out, brushing roughly past Nerfal and Vexanious. The stallion let out a very horse-like squeal and lashed out with a hind hoof that just missed the guard's posterior. The man picked up his pace and rushed from the barn.

"I truly beg yer pardon, my Lord!" exclaimed the big man. "And my Lady, tish, ye must be soaked through by the rain. Let me take yer things."

He took Deirdre's cloak and hung it to dry on a peg near the large fireplace.

"The daft lout," said the man, half to himself as he turned around and looked Nerfal straight in the eye. "Captain Rialain left orders to bring ye in by the garden gate, so as not to make as big a fuss over yer arrival. That man musta thought that y'were of no import, though I know different."

"Deirdre, may I introduce Bartholomew Wethersby, master of Her Majesty's horses and one of the Kin. Bartholomew, my daughter, the Lady Deirdre Ettar."

"My Lady," said Bartholomew, taking her hand into his broad calloused one, "it is a pleasure. I am yer father's second cousin, believe it or not, and I used t'live in Mountain Reaches though ye cannot," and here he ran his hand through his hair to emphasize its hornless-ness, "really tell."

He suddenly caught sight of the white wolf standing at Nerfal's side, and took a good look at Vexanious.

"Lady Nersh! Always a pleasure! And unless I miss my guess..."

"Hello Bartholomew," said Vexanious quietly.

"Vex!" exclaimed the man. "I cannot believe my eyes! What happened to yer never coming back here?"

"The lady needed a good mount as riding was not one of her strongest skills. I was asked as she needs all the protection we can give."

"I never thought to see y'again. Not after Benjamin..."

"For safety's sake, Bart," hissed Vexanious in an undertone, "treat me as you would any other horse. I do not think it would prudent if certain parties knew that I was here."

"Gotcha, right!" said Bartholomew. "Lads!"

Two young boys poked their heads out of the farthest stalls expectantly.

"Take these two fine animals, warm 'em, rub 'em down good, and give them a warm mash. Blanket 'em, too, once they are dry."

The boys trotted down the aisle, slowing well before they reached the horses, and took them to be fed. Nerfal, having retrieved their luggage and packs, turned to Bartholomew.

"What news?" he said.

Bartholomew sighed.

"It is the Kin, ye see," he said, slowly, "Not me, you ken, but the other ladies, wondering why one of them will not do. My Lady should be on her knowing that they will not make it easy for ye. Several of them are jealous of ye already and being a bastard on top of that... 'Tis a good thing that ye have horns on yer head; they will not do anything for fear of yer father."

"Has it gotten that bad?" asked Nerfal, looking his cousin in the eye.

"Aye," said Bartholomew, soberly. He turned to Deirdre. "The humans and the shapers have always been a bit at odds, y'ken, but never like this. The past two months... Factions have been fostering unrest. Very few Shapers and wild folk come to the castle now. The Kin are not helping matters any, either, what with their fabricated stories of what goes on in Mountain Reaches..."

His face softened, and he reached for Deirdre's cloak.

"I best not be keeping ye standing here any longer," he said. "Ye look like ye all need some rest and some food, not necessarily in that order. Come, Nerfal, I will take y'to Queen Brena. She is waiting above."

He turned and pulled open a heavy oak door that had been hidden in the shadows thrown by the fireplace. Nerfal picked up their packs and followed his cousin with Nersh and Deirdre close behind.

"Bart," said Nerfal softly as they followed the head stableman into a dimly-lit corridor that ended in a staircase. "Do you think that the guard...was that an intentional snub?"

His cousin didn't turn, but his short answer carried back clearly.

"Aye, I do."

They followed him up the stairs and through another heavy door, this one bound with iron strap work and studded with faceted nail heads. Their guide tugged it open as if it was made of cloth, and the door swung back to reveal another corridor, this one brighter and cleaner than the one before. Torches burned merrily in wrought-iron basket holders, and there were several round top doors leading off to various unknown rooms.

They came to the end of the corridor, passed through another door, and found themselves entering out into an enormous hall, the scale of which took Deirdre's breath away. The ceiling spiraled up at least six stories and was clearly the tallest spire that she had glimpsed from outside. It was the heart of the castle, without a doubt, and Deirdre looked around herself in wonder.

The whole room was paneled, carved, and sculpted of milky white quartz. Tsavons and unicorns were the main theme, but satyrs, centaurs, and even a huge bas relief dragon filled the room with a feeling of majesty. There were gigantic tropical plants growing in planter benches all around the room, and the mix of the greenery with the glowing quartz was almost overwhelming. People walked in and out amongst the plants, some sitting on the benches, some standing about talking to each other with a fairly formal attitude, though they seemed very familiar with the room itself.

Large fountains were prominent on all four of the walls and steaming water poured from tsavon's mouths and arched beneath leaping dolphins. There was a metallic smell to the moist, hot air as well, Deirdre found, and she realized that there must be a hot spring running under the castle that had been harnessed and put to good use. The hall was so big it had probably been the most economical way to heat it, as no amount of fireplaces could have done the job efficiently. Although there were two small hearths, they were obviously for ambiance only.

Nerfal glanced at her and smiled.

"In the summer,' he said, "they have a device that turns off the fountains and diverts it into a pump system that pulls water from a nearby stream. That stream runs down from the mountains and when the fountains are changed over, they run cold and keep the hall cool even on the hottest days."

"Incredible," breathed Deirdre, looking at the ivy scaling the trellises and walls of the hall. "Absolutely wonderful."

They progressed further into the room, and Nersh sighed contentedly.

"The heat certainly feels good," she said. "All of these plants are from below the Southern Mountains where it is warm all the time. The various rulers tried scores of our native plants, but none of them would grow for long, so they have been slowly importing species that looked promising and would not poison the staff. They brought one plant that looked to be the cousin of the stinging nettle, but one hapless chef's assistant brushed against it one day, and they found out how bad some of the plants could be."

"They have been a lot more careful since then; the poor boy died within an hour," said Nerfal. "There is a lot of danger below the Southern Mountains. It is no wonder the dragons stayed there. No one would risk the journey lightly."

Bartholomew glanced sharply at his cousin.

"Perhaps ye and I ought to share a drink before retiring," he said, slowly. "I think it would be a good precaution...against the cold and damp."

"Yes," said Nerfal, as they approached the dais. "Yes, I think you are right."

Deirdre looked askance at her father, but he gave a minute shake of his head and nodded at the low platform that stood before them. Deirdre looked and found herself facing two thrones, on one of which sat a woman not much older than her own twenty-four years. She had long, brown hair plaited back into a single braid and was dressed in a light blue satin gown. On her brow, she wore a small coronet with two small, silver antlers rising from the center.

Bartholomew stepped forward and went down on one knee. Deirdre noticed that all the conversations around them had stopped, and that people were moving in closer to see what was happening.

"Yer Majesty, may I present Lord Nerfal Ettar, Keeper of the Mountain Reaches, the Lady Nersh d'Wulvra of the Talking Folk, and Lord Nerfal's daughter, the Lady Deirdre Ettar, yer new Ivory Lady of the Realm."

Deirdre curtsied to the queen as Bartholomew continued.

"Lady Deirdre, may I present to ye Her Royal Highness, Queen Brena, ruler of Keyralithsmus and caretaker of the Realms.

"Yer majesty might be interested to know that yer new lady was left in the rain at my doorstep. The guard had told me that they had been instructed to bring them in by the Garden Gate, not the main."

"Yes," said the Queen, her voice carrying pleasantly out over the gathered court. "We instructed our captain to do so to further hinder our enemies by making her Ladyship less accessible to the people, in hopes that they might not immediately come to realize that she was among us. We did not instruct him to insult you, however. That will be dealt with shortly."

The queen rose from the mahogany throne on which she sat and came down to where Deirdre stood.

"You are tired, and we would believe hungry after your journey," said the Queen. Her eyes flickered to the horns on Deirdre's brow and then moved on to Nerfal's to catch his brief nod. "We will give you some time to change into dry clothes and then join us and our council in the small dining room in one half hour."

She clapped her hands, and two male servants bounded forward to come before her on bended knee. Both wore black tunics and hose with a bright blue sash.

"Take our distinguished guests to their quarters and help them get themselves settled. Lady Margret?"

A young, plump woman from the circle of castle folk stepped forwards and curtsied.

"Lady Margret, would you do our royal cousin the service of being her lady-in-waiting while she is among us?"

"Yes, your Highness," said the lady, curtsying again.

"Excellent," said Brena. She turned back to Deirdre. "The Lady Margret will see to all of your needs while you are here. She is one of our personal maids, and we can assure you, is quite discrete. Lord Nerfal, your usual manservant will attend your needs while you are here. We will see you in our chambers when you are changed. Bartholomew, you have our thanks."

The queen turned, walked back up the dais, and passed through a door behind the thrones. The servants bowed to Deirdre and Nerfal.

"If you follow me, my Lady Deirdre, my Lady Nersh," said one, "I will show you to your apartments."

Deirdre nodded and, with a last look at Nerfal, followed the man with Nersh at her side. Lady Margret fell into step behind them, followed by another servant carrying Deirdre's bags, and they proceeded down the length of the hall and out a set of double doors opened for them by two of the royal guards.

The air of the antechamber felt almost cold after the warmth of the Great Hall, and Deirdre was all the more aware of the dampness of her clothes as the chill air quickly sucked the heat away from her skin. The servant set a brisk pace, leading them through the small antechamber into a large, albeit still small-feeling hall that looked to be an entry-way, and swiftly up an enormous staircase that split midway and spread out like a pair of wings to connect to the floor above. The servant chose the left side of the stairs and, at the top, took the first passageway next to the rotunda. From there, with Deirdre almost jogging to keep up with him, he made two more quick rights and a left through gorgeously tapestried corridors before he stopped at a set of doors marked with a small plaque on which gilt words were embossed.

It read: "The Ivory Suite"

"My Lady," said the servant, "I will return in one half hour to escort you to dinner. Lady Margret, I will see to the moving of your effects at once."

He bowed and was gone. The other servant placed Deirdre's bags by the door, bowed with a sense of apology, at a nod from Lady Margret, followed the other servant back down the hall.

Deirdre stared after him a moment.

"You should not have let the first man order you about like that, my Lady," came a soft voice at her elbow.

Deirdre turned to find Lady Margret nodding towards the departed figures

"I thought that he was polite enough," said Deirdre.

"He snubbed you just now. He should have waited for you to give him permission to go. I will warn you now, my Lady, not many people in this castle hold much love for Shapers. Shall we go in by the fire and get you warm and dry? I will tell you a little more as time permits."

Deirdre nodded, and Lady Margret opened the door for her to proceed through. Deirdre did so with Nersh close behind, and the lady followed them in, carrying Deirdre's bags.

"You travel fairly lightly, but I assume that once the rest of your luggage arrives, you will have quite the selection," said Lady Margret. She went past Deirdre, disappearing into one of the other rooms.

Deirdre stood, gazing around herself in the first room, feeling out of place all over again. Four doors branched off from the room in which she stood, but the one she was in had captured all of her attention for its sheer lack of color. Everything, every little detail, was captured in an ivory hue. Three lavish couches bracketed the fireplace, carved of white marble into the shapes of huge tsavons, the front halves of which curved around to form the armrests. Their carved heads rested on the forepaws, and rather than being fierce, they conveyed the feeling of patient guardians. Deirdre walked over to one of the three and ran her hand along the face of the beast, marveling at the intricate details that flowed under her fingertips. She sat down on one of the velvet cushions that graced them, tracing the curved lines of the crested mane with her index finger, almost afraid to touch such magnificent art.

Lady Margret cleared her throat, and Deirdre turned to see her standing in one of the doorways.

"They do not have such things where you come from?" she asked.

"Not in any place I have ever lived," replied Deirdre.

"Her Majesty told me to expect you to be different. She mentioned that your home, your world, was a very different place...and no, she has not told everyone. I am to be your tutor, at least in some of the more subtle politics that Count Nerfal might have been unaware of. Feelings towards shapers have been changing at the castle and the city beyond. The Kin have divided. Some of us, like Bartholomew and myself, are loyal to the Queen and the Pact. Others have been whispering rumors of conspiracies, causing the ignorant and the undecided to hesitate and contemplate their lies."

She walked over to where Deirdre sat and perched on the couch next to her.

"Some," she said softly, "are trying to convince Brena to break the Pact, and if they cannot do that, they talk of overthrowing her. It is said that several guards were present the night that Darlena was killed and that they did nothing until it was too late."

Deirdre stared at Lady Margret's sober, unflinching gaze, and the lady nodded.

"They *let* her be killed," said Lady Margret, "but...there is no proof, you see."

A chill ran down Deirdre's back, and she exchanged a startled glance with Nersh.

Margret rose abruptly, breaking the mood, and waved her hand around to encompass the room.

"All of this is yours," said the lady. "You have a dressing room, a bath, a bedchamber, and through that fourth door is where I shall be staying. I will be the one to answer your door, draw your baths, and assist you in a myriad of small ways. If you have any questions, please ask, as I am sure that some of our ways will be strange to you."

"They are already," said Deirdre, rising from the soft velvet. "I am grateful to have someone who understands my...situation."

Lady Margret nodded.

"Now," she said, "may I assist your Majesty in changing? You have paltry few dresses in your luggage. When will the rest arrive?"

"That is all I have," sighed Deirdre. "I suspect that a trip to the tailor is in order."

"Did you bring a copy of your measurements, my Lady?" asked Lady Margret.

"I believe so, yes," said Deirdre and paused. "Margret, can we, at least in private, dispense with the formalities? I assure you, you are doing me no disservice by calling me Deirdre."

"Deirdre, then," said Margret, smiling, "And you will call me Margret? Lady is far too formal among friends."

"Agreed. I realize why we have to maintain a formal front in court, but it seems so...strange."

"Not so much to me, but I know what you mean. I was born here and am a member of the Kin, but there is some small part of me that wished for a simpler life sometimes. Lady Nersh, I will arrange for your dinner to be sent up here, if you like. You look about done in."

"That would be wonderful, thank you," said Nersh, stretching out by the fire.

Walking over to the wall, Margret pulled on a small, ornate tapestry, and a little bell jingled nearby. Almost at once, there was a knock. Margret answered it, and spoke briefly to a person out of Deirdre's line of sight. Closing the door again, Margret smiled and held a hand out to Deirdre.

"All is arranged," she said to Nersh, and turned to her new charge. "Come, then, let us get you dressed for dinner. We have not much time left."

———

Margret had barely finished braiding Deirdre's long hair into a simple, yet elegant design when the knock came at the door. Nersh glanced up, then returned to where she was dozing, a now-empty platter beside her. Margret answered the door, transforming into the elegant Lady Margret so quickly that Deirdre almost had to laugh. The same servant stood in the doorway, his attitude slightly haughty.

"Dinner is to be served. Will you come?"

Deirdre stepped forward and drew herself up to stand very tall.

"You did us an insult earlier. We shall expect to be treated more courteously and with the respect due our station in the future."

She managed not to smile as she recited the speech that she and Margret had worked out while she dressed and was satisfied to see the look on the man's face alter from smug to uncertain.

"I beg your Highness's pardon," he said, "I meant no disrespect and do apologize."

He bowed low.

"When you are ready," he said, "I will escort your Highness to dinner."

Deirdre nodded her head to him, and said,

"Lead on."

The man turned and led the way out of the room. Deirdre followed him with Margret a step behind her. They proceeded back to the staircase and down the steps to the foyer. Instead of going towards the Great Hall, however, they followed a wide passageway that led beneath the staircase to the end where a pair of large arched double doors stood flanked by two guards. The men opened the doors as they approached and stepped to the sides, looking neither right nor left.

"The Queen's elite," whispered Margret when they had passed into the dimly lit antechamber. "All of them are Kin and, regardless of their thoughts on Shapers, are loyal to the Queen."

The servant led them to another arched set of double doors and knocked twice. The doors swung inwards, and Deirdre found herself looking upon a small group of people all seated around a formal dining table.

Her father was there, dry and looking much warmer for it. Next to him sat the Queen, now dressed in a white silk dress with pearlescent threads interwoven throughout the fabric. The others stared at Deirdre with varying degrees of approval. One, a youngish man with tousled brown hair and a quirky, delightful smile, looked almost too formal in his grey robes embroidered with green leaves at the wrist and throat. He seemed so pleased to see her that she found herself returning his smile with genuine delight.

Another man cleared his throat, and Deirdre glanced at a dark, curly haired man in an officer's uniform. His face was angular and handsome, with the chiseled features and a stern glance of a soldier. He looked at her as if he could see through her, and for a moment, she actually felt a twinge of fear. A strong desire to leave the room overcame her, but then he smiled a beautiful smile, and she wondered if the stern-faced, fearful apparition had really been there at all. Then she noted his eyes, pearl grey and cold, and knew that she had not imagined it.

Her father rose, and both his servant and the now-very proper Lady Margret bowed and departed from the room, closing the door behind them.

"My dear Deirdre," said Nerfal, "Queen Brena Tanols you have already met. May I introduce you to Lord Tomille, our Master Magician, and Captain Marshall Rialain, the head of the royal guard and consort pro-temps to the Ivory seat. To his right is his second-in-command, Ramor Vence. Going around the table, there is also the esteemed Mistress of the Purse, Frin Fanar; the Minister of Information, Dugal Wore'm; the Royal Chaplain, Elder Drenaes; the Chief

Magistrate, Master Trule'; and the Minister of the Realms, Chancellor Orek."

Nerfal turned back to the others, "My Lords, My Lady, My Queen, may I present the Lady Deirdre Ettar."

The Queen rose and walked over to where Deirdre stood and took both of Deirdre's hands in her own.

"You are more welcome than you can know, Deirdre," she said, looking steadily into Deirdre's eyes. "In fact, probably more than you can believe. Thank you for choosing to help us. Please, be seated."

Deirdre took the empty seat next to Nerfal, and the Queen returned to her own place at the table. Reaching behind her, she tugged on what Deirdre now recognized as an embroidered bell pull, and servants immediately filed into the room from a door opposite the entryway bearing steaming platters of food. They served the company swiftly and left almost as quickly as they had entered. Deirdre ate the hot baked fish and roast vegetables with real hunger. The others did the same.

Between bites, Deirdre took the opportunity to subtly glance at the councilors and try to get a feel for them. The tousle-haired Lord Tomille was first. His hands never stopped moving, and he spoke so fast and with such intensity that he stuttered over half of his words when he was excited. He reminded her of a nervous rabbit, all excitement and movement. Nevertheless, she found herself drawn to him more than any of the others. His grey robes almost seemed to have a rainbow gleam to them as he moved, and whether this was a trick of the light or something else entirely, she did not know. She only knew that she liked him instinctively and felt she could trust him, which was odd for her in any situation where she had not spoken more than two words to someone.

The Mistress of the Purse, Frin Fanar, was a short, round woman with a peculiar pinched face that looked as if she was smelling something bad all the time, even when she smiled. She wore her robes of office proudly, but Deirdre could not help but notice that they were a bit threadbare. She wondered why, if Frin was so good with money, she could not spare some for new robes, and then realized that this was likely part of the woman's plan. If she had indulged in new robes, how could she turn down requests without looking like a hypocrite? Deirdre smiled at the woman's cleverness and hoped to never have to go head-to-head with the Purse Mistress.

On the opposite end of the spectrum was Elder Drenaes, a thin, balding man who never seemed to smile. His robes were immaculate, and the golden embroidery around the sleeves must have cost a small fortune. He seemed to have nothing much to say about anything. Most chaplains of Deirdre's acquaintance always had something to say, usually with a religious bent, but Drenaes appeared a man who had become very disillusioned with his faith.

Chancellor Orek, on the other hand, was a garrulous man who never stopped talking, which might be why the Elder didn't bother. Orek was good at pontificating loudly about whatever subject was being discussed. He wore robes bearing a very old wine stain on them that had been scrubbed to no avail, and he brushed his thinning hair out of his eyes multiple times. Deirdre could not keep a straight face while looking at him; he reminded her of Fred Gwinn's character in Mark Twain's *The Mysterious Stranger*, but he seemed, from what she could tell, to be well loved by those around him.

Dugal Wore'm, the Minister of Information, was a small fair-haired man who dressed in all black, and said little more than, "Hear, hear," in frequent agreement with Orek. He offered no opinions of his own, but Deirdre could tell that he missed nothing as he watched the people around the table.

"That one," Nerfal told Deirdre in a quiet aside, "listens to everything that is said and has a perfect recall of conversations. If ever the Queen needs to remember something, he would be able to recite it verbatim, and that makes him an invaluable asset."

The only man who seemed unhappy and withdrawn was the Chief Magistrate, and his few comments indicated that this very tall, very thin man was extremely worried by what had been happening in and around the region. He was very somber, and his few remarks were pointed and exact. He was one of the most nondescript people Deirdre had ever seen, and if she had had to point him out in a crowd, she was fairly sure that she would fail.

In contrast, Marshall's Second-in-Command, Ramor Vence, was very striking. Dressed all in a black uniform and bearing several visible weapons, Ramor seemed a dangerous man to cross. He smiled only slightly at Orek's witty jests, and his eyes leapt about the room like bright frogs, trying to catch each facial expression that people made, each nuance of their speech. Several times, people glanced his way and just as quickly looked away, as if not wanting to be trapped in his gaze. He made Deirdre very nervous, and she felt as if he was trying to dissect her with his eyes.

She turned away from him, and once again met the pearly gaze of the Captain of the Royal Guard. He smiled at her and sat up straighter in his chair. Deirdre's original impression of him hadn't changed; she still didn't like him.

Dinner continued for a while, the counselor's talking about relatively trivial matters, but as the servants were gathering the plates, Marshall Rialain turned his full attention to Deirdre.

"So," said the Captain, dabbing at the corners of his mouth with a linen napkin, "how do you find our fair land, Lady Deirdre? Is it so much different from your own?"

Deirdre glanced at her father.

"It is safe to speak freely here, Deirdre. Our council knows of your situation. Aside from them, only Margret has been let in on your origins, and I have asked Her Majesty to send the lady on with you to the Ivory Castle."

Deirdre nodded and looked over at the captain. Though his countenance was pleasant, his eyes hadn't changed at all. She flickered a glance at Lord Tomille who caught it and smiled encouragingly.

"It is very different," she said. "We don't have shapers and talking beasts in my land, at least, not anymore."

"Tell me, Lady," said Tomille, and Deirdre shifted her attention to him gratefully, "is there magic where you come from?"

"Not like here," said Deirdre. "Not that I have seen much, mind you, but...I can feel it here, somehow. Like a buzzing in my brain, and I feel I could tap it if only I knew how. Our world has magic, but it is buried deep, and I have only sensed it once or twice."

"Odd," said Tomille. He gestured towards the marble fireplace at the far end of the room, and the fire that had been burning on the heath guttered and went out. A second gesture, and it came back, dancing as merrily as if never gone. "Here it is not common but accepted as a certainty. If you can feel it that strongly, we should talk together before you travel south."

"Yes," said Marshall, eyeing her thoughtfully, "I, too, have a wish to speak with you, my Lady."

"Such things will have to wait now, Captain and good master Magician," said Brena, "Count Nerfal informs me that you believe that the dragons in the South may be aware of what is going on here, Deirdre. Surely you realize that no one has seen a dragon in these lands for over two hundred years?"

"*Almost* no one," said Tomille, looking knowingly at Queen Brena.

Brena turned to look at the magician, her eyes cold. He met her gaze without flinching, and finally, the Queen turned her attention back to Deirdre.

"We will send a party in search of the Dragons," she said, "but it is a long way to the Jungle of Esalon, and there are many dangers."

"I should like to go, your Majesty," said Deirdre.

"No," said the Queen. "It is out of the question."

Elder Drenaes shook his head emphatically.

"You are far too important for us to risk, my Lady. You are the last living heir to the Ivory seat, and we need you here. Below the Southern Mountains is the Alari Desert, and beyond that is the Esalon Jungle, a place of great peril. We cannot chance sending you."

"Hear, hear," said Chancellor Orek, raising his cup and draining it. "Stay with us. Give the populace something positive to think on."

"Yes, it will be far more useful for you to go to Lady Judeth's ball and bolster the spirits of the other Ladies and Lords," said Brena. "They have been unsettled since we lost Darlena. They need to see for themselves that you are real."

She rose and gave the embroidered bell pull on the wall another short tug.

"I will have Lady Margret show you back to your rooms. You must be tired. A good night's rest, and you will feel much better. The ball is in a fortnight. That will give you a week to prepare and then another to travel there. In the meantime, we can finish outfitting you as I am told that you have nothing appropriate to your station to wear for the ball."

The servants' door opened, and one of the liveried men stepped in and bowed.

"Please fetch Lady Margret to lead Lady Deirdre to her chambers for the night."

The servant bowed again and departed, and Deirdre sat, listening to her father and the queen talk about local affairs. Lady Margret appeared a few minutes later, and Deirdre bid everyone a good evening, grateful to return to her rooms where Nersh lay curled by the dying fire. Margret helped her change into a clean nightgown, and Deirdre fell asleep almost as soon as she laid her head upon the pillows.

7

The morning sun lanced over the walls of the castle, striking the garden paths with golden light. The last dried leaves on the rose bushes glistened with a fine layer of frost, and the air was cold and very clean after the rain the night before. The grass underfoot gleamed white and crystal with frozen moisture, and the gravel paths were silvered with a fine sheen of ice.

Deirdre inhaled deeply and then let out a visible cloud of breath in the chill morning air. Lady Margret walked at her side, pointing out statues of heroes and figures that to Deirdre, still seemed half real. Centaurs bearing lances reared above the hedges, and firebirds swooped through fountains of red-dyed water. Here a wolf - a member of Nersh's clan according to Margret - leapt after a stone butterfly.

Breakfast that morning had been brought by servants, a thoughtful gesture on Margret's part it turned out, as the lady had seen how stressed Deirdre had been the night before. Eating in her rooms with Margret and Nersh, Deirdre had listened to more about the court life and how complicated things could be.

Once they had finished, Nersh had gone in search of Nerfal. Margret had assisted Deirdre in dressing, and they had gone straight to the royal tailor who took Deirdre's measurements, ignoring the ones she had brought with her, and brought out several sample styles to show her what could be made. At Margret's insistence, Deirdre had ordered six more gowns, including a gloriously extravagant ball gown with enough flounce and petticoats to put a peacock to shame. The tailor had asked her to come back in two days' time to discuss lace and embroidery and had immediately put her four assistants and three apprentices to work.

Deirdre and Margret had then fetched their cloaks and gone into the gardens to talk, feeling that it was the most peaceful area available. Deirdre had asked about the wolf statue, and Margret had delightedly begun a tour of the statuary. About halfway through the garden, they came to one that caught Deirdre's attention at once. It was of a young man, and the face seemed so familiar that she gasped when she realized that it was the man from her vision.

"Who is this?" she asked.

"That is Prince Benjamin," said Margret, her voice cracking.

Deirdre stared at the statue. The man stood proudly, holding a drawn sword in one hand while the other held a hunting horn. He looked to be dressed in a uniform very much like that of the guard. It was hard to tell, but he almost seemed to be smiling. Deirdre found that she liked him very much.

"You have heard of how he was killed?" asked Margret quietly.

Deirdre shook her head.

"He was run through by the sword of a rogue minotaur," Margret sighed. "He was a wonderful man, such a character and gallant to every lady and serving woman in the castle. I wish you could have known him."

"Yes," said the voice from behind them, "my cousin was the most decent of fellows."

Deirdre and Margret turned to see Marshall Rialain standing behind them, arms clasped behind his back. Ramor Vence was at his heels, saying nothing but watching them in a way that made Deirdre's skin crawl. Margret shifted a little and dropped her eyes.

"Lady Margret, I would like a few moments alone with my royal cousin. Please go prepare her rooms for her return. I will escort her to lunch."

Margret glanced at Deirdre and, at her nod, curtsied and returned to the castle. Deirdre watched her go and turned to face the captain with a slight feeling of trepidation. The captain signaled curtly to his second, who also took his leave of the courtyard. Captain Rialain smiled at her, but Deirdre saw that it once again went nowhere near his eyes. Perhaps, she thought, it was the result of losing so many that you love. She wouldn't feel like smiling either after that.

"My Lady, will you walk with me?" he asked, offering his arm.

Deirdre nodded and took his arm with only slight hesitation. They began to pace down the grassy paths, past the rose bushes with their dying leaves.

"I am," said Marshall, "very glad that you have come. It was our fear that you would decide that a foreign land peopled with complete strangers would not be worth the risk."

"I agreed to try," said Deirdre. "That's all I can do."

"Precisely," he said, "and the Queen and I are very grateful that you have. I, especially, am pleased with your choice. It takes a great deal of bravery to do what you have done, my Lady. May I ask if you have plans to return should we prevail?"

"I am undecided on that point, sir," said Deirdre.

"I see," nodded Marshall. "You do know that should you stay, you will be expected to find yourself a consort at some point. Most of the council feel that your bloodline should be continued on for the good of all. It would also strengthen your position, and there is a great deal you could do to bridge the rift between the Shapers and the Kin."

"Is that a statement of interest?" asked Deirdre boldly. "I am aware that you were planning to marry my half-sister, and I assume that such an alliance would elevate your status as well."

"Not half as much as yours," laughed Marshall, patting her arm in what felt to Deirdre like a condescending manner. "If Her Majesty should happen to die in the upcoming war, you will become our

Queen. That's the law of succession. I am technically consort by position only, but marriage might benefit us both if it became a reality."

"It might," said Deirdre flatly, removing her arm from his, "but only if I stay. I may wish to return to my home."

"Can you do that, in truth?" asked Marshall, stopping and looking pointedly at the horns on her brow. "Can you really go back to your world, looking as you do?"

"That remains to be seen," said Deirdre. "Who is to say if I will even succeed in my quest?"

"There is that," admitted Marshall, turning to walk on, "but we have to look beyond that, to see the possibilities. Say, for the sake of argument, that we win the war. I am the only eligible man of the blood to ensure an accepted match."

"Or," said Deirdre, "I can simply decide not to marry. I frankly find you to be rather rude. Maybe the ladies here are used to being spoken about as if they were cattle to be bred and sold. I am not. In my world, a man who talked to a woman in such a fashion would have very little chance of success. Good day to you, Captain."

Deirdre turned and stormed away from the captain of the guard as fast as she could. Footsteps sounded behind her, and she turned to find Marshall hurrying after her.

"Lady Deirdre, my apologies. I had no idea my words were bothering you so much!"

He looked to all appearances chastised, and his smile was both charming and self-effacing in its brightness. But again, the smile never touched his eyes, and Deirdre felt a tinge of uneasiness looking into them. They were now a darker shade of grey and so intense that they made her desire to run away and quickly.

"I am going in now, Captain," she said. He moved closer, and she added, "I thank you, but I can find my own way back to my chambers."

She turned, and headed into the castle. This time, there were no footsteps behind her.

———

The guards in the halls appeared to take little notice as Deirdre stalked past them on her way to her rooms. With as much dignity as she could muster, she walked up the grand staircase and down the corridor to her suite. Once there, she angrily slammed the door both open and closed and stood by one of the ornate couches, steaming.

Margret appeared from her own room and slowed when Deirdre turned her furious gaze in the lady's direction.

"I can't believe the nerve of that guy!" snarled Deirdre. "What an absolute jerk!"

As Deirdre continued to fume, the lady motioned for her to join her in the small study off the main chamber. Deirdre followed her and found, to her surprise, Lord Tomille reclining in one of the two carved oaken chairs. Deirdre stopped her complaints in mid-sentence, embarrassed.

"My Lady," said the magician, rising to greet her. He took her hand and kissed the back lightly.

"My Lord Tomille," said Deirdre, "what a pleasant and unexpected surprise."

"Lord Tomille and I were just discussing our encounter with Captain Rialain," said Margret.

"Yes," said Lord Tomille, "and I would very much like to hear what the captain had to say to you, but here is not the place. Come, we will luncheon in my suite in the tower. No one will bother us there."

"But won't they see us go?" asked Deirdre.

"I do not believe so," said Lord Tomille with a smile, "Close your eyes, my Ladies"

Deirdre complied and heard Tomille chant a brief phrase in a language that flowed, liquid and sibilant, around her. The buzzing in her head increased sharply for a second and then stopped. Deirdre half opened one eye and was not at all surprised to find herself in a different room. She opened both eyes wide and took in the new surroundings.

They stood in a round chamber with stonework walls hung with charts and tapestries that looked a bit neglected and careworn. Several comfortable chairs upholstered in rich burgundy velvet were set near the small fire that crackled on the hearth, and a small pillar table stood near them bearing a decanter of deep red wine and four cut crystal goblets.

Lord Tomille smiled at Lady Margret's awestruck expression and Deirdre's furrowed brow.

"My lady?" he asked, eyes twinkling.

"The buzzing in my head got louder, but not by much and not for long. Was that a gating spell? It felt like the portal from my world into yours."

"Well!" exclaimed Lord Tomille. "For one who comes from a place with so little magic, you seem to know a lot about it! No, it was merely a call-me-home spell, and it only works in this castle and the city beyond. It is a way for me to get back here quickly without attracting too much attention. A full gate would be much more complex and costly in both time and magic."

He led the way to the chairs and poured them each a glass of wine. Motioning them to sit, he walked over to a door in the wall and opened it, revealing a small cupboard. From a nearby shelf, he took a slip of parchment and a quill pen, dipped the pen in an inkwell, and proceeded to scrawl a quick note, which he then placed in the cupboard. Closing the door, he gave a tug on another of the ubiquitous bell-pulls, and slight squeaking noises issued from behind the little door. He came back and sat down.

"I told them to send lunch," he said, smiling, "and asked for three plates."

"A dumbwaiter!" exclaimed Deirdre, "I don't think I've ever seen one in operation before."

"Saves trips up the stairs for the kitchen staff," said Lord Tomille, sipping his wine, "and, if I am in the midst of a ritual or a spell, saves anyone from getting in the way."

He smiled broadly, and Deirdre was relieved to see that his smile was reflected in his eyes. She began to relax in his reassuring presence.

"So, tell me about Marshall. I was under the impression that he was going to escort you to lunch?" Lord Tomille sat back in his chair, and steepled his hands in front of him.

"Yes, well, he got rather pushy, and I decided to leave. He started talking about lines of succession and the best marriage options and what ifs, pointing out how much trouble these little horns could bring me in my own world." Deirdre sighed and sipped the dry red wine. "Not exactly encouraging sorts of things that one might say to a future prospect for marriage, at least where I am from."

"Marshall is not known for tact in the best of times," said Tomille, "but this goes beyond his usual blunt behavior. Did he say anything that really caught your attention?"

"Not really. The only thing that stood out was that if the queen should die in the war, I would be next in line."

"Yes, and being married to you would put him in an extremely good position, politically," said Lord Tomille. "We wondered if his motivations were pure, but we had no proof. We still have no proof, mind you. This could just be a sign of his ambitions, but now we know to watch him even more closely."

"He did not always act this way," said Margret. "Before Prince Benjamin was killed, he was one of the most trustworthy of the Queen's guard. No one was surprised when he became captain. It was after that that he became so..."

"Rude? Overbearing?" supplied Deirdre. She turned to the magician. "My apologies if my words before offended you, Lord Tomille."

"No, they did not offend me, my Lady, and please, as with Margret, let it just be Tomille in private. There really is no need to be so formal all the time," he said, smiling, "In return, if I may call you Deirdre...?"

"Yes, of course," said Deirdre. "Perhaps being moved closer to the line of succession made him change, or maybe the loss of the prince? I had heard that the two were close."

"Perhaps. Whatever the reason, he did change. If Brena were to die, you would be next in line, and if you were to die, accidentally or otherwise..." Tomille paused to let the thought set in and then leaned forward a little, his voice low and full of earnest intent, "Do not agree to marry him. Find someone else. No matter how good the political match, I have the feeling that you would be better off with another husband, one not involved in the power struggle. Most people are loyal to the Queen, but some dislike her continuance of a tradition they feel outdated. Each year, people grow less tolerant of magical beasts. Very few of these creatures roam Keyralithsmus anymore. Why keep up the pact made over three hundred years ago? Why not exile the Shapers and talking beasts to below the Southern Mountains? With each generation, fewer stories of Rathal and Tali are told, and the people forget."

"Except now they may have some new ones," said Margret.

Tomille nodded.

"I have heard the rumors that a unicorn has been sighted on the Great Plains to the west," he said. "If this is true, it is only the beginning of something very important."

A concealed bell rang and from the dumbwaiter came a bump and scrape as the contraption made its way back to the tower room. Tomille rose, took the tray, and walked over to place it on a small table across the room. Two chairs were already there, and a brief search found a stool hosting a pile of books that were swiftly moved elsewhere. Tomille perched his lean frame upon the stool, and all three of them began the meal with as much restrained enthusiasm as their hunger would allow.

"Rathal or some other unicorn was seen," reiterated Tomille, taking a breather from his swift consumption of the meal, "and Nerfal tells me of a strange visitor with a star mark upon his forehead."

He paused a moment, locking eyes with both of them in turn, then continued, "I believe that we are on the verge of more than just war here. I believe that the Land itself will rebel if we just sit still and let this pass us by unheeded. You have a very good chance of succeeding, but you have several obstacles to overcome first."

"Which are...?" asked Deirdre, gingerly pulling strips of meat from a rapidly disappearing roasted duck.

"One is your newness to your powers. You need to be trained to shapeshift. I know that Nerfal wants you to wait until after Lady Judeth's party, but I find that to be unwise. You should be trained now, while we have the time. Waiting can only hinder us.

"Another is magic. I should start to teach you now, but there is only so much I can do in four days. Again, the blasted party is taking priority. I know that it is not a bad thing to introduce you to the other castle Lords and Ladies, but at this time? Ridiculous! Be that as it may, with your permission, I will instruct you on as much as I can, but at best...well, there is little that I can teach you in the time we have."

"Can I just not go to the party?"

"Not now, no," said Tomille. "In the beginning, perhaps, but now? It would not be viewed favorably by the others, and we need their support.

"Then, there is a third reason. Us. Brena, Marshall, even I will try to keep you out of harm's way, but that is not the best solution. Candidly, I should like to tell you to get to the party and then run wherever you think would get you to your goal the fastest. I think that you can call the dragons, but only if you let none of us stand in your way. You know what I am talking about, do you not? It scares you more than anything else because it means being on your own, not knowing who is your friend and who is your foe."

Deirdre sat very still, clutching her wine glass in her hand. She stared into Tomille's unwavering brown eyes and nodded.

"I am not saying to go off alone necessarily," he said, looking over at Margret, "Just know when it is time to go, do not tell anyone likely to stop you, and do not look back. Someone, perhaps even myself, might have to stop you. Right now, we need you to help us. We might not be able to let you if we know."

Deirdre nodded, thinking about what the voice of the Land had said about love blinding people to the real needs. There was a lot of truth in that statement, and she recalled that even love could have drawbacks.

"If you like," Tomille continued, "I will begin your instruction in magic now. I might be able to teach you a couple of small things that you can use to defend yourself."

Deirdre nodded and set down her wine glass.

"We might as well begin, then," said Tomille. "Margret, would you like to stay?"

"No, thank you, Lord Tomille," said Margret, rising to collect the dishes and put them onto the tray, then putting it in the dumbwaiter. "Someone should reassure the Queen that her missing lady is not really missing. If you do not mind, I think I will take a more conventional way back."

Margret moved to the door opposite the fireplace and opened it to reveal a set of stairs that lead down. She waved goodbye to Deirdre and closed the door behind her.

Deirdre watched her friend leave, then took a deep breath and turned to Tomille. The magician gazed back at her and offered a reassuring smile.

"Well," he said, "we cannot very well work here, that is for sure. No telling what might catch fire or explode in this room. Come, we will go upstairs to my work room."

He led the way to the door that Margret had just passed through and opened it. Deirdre looked past him to see the same stairwell, but this time, the stairs led up instead of down.

"My lady," he said, bowing.

His eyes again twinkled merrily as hers met them, and she suppressed the urge to ask how he had done it. She wasn't all that sure she was ready for that answer just yet.

———

The magician spent the afternoon explaining technique, the necessity of practice, and his own hope that once the war was over, that she would stay on in Keyralithsmus and be his pupil for at least a time. Most of the afternoon was spent honing her ability to sense magic. The peculiar buzzing that she felt more than heard indicated when magical energy was present, and she discovered that she could link to the power in the earth, the ley lines which ran like rivers of pure energy in a crisscrossing network of tributaries and streams. That in itself had taken over an hour. Learning to sense them had been difficult, but by focusing on the major line below the castle that ran to the sea, and then following a connecting 'stream' from one line to the next, she was able to see and feel the patterns.

Tomille then taught her to center. This was another tedious process, for it required her to locate her point of spiritual balance within, and when she finally did, it wavered so wildly that she wondered if it would ever stay in one place.

"It will take practice, but it will come," he reassured her. "You are learning to manipulate the energies within yourself and within the earth. Eventually, your center will become so stable and so calm that if you meditate on that silence, it will bring you peace beyond measure."

She practiced for a while listening to the quiet within and thought that she could begin to understand what he was saying.

Grounding was the third and final step, and it required her to find her center and reach for a ley line, connecting the two. This created a two-way link to the earth power taking in energy and sending it back out, like the way blood moved or sap flowed through a tree. This, too, took time and when she finally learned it, she was amazed to feel the amount of power available.

"Good!" he said, "Now damp it back a little, control it. Narrow it to a fine focus."

She complied and found that it felt like a thin rapier or laser beam, powerful, yet defined.

"Now," he said, pointing across the room, "take a fraction of that power and light the candle on the table."

She looked at him in disbelief. Her connection to the earth snapped, and she sat down hard on the floor, surprised at the loss of strength.

Tomille sighed.

"You have a problem," he said, "and be assured that you are not the first to have this. You cannot envision doing what you cannot feel physically, can you? If it is not tangible, it is not real to you."

Deirdre nodded and accepted Tomille's proffered hand up.

"I had the same problem," he said. "My teacher explained it to me this way. 'If,' he said, 'you can feel it, and it is real on the inside, then it is real on the outside' The power you just gathered was not imaginary, Deirdre. And regardless of what happens in your world with the lack of magic that it has, here the magic is real. Try again and forget all about your world for a minute. In your world, you would not have horns. Think of it that way."

Deirdre reached up and touched her forehead, feeling the solid reality of the small horns that adorned her brow. She reconnected to the earth, and the process went much smoother. Seconds later, the candlewick burst enthusiastically into flames.

Tomille cheered and congratulated her gleefully, all pretense of dignity forgone and forgotten. He told her that what she had accomplished in one afternoon had taken him a full week, but he hadn't wanted to say that before as he was afraid that she might hold herself back, unwittingly. Almost as an afterthought, he told her that she had to break the connection with the ley line when she was finished with it.

They went back down the staircase, and Deirdre was not surprised when the door opened this time into a corridor just off the great hall. Tomille had bowed her out and remarked that he hoped they could resume the next day. Deirdre readily agreed, and the magician left her.

After all that had happened, she had no wish to dine anywhere but in her rooms, and she hurried upstairs to confer this request to Margret. Over dinner, Deirdre showed an enthusiastic Margret that Tomille had in fact managed to teach her something. She was able to light several candles with some effort, and Margret was totally delighted.

Dinner had been delivered, and they were chatting over their repast when there came a knock at the door. Margret and Deirdre looked at each other, and under her breath, Deirdre said, "If it is Captain Rialain, tell him that I do *not* want to see him."

Margret nodded and went to answer the door. A brief conversation ensued. It was indeed the captain, demanding to know where Deirdre had been all day. Margret politely returned that the lady had been rest- ing, and that they were having a private dinner. The captain seemed to withdraw with good grace, but he promised to return later that evening to visit the lady and see how she was for himself.

"I am really beginning to dislike him," said Deirdre as Margret returned to her seat.

"He was doing his duty, checking up on you. Whether it is neces- sary for him to return later is debatable."

"I think," said Deirdre, "that I will retire early tonight. I am sure that my father and the Queen will want to see me in the morning. I was surprised that they didn't call for me today."

Margret nodded. "I am sure that it has something to do with the war council," she said, pushing the contents of her food around in small figure eights. "That and giving you a day to settle in. Nersh did come by to check on you this afternoon, by the way. I told her that you were with Tomille."

"Oh, and what was her response?"

"She seemed a bit surprised," laughed Margret, "Her ears went up, then back, then up again. Then she resumed her neutral demeanor and said that she would notify the Queen."

"Hmm."

"Yes?"

"Then Marshall knew I was perfectly all right," scowled Deirdre. "I wonder what he's up to. Was this his way of apologizing for his rude- ness this morning?"

"Possibly," said Margret, rising to collect the dishes. "I laid out your night clothes, so as soon as you are for bed, everything is ready. Or would you prefer a hot bath first?"

"Oh! I would love a bath!"

"I will run it for you then," said Margret, "The water pipes in from springs below the castle, you know, so we are never short of hot water."

"Good," she said, "I need it after today."

Margret smiled and went to run the bath.

———

In her dreams that night, Deirdre wandered into the dark cave of the dragon, heart pounding, apprehensive to come before the huge beast yet again. Rounding the corner that led into the cavern, she found it empty save for the giant torches that cast bright reflections off the jewels and gold all around. She began to climb the pile in front of her, wanting to check the top of the golden bed for any clue as to the dragon's whereabouts, both hoping and fearing to find it.

A huge book lay atop the gold, its dull brown leather cover creating a contrast between the mundane and the marvelous. Deirdre sat down in front of it and slowly opened the enormous cover. The first page was blank, and as she flipped through the pages, she noted that the rest seemed to be too. It wasn't until she reached the last page, that anything at all was written.

Four lines of verse stared back at her, two of which she knew. She began to read the words out loud.

"Not-Dragon fears the flame

Not-Dragon knows not its name"

During the second half of the riddle, a male voice joined in with hers, but she didn't turn around, and instead continued to read,

"Not-Dragon from history back,

Not-Dragon search out the track"

She turned then and found herself facing a man who looked oddly familiar, but she could not place where she knew him from. He was dressed only in a loincloth of a patterned weave, and he stared at her like he had never seen a woman before.

"Who are you?" he rasped.

"I am Deirdre," she said in a low voice, "And you? Who are you? Are you a ghost?"

"Not dead," he moaned, "Not dead, lost. Lost in the most accursed way a man can be lost. Not dead, though, no."

Deirdre looked at him and saw sorrow in his green eyes.

"Do you know more of the riddle?" she asked.

He shook his head, hair falling over his eyes.

"Lost," he whispered. "Help me."

"I will," said Deirdre, "I promise."

The dream faded, and Deirdre's night continued on dreamless and uneventful.

8

All too soon, the time came that Deirdre dreaded the most: leaving for Lady Judeth's ball. She would be going to a strange castle with strange people in a strange land. A company of the Royal Guard was going with her, it was true, as were Lady Margret and several of the minor lords and ladies she had glimpsed at court, but the previous night, Lord Nerfal had announced that he would not be able to go due to the ongoing war council. It was to be her first trip without her father and, in some ways, it terrified her. Lady Nersh elected to go in his stead, saying that sitting around the Carathusin Castle reading tomes for the next six months just did not suit her style. She arrived that morning bearing a leather set of panniers made just for her, and what she carried in them was anyone's guess.

A great crowd of the castle folk came to see them off. Nerfal and Deirdre stood by Vexanious's flank, watching the chaos sort itself into some semblance of order. Guards led pack mules, and mounted troops wove in and out of the crowds. Vexanious snorted and stamped his hooves, ready to be away from the confusion.

Lord Tomille fought his way over to them, and smiling broadly, gave Deirdre a big hug.

"Remember what I told you," he whispered in her ear, then said louder, "Good luck, my Lady. I think, with more practice, you will make a fine magician. Have a safe trip and keep up your practice."

Deirdre nodded and smiled fondly at the lanky magician. His hair slipped over one of his eyes, and he smiled back again, a quirky smile that easily hid any of the seriousness connected to his reminder.

A horn sounded, and all of those not already mounted began to find their ways into their horses' saddles. Nerfal hugged Deirdre tightly.

"I wish I could be going with you," he said, "but there is just no way for me to leave in the middle of these meetings. My input as the warden of the north is just too important right now. You will be fine, and Nersh will be with you the whole time. When you get back, we will begin training."

Deirdre smiled at him, and then he boosted her onto Vexanious's broad back. She settled herself, adjusting the lay of her new riding habit so that it did not bind. The hunter green outfit with its side split skirt was of medium weight wool; between it and the matching woolen leggings, Deirdre felt she'd be warm enough for the ride ahead. She glanced up at the sky where small clouds scudded overhead, occasionally causing the bright fall sunshine to dim slightly. Otherwise, the day was pleasant still, with only a hint of winter's bite to spice the air with a tang of frost and ginger.

Deirdre smiled at her father, and he took her hand in his.

"Do you have Brena's letter of introduction?" he asked.

Deirdre patted the small pouch she carried on her belt.

"Excellent," he said. "Good luck on your journey. It is better, I think, that you have a last chance to be without so much of the burden that you must soon bear. I fear that will be all too brief as it is." He cleared his throat and a smile creased his careworn face. "Come back safely to me. I am proud to have you as my daughter."

The milling pack of men and beasts began to form into an orderly procession. Lady Margret rode up to stand her dapple-grey palfrey next to Vexanious. The mare neighed a greeting, and Vexanious acknowledged her in kind.

"Are you ready, your Majesty?" Margret said. "The guard has asked to place you within the procession now. We are to ride near the center, between the two sets of guards. The other lords and ladies will be riding with us and are already in place." In a quiet aside, she added, "They will be feeling you out the whole trip, so be very careful and try to take no notice of their quips and slights."

Deirdre nodded and gave her father's hand a last squeeze. He let her go with reluctance, and Deirdre rode with Lady Margret to the place left for them in the now-organized group of nobles, guards and servants. They passed several burdened carts to the rear of the procession loaded down with trunks and baggage as well as casks of wine and other provisions. What looked to be rolled up canvas tents filled one wagon, and Deirdre looked at Margret askance.

"We will be staying in the village of Tembaril the first night out, but the next three nights, we will need to camp out of doors as there are no towns in the Western Wilds for quite a distance, not the way we are traveling at any rate. We will be safe with such a large group, though, have no fears, my Lady."

Behind her, Deirdre heard two of the other ladies talking and heard her own name followed by a very derisive sniff. Deirdre simply lifted her head a little higher and pretended not to have noticed.

The horn sounded again, this time from beneath the Queen's balcony overlooking the gardens, and Deirdre looked up to where Queen Brena stood watching them prepare to leave. The company moved out, leaving through the garden gate and giving obeisance to the Queen as they passed.

Deirdre looked back only once to see her father and Tomille standing in quiet conference and nearby, not obviously eavesdropping, but definitely close enough to overhear, sat Marshall Rialain, glowering at her from the saddle of his chestnut warhorse. Deirdre had managed to elude or derail him successfully for the past three days, seeing him only at mealtimes. In fact, he had been constantly trying to find her, but she kept avoiding him by leaving the area bare minutes before he arrived, mostly thanks to quiet words from various servants who were working with Margret to keep Deirdre out of his reach. The lady herself had told her of this ploy and had witnessed at least one example of an irate Marshall Rialain stalking along the corridors. Deirdre had laughed uneasily and had thanked Margret for her efforts.

Deirdre and Vexanious rode beneath the Queen's balcony, and the queen waved cheerfully to them as they passed. Her gaiety belied her underlying worries, and although most could not tell, Deirdre noted a stiffness to the Queen's actions as she waved them off.

The gate loomed large and mouth-like before them, and then they were again in the tunnel. Deirdre cast a wary eye at the murder holes in the ceiling above and was very thankful to pass through the outer portcullis and into the city beyond.

Crowds lined the streets, watching as the procession rode by. They cheered and waved at the men and women on horseback and tried to catch the attention of the lords and ladies in their finery. Deirdre sat very still upon Vexanious, causing the stallion to half buck to get her attention back to her supposed 'dumb horse.' The people looking at her, cheering and staring, made her nervous. This was their first real glimpse of her, and they stared openly, marking the horns on top of her head, and either frowning slightly or smiling more than before. It truly was a divided city, Deirdre thought, and she was relieved when they had descended the switchback trail and were out on the road, away from the populace.

The pace was slow, restricted by the baggage and provision wagons at the rear of the group. Vexanious and Margret's grey mare settled into a dozy pace that was restful, though too slow by Deirdre's reckoning. The air was growing warmer as more sunlight peered down through the thinning clouds. Nersh trotted alongside Vexanious, making conversation, and occasionally asking Deirdre what she thought of the day, the company, the conditions of the road, and what she was expecting to see at the ball.

Lunchtime came, and the entire party stopped. In a short period of time, they were eating a light fare of mixed berry tarts and thinly sliced venison between thick pieces of brown bread. It was spread with a spicy sauce which reminded Deirdre of horseradish and caused her to choke a bit when the taste first hit her. Servants handed pewter goblets of wine to the lords and ladies, while the guards imbibed dark brown beer out of earthenware mugs. Deirdre looked at the pewter and wondered absently if it was lead-free. It was such an odd, out of place thought that she laughed aloud, drawing sideways glances from the other ladies sitting primly nearby.

Nersh lay, yellow eyes half closed, on the blanket spread for Margret and Deirdre's use. She turned her gaze upon the covey of ladies seated nearby and yawned briefly, giving them a good glimpse of her long canines. She turned back to smile at Deirdre and winked solemnly.

"They," she said loftily, "have a lot of learning to do. You will potentially be their savior. A wiser lady would treat you with the respect that you deserve. Their little jibes are meaningless, but they are a good barometer of public opinion. If you succeed in calling the dragons, this little bevy will become your loudest, staunchest supporters, mark my words."

"And right now, it's not so high," sighed Deirdre.

"Well, it is not great, no, but I suspect that it will rise dramatically. Look, the rest are starting to pack up again. We had better get back to the horses."

They returned to where their mounts were staked and watched the group begin to pull itself together. Vexanious greeted Deirdre with a neigh and motioned her near with a quick toss of his forelock. While she scratched behind his ears, he muttered, "One of your admirers tried to stick a burr under my girth strap. Were I a normal beast, I might have bucked you off."

"What did you do?" asked Deirdre, pretending to feed him a piece of carrot.

He lipped her palm.

"Stomped his foot a good one," said the horse. "He will be limping for days. I will do it again, too. Should the need arise, that is."

"'And may God turn our enemies' ankles, so we'll know them by their limping,'" said Deirdre, grinning at Vexanious.

Vexanious snorted his amusement. Chuckling to herself, Deirdre settled into the saddle, and a few minutes later, they were underway again.

In a strange sense, the trip was very pastoral, reminding Deirdre of many of the medieval landscape paintings in the Museum of Fine Arts in Boston. They passed through gently rolling hills scattered with trees, the leaves of which had only just begun to turn to fall oranges and reds and spice the air with cinnamon. Farms dotted the country-side, the last vestiges of crops drying in the fields. A meandering brook here, a scenically-placed boulder there... The afternoon took on a surreal quality, and the overall feeling that Deirdre had was a sense of endings. It felt as if everything and everyone she had known in her younger years were just characters in a book, and that the only reality was the here and now. The feeling intensified throughout the after-noon, and by the time they reached the town of Tembaril, it was all she could do just to climb out of the saddle and walk into the big, two story building they were staying at.

One of the inn's servants led the lords and ladies to a private dining room in the back of the building and brought them specially prepared dishes. The guards and other folk from their group ate in the common room, and loud shouts and boisterous songs leaked past the oaken door.

Deirdre and Margret chatted amiably together, with Nersh chiming in occasionally. The other nobles concentrated on eating. Most of them looked tired and drawn, and it occurred to Deirdre that many of them probably spent very little time in the saddle and were likely more than a little sore. The fact that she was more distracted than tired made Deirdre smile to herself and, despite the snubbing she received from the others, she was able to sleep well and comfortably that evening in the room she shared with Margret and Nersh at the top of the stairs.

———

After a hearty breakfast at the inn, the trip the second day seemed very much like the first when they started off, but shortly after mid-day, they reached the beginning of the Western Wilds, a dense forest that they would have to traverse in order to reach Garey Manor. Nevertheless, the road looked often traveled and well-maintained, and they entered the forest without hesitation.

It was much cooler within the woodland - a good ten degrees by Deirdre's reckoning - and it was darker as well under the thick, leafy canopy. Twice that afternoon, Deirdre saw deer bound away from the travelers, and several times, rabbits and quail broke from their hiding places to leap or whir away.

Rested after a good night's sleep, the surreal feeling of the previous day had lifted, and Deirdre found herself enjoying the pleasant ride into the green. The guards rode in relaxed postures, seemingly confident that nothing could threaten so large a party. Deirdre felt slightly uncomfortable with their cocksure attitudes but tried to relax and have faith that they knew more of the realm than she did. After a while, she forgot all about her misgivings.

Camp was set up in the late afternoon, with all the tents strung beneath the trees, and a brief hunt by some of the guards secured a large buck that was prepared and roasting over a fire by nightfall. The cook's assistants had foraged successfully for wild mushrooms, onions, and watercress, all of which were used to stuff the deer. It turned on the spit until the fat melted and ran, hissing into the fire, and the flesh was crisped and browned on the outside. Dinner, albeit later than expected, was excellent.

After they had eaten, one of the guards escorted Deirdre, Margret, and Nersh to one of the big tents. Two cots with down pallets and wool blankets awaited them, with a third pallet on the floor for Nersh. The old wolf sank into it, falling asleep almost immediately. Deirdre and Margret changed into their nightgowns and sat talking while Margret braided first Deirdre's hair, then her own in the light of the tent's lantern.

"Is this not much better than being in the castle?" asked Margret, turning slightly to reach the back of her head. "The other ladies are most likely complaining to their servants right now about the beds not being soft enough or the blankets not being warm enough. They always act like everything is done to slight them. It is not the case at all. They are treated very well given that they are lesser nobles at best. One of them is not even a member of the landed gentry. Her father is a merchant who was knighted in return for his service during the last war and given a house in the city, but no lands of which to speak. Of all the ladies traveling with us, she should be the most careful."

"Don't they snub her too?" asked Deirdre. "After all, she really isn't one of them."

"Ah, but with you around, she is accepted as the lesser of two imposters," smiled Margret, sadly. "She cannot approach you, as I believe she might have, without losing face with them."

"I see. She's the thin blonde, right?"

"Yes, her name is Affrey. I think she may come around before long. Once we get to Garey Manor, the others will go join their little groups and leave her out. Do not judge her too harshly."

"You sound like you know from experience," said Deirdre, eyeing her friend.

"Oh, I am a crow among the doves as well, but as I am held in such high regard by the Queen, they have to accept me, more or less. But yes, I was once in her shoes. Affrey's fall from grace will come very suddenly, and we will end up picking up the pieces, I have no doubt."

Deirdre said nothing for a few minutes, just played with her braid thoughtfully.

"You know," she said, speaking softly so that no one outside could hear her, "there is something I have been meaning to ask you. The first day I was at the castle, at dinner with the queen, something was said about no one seeing dragons for a long time. Then Tomille piped up and said 'almost no one.' The Queen glared daggers at him for that. What did he mean?"

Margret put her finger to her lips and patted her cot for Deirdre to join her. When Deirdre was sitting cross-legged next to her, Margret turned the lantern down so that the tent was almost pitch dark.

"I want them to think that we are asleep," she whispered. "This subject is considered very impolite to talk about, but since you do not know the story, it is better that you hear it from a true friend of the Queen's rather than one of the people who just pretend to be her friends.

"A few years ago, the guards caught a man sneaking into the castle, a dashing young rogue by the name of Jack Parns. He had come to see the queen privately, he claimed, and was brought then before Brena. She instantly ordered his release and took him into the council chambers along with your father, Benjamin, Marshall, and Tomille.

"We know now that he brought information for Brena on the whereabouts of the dragons below the Southern Mountains and across the desert beyond. From his information, the dragons were alive and seemed inclined to help if the fourth shape, that of a dragon, could be reached.

"Then, one day, it was discovered by Marshall's lieutenant that several large gemstones were missing from the treasury. Somehow, Jack was implicated, though how he could have managed to get in and out of the guarded vault was never answered to many people's satisfaction. The queen was forced to order his arrest, after which he disappeared rather dramatically, saying that he would no more share the secrets that the dragons had imparted unto him with Brena and the court than he would fly. No one knows exactly how he managed to escape, but he has not been seen since."

"I take it that there is something else there that you are glossing over just a bit?"

"Yes. I was alone with Queen Brena after Jack escaped. It turns out that he had become a very dear friend and her occasional lover. That is very secret. Only you, Tomille, and myself know about that. I do not think that Marshall does more than suspect it."

Deirdre sat quietly for a moment before turning to look Margret in the eyes, trying to judge in the dark what her friend was thinking.

"We have to find him," said Deirdre, finally. "It seems to me that Queen Brena won't be able to help me solve this riddle."

"What riddle?" asked Margret

"The way to become a dragon," said Deirdre. "Remember when Tomille recommended that I might have to take matters into my own hands? After the ball, I shall have to seek out Jack Parns."

"You mean sneak off and look for him yourself?" asked Margret, "That will not be easy, you know. The guards have instructions to watch you as sharp as falcons. You will have to be very sneaky."

"I take it that you aren't going to try to stop me."

"If Tomille thinks that you might be better off taking a different course than the one they have laid out for you, I would be much more apt to go with you than stop you," said Margret fiercely.

Deirdre nodded and rose.

"I think that I should get some sleep now. We have another long day of riding ahead of us."

"Yes, sleep," said Margret, snuggling down in her blankets. "The days ahead could bring almost anything."

———

The next morning dawned bright and clear. The noise of the camp began before the sun had even slid over the horizon, and when Deirdre awoke to a servant bringing them fresh fruit and bread, the sky had only just begun to brighten. She and Margret ate in silence, then quickly got dressed. As soon as they left the tent, there were workers swarming over it, and it was swiftly dismantled and rolled into a compact bundle to fit into the back of one of the wagons.

Vexanious, groomed and shining in the morning sun, waited for her to mount. He stomped his hooves once she was seated and tossed his head a bit.

"Feeling frisky?" she asked him. "More nighttime visitors?"

He tossed his head, his tack jingling merrily, and snorted his mirth.

A horn blew, calling them to their place in the line. Margret joined her, and within what seemed to Deirdre a miraculously short time, the whole party, some groaning a little at being in the saddle so early, was once more traveling down the forest track.

Deirdre inhaled the crisp morning air, reveling in its freshness, and then exhaled with a sigh, watching the wisps of breath waft away in the wake of their passage. She grinned at Margret. The day was absolutely beautiful with the light lancing down through the trees in bright beams of gold, and the dew that had gathered on the grass gleaming as the rays touched it. Deirdre felt as if nothing could ruin the magic of so bright a morning. Vexanious lifted his feet and pranced alongside Margret's mare, who caught the spirit and matched him as they went along.

Nersh bounded over to them and bowed a greeting.

"Good morning to you," she said. "I trust you slept well on your first night in the wilderness, Deirdre? No thoughts of finding dragons disturbing your slumber?"

Deirdre glanced down at the wolf, who nodded.

"Every word," she said. "Count me in, too"

With that, Nersh trotted on ahead to chat amiably with the lieutenant in the lead of the group who seemed to be an old friend to the wolf. Margret and Deirdre exchanged worried glances, and Vexanious snorted quietly, giving them a knowing glance.

"You too?" asked Deirdre in a whisper.

The stallion dipped his head and went back to briskly walking along.

Deirdre sighed.

"Did everyone overhear?" she said bemusedly to Margret.

"Only the sharpest ears," smiled Margret, "or the best informed. Think of this as being to our benefit."

"I'll do that," said Deirdre. "So much for secrecy."

They rode on, stopped briefly at lunchtime to give the riders a break and water the horses, then continued on. The forest had become very dense since morning, and the further they traveled, the dimmer the light filtering through became. By midafternoon, the road ahead was deep in shadows, and some of the horses had begun to shy, although nothing was to be seen among the trees. One tried to bolt, and its rider had a hard time getting it back under control. The guards looked about them, alert, but there was nothing tangible.

Deirdre glanced up to look at the sky and noticed that some heavy clouds had come in, partially blocking the sun. The sunlight came and went at random intervals, and when the sun was covered, the air turned chill and unfriendly.

"Gee," she said to Margret, "what happened to that nice day we were having?"

A bird cried ahead of them, and Deirdre looked just in time to see a peregrine falcon wing its way through the trees. She suddenly recalled the vision in the cave and opened her mouth to yell a warning.

Time slowed. From the depths of the woods, from the very shadows themselves, shapes oozed and flowed, forming into inky black wolves that snarled silently through dim mouths at the guards and the other riders. Horses screamed as the black creatures with their ember red eyes leapt for guard and noble alike, killing several people before any could raise a hand to stop them. A woman behind her screamed, and Deirdre turned, panic rising in her, as one of the creatures leapt, taking the woman's head off in passing before lunging at a nearby guard.

Looking down, she saw Nersh standing by Vexanious's hooves as the stallion was backing and tensing to rear. The wolf's hackles were raised, and her lips pulled back in a terrifying snarl. Nersh hesitated a

moment longer before leaping into the middle of the shadow creatures. Horses milled about in confusion, and several bolted, taking
some of the less experienced riders helplessly with them or dumping
them bonelessly on the ground.

"Hold tight!" yelled Vexanious and reared to his full height, lashing
out at the nearest dark shape with his iron-shod hooves.

To Deirdre's horror, the deadly blow passed right through the creature, and Vexanious, prepared for an impact, lost his balance and
stumbled. He came down abruptly, throwing Deirdre forwards onto
his neck. She barely managed to twist her head to the side, smashing
her ear instead of her nose into the crest of his neck, and felt her grip
on the stallion's mane loosen. Her ear bloomed with warmth, and she
frantically pushed herself upright, clutching at his coarse black mane.

To her right, she saw Margret's horse wrest control from her
mistress and bolt, racing down the road as Margret screamed. Deirdre
looked to her left and saw Nersh darting from cover to cover, trying to
draw the creatures away from the people who lay strewn upon the
ground. More horses, mounted and not, streamed past her, lathered
with foam, their eyes rolling wildly. Many of the guards were lying
dead, and only the cart horses and wagons remained. Shrill neighs and
the yells of the frightened men told her that the carters were losing the
fight to keep the panicked animals under control. Vexanious steadied
and then reared suddenly as one of the carts thundered past, the
wagon rocking perilously from side to side, the horses mad with fear.

Deirdre clutched desperately at Vexanious's mane as the horse
came down again and had just started to move her hands tighter when
the stallion reared up for a third time in a vain attempt to keep the
shadow beasts from reaching her. Deirdre, her grip already loose, had
no time to do more than claw uselessly at the stallion's lathered neck.
Her hands, slick with sweat, found no purchase, and she began to fall.

"Deirdre!" screamed Vexanious as he felt her leave the saddle.

As she fell, a bright blue light appeared from the wood borne by a
huge beast who towered over the attackers. She saw the shadow

wolves turn in eerie unison to face the newcomer and glimpsed Nersh lying on the ground, red blood staining her white coat. Deirdre landed on the hardened ground of the road, and there was a sharp pain to her head. The world went black, and the last sound she heard was a guttural roar of rage, and then the world and all of her worries were no longer her concern.

9

She woke in the dark to pain in her head, and the smell of burning wood. A damp pressure on her eyes told her that a coarse, wet cloth was laid across them. From the way her head ached, she guessed that the cloth was more to keep her head from pounding than from any wound.

She stirred, the bedding beneath her rustling and releasing the pungent, sweet smell she had come to associate with the rushes at the Keep. She moved her right hand slowly, feeling the coarse fibers of the blanket that covered her. It smelled a little like horse, but more of cow, a strong odor for one not used to being around farm animals, and she wondered muzzily who might keep cows in the middle of the forest.

Lifting her hand from the blanket, she reached to touch the cloth over her eyes. There was a sound of motion nearby, and a large hand caught hers and placed it gently back on her chest. The hand covered hers for a moment, and then was withdrawn.

"Not yet, huh?' she said, her voice sounding raspy and frighteningly weak to her ears. She licked her dry lips, realizing her thirst for the first time since waking.

Her host made a low groan and moved slightly. She felt a hand slide gingerly under her head and raise it. A cup touched her lips, and she took small sips of water until she slaked her thirst. Gently, her head was lowered again, and she listened as her caretaker rose and moved a little ways away. She could sense whoever it was nearby, watching her, and it made her feel uncomfortable, yet safe at the same time. Before she could make up her mind which was better, she had drifted off again.

———

A bandage of some light material had replaced the cloth the next time she awoke. Her head was clearer but still ached abominably, making her glad for the darkness provided by the wrap. The fire threw off more heat than before, and she heard the thump of wood being added to the blaze. She managed with great effort to sit up a little on her elbows and waited for the pain to subside before sitting up a little more. A wall behind her proved to be better support than her own muscles, and she heard her host breathing nearby, watching her intently.

"I know you are here," she said. "I want to thank you for your help. My name is Deirdre."

A soft snort came from across the room, and after a moment of intense silence, broken only by the snap of the wood burning, she heard the sound of footsteps coming towards her. The smell of cow intensified as her benefactor knelt down near her, and she felt the flask pressed into her hands. She drank slowly, listening to the measured breathing of her host, and began to get the distinct impression that whoever it was wasn't completely human. Male, yes — she got no feeling of feminine from the being — but not totally human. The smell of him still confused her, though, and brought to mind vague possibilities that she could not quite get a grip on. Something wasn't clicking, and she hurt too much to think about it just then.

When she'd finished with the water, she handed the flask back and felt a piece of cooked meat pressed into her hand. The taste was wild and sharp, much like the venison she had eaten the previous night. It was tough to chew, though satisfying, and just gnawing on the meat tired her enough that she had to lay down again once she had finished. She felt the blanket being placed over her, and its warmth, combined with that of the fire, made her start to doze again.

"Thank you," she murmured as she drifted off, and she fell asleep once more.

————

The next few times she awoke were much the same. She'd be handed food and water, and after eating, would almost immediately fall asleep again. When needed, she let herself be guided to a crude privy and was left briefly so that she could have her privacy. She began to get a feel for her host: quiet, sad, and unable or unwilling to speak. He was ever gentle with her, and although he did not speak, he was able to convey a great deal of meaning in every action.

As she grew stronger, she told him a little about herself, about Nerfal, and how she had come to be Ivory Lady. She didn't tell him about her true home, but instead mentioned that she was from an unrecognized union, suddenly discovered. None of this seemed to bring a response from her friend until she mentioned Darlena's death. She could tell even without the benefit of vision how agitated he had suddenly become, and his quick departure and distant roar of fury frightened her tremendously. Momentarily, she really thought about the size of his hands, and wondered if he was just the gentle mute she had assumed.

She laid back down then, not the least bit sleepy, and wondered, not for the first time, if Nersh and Vexanious were alive and looking for her. Had they perished after she had fallen, killed by the shadow wolves or the being with the glowing sword? How had she gotten away from the massacre, and where had her rescuer come from? Her head began to hurt again as she thought about all of the possibilities. She tried to relax, waiting for the pain to subside.

When she felt a little better, she gingerly touched her head, probing at the lump and the bandaged gash. It was tender, but nowhere near as painful as it had been a couple of times she had woken previously.

Sometime later, she heard her host's footsteps echoing on the stone of the floor. She turned to smile at him as he entered

"Hello," she said. "I'm sorry if I upset you. I didn't mean to."

She heard him slow, and his steps falter. He hesitantly approached the bed, and she sat up to greet him, reaching out as he sat down next to her. His hand met hers, and for a moment, they simply sat there. She wondered again at the size of his hand and the way it enveloped her own. Then he guided her towards him and let her touch his face. She could feel him tensing as she made contact, but he made no move to stop her or turn away.

Her fingers found fur, and she pulled back a bit in surprise. Fur! Tentatively, she made contact again, tracing the fur along a broad muzzle and up a gently angled brow. A thatch of coarse hair, slightly softer than Vexanious's, fell across his forehead, and she reached up further. Large, cupped ears that twitched when she touched them, and finally, what she had suspected but dared not voice, even to herself. Horns. Massive, curving horns that narrowed to a slightly rounded point. He bent his head as she explored his face, trembling slightly but allowing her to discover the truth without hindrance. He took her free hand in one of his.

His other hand moved to her head and began to unwrap the bandage that covered her eyes. She moved to aid in the removal, and soon was blinking in the almost too bright light of the small fire. She took a moment, focusing on the face that she could finally see.

Black furred, broad-browed and intensely bovine, her host's face was less than a foot from her own. His muzzle narrowed towards the end but flared wider to where the nostrils sat above lips that looked more mobile than those of a cow. Huge, white horns tipped with black arched above almost comically large ears, and a thatch of hair fell between deep-set brown eyes that looked intelligently back into hers. It was his eyes that turned her wariness to wonder, for they held no trace of menace or cruelty in their depths. They were sad, worried perhaps, but otherwise guileless and completely without the wicked cunning she would have suspected to find in the eyes of a minotaur.

A minotaur! Deirdre held back her alarm and looked at the rest of him; he was very much human, if larger in proportion. She guessed that he stood over seven feet tall when at full height, and he seemed very broad across his moderately furred chest. He sat in a chair by her bedding. What she could see of his body seemed mostly human, save for the black bull's tail that twitched behind him in agitation

His only clothing was a tattered loincloth which was held in place by a broad belt from which hung a heavy-looking sword in a cracked and rotting leather scabbard. The sword made her head buzz like a swarm of bees, and she nearly laughed, realizing that she was actually near a magic sword, the grand cliché of her own world's fantasy novels. It was strange how ordinary it looked just hanging from his belt. If she hadn't been able to sense the magic from it, she might never have noticed.

"Well," said Deirdre, and stopped. She scratched her head thoughtfully and glanced back into the creature's eyes. The pleading look in them moved her to pity, and in spite of his form, she wanted to trust him. She looked to where he still held her other hand. He followed her glance and looked back at her hesitantly. Deirdre managed a smile and squeezed his hand gently. "Well, I assume that you aren't going to eat me or attempt to do something awful to me, right?"

He shook his head emphatically.

"Can you talk?"

Again, the vigorous shake. He opened his mouth to reveal sharp canines, huge molars, and no tongue. There had once been a tongue, but only a long-healed stump remained to prove its past existence. Deirdre gasped, and she gave the minotaur a look of sympathy.

He moaned gently and shook his head, pointing to his chest.

"I shouldn't feel bad for you?" she asked.

He shook his head again and picked up a piece of fallen stone. Leaning over, he began to scratch something on the stone floor.

Deirdre peered past his shoulder to see him making crude drawings. One was of a minotaur; the other was of a man. Between them he drew a pair of crossing arrows. He pointed to the man and pointed to himself. He then pointed to the minotaur, and made a pushing gesture. He clapped his hands together then, and pointed to the minotaur. Lastly, he pointed to himself, and made a pushing away gesture towards the man.

Deirdre scowled at the drawing for a second, and her eyes went round in dawning comprehension.

"Oh! You were once a man?" she asked.

The minotaur nodded, squeezing her hand, his eyes wide and moist.

"And you were turned into a minotaur."

He shook his head and pointed at the arrows.

"You changed places?"

A nod.

"Bad magic?"

Another nod.

"And then they cut out your tongue so that you could not tell anyone?

He gave a rather emphatic nod and looked at her sadly.

"You poor man," said Deirdre.

She looked at the thankful expression on his face and concluded that he wasn't lying to her. His eyes were so sad, she thought again, and she felt that, as he had saved her life, she had to help him in return somehow.

"Can you read and write?"

He looked at her warily and glanced at her head for a long, considering moment, looking at her horns. Then he slowly nodded and picked up the stone again.

"I am Tor. It is not my real name," he scratched. "I was once a man. I fought in the war. Minotaur attacked me. I fought, was run through by sword. Saw out of these eyes my own body dying. Men came while I watched myself die. Bound me, took me North, cut out my tongue, and set me free. They laughed."

He waited until she was done and smudged the message with an abrupt stroke of his hand.

"So they let you go, and you came here?" Deirdre looked up to meet his gaze. "But why go to so much trouble? Wouldn't it just have been easier to kill you?"

Tor shrugged and looked at the fire. Deirdre bit her lip and gently extracted her hand from his to reach for the water flask. He looked back at her, but she only sipped the water and replaced the flask. She also returned her hand to his, something that caused him to start with surprise.

"So what are we going to do?" she said. "I mean, I am sure that people have been looking for me. How long has it been?"

Tor held up two fingers.

"Two days?" said Deirdre. "I am sure that if Margret, Nersh, and Vexanious are still alive, they would have been searching for me."

The minotaur nodded, moaning softly.

"You have seen searchers?"

He nodded again, pointed to himself, and shook his head. At her blank stare, he scratched on the stone, writing, "I saw them but could not talk to them. Was afraid to approach them. Would not have done any good."

Deirdre nodded thoughtfully.

"I need to get to Garey Manor, since it's the closest from here, from what I can recall. Can you help me?" At his hesitation, she added, "I'll do something, grant you immunity or sanctuary... Isn't there something a noble can do?"

He looked at her sharply, and she recognized her omission and felt the warmth rise in her face.

"I haven't told you everything. I mean, too many people know as it is. I am the illegitimate daughter of Count Nerfal, which is true, so by blood, I am a noble, and I am the Ivory Lady, but in all honesty, I have only been on this world for about a month. It's a ... well, it's a long story."

He inclined his head to her, and she told him briefly about what had happened to her up to the fight in the forest. At the mention of her dreams, he looked at her intently and indicated that she describe them further, and so she did, with a sense of relief that she finally had finally had someone to share them with. When she was finished, Tor sat in thought and scratched the tip of the stone on the floor.

"You will hunt for Jack Parns after the ball."

"Yes," said Deirdre, looking at where he was still writing with sudden hope.

"I will come with you," he wrote. "I know where you can find him."

Deirdre's mouth dropped open just a little.

"You know him?"

"He and I are old friends. I know where he hides," he wrote.

"Then you were no ordinary soldier," said Deirdre. "You read, you fought in the wars, you caroused with very suspicious characters..."

"I am Kin," he acknowledged. "We share blood or used to. I am one of the Hornless, though not anymore!"

Deirdre smiled at his attempt at humor, and asked, "From the Mountain Reaches?"

"Remembrance," he wrote, "City Kin, but loyal to the Queen and the alliance."

"Hmm..." said Deirdre. "Tell me, does a lady of Keyralithsmus have the right to choose her bodyguard?"

"Should," he wrote.

"Then I wish to appoint you my personal bodyguard. You've done so much for me, and I want to repay you. I mean, they can't argue that you saved me when they couldn't, right? It should serve to protect you from instant imprisonment, though I can only guess what else they'll try to do to you. In return for my protection, can you get me to the Garey Manor and then to Jack Parns?"

He nodded and drew his sword, proffering it to her hilt first. She took it and looked at him questioningly. Tor gave her a quirky smile and nicked the side of his left thumb with the point. With his other hand, he wrote, "I swear to protect you," in bold letters.

The sword, dull metal when she'd taken it, began to glow a bright blue. Deirdre handed the sword back to Tor and followed his example. The thought of deliberately cutting herself made her feel slightly queasy, but she took a deep breath, and gave the skin below her thumb a slight jab. It was enough, and the sharp edge cut a shallow line below the knuckle, letting her blood flow down to mingle with Tor's.

"I swear to protect you," she said and glanced up to see a dumbfounded look cross his bovine face. She grasped his hand, letting their blood intermingle. The blade glowed brighter and brighter, becoming impossible to look at, and when it finally winked out, their combined blood that had smeared it was gone. In its place were lines of runes.

Tor's eyes were huge as he looked upon the sword. He held it up higher and let the firelight reflect off its polished surface.

"Can you read it?" asked Deirdre, reaching for the cloth he'd so recently used on her eyes. She found it by touch, ripped it in half, and lifted her injured hand to examine the wound. It was shallow and already appeared to be half healed. She wrapped her hand and turned her attention to the sword, peering at the lines of runes now written across the surface of the blade in gentle waves.

Tor nodded absently and after a few moments, picked up the stone, and began to write.

"It says, 'Two become one
Joined by need,
Journey begun,
So to be freed.
To the west and the south
Then back north again
The cure is in the deed
Not now, but then.'"

"Great," said Deirdre sarcastically. "Just what I need. More riddles. It isn't as if the dreams I have been having aren't bad enough."

Tor nodded and took the other half of the bandage to wrap around his own hand.

"Rest," he wrote, "It is almost night. We can depart in the morning."

Deirdre lay back down, feeling as if the mere mention of sleep had made her tired. As she drifted off, she found herself looking at her companion in drowsy awe, that living figure from myth sitting calmly nearby watching her. She smiled at him, and he nodded in return. Closing her eyes, it wasn't long before she was fast asleep.

10

A light mist was falling when Deirdre finally saw daylight the following morning. The air clung damply to her skin, but the cold was invigorating. The whole forest smelled crisp and alive, and the scent of the leaves as she crushed them underfoot gave the day a tang of wildness.

Tor had apparently been able to scavenge some things from the wreck before the guards came back to claim it all, for he had presented her with new clothes that morning, including thick leggings, a long tunic, and a woolen cloak. She pulled the cloak tightly around herself, grateful for its warmth, and looked up at the edifice she had rested in for the past three days. It was an immense black building that seemed to absorb all light around it into the stones. It was designed almost like a Mayan step pyramid, and she wondered what something like that was doing in this world.

She turned back to look at her surroundings and assessed how she was feeling. Other than a little cold, she felt good. Her riding boots were insulated enough to keep her feet warm, and with the cloak about her, she believed she just might live. She felt a little anxious at seeing Tor in the daylight for the first time, however. Firelight always came with shadows and hid things that sunlight did not.

He emerged suddenly from the gloom, carrying the pack containing supplies, some extra clothes, and two dresses he had managed to salvage from the wreckage of the baggage train. He had steadfastly refused to let her carry anything more than her sword, insisting that he could handle the pack easily, of which she had no doubt. The manor was only a day and a half away, Tor had told her. They should make it just in time for the ball. Deirdre had laughed, though it hadn't seemed very funny, and said sarcastically that beyond all other things, the ball could not be missed.

The last and most important thing that Tor had found was the little leather case holding Queen Brena's official document recognizing Deirdre as a Lady of the Realm. This Deirdre carried in her cloak pocket, wanting to have access to it immediately if need be.

"Ready to go?" she asked, looking at him intently.

By light of day, he seemed a little smaller, but his horns looked whiter than ever. Although he still stood over her by a good foot and a half, the tattered cloak he wore and the rags tied around his feet made him seem more a figure to be pitied than feared. He nodded and led the way down a short flight of stairs to the forest floor. She followed, pulling the hood of her cloak up to keep off the rain.

It didn't take them long to reach the road, and by then, the drizzle had tapered off, and the sun was trying vainly to poke its rays through the cloud cover. Deirdre stepped onto the track, looking around and half-expecting to be attacked by the creatures from before; however, according to Tor, the building was nowhere near the site of the ambush, and nothing moved in the shadows, real or supernatural. When several moments had passed and all appeared still, they began to walk down the path. Tor remained alert, looking about them as they traveled, ears flicking to catch any unusual sound, but as they progressed on undisturbed, he seemed to be less concerned.

A low ground fog began to rise as the air warmed in the struggling sun, and the woods developed an almost haunted feel. Soon, they found themselves knee deep in a white mist, and the track was only discernible due to the gap in the trees. Deirdre stumbled twice over roots made invisible by the mist, and after the third time, went on more cautiously with one hand lightly resting on Tor's arm. He looked momentarily surprised when she touched him but soon accepted it, and they continued on.

The mist swirled around the bases of the trees, coasting against them and moving away again like waves on the sea. Sounds echoed oddly, dampened by the mist, and seemingly coming from all directions at once. Even with the amount of time Deirdre had spent in the woods near Randolph's house, the trees seemed the only familiar objects. These woods felt stranger than any other landscape she had yet seen. Large boulders loomed out of the haze, seemingly from nowhere. There were no animal sounds, no birds singing, and the branches themselves appeared to bend towards them as they passed. She shivered with a combination of the cold and nerves, her own imagination getting the best of her.

They stopped for lunch when the sun was high. Tor had spotted some low rocks on the side of the path, and they ate their meal atop them. The sunlight had finally pierced the gloom, slowly eroding the mist and warming the air. Broken clouds scudded above the trees, and the wind that gusted high aloft blew more gently through the thinning leaves below. The moisture began to dissipate, leaving behind a crisp autumn air that was much easier to breathe. As the sun drove away the last of the damp, Deirdre began to feel more like herself, not so fearful or hesitant, for the first time in days.

She glanced at Tor where he sat next to her on the rocks. This was her first real opportunity to get a good look at him, and she watched him gnaw on the haunch of rabbit they had brought along. She smiled to herself, noting how carefully he ate his food, shooting sidelong glances towards her when he thought she wasn't looking. The thatch of hair on his forehead had been pushed aside by the breeze, and she saw that there was a white patch on his forehead, what Nerfal would have called a star if it was on a horse. His coarse hair was somewhat matted, and there were the occasional twigs and burrs tangled within its thick lengths. His cow-like nose glistened damply, and the nostrils flared when they caught smells on the breeze. The brown eyes remained unchanged: sad, concerned, and wary.

He had been hesitant around her all morning during preparations and had been very tense during the early part of their journey. Briefly she had wondered why and had hit on the assumption that he was still worried she might simply turn him over to the guard once they got to Garey Manor and was trying to appear as non-threatening as possible. Bearing that in mind, she had held his arm not only for support, but also as a sign that she trusted him. Obviously, she thought, from the way he watched her, he wasn't convinced that she totally believed him, even after the whole affair with the sword. Sighing, she took another piece of rabbit and chewed it thoughtfully. She would just have to show him otherwise.

"Have you thought of what we are going to do tonight for shelter?" she asked, looking straight at him and realizing that she was finally getting used to sitting with a creature so firmly rooted in myth.

He nodded and took a stick to draw a mountain shape in the dirt, and then indicated a small opening.

"A cave?"

He shrugged and wrote, "Sort of."

Deirdre nodded, and they finished their meal in silence. When they were done, they resumed their journey. Unimpeded now by fog, they managed to make pretty good time the rest of the day.

The sun was beginning to creep low behind the trees as they left the path to follow a tiny stream into the underbrush. The dimness of the woods, not to mention a sense of growing exhaustion, caused Deirdre to reach for Tor's arm again. Thick undergrowth quickly forced him to gently remove her hand from where it lay and clasp it in his own. In that manner, he guided her over and around the worst of the tangles of thorn and bramble, coming finally to a low opening in the side of a root-gnarled hill.

Tor let go of her hand and pulled from his pack a piece of flint, a crude torch, and a handful of tinder. Placing the tinder on top of the torch, he struck the flint against his knife until a spark caught and set it alight. Shortly after, when the main part of the torch had started to burn, Tor lifted it and led the way half-crouched into the shelter. As he led the way in, Deirdre belatedly realized that she could have helped save him the trouble by using magic. Tor had made the lighting of the torch look so easy that she'd never even thought of it.

Tor waved the torch around the inside of the small enclosure, sending several animals scurrying into hiding. To Deirdre, it looked like an upside-down bowl. The back of the wall was a natural indent into the side of a stony hill, but the roots and tangles that made up the front looked more cultivated and planned, like they had been grown or trained into the bowl-like shape. In the center, even Tor could stand at full height, but the sides quickly sloped down at a steep angle. She turned from her examination of her surroundings to find that Tor had stuck the torch into the floor and was making a fire in the center. The ashes in which he built the fire, along with the pile of dried out wood stored along the wall, made her realize that this was one of Tor's hiding places. It was somewhere that he could hole up without being found, and the knowledge that he would trust her enough to show her his refuge made her look at him again in wonder. He'd placed his very existence in her care, she thought, and shuddered, not from fear, but from the weight of that idea. It was very new, that weight, and she suddenly had a flash into what the Queen must feel on a daily basis. It was terribly personal.

She watched him silently as he picked up the torch and lit the fire with practiced ease. Taking several pieces of the dried firewood, she brought them over to Tor, and he approximated a smile as she handed them to him. She looked around to see what else might need to be done and set about arranging their supplies while he built up the fire. He finally seemed content with the almost smokeless fire crackling warmly on the floor, and he sat down, beckoning her to join him and get warm.

Deirdre sat near the fire, removing her damp cloak and propping it up on one of the thick tree roots that hung low from the walls of the cavern. Tor did likewise, and they made a meal of tubers and bits of smoked meat that Tor produced from the pack. After, weary from a long day of walking, they sat in a comfortable silence by the fire.

Tor eventually rose and, from the pack, pulled two blankets that he spread on the ground, one on top of the other. He then motioned to Deirdre's cloak, pointed to the blankets, and then made a covering gesture towards the cloak.

"Right," said Deirdre, yawning. "It is most definitely bedtime. Thank you."

She pulled the slightly dried cloak from its impromptu hook and dragged it over her shoulders. She lay down on the blankets, resting her head on one arm. The ground was firm, but not hard enough to keep her from sleep, and although it was still cool, the heat from the fire staved off most of the chill. She saw Tor wrap his cloak around himself and prop himself against the wall with his sword drawn and resting across his lap. 'A weight on us both,' she thought, and, closing her eyes, drifted swiftly off to sleep.

———

The dim glow of early light and the smell of cooking fish greeted her as she awoke the next morning. She lay still for a few minutes, simply allowing the sensations to wash over her, smelling the fish, feeling the warmth of the low sun as it crept through the cave's small mouth. She sat up, the night on the ground making her a bit stiff all over, and stretched muscles that had chosen that exact moment to remind her of their existence. They were distinctly not happy.

Tor sat by the remains of the fire, poking it with a stick and occasionally using the stick to turn leaf-wrapped packets over on the hot coals. In the diffuse lighting of the cave, he looked like something out of a prehistoric shaman's dream, hunched over the fire wearing only a primitive loincloth, his feet wrapped in rags. His face, expressionless by human standards, nevertheless communicated that he was lost in his thoughts. His eyes seemed fixed on some faraway place, and he didn't seem to notice her movements. Deirdre wondered if he was thinking of his past, and she decided to do what she could to make his life better, hoping profusely that she could help him.

Smoke wafted from the fire to tickle her nose, and she sneezed. Tor glanced over and approximated a smile by twitching the corners of his mouth, though his body language became more closed to her than it had been moments before. His posture became more upright, and his movements more stilted. Deirdre sat up and rubbed her eyes free of sleep. She pointed to the packets in the coals, and said, "Fish?"

Tor nodded, and used a small knife from his pack to skewer one of the portions from the fire. Deirdre did the same and found the fish too hot to eat right away. Tor had set his on the edge of his cloak to cool a little, and Deirdre did likewise, figuring that the fish would be better off on her cloak than on the ground. It was when he passed Deirdre a water canteen that she realized how full her bladder was. She smiled at him and nodded to the entrance to the cave. He nodded back, and she ducked out.

When she returned, Tor had started on his fish, and Deirdre sat to eat the still-hot meat with quiet pleasure. It tasted much better than she could have imagined - the flesh tender, and the taste like a cross between salmon and cod - and she snagged another portion and set it to cool as she helped Tor pack up the blankets and other supplies they had used the previous night. A half an hour later, fully fed and packed, they put out the fire and left the cave, heading back through the brush to the road.

Bright sun shone down through autumn leaves as colorful as any on New England trees. Deirdre stared at the variegated red and gold leaves of the Keyralithian trees with renewed appreciation for their beauty. It hadn't occurred to her until then that she might never see a New Hampshire fall again, and she felt suddenly homesick, though not as much as she believed she might. It seemed, she mused, as though she had adjusted to the idea of staying. Realistically, though, how could she go back anyway? She had horns growing from her brow and now some sort of blood bond with an enchanted minotaur. Add to that her father and numerous other people who were counting on her, and it seemed to her that clearly she was meant to stay in this fantastical land, at least for the foreseeable future.

She sighed and looked down the road, watching it wind through the forest. Although the ground was fairly level, they were beginning to see more low, rocky hills like the one they had sheltered against the night before. The trees were spread out a bit more than the previous day, allowing the sun to penetrate the canopy, spotlighting sections of the forest floor, and there was a lot more undergrowth now among the trees. The light turned the air golden, making everything feel peaceful and somewhat magical. It was truly a spectacular land, she thought, and found that her own world paled in her memory by comparison.

Glancing at Tor, she suddenly found herself thinking very hard of what she had to go back to. He looked at her curiously, and she laughed.

"Just thinking," she said. "In my world, there were few who would help a complete stranger, taking them in, to their own possible detriment. Trust seems like a rare thing back home. I think that only Randolph, my grandfather, will really miss me, and in truth, he'd be the only person I'd really miss. Maybe, when this is all over, I could get him to come here."

Tor looked at her questioningly. Deirdre smiled and shook her head slightly.

"Just kind of wondering why I'd want to go back. Can't think of many things I really would miss."

He cocked his head to the side, and she looked back down the path.

"I have some old art school friends who only come up to drink and borrow money, old boyfriends with whom I parted with amiably enough, but who never call, and a grandmother I only see when it is convenient to be seen with a granddaughter. I honestly think I would really only miss Randolph. Nothing else matters enough to go back for."

A strong hand touched her shoulder, and she glanced over at Tor to see him looking at her in concern. Suddenly, the simple fact that he cared overwhelmed her, and she sat down on a fallen log and began to cry in great hitching sobs. Tor dropped his pack, knelt down next to her and took her hands in his, holding them and squeezing them gently. This made her cry even harder, and he stayed kneeling by her until she had cried herself out.

Deirdre finally calmed enough to look up at the minotaur and saw that his brown eyes also had tears in them. Slowly she got herself back under control, freeing a hand to wipe her eyes and breathing more regularly.

"I'm sorry," she managed, finally. "I'm not prone to breaking down like that, but between the attack and everything else..."

Tor nodded and squeezed her hand before letting go. She dried her face on a corner of her cloak and stood up, feeling oddly cleansed. Tor assisted her to her feet and shouldered the pack he had put aside. He turned back the way they had come, then looked around, large ears swiveling rapidly. Deirdre watched him, and he pointed down the road, motioning for her to be quiet.

For a long moment, there was no sound, but gradually, Deirdre realized that she could hear the echoing hoof beats of a galloping horse. She looked wildly about, and Tor motioned her into the brush. Together, they crouched down to watch.

The sounds of hooves grew louder, but there was no jangle of tack, no creak of leather to accompany it. Deirdre peered eagerly through the leaves, hoping to see a familiar form, but not daring to believe that she would. Seconds later, she was rewarded by not one, but two familiar racing figures on the path, both of which were well-known to her.

"Stay here" she whispered to Tor.

Before he could stop her, she stood up, waving her arms and running out to greet her friends, calling their names aloud.

"Vexanious! Nersh! Wait!"

Vexanious skidded to a stop, his haunches so far under him that he looked as if he would sit down. Nersh was able to slow more gracefully, and her yip of surprise covered, or almost covered, Vexanious's colorful phrasing as he slowly stood straight again and made his way stiffly to where Deirdre stood.

"Deirdre!" exclaimed Nersh, leaping up to place both forepaws on Deirdre's shoulders. "Thank goodness you are all right!"

"I'm thankful you are too!" said Deirdre joyfully, embracing the wolf.

Vexanious butted his heavily maned head against Deirdre's side, and she reached up to scratch behind the stallion's big black ears with delight. The stallion responded by pushing against her even harder.

"We never thought to see you again," said the horse, not raising his head. "We have been searching for days!"

Nersh dropped back onto all fours, and Deirdre noticed how ragged she looked and how unkempt her fur was. Vexanious wasn't much better, splattered to his belly with a thick crusting of mud. His tail was full of burrs and knots, and his mane had bits of brush and leaves caught in it.

"What happened to you two?" asked Deirdre.

"When you fell," said Vexanious, "I was attacked by three of the shadow beasts at once. I fought through them as a new menace arrived, a great black minotaur with a blinding blue sword. He swung at the beasts, killing several somehow, and they retreated from him. Then I was very busy fighting off my own attackers and trying to get back to you. They all fled suddenly, and when I turned to look, you and the minotaur were both gone."

"I was unconscious by the time the minotaur showed up," said Nersh, "However did you escape him?"

"I didn't," said Deirdre. "He rescued me and took me to a big black building in the woods where he has looked after me for the past few days."

"The Nordoust Temple?" asked Nersh. "That was where we were headed today. Are you all right? He did not hurt you, did he?"

"No," said Deirdre, feeling odd at the idea of Tor trying to hurt anyone; she couldn't fathom it. "No, he bandaged me and took care of me. We started off for Garey Manor yesterday."

"Do you mean that he is here?" exclaimed Vexanious, backing up a step and lifting his head as high as he could. Nersh crouched and began to growl low in her chest, her hackles rising, ears flat against her head.

"Wait! Wait!" said Deirdre, holding up her hands. "He isn't like that. He was in the war Nerfal told me about and used to be human. Some sort of enchanted blade caused him to exchange bodies with the minotaur that killed him. The enemy had planned it, and they cut out his tongue so he couldn't tell anyone who he was. Please! He's taken very good care of me at his own risk. Give him a chance."

Nersh and Vexanious glanced at each other, and then looked towards the forest behind Deirdre.

"He was once human?" asked Nersh, hesitantly.

"Kin, though hornless, from Remembrance. He knows Jack Parns and thinks he knows where we might be able to find him. I...took the liberty of appointing him my personal bodyguard. We swore on his sword to protect each other."

Vexanious looked Deirdre in the eye with one of his big brown ones.

"You swore?" he said, soberly. "On the magic sword?"

"Yes," said Deirdre evenly.

"Blood magic?" asked Nersh.

Deirdre nodded.

"You do realize what that means," said Nersh, "do you not?"

"Umm..."

Nersh sighed.

"Call him out," she said. "We will not hurt him. The two of you are now bound to protect each other. Since you did not specify how long... just...call him out."

"Tor!" called Deirdre, "Come on out! It's alright!"

"Tor," muttered Vexanious. "How original."

Deirdre shot him a black look.

Tor stood up from behind the sheltering shrubbery and looked cautiously to where Deirdre was hailing him. He squared his shoulders and slowly made his way to the road to stand next to Deirdre, his attitude hesitant as he looked uncertainly at the animals. Both Nersh and Vexanious scrutinized him carefully without saying a word, and he watched them, waiting for their verdict.

Nersh sat back finally and nodded to Vexanious. The stallion backed off a few paces and snorted noncommittally.

"There is, of course, no way to verify your story," he said. "You smell like a minotaur, and there is no trace of enchantment on you that I can detect."

Nersh nodded.

"Nor, since you have not given us your true name, can we check out the story through other means."

Tor looked at her without blinking, his expression bland.

"However, you did rescue us all, and it appears you have tended to Deirdre's injuries," continued the wolf. "Providing that you *are* Kin from Remembrance, we have no option but to welcome you. The bond that you made with Deirdre is stronger than blood."

Deirdre and Tor glanced at each other in surprise.

"You may not feel the effects of it yet, but it is also a bond of magic. Neither of you can betray the other, else risking some sort of magical retribution. The sword you used radiates a terribly powerful aura. May I see it?"

Tor drew his sword and held it out on his palms for Nersh to see. Both the wolf and the horse studied the weapon with great interest.

"The runes appeared after we blooded the blade," said Deirdre.

"Did you read the runes?" Nersh asked Tor, looking at him.

The minotaur nodded.

"You two are bound by your vow until the end of your quest, at the very least," said Nersh. "As for after that, I think it will depend on you. Being the lady's bodyguard does offer you certain advantages. You will not be imprisoned or shipped off to Coliseum. I warn you that you will not be treated graciously, but because of Deirdre, you will not be treated completely like a beast either. You understand the distinction, I am sure."

Tor nodded and gestured at Deirdre.

"Well, this is going to cause total chaos at the court and will both lower and raise her standing with the nobles," said Nersh. "Lower it because of what minotaurs have done to her family, but raise it because no one in Keyralithian history has ever had a minotaur as a bodyguard. People know that not all minotaurs are stupid, and what most are going to assume is that you have agreed to protect her for your own safety in return. They also, due to the length of your absence, are likely to assume that you are lovers."

Deirdre and Tor looked at each other in amazement. Tor snorted, shaking his head, and Deirdre felt warmth steal over her face and realized that she must be turning very pink. Nersh looked at the dumbfounded pair and laughed.

"This again has good and bad sides," she said. "Bad due to the fact that most Keyralithians already think that the people of the Mountain Reaches mate with the Talking Folk..."

"Wait, what?" asked Deirdre.

"It has happened, Deirdre," continued the wolf, "but not with the frequency they think it does. Your supposed romance with Tor will spark more rumors than I care to contemplate, and unless Lady Judeth makes him sleep in the barn or in the barracks, he will be sleeping in your rooms. Not in your bedroom, but even in your sitting room will be enough to fire up the gossipers."

"Maybe we should specify that he stays in the barn," said Vexanious, thoughtfully. "Deirdre, does he know?"

"About our escape?" she asked. "Yes, I told him, and you are right." She turned to Tor. "We could sneak you out of the barn much easier than we could out of the main house, and you could tack up Vexanious and undo the latches. Are you still playing "horse," Vexanious?"

"Oh, yes, I am most certainly "playing horse." I have been in the forest this whole time, looking for you. Nersh stored my tack near the

Orkra Falls. Your packs are there, too, Dee, with some more suitable clothing. No offence, but you do not look very royal right now."

Deirdre looked at her ensemble and laughed.

"We did the best that we could," she said. "My dress wasn't in much better shape after Tor found me, and anything else Tor could salvage was far too fancy for hiking."

Nersh nodded.

"All of that will be taken care of. We should get going if we want to be there by suppertime. It is not much farther to the falls, and you can at least wash your face there and put on some clean clothes." She then turned to Tor and smiled a toothy smile, "I will vouch for you to the Lady Judeth, but I am going to conceal the fact that you were once human. Whoever you were, I trust you will tell us when you are ready, but someone went to a lot of trouble to put you in this body and make it difficult for you to communicate. I do not want to give that same someone the idea that a more permanent solution is needed."

Tor shook his head and held out his hand to the wolf. She placed a forepaw in his huge hand, and he shook it gently.

Vexanious snorted and moved over to a low branching tree. Deirdre took the hint, climbing up the trunk and onto Vexanious' broad back. She grasped his mane and relaxed as they started off down the road. Riding without a saddle wasn't too bad, Deirdre thought, but a little slippery and bony, not to mention jarring. She looked forward to arriving at the falls and being able to ride with tack again.

It wasn't long before they reached a swiftly flowing river and turned from the road to follow it. Deirdre watched the water foam white as it splashed and rushed along among the stones, and she soon noticed a low roaring noise coming from the direction they were travelling. The sound grew increasingly louder as they followed the slight winding of the river's path.

Deirdre asked Vexanious to stop long enough to slide from the horse's slick back, and they led the way along the narrow track that bordered the river. Nersh walked with the minotaur, eyeing him now and again until Deirdre and Vexanious were far enough ahead to be out of earshot.

"Who are you really?" she asked.

He kept walking, shrugging his shoulders and looking at her with sadness in his brown eyes. She kept pace with him, staring back at him intently.

"Very few people know what you know. If you want me to trust you totally, I need a little more to go on than what you have given me so far. Deirdre is very naïve in certain areas, mostly those concerning the plotting and scheming that takes place at court. I am going to have to advise her at the ball tonight and will not have a lot of time to prepare for our departure. I want to trust you, Tor, but I need to know if I can afford to."

He looked at her, stopped, and knelt down next to her. Drawing his dagger, he scratched at the dirt.

"This can go no further until I am ready."

"I agree to that," she said, "My word as a d'Wulvra"

He nodded and from a small pouch that hung from his belt he drew a brilliant blue gem, cut into the shape of a faceted heart. Nersh's eyes grew round at the sight of it and she watched him write in the dirt with his dagger:

"Knew I could not fool you, old wolf."

"Old?" Nersh exclaimed indignantly, with a false air of arrogance, her voice breaking. "I am very, very young, and grow younger still knowing that you are yet among the living. How did you salvage it?"

"Hid it before war. Lucky for me I did. Would have been odd, searching my own corpse."

"How long?" asked the wolf, scanning Tor's bovine features.

"Since that day," he wrote, and shook his head. "It was horrible."

"I can guess," said Nersh. "Lots of things have changed in Remembrance since then."

"I have heard of some of them. Seems like Marshall is showing his true colors."

"You should be glad you left his company before the war began," said Nersh. "His command lost the most men, all accountable to mino-taur blades."

"A distraction?"

"Maybe," Nersh sighed. "He is so very good at being good, but he still is not well liked by many. He tried to reel in Deirdre, you know. She spent most of her hours dodging him, usually in Tomille's tower. Darlena was not that quick to catch on, I am afraid."

"I heard," Tor wrote. "If only I had survived the battle as myself, none of this would have happened."

"Oh, Marshall might have gotten rid of you another way," said Nersh, looking him square in the eye. "You were too much in his path, my prince. We want to tell Brena our suspicions, but all we have to go on is rumors, oddly phrased sentences, and our gut instincts. It is not enough. All we can do is watch him and try to anticipate him. Now I know we cannot tell anyone you were once human. Your lack of a tongue will mark you to any who know the details of your transforma-tion. You are going to have to do one hell of a job acting the dumb brute."

"I can do it. As you said, some minotaurs are not that dumb."

"True. So, when are you going to tell Deirdre?"

"Not just yet," he wrote. "It is not easy to tell the secret I have kept for so long. I want to be sure of her as well."

"You can trust her," said Nersh. "She has plenty of secrets of her own to keep."

"She has told me some. I make a good confessor."

Nersh laughed, and Tor reached over to give her a huge hug.

"It is so good to see you," he wrote when they broke the embrace. "I never thought to see any of you again."

"Same here," said Nersh, looking back up the trail. "Come, they must have reached the falls by now. Let us catch up."

Tor nodded, rose, and together, they went to follow their companions.

———

Deirdre and Vexanious walked down the path, chatting amiably, their voices rising even louder to make their words be heard above the roar of the swiftly flowing water.

The air was very damp and cool, and with a last turning of the path they were on, the source of all the noise and moisture came into view: a thirty foot waterfall that jettisoned cascades of water from atop its craggy landing. A breeze from the falling water blew a moist mist into their faces.

"That rock," shouted Vexanious, "is part of the ring of mountains surrounding the Convere Valley where Lady Judeth Garey's castle resides. If all goes well, we will be there in about two hours!"

"That is good to know!" hollered Deirdre, looking at the foaming froth at the base of the falls. She shivered as the cold dampness pervading her warm clothes. "I'd love a warm bed tonight."

"Come on!" called Vexanious. "We have to go behind the falls. That is where Nersh stored everything."

"Of course," muttered Deirdre, catching up to the stallion with a bounding step. "After all, doesn't every waterfall have a cave behind it?"

"What was that?" yelled Vexanious, turning to look at her through his heavy forelock.

"Nothing!" shouted Deirdre. "Just practicing my cynicism, that's all."

Vexanious snorted, and they made their way behind the waterfall to a small concealed crevice. Deirdre would never have guessed it was there if she hadn't been told.

"I am too big to go in," shouted Vexanious. "You will have to go in by yourself."

Deirdre nodded and ducked inside. The cave was dark, but she easily located the tack where it lay wrapped in an oil cloth. Deirdre refolded the cloth, took the gear, and left the way she had come. They returned to a spot just beyond the reach of the mist to put the tack on Vexanious.

Deirdre had just gotten the blanket adjusted and was reaching for the saddle when Vexanious snorted and looked around, alert. He straightened, ears pricked forwards, and that was when she heard it, a strange sound that began to filter past the noise of the falls. Moment by moment, the sound grew louder and resolved itself into singing unlike anything Deirdre had ever heard before. Vexanious suddenly glanced up, and Deirdre looked to where the horse was staring. At the very top of the falls, standing gracefully perched atop the narrow edge, a unicorn was singing.

Deirdre felt her mouth fall open, and she was having trouble believing what she was seeing. Never before had she heard a sound so unearthly as what this creature was creating, and seeing the unicorn, Deirdre felt that only something so magickal could have sung in such a manner, so encompassing and eerily lovely. The sound filled her with extremes of emotion and made her want to weep at the beauty of it.

The unicorn sang on in words Deirdre could not understand. With the unconscious grace of a dancer, it picked its way across the top of the falls, moving with slow, sure steps. Its mane and the leonine tip of its tail rippled in the wind of the falls, and its white goatee floated back to touch its shoulder. Iridescent dapples shimmered at shoulder and flank, and even from so great a distance, Deirdre could see that its sky blue eyes were fixed on them.

Barely breathing, Deirdre watched it leap to the shore next to the falls and disappear into the brush, its song trailing off and fading away. She slowly became aware of the roar of the falls again, yet compared to the song of the unicorn, it seemed to her that the water was almost silent. For a long moment, neither she nor Vexanious moved, and if the sounds of footsteps on the path behind them hadn't shattered the mood, they might have stayed longer, so lost were they in awe.

A small noise behind them broke their reverie, and they turned to find that Nersh and Tor had arrived and were eyeing them speculatively.

Nersh looked from one to the other, and sighed.

"Want to tell us about it?" she said.

11

Vexanious shook his head, tack jingling merrily as they traveled along the road edging the mountains. Deirdre sat in the saddle, feeling better than had she felt since...well, since before she had left the Mountain Reaches anyway. The sun overhead shone brightly on the road, sliding slowly down the azure sky; lunchtime had come and gone long since. In the distance, Deirdre could see a grand estate made of multiple buildings situated in the center of the little valley.

"Not long now," said Nersh cheerfully. "Warm beds, warm food... Lady Judeth will no doubt send us all straight to bed so that we may be rested for the ball. One of the baggage carts was salvaged, Deirdre, and I believe your gown is safely awaiting your arrival."

"No doubt many things are awaiting your arrival," snorted Vexanious. "Those beasts that attacked us belong to the realm of the Lord of Ganley Keep, and his no-good, spendthrift son will be in attendance."

"How do you know that?" asked Nersh.

"Talk I have overheard from search parties," said Vexanious. "I followed one for five miles yesterday. Everyone thinks Deirdre is dead, and that Avar is responsible. His son may well be spying for him."

Vexanious huffed, "Watch him, Deirdre. He has a nimble tongue and a taste for women."

"Have you ever met him?" asked Deirdre.

"Jasper? No, but the stories of his escapades are numerous and unpleasant. He gambles, is a vicious hunter, and the things that he is said to do to women are best not repeated." The horse snorted. "If he ever bothers you, let me know, and he will not be bothering anyone for a long time, if ever, again!"

Tor turned to Deirdre and nodded his head in agreement. She smiled her thanks and saw a flicker of some unidentifiable emotion in his eyes - possibly trust or affection - she wasn't sure.

"We should discuss our plans while we have a last few uninterrupted moments," said Nersh. "That guard post up ahead is not more than two miles away. We will be there in about a half hour."

"We should leave tonight as soon as we can," said Vexanious, tossing his head. "Tor and I will be in the barn. I should be tacked and ready to go when you get there."

"I will come to the ball with you, Deirdre," said Nersh. "Hopefully, we will be able to tell Margret in time for her to pack. She will be so relieved. The poor girl was beside herself last I saw her."

"Then what?" prompted Deirdre. "Do we leave after the ball?"

Nersh shook her head.

"The ball could go all night, so it would be best to just leave late and slip out while people are still occupied," said Nersh. "Around midnight, you should leave the ball, claiming exhaustion. No one will question you. Margret and I will escort you to your rooms. Pack before we leave. We will plan to be changed and on the way in about fifteen minutes. Think practical and bring nothing fancy, as we are likely to be on the road a long time before we hit civilization again. When we leave, we should head straight for the city of Malepoer, as fast as possible."

Deirdre nodded and felt Vexanious stiffen and stop short. She looked ahead and saw two uniformed men on horseback cantering towards them, swords drawn. Vexanious half-reared; Deirdre grasped at his mane, and as he came down abruptly, she bit her tongue.

Nersh trotted out to meet them with a raised head and tail, her stance conveying the presence of a visiting dignitary. The riders slowed to a walk when they recognized the wolf coming towards them, her silver chain of office gleaming around her neck.

Vexanious stood still, trembling with nervous tension, and Tor watched anxiously, one hand resting on the hilt of his sword. Deirdre reached down and gently removed his hand from the hilt, taking it into her own. They interlaced fingers in an unspoken accord, and this time when Deirdre looked into his eyes, there was gratitude there too.

Nersh led the riders back up the road, their pace unhurried. The men had placed their swords into their sheaths, but their hands never strayed from the hilts, their eyes watching the minotaur's every move. For the first time, Deirdre got a real feel for just how much people feared and loathed minotaurs.

The guards stopped their horses a few yards away, their mounts scenting the minotaur and neighing shrilly, protesting their riders' attempts to get any closer. Nersh trotted back to stand next to Vexanious. The men looked expectantly at Deirdre, appearing neat and official in their dark blue uniforms. She saw their eyes flicker to where her hand rested in Tor's against the leg flap of her saddle.

Deirdre swallowed nervously under the scrutiny of their gaze and lifted her chin a little.

"I am Deirdre, Lady of the Ivory Castle and the daughter of Count Ettar of the Mountain Reaches. My party was attacked in the woods by shadowy wolves that could kill but not be wounded. This minotaur, Tor by name, rescued the party and took care of my injuries for several days until they healed. He was guiding me to this very castle when Lady Nersh found us. In gratitude, I have granted him the status of my personal bodyguard and have accorded him sanctuary while serving me. You will treat him civilly, sirs, as he has done me a great service in saving my life and the lives of others."

When she was done, Deirdre exhaled and tried not to convey how nervous she actually was. One of the guards nudged his protesting mount a few steps closer; the horse's eyes rolled wildly, and it snorted loudly as it neared the minotaur; the guard controlled it, overcoming his mount's urge to flee by sheer strength.

"I bid you a warm welcome, Lady, and I must admit that it is a great relief to see you safely here at last. Lady Judeth has been wringing her hands for days, and we have had a flurry of messages by pigeon to and from the capital the likes we have never seen. I am Inier Evarl, captain of Lady Judeth's guards. Your companion is going to cause quite a stir, my Lady, as I am sure you are aware. As your body-guard, he is entitled to remain in your rooms, but we might be able to forestall certain...problems...by providing him with quarters elsewhere."

"Thank you, Captain, for your welcome," said Deirdre, smiling in what she hoped was a reassuring way. "My companion will be satisfied to bed down in the stables, I think, and I should be safe enough in my own rooms. All I ask is that none of your men harass or try to harm him. He is a good-hearted soul, and I would hate to see him done any injustice after all he has done for me. Now, if we can get to the castle, I am in need of food and rest, but most importantly, I would like to set at ease the minds of my father and the Queen."

"Please then follow me, Lady, and we shall have your needs attended to presently," said Captain Evarl, and they turned their horses, who were visibly calmer to be moving away from Tor, to lead the way to the manor.

Deirdre gently released Tor's hand and took up Vexanious's reins again. She found that she missed the minotaur's hand in her own. She glanced sidelong at Tor, but could tell nothing from his expression, no hints of similar feelings. Maybe it was the blood oath, she thought to herself. It had connected them, so perhaps touch would strengthen it. She let the matter be and turned her focus to the road dropping gently down into the valley as Garey Manor came into full view a short distance below them.

It looked more like a Southern plantation than a castle in design.

The house was a huge, sprawling concoction of gingerbread and colon-nades, multiple additions and gardens that took up well over three acres on its own. Nearby out-buildings included a barn, a blacksmith, a conservatory, a huge gazebo, and what looked to be a carriage house. There also seemed to be a small market square that bore bright banners and flags.

The areas surrounding the main buildings looked to be farmlands, dotted here and there with small houses and barns. Deirdre could see sledges and dray horses being used to collect the harvested crops, and workers in the fields were plentiful. It was like looking into the past of her own world, sometime in the late 1700's, but the manor seemed very out of keeping with everything else she had seen so far in terms of architecture.

As they neared the estate, Captain Evarl signaled to his companion.

"Drop back behind the minotaur so that the other guards will not attack him on sight thinking he is holding anyone hostage," he said.

The other guard nodded and rode back behind the group, making a wide arc around the minotaur. The captain slowed his own horse to ride next to Deirdre as they continued their journey, Nersh trotting alongside them.

"What an interesting manor!" Deirdre exclaimed to the captain as he came beside her.

"Yes, quite remarkable, is it not?" smiled the captain. "One of the Lady's ancestors spent a year in some other realm in his youth, or so the story goes. He came back with sketches, plans, and all sorts of odd things, and had this mansion built. He figured that being in this secluded valley would be protection enough. It is not quite as imposing as a stone castle, but it is much more charming, would you not agree?"

Deirdre nodded and watched as Garey Manor grew closer as they descended into the valley below. It would be easy to get out of the main house but once outside, leaving the valley would be a much greater risk. Sentries would always be looking up the road, and it was in that direction that they would have to travel.

The temperature was also growing colder the further down they

went, and Deirdre glanced at Tor. Despite his stoic appearance, she
wondered if he was warm enough in his tattered cloak and guessed
not. There had been no clothing or boots in the wreckage of the
caravan that would fit a seven-foot-tall minotaur. Deirdre decided to
make speaking to Lady Judeth about proper clothing for Tor one of her
priorities.

Finally, mid-afternoon, they arrived at the edge of the market. The
captain stood in his stirrups, yelling for people to make way for the
party, and his orders were hurriedly obeyed, though it seemed to
Deirdre their speed had more to do with the minotaur's appearance
than from listening to Evarl. Deirdre saw many faces peering fearfully
from behind curtains at Tor as her party rode by, and she swallowed
hard, as there was hostility amid the fear as well.

The manse came now fully into view, and Deirdre stared at its
three-story-high front portico supported by white lyric columns and
housing an immense, paneled red front door. A groom ran over to
assist Deirdre down from Vexanious's saddle, but stopped abruptly as
he came face to face with Tor. The man's terror was plain on his ashen
countenance, and he seemed unable to move.

Evarl dismounted and walked over to assist Deirdre himself,
making a show of turning his back to Tor. She smiled at his unspoken
statement of trust and allowed him to take her hand and lightly assist
her to the ground. He then collected the reins of the horses and handed
them to the groom.

"Take the horses to the barn," he instructed the groom, "and make
sure the black is well-tended as he has been out in the wilderness for
several days."

The groom hastily took the reins of all three of the horses and
guided them to the barn. Evarl then led the way to the house, his fellow
guard once more falling in behind Tor. Nersh paced beside Deirdre, and
the wolf's confidence soothed Deirdre's growing nervousness. The
men stationed at the doors began to unsheathe their weapons, but at
Evarl's wave, reseated them and uneasily watched the minotaur go by.

Deirdre looked around herself as they passed through the doors. The hall that they entered was cavernous with a vaulted ceiling rising three stories to a high, arched dome over the parquet floor. Directly in front of them, a grand, sweeping staircase rose up to the second floor, then split and doubled back like wings to rise to the third. Carved banisters, the wood polished and gleaming with many coats of beeswax, reflected brightly in the afternoon sun that streamed through the huge stained glass doors depicting mermaids perched on rocks gazing out over the sea. Deirdre gazed in wonder at the intricate glasswork, noting in particular the mermaid with long, red hair whose wistful countenance was focused on a spot beyond the horizon. Looking through the glass, Deirdre could make out the shapes of chairs and sofas in the room beyond.

The wood-paneled walls were tastefully hung with a variety of detailed portraits of seemingly good-natured people. Here and there, hiding in arched niches, stood statues of dryads and fauns, all life-sized and incredibly detailed. The house looked like a mixture of Victorian and Art Nuevo in its layout and decor.

Two doors, made of the rich, dark wood that also paneled the walls, were visible past the stairway. The captain led them around the bottom of the staircase and towards the doors. As they came near to them, the left hand opened, and a slender blonde woman rushed into the hall.

She was dressed for all-the-world in what looked to be a very ornate eighteenth century Colonial period dress. It was a light peach color and trimmed with fragile-looking lace around the low-cut collar and the bottom of the narrow sleeves. Her skirts were buoyed out by layers of petticoats, and her waist was cinched close.

Right behind her followed a bespectacled young man in tan breeches, a white shirt, and a brown tweed waistcoat. He carried a quill pen in one hand and half a dozen sheets of parchment in the other. He had the air of a scholar about him, and strands of his sandy-blonde hair struggled to get out of his control even as he tried to push them back with the hand that held the quill. Deirdre smiled, picturing the result had the pen been full of ink.

The woman slowed when she saw Tor, but managed to maintain her composure to smile warmly at the group. Upon reaching Deirdre, she curtsied deeply, her blue eyes sparkling and joyous. Deirdre curstied in return, noticing the smooth satin of the woman's dress and thought of her own less than regal state with chagrin.

"My Lady Deirdre, I am incredibly relieved to see that you have made it to my home in one piece. I shall send word to your father and the Queen at once of your safe arrival."

Captain Evarl cleared his throat, causing Nersh to start, and Tor to lay back his ears for a moment. The captain bowed to the Deirdre and said,

"May I introduce your Ladyship to the Lady Judeth of Garey Manor, and her master of household affairs, Jan Trillingly. Lady Judeth, may I present to you Lady Deirdre Ettar of Keyralithsmus, Lady Nersh of the Mountain Reaches, and the minotaur, Tor, savior of her Ladyship and her recently appointed bodyguard."

Deirdre noted the minute sarcasm in the captain's voice and wondered vaguely if coming to the ball might not have been a mistake after all. Nersh grinned a toothy grin at her, however, and Deirdre resolved not to allow the captain to get the best of her.

"Ah," said Judeth, "that is why you are accompanied by a minotaur. Sir, you must be an uncommon minotaur to have rescued our lady, as most of your kind would more likely have joined in the fray on the side of the shadow beasts. I offer you the hospitality of my house and bid you welcome in. What can I do to make your time here more comfortable?"

Deirdre looked at Tor, then back to Judeth, and said, "My Lady, he cannot speak. I think, though, if you could find him some warmer apparel and settle him comfortably in the barn near my horse, he and I would be most grateful."

"I shall do so," said Judeth. "Footwear might be a problem, but clothing can be found or assembled easily enough." She turned to the young man. "Jan, fetch the tailor and bid him come to the Lady's chambers immediately. Margret is preparing them for you now, Lady. Also, have the chef send up a light fare to tide us over until dinner. Evarl, if you would be so kind as to send word to the Queen and Count Nerfal, I will escort Deirdre to the Ivory Suite and get her settled in so that she may bathe and have a short nap before dinner."

The young scholarly man bowed and left the room the same way he had come in. Evarl likewise bowed and exited through the front door, presumably to go to the dovecote. Judeth smiled and led the way up the gently curving staircase. Deirdre craned her neck to marvel at the crystal chandeliers and gilt frescoes on the ceiling and upper cornices. She glanced at Tor and found that he was also giving the wonders a good look, though it seemed to her that it was with a hint of familiarity, as if he had seen them before and was only renewing his acquaintance with them. It made her wonder.

On the second story landing, they left the stairs and walked down a long corridor with many doors leading off of it and even more paintings lining the walls. There was one in particular, however, that gave Deirdre pause. The painting was of the same waterfall that was outside the valley. The artist had captured it faithfully, with rays of sun shining off of the mist to create a rainbow that shimmered fitfully across the width of the spray. It was painted to look like the scene was occurring in full summer, but here and there among the lush, verdant undergrowth, there appeared a hint of a hoof or horn. The more she looked, the more there were, and she looked askance at Judeth who had stopped a few feet away.

"It is a beautiful picture," said Deirdre.

"It is," replied Judeth. "This was painted nearly three hundred years ago by an ancestor of mine named Rondarick Garey, the very man who built this place. He named it *Unicorn Falls*, but I cannot find any reference as to why he did so. There have been many theories, but no one is sure for certain."

"Do you see the unicorns in the painting?" asked Deirdre, pointing them out to her.

"Almost," said Judeth. "How odd! I almost start to, and then it is like my eyes slide to the left, and it is gone. Do you see them?"

"Clearly," said Deirdre. "Nersh?"

"Not I," said the wolf, "but I do detect a hint of magic around the painting. Can you feel it?"

"Yes!" said Deirdre. "My head is buzzing! It must be enchanted so that only someone who has..."

"Seen a unicorn can see them!" chimed Nersh. "This is a true test as to whether or not someone had actually seen one. Probably Lord Garey wanted a foolproof way to test his allies, and he had this created by an artist working with a unicorn to enchant it. That would have been before they all went across the sea. How extraordinary!"

"You have seen a unicorn?" asked Judeth, excitedly. "When? Where?"

"At the falls earlier today," said Deirdre. "I am not sure, but it may well have been Rathal himself, for it was he who brought my existence to my father's attention, though he appeared to him as a man with a bright birthmark on his forehead."

"Ah," nodded Judeth, turning to stare again at the picture. She looked back at Deirdre thoughtfully. "One warning, my lady. Although your parentage is known to us all, do not bring it up around the lords and ladies you will meet today. The more you act like the rightful heir to the Ivory seat, the more they will respect you. And, mark me, make sure those little horns are visible at all times. That will give them pause for thought. You need to win as many of them over as you can, and being illegitimate is already a detriment. Come, it is nearly two of the clock now. Let us get you to your rooms for some rest and some food. Dinner is from six to seven, and then you will have an hour to dress for the ball. This way."

Judeth led them the rest of the way upstairs and down a short corridor, stopping at a set of white double doors. She opened them inwards to reveal a huge sitting room furnished in an opulent style that had a strong Victorian flair to it. Plush white velvet settees and armchairs surrounded the room in little groups, and a fancy writing desk stood ready, complete with feather plume and paper.

Deirdre stood looking at the luxurious surroundings and shook her head. Every time she thought she was getting used to living this way, something new would change her mind again and prove her wrong. The splendor of the deeply polished wood floor and darkly varnished furniture set off the white material strikingly and gave the room an air of reverence and palatial grace. She glanced at Tor and found him glancing around the room with mild curiosity and the attitude of one long accustomed to similar surroundings. He seemed at ease with the setting, much more than she did herself.

She suddenly found herself longing for a bath and clean clothes more than anything else, and she turned to smile at Judeth, ruefully.

"I am afraid to touch anything, "she said, indicating the state of her clothing.

"Of course," smiled Judeth, and called out, "Lady Margret, look who has joined us at long last!"

One of the three doors off of the sitting room opened, and Lady Margret burst out in a run, beaming at the sight of Deirdre standing there.

"Lady Deirdre!" she cried, and then spied Tor standing by the door. She stopped, and clasped her hands to her mouth, her eyes growing round and fearful.

"It's all right, Lady Margret," said Deirdre hastily. "His name is Tor, and he saved my life when we were attacked. I have asked him to be my bodyguard for the trip ahead."

Margret slowly lowered her hands, and Deirdre glanced at Tor to see his reaction. He looked suddenly tired and lost, and his eyes sad as he seemed to slouch a little more.

Lady Judeth finally cleared her throat and broke the long moment of silence,

"Lady Margret, would you be so kind as to draw the Lady a bath?"

"Certainly," said Margret. "I will bathe you and get you settled, if you like."

"Yes," said Deirdre, "I would love to be ministered to, Margret. I am far too tired to even lift a brush at this point."

Margret curtsied and left the room through another of the doors. Deirdre heard water begin to flow from beyond and looked at Judeth quizzically.

"We have pipes to carry hot water here," said Judeth. "One of the adaptations that my many-times great-grandfather made. Water is carried by dumbwaiters to the roof, and dumped into a cistern where it is kept warm by reflected sunlight and fires. The cistern attendants keep the fire going and direct the flow of water to whatever part of the house needs it. We reuse as much of the water in the fields as we can so as not to waste it."

A knock came at the door, and Judeth opened it to reveal a thin man with a wilting moustache who peered anxiously about the room before spotting Tor and turning sheet-white.

"This is Montre of Congel, our resident tailor," said Judeth, ushering the man inside almost bodily. "Go on, Montre. Lady Deirdre has assured me he's perfectly safe. You can take Tor's measures and have at least a few items done by...early evening?"

Montre nodded weakly.

"The shoes may take a little longer, I am afraid," continued Judeth. "The cobbler is very busy with the ladies getting last minute fittings for the ball. Montre, if you please..."

Judeth almost had to drag the little man over to the minotaur and stood close by his elbow as he collected the measurements he needed in a small notebook before scurrying out the door. Deirdre noted that Tor looked even more shrunken than before and began to worry that she had done the wrong thing to bring him to the manor. She caught his attention and gave him a reassuring smile. He straightened a little then and nodded his head to her.

"Before the dance, I will send someone to lead you to the stables, sir," said Judeth. "Lady Deirdre, I will leave you now to get some rest and will return at ten of six to lead you to dinner."

She turned and left the rooms, closing the doors softly behind her.

Deirdre and Tor looked at each other and then at Nersh; the old wolf breathed a deep sigh and sagged visibly.

"I am going to curl up by the fire over there and sleep some of the last seventy-two hours out of my bones," she said. "I urge the two of you to do the same. Get some rest while you can and remember what we talked about earlier."

Lady Margret appeared at the doorway of the bathroom, and beckoned to Deirdre.

"The bathtub is full, my Lady," she said. "Come and get cleaned up. You look a sight."

Deirdre walked tiredly into the bathroom, making no attempt to stop Margret's fussing over her. Once the door was closed, Margret helped her to undress and assisted her to step into the deep, footed bathtub. Deirdre sank down, letting only her head remain above the warm water. Margret had rolled up her sleeves and proceeded to scrub Deirdre from head to foot. Once Margret was convinced that Deirdre was suitably clean, she drained and refilled the tub with clean water, leaving Deirdre to soak while she fetched some dry clothes and towels.

Deirdre luxuriated in the hot water, nearly asleep and warmer than she had been in days. She didn't realize how grimy and tired she had been until now, and it was a struggle to stay awake. Margret bustled back in with a long cotton nightgown and three large towels. She helped Deirdre climb limply out of the tub and dried her off.

"Honestly, Margret, I can dry myself," said Deirdre, amused.

"Nonsense. Let me be a proper lady-in-waiting tonight. Tomorrow I shall be a fugitive on the run and will be too busy looking after myself," Margret said dramatically, and then smiled. "I am still in on this, I should hope."

"Of course," said Deirdre, sliding the nightgown over her head. "There. I'm off to sleep, not even hungry."

"Good thing, too," grinned Margret. "Our friends out there ate almost the whole tray of food that was sent up. Both of them are sound asleep, so we will have to get Nersh cleaned up before the ball and arrange a bath for your new bodyguard. You would think they were the ones who had been thrown from a horse and dragged through the wilderness."

Deirdre gave a weak laugh that never really took to the air before following Margret out of the bathroom and through the sitting room where Nersh and Tor slept peacefully. The wolf was snoring loudly, flat on the floor by the fire, and the minotaur was draped artlessly over a couch clearly not designed for sleeping. Margret opened another door, and Deirdre beheld a heavily curtained and draped poster bed hung with fine embroidered ivory fabrics of exotic weave and texture. The patterns of the stitch-work were familiar, and Deirdre ran her fingers over the William Morris-work designs with a look of awe on her face.

"Earth," she marveled softly. "These are from Earth."

"Your home?" asked Margret. "How did they get here?"

"I don't know," said Deirdre. "They look very much like the patterns of a famous artist from Earth."

She passed her hand over her eyes, her vision blurred with a lack of sleep.

"I am too tired for this," she said. "I need some rest."

"Rest then," Margret said, pulling back the heavy blankets.

Deirdre took the invite, clambering into the high bed and slipping under the covers. She found herself fully relaxing for the first time in days, all of her muscles releasing tension she hadn't known she had. She fell asleep almost immediately and soon dreamed peacefully of earth, Randolph, and a time without horns.

———

Lady Margret laced up the back of Deirdre's dress, a flowing linen gown made of ivory-colored cloth of a very fine weave. She looked into the large mirror that the dressing room boasted. It felt thick enough to keep her warm, was graceful in design, and elegant in its fit - much simpler than the elaborately tiered and bustled ball gown she would be wearing later that evening.

When the dress was fastened snugly, Margret turned her attention to Deirdre's hair. Once it was brushed smooth, Margret managed a complex braid, deftly weaving Deirdre's hair into a delicate pattern of large and small braids that made the bottom look almost like filigree. Deirdre admired the view using both the large mirror and a small hand mirror. It was very elegant, and she spent a few minutes preening and getting a good look at her reflection. It had been a long time since she had felt anything approaching attractive.

Lady Margret laughed at Deirdre's bemused expression.

"Just wait until you see what I do with it before the ball!" she exclaimed, eyes sparkling.

"Will you have time to get dressed?" asked Deirdre.

"Oh yes. I will get dressed while you are at dinner. Lady Judeth is lending me one of her dresses, a plum wine-colored satin affair in the style that they wear here. It should be interesting to be all dressed up with the rest of the brightly-plumed birds!"

Deirdre turned to look at Margret, placing the hand mirror carefully on the vanity table as she turned.

"Should we really be celebrating? All those people killed..."

Margret sighed and set down the combs and brushes besides the mirror.

"In truth," she said, "we lost half of our party, most of them guards. People died. I think the others regard the ball as a reaffirmation of life. I know that I do. It makes it more than a meaningless celebration meant to get the minds of the nobles off of the upcoming war. Getting you back in one piece also gives us a good reason to celebrate. If you are feeling guilty tonight, stop and give thanks to those who gave their lives for you to be here. Your presence means a lot to the lords and ladies here tonight."

Margret rose and led the way out of Deirdre's dressing room and back into the sitting room. Tor turned at their entrance and stared at Deirdre, seeing her in a real dress for the first time. Nersh looked over at the minotaur's open mouthed expression and grinned, but said nothing. The look he was giving to Deirdre was evidence enough for the wolf as to his feelings for the lady.

Noticing Tor's scrutiny, Deirdre suddenly felt very self-conscious and spent several minutes fiddling with the skirts before regaining her composure. It was, however, disconcerting that someone like Tor, who had seen her at her most vulnerable, could throw her so much off balance. It was looking to be a very long evening.

Nersh suddenly stood and cocked her head to the side in a very dog-like manner. A few moments later, Deirdre could also hear voices coming down the hall, growing louder.

"...do not care what Evarl told you! I will not have people stationed outside the Lady's room like a couple of statues!"

"My lady, Evarl was worried about the..." the soldier's voice dropped below an audible level on the last.

"Phaugh!" exclaimed Judeth, sounding disgusted. "Get down to the barracks and tell Evarl I wish to see him directly in my study after dinner."

"Yes, lady."

The door opened abruptly, and Lady Judeth swept into the room, visibly calming herself as she entered. She wore a light peach dress of similar style to the one Deirdre was wearing and looked far more composed than she had sounded. The same small, bespectacled scribe followed her in, his eyes wide and sparkling with barely suppressed amusement.

"I beg your pardons for the disruption," said Judeth. "My captain seems to have less faith than I in the good intentions of your companion, I fear. I will speak to him about that presently. My lady Deirdre, you look lovely. Are you ready to go to dinner? Lady Nersh, will you be joining us?"

"No, my lady. If you would send up fare for Lady Margret and myself, we will dine here," smiled the wolf. "I need to get cleaned up and mean to bask in front of the fire a while longer."

Judeth nodded, and said, "We will take ourselves off then. Jan, would you order up some dinner for the Lady Nersh and the Lady Margret after you escort our minotaur guest to the stables? Arrange a bath for him and see if you can get Cook to carve up some rare meat for him. That is, unless you would prefer raw, sir. I have not had much experience with minotaur diets."

Tor nodded his acceptance and rose, turning to Deirdre. She smiled and took his hands, squeezing them reassuringly. He smiled back and followed Jan out of the rooms. Deirdre watched them go, admiring the young man's bravery in walking with the minotaur armed only with a pen and a small dagger on his hip. She felt an odd pang as she watched Tor leave, almost as if a part of herself was leaving. It was undeniably odd. She looked at Nersh, and saw the old wolf eyeing her narrowly. Nersh nodded to her, once, in recognition of her unspoken question.

"Shall we, my lady?" asked their hostess.

"Yes," said Deirdre. "I'm ready."

12

As they traveled through the halls, Deirdre tried to assuage her nervousness at meeting the other lords and ladies. She was not sure what they would make of her, and as Judeth was the only one that she was even a little familiar with, her discomfort was growing and her step became more hesitant.

"Nervous, my Lady?" asked Judeth, turning to look at her with a smile. "I think I have something that will prepare you for this dinner."

They reached the stairs, but they didn't go down as Deirdre had expected; instead Judeth led her halfway around the landing again to another corridor, this one darker and narrower.

"Where are we going?" asked Deirdre.

Lady Judeth shushed her quietly and opened the first door they came to. She ushered Deirdre inside, closing the door behind them. It was pitch black inside, but Judeth took her hand and pulled her along effortlessly. Deirdre heard the soft sound of a curtain being pulled aside and was startled to see two small holes of light appear in the wall near the floor. Voices wafted up from below.

In the dim light, Deirdre could see the earnest look on Judeth's face as she motioned Deirdre to sit.

"Lady Margret and I have known each other a long time," Lady Judeth whispered. "She has given me a little of your background and has confided in me what you plan to do. I am with you on this. No offense to the queen, but locking you away in the castle will make you an easy target. You would surely fall into a routine and become vulnerable, just like Darlena."

"How much did she tell you?" asked Deirdre softly.

"She did not reveal too much, but I do know that your plan involves finding Jack Parns. I can help you find him. Jack Parns has a wealth of knowledge in all things regarding the southern areas of Keyralithsmus. He would know where to find just about anything and anyone. Therefore, I am going with you."

"Wait, what? What about your lands?" asked Deirdre. "What will happen to them if you help me?"

"They are forfeit anyway if the Perstalians conquer the country. I would rather take my chances with you. Jan is assembling clothing, food, and other staples for the road. I will make sure we are well-provisioned. Evarl will stay here and guard the lands until, or if, I return.

"I also have a horse that the minotaur can ride if he is able. How did you ever...or am I being too nosy?"

"We have agreed to protect each other," said Deirdre. "He knows what will happen to him if he gets caught alone. Can Jan be trusted?"

"He is as mute as your friend, loyal to me, and smarter than anyone I have ever known," Judeth nodded. "We are...very fond of each other, Jan and I."

A muted sound reached their ears, and Judeth pointed abruptly to the round holes in the walls.

"Take a look," she said.

Deirdre crept over to one of the holes and did as she was instructed. Sitting slightly below her vantage point was an assembly of men and women around a large, ornately set dining table. They were talking in loud voices, making no efforts to be quiet.

"So where are they?" asked a russet haired man with a look of perpetual boredom on his face. "How long does it take to fetch someone?"

"Lord Jasper of Ganley Keep," whispered Judeth in Deirdre's ear. "Quite the scoundrel. Not someone to tangle with. He is a lot more aware than he appears."

A woman with sandy blond shoulder-length hair and piercing blue eyes made an exasperated sound. She appeared to be about Deirdre's age and was dressed in royal blue with lighter blue lace at the throat and wrist. She set down her glass with an overly loud thump and glared at Jasper.

"My Lord," said the lady, "the Lady Deirdre has been through some very hard trials as of late, some of which are potentially linked with your house and your father. She has every right to be late if she so chooses."

Jasper lounged in his seat, one arm thrown over the back of the chair, the other raising his half-drained wine glass to his lips. In contrast to his black velvet doublet and pale face, the dark red wine possessed great vitality. Draining the goblet, he set the heavy crystal down hard, echoing the lady's action.

"What my father does or does not do is no concern of mine. The house of Ganley can rot for all I care. My father is more than content to rule his domain, and he tells me little of it. I, however, much prefer the gentle companies of ladies and the lucky roll of the dice now and again."

Deirdre watched the red haired man with a combination of amusement and concern as a servant hurried to refill his glass. She had seen men like him before. This Jasper Ganley was a great actor, but something in his attitude made her wonder what his real motives were. Was he here to spy for his father? What was his real agenda?

The lady in blue spoke again, her whole attitude one of anger.

"It is of no surprise to you that your father is not well-loved by any in this company," she snapped. "However, like it or not, you still have the job to act as his emissary while you are here. What you do in your spare time is none of our affairs."

"Hear, hear," spoke up a thin man dressed in green. "I must agree with the Lady Lorelei. None here need to be reminded of your 'hobbies'. What all of us are concerned about is that your family may be involved in this attack!"

His words had risen to a crescendo and when he was done, the air rang momentarily, leaving a brief, uncomfortable silence. Lord Jasper leaned forward, folded his hands in front of him on the table, and looked at the speaker long and hard, a half-sneer twisting his face.

"Do you really believe for one minute, Lord Percy, that Lady Deirdre, a half-spawned bastard from some backwoods farm in the Mountain Reaches, that unlanded Lady, that...minotaur-lover...could save anyone, much less herself? If my father's wolves had attacked her, which I very much doubt, she would be dead by now. Dark Wolves indeed!" spat Lord Jasper.

He raised his glass and drained it, slamming it angrily on the table once again.

Deirdre stared at him, aghast. Nerfal had warned her that people might think of her in such terms, but this was the first she had heard it spoken. She was shocked, however, that he would try to discredit her and imply that she was in no mortal danger. That was akin to tossing her to those very wolves she had avoided.

"We should get down there," said Lady Judeth softly. "This could get out of hand."

Deirdre let Lady Judeth guide her back to the door and, after closing it behind them, they went swiftly along the corridor to the staircase. Lady Judeth lifted the hem of her skirts and fairly flew down the stairs, forcing Deirdre to do the same in order to keep up. At the bottom, they turned and entered the hallway that Deirdre had seen Lady Judeth originally emerge from when they arrived. It opened into another corridor, this one brightly lit with many doors, outside one of which stood Jan. When he saw Lady Judeth, he gestured wildly at the closed portal behind which came sounds of muffled arguing. Lady Judeth pointed up and said, "Dinner." Jan nodded and raced down to the other end of the corridor.

"Ready?" said Judeth softly.

Deirdre nodded, and they entered the room. Inside was a small antechamber, richly paneled in light maple, and another door through which came the sounds of the altercation, now even more alarming. Lady Judeth opened the second portal without hesitation, barging into an argument in full swing. Deirdre followed her but hung back a little, not sure if she were ready to be part of the scene.

The tension in the room had escalated to the point where several of the guests were out of their chairs, some with their hands resting on the pommels of their daggers. All were glaring at Lord Jasper with a mixture of disgust and outright malice. Lord Jasper was poised in a ready stance, glaring at his accusers with equal animosity.

"What is going on?" demanded Lady Judeth. "We are supposed to be having a formal dinner, not an opportunity for you to air your grievances! What is the meaning of this?"

She turned to Deirdre and gave her a deep curtsy accompanied by a small wink.

"My Lady Deirdre, I do apologize! This is not the normal occurrence at my residence. Please take your seat, and I will sort this out immediately. Your trials have already taken enough from you as it is."

Lady Judeth turned back to the others, most of whom had bowed or curtsied and taken their seats again. Deirdre stepped forward to look at the other dinner guests. With the exception of Jasper, they looked back at her with polite curiosity. Jasper, however, remained standing, glaring at Deirdre. She wondered what she had done for him to view her with such animosity.

"Please be seated," said Lady Judeth. "Lady Lorelei, would you enlighten us as to why we have been treated to this display of aggression?"

"Certainly, my Lady," said Lady Lorelei with a touch of glee. She turned to look at Lord Jasper. "My lord was enlightening us as to his opinion of Lady Deirdre, and his unequaled faith, or lack thereof, concerning her position in the upcoming war."

"He insulted her," spat the man in green, Lord Percy, rising to his feet again. "Why be tactful, my Lady? He insulted Lady Deirdre fully and without cause. We all heard the survivor's reports. Only Dark Wolves could have caused the chaos that was loosed on the party three days ago. Yet he implies that it was a band of rogue wolves that attacked! Rubbish!"

"Lord Jasper?" Lady Judeth turned to the heir of the Ganley seat, "Is that the truth?"

"I believe that that covers it nicely, yes," sneered Lord Jasper. "My opinions, however, are my own, Lady Judeth. The council I keep, I think, shall be the same."

He pushed his chair back and stormed out of the room, giving Deirdre a cold look as he passed. The door slammed behind him, and they could all hear him stomping off down the corridor.

No one breathed for a long moment, and then Lady Judeth cleared her throat.

"Be seated again, my Lord of Chadwick," she said. "My lady, sit here next to me, to my right. Lord Jasper seems to have had a great deal to say, my Lords and Ladies. It looks as though we shall be spared his thoughts for now, at least until the ball."

She gently tugged on the elaborately embroidered bell-pull to her left and took her seat. The other lords and ladies also returned to their seats and the uncomfortable quiet lingered as they made themselves busy adjusting napkins for a few long moments.

"While we await dinner, may I make introductions? From my left is Lord Percy of Chadwick Castle, Lady Kara of Craddock Keep, Lord Lorell from Owens Dwell, Lady Jaime of Pendelton Horn, Lady Alleen of Bartlett Castle, Lady Marlea of Onslow Manor, Lord Dean of Casing Hold, Lord Liliek of Blakely Castle, and Lady Sadia of Jacobs Keep. Along with yours, they make up the ruling families of Keyralithsmus under the Tanols. My Lords and Ladies, may I introduce you to Lady Deirdre Ettar, Lady of Keyralithsmus, Vicomtess of the Mountain Reaches, and Lady of the Ivory Castle."

All of the lords and ladies greeted her politely, some with more enthusiasm than others, but all with smiles that seemed genuine.

Deirdre graciously inclined her head to them, momentarily taken aback by the eyes that so intently studied her. No one seemed hostile towards her. A little indifferent in some cases, a trifle unsure, but in all of them, she sensed a rising hope that she could help them. Their expectations surprised and humbled her. It was a relief when the door opened moments later, and servants filed into the room bearing dinner.

Subtly, she watched Lady Judeth. She was gracious, witty, and seemingly at perfect ease with everyone around the table. She knew countless pieces of family history, asking after Lady Jaime's ailing father or inquiring as to how Lord Lileks's daughter liked her new pony. Nothing seemed to escape her notice, and Deirdre began to wonder if the Lady kept a magic mirror hidden somewhere with which to keep up with the news. Deirdre smiled to herself at the thought.

The dishes being placed on the long table soon distracted her attention. The food set before them made her mouth water as each one was announced. Roast duck, breaded veal, sliced pears in a raisin plum glaze, braised beef ribs, freshwater mussels – the list seemed endless. Some things she had never even heard of, much less eaten.

"What are these?" she asked, sampling a dish that looked almost like fettuccine.

"Those are sweetling saplings cut down with the sap flowing thick in them, sliced into thin pieces and then steamed tender," replied Judeth. "They are delightful, are they not?"

Deirdre nodded, and sampled some of the other dishes. There were unfamiliar tangy fruit slices wrapped around a haunch of venison and baked with cinnamon and sliced sugar cane to produce the most flavorful meat she had ever had. A close second were apples cored and stuffed with cheese and bacon, then roasted in a pan with brown sugar. The smells intermingled into a heavenly mix of sharp, tangy bacon and savory cinnamon to make an aroma that was mouth-watering.

Famished after several days of meager rations, Deirdre tried a little from even the most inedible looking dishes, finding that each was as palatable as the last. About halfway through the meal, Lord Percy made a joke to Lord Lorell about rolling their way to the ball, and Deirdre looked around discretely to see if her peers were eating less vigorously than she was. They were not. In fact, some of them were eating even more voraciously.

"I must compliment you, Lady Judeth," said Lord Dean, a tall, gangly man with blond hair that fell halfway to his broad shoulders. "This year's banquet is even better than last year's. I must get some of these recipes from your cook for my wife's next dinner party."

Everyone laughed, and Lady Judeth whispered in Deirdre's ear, "The Lady of Casing Hold has served the same thing at every feast for the past ten years. Lord Dean is getting desperate."

Deirdre chuckled and turned to see the servants entering with yet another round of dishes. It was definitely time to slow down the mad rush to eat the whole table.

The conversation moved on around her, and Deirdre could tell that they had questions but were hesitant to ask. Lord Lorell broke the tension first during a lull in the conversation following an animated discussion about the lineage of Lord Percy's horses. The lord smiled at Deirdre in greeting and looked to her for acknowledgement. Deirdre smiled back accordingly.

"I fear that my fellow nobles are a bit unsure of what to say to you, Lady Deirdre," he said, "so I will ask what we all are curious to know. Is it true you tamed a minotaur?"

"Not exactly," said Deirdre, looking around at all the eyes watching her and feeling her stomach tense. "He is not tame; he is simply not your typical minotaur. He does not speak, so maybe he was made an outcast for some reason. He saved my life, though, and I promised to protect him in return for his good act. His name is Tor, and he is my bodyguard."

Lord Lorell nodded, and several of the others exchanged glances that made Deirdre remember Nersh's warning as to what people might assume of the relationship she had with the minotaur. She wondered if she should say something so they'd believe that there was nothing else going on between Tor and herself, but stopped when she saw the smile on Lady Judeth's face.

The Lady shook her head and said softly so that only Deirdre could hear, "Let them think what they like. Let them wonder."

"Were you not afraid when you first saw him?" asked Lady Marlea. "I know I would be terrified of seeing such a brute up close!"

"He is not a brute, my lady," said Deirdre, trying to hide her annoyance at hearing Tor referred to so coarsely. "I hit my head in the fall, and he bandaged my eyes so the light would not cause me pain. I didn't know he was a minotaur at first, so I had time to get to know him as a friend."

There was an uncomfortable silence as the other lords and ladies looked around at each other in bewilderment. Clearly, they had never conceived of there being an intelligent minotaur before, and she wondered what they might think if they knew he had been human.

"Lady Deirdre, let us change the topic rather than discomfit you further," said Lady Jaime, a thin woman with a pleasant, low voice. "Were the beasts that attacked you truly Dark Wolves? We have only heard snippets of the tales the party members told."

"As I have never experienced anything like them before, I can only tell you what I witnessed," said Deirdre. "Swords and spears passed right through them as if they were made of smoke. Horses couldn't kick them and nothing could touch them. Lady Nersh said that until Tor showed up with his glowing sword, they were merciless, but the sword made them flee."

"They sound like Dark Wolves to me," said Lord Percy in a disgusted voice. "All the other survivors tell stories identical to yours, my Lady. I wonder what else the Lord of Ganley Keep has in store and what side he is really on."

"Their family has been loyal to the alliance for over three hundred years. I wonder why it has changed?" said Lord Lorell.

"If it actually *has* changed," said Lady Alleen. "We have no real proof that there has been a true break of the alliance."

Lord Percy set his wine glass down and dabbed at the corners of his mouth with a napkin. Pushing his chair back, he rose.

"I, for one, am willing to let this discussion rest until the morrow. Right now, I have a ball to prepare for. Ladies, Lords, I will see you shortly. Perhaps my Lady Deirdre will save me a dance!"

Bowing first to Deirdre and then to Lady Judeth, he left the room.

The clock opposite the door began to strike, and the other lords and ladies took their leave one by one until only Deirdre and Judeth remained in the room.

"Well," said Lady Judeth, folding her napkin and setting it on her plate, "that did not go too poorly."

"No," admitted Deirdre, draining the last of her wine. "After Jasper left, things got a lot better. He'll be at the ball, I assume?"

"Oh, yes, he surely will. Many will have already heard about tonight's performance, I suspect. I will watch him for you, and there will be many other eyes on him as well. He will not be able to try anything in so large a crowd."

She turned and led the way out of the room, back through the two doors, and into the corridor.

"I will walk you back to your rooms, and Evarl will arrive in two hours to escort you to the ball. You should be able to get ready in two hours, yes?"

13

"Two hours! It's been almost two hours!" exclaimed Deirdre. "Margret, how long does it take to braid hair?"

"Well, my lady, it depends on how complicated it is," chuckled Margret. "I did my own, and it took me over a half hour without the ribbons and silk flowers. I am really almost finished, I promise."

Deirdre nervously ran her hands over the ivory satin ball gown trimmed with tiny silver bells and enough lace to make a dozen ornate placemats. She felt absurdly like a Disney Princess: Belle, perhaps, or Cinderella. She had never worn anything quite so elaborate in her life, and she wasn't sure that she could walk in it, much less dance. To further complicate matters, it had a bustle in the back and enough starched petticoats that she felt like an onion she was layered so.

Deirdre looked at the braid her long hair was being twisted into, a complicated weave even more elaborate than the one she had worn to dinner. She had begun to feel her neck stiffen after the first fifteen minutes of holding still. Margret had scolded her every time she moved, and she was positive that she would be unable to do more than nod for the rest of the evening.

"There!" Lady Margret exclaimed, standing back to admire her own handiwork. "Perfect. I am glad that I applied your makeup first. Evarl will be here any minute."

Deirdre did some shoulder rolls to see how tense her neck was and laughed at Lady Margret's look of mock indignation. She turned to look at herself in the mirror, and Lady Margret held up a hand glass so that she could see the intricate braid work at the back of her head. It was a masterpiece of ribbon, silk tea roses, and interwoven braids. The ribbons and flowers matched her dress and shimmered with tiny seed pearls in grey and ivory hues. Deirdre was amazed and revised her estimate immediately. Something that complicated should have taken much longer to create.

A second look in the dressing room's full-length mirror made Deirdre shake her head in disbelief. Had it only been five weeks since she had come through the gate? The person staring back at her was a little thinner, looked more fit, had small horns, and held an air of self-confidence that had not been there before the crossing. Add the makeup to the look, and in the mirror stood a woman that Deirdre never before could have imagined being. A quote came to her then from Shakespeare.

"'And since you know you cannot see yourself so well as by reflection, I, your glass will modestly discover to yourself that of yourself which you yet know not of,'" she said, laughing.

"It is really you," said Lady Margret, a broad smile on her face. "A bit surprising, is it not? You look different to me than you did even a week ago, more sure of yourself...the image of a Lady. Tonight's ball will be a test of your mettle. I think you are up to it."

She paused and set the brush down on the little vanity table.

"How far can Tor be trusted, my lady?" she asked suddenly, her expression one of concern.

"So formal," said Deirdre in a teasing tone, then sobered when Margret's expression didn't change. "I trust him with my life, Margret. He's already saved it once."

Lady Margret nodded unhappily, clearly unsatisfied with the answer and looked at her own reflection in the mirror.

"It is just that...he is a minotaur, Deirdre. You know what they are saying about you, do you not?" she said, looking sideways at Deirdre. "With the lesser nobles, it was the primary topic of conversation at dinner tonight."

"I'm sure it was," said Deirdre with a sigh, turning to look up at her friend. "It isn't true, Margret, and even if it were, what business is it of theirs? Let them think what they want. After tonight, they will have even more things to gossip about."

"So how *did* you tame a minotaur?" asked Lady Margret.

"For now, let that be my secret, all right?" smiled Deirdre. "I didn't have to do anything in any way lurid, if that is what you were concerned about."

She rose from her chair and walked out into the sitting room, feeling the weight of the ball gown fully for the first time. It was surprisingly heavy, what with all the trimmings and petticoats. She did an experimental twirl, and found that the skirts were perfectly balanced. Lady Margret followed, closing the dressing room door behind her. Evarl hadn't arrived yet, so they sat down on the couch to wait. By the fire, Nersh slept peacefully, her coat gleaming from a bath and a good brushing as she basked in the radiant warmth. An empty dinner plate rested on the floor beside her.

"Should we wake her?" asked Lady Margret, softly. "She wanted to go to the ball, but she seems so tired."

"Let's wait until we come back. We leave for the South tonight, and she needs all the rest she can get," replied Deirdre. "We need to stay focused. Even you are too worried about what the nobles think. After tonight, it won't matter."

A knock on the door startled them.

"Let the games begin," Deirdre said, drawing a deep breath.

Lady Margret gave her a reassuring smile and went to answer it with a swift grace that made Deirdre envious.

Evarl stepped into the room, resplendent in his dress uniform, and bowed to them. He straightened and proffered an arm to Deirdre. She curtsied back and accepted his arm, grateful for the support as the thought of descending the stairs in the multilayered skirts was a bit intimidating. With a last glance around at the relative safety of the room, Deirdre allowed herself to be escorted to the ball.

The night air was cool as they exited the main building and made their way along the flagstone path that led to a structure separated from the main house. The short walk had left Deirdre slightly chilled, and she was glad when they reached the grand entrance. It was flanked by two liveried servants dressed in the house colors, and these two whisked the double doors open, bowing as the group approached. With Evarl's arm still lending her support and Margret by her side, Deirdre stepped inside the brightly lit foyer and over to the second set of doors beyond which strains of music with a tempo similar to that of a waltz could be heard. A thousand butterflies suddenly fluttered in her stomach, and she felt her hands go clammy inside their white gloves.

Another set of doormen bowed as they approached and opened the gleaming oak doors for them. The music enveloped her fully, and the perfume of beeswax candles filled the air. Deirdre took a deep breath as they crossed the threshold and looked at Margret for reassurance. Margret glanced at her, winked, and then Deirdre turned and fully viewed the room into which they had stepped.

The main part of the hall lay a few steps down from the entrance they had come in from, and there were already a decent number of dancers doing a lively waltz on the polished parquet floor. Other nobles milled around, being offered light hors d'oeuvres or sparkling cordials by servants. The musicians were set upon a dais to the right of the entrance, and Deirdre noted that the instruments they played were also of the familiar styles from the same era as the rest of the estate. Bass cellos, soaring violins, and even a flat backed mandolin were being played by the very adept musicians, and Deirdre wondered again at the similarities between this estate and her home world.

A liveried man right inside the door took immediate note of Evarl, raised a horn to his lips, and blew a short fanfare. The musicians wrapped up their song with a flourish, and all eyes in the room suddenly turned to where they stood. Conversations died, and Deirdre momentarily quailed at facing all of them at once. She squared her shoulders and did her best to hide her fear.

"May I present Deirdre Ettar, Lady of the Ivory Tower, and Vicomtess of the Northern Reaches; her escort, Captain Inier Evarl, commander of the forces at Garey Manor; and Lady Margret Breen of Remembrance."

The ladies and lords around the hall bowed and curtsied towards Deirdre, and she tried not to clutch Evarl's arm tighter, fearing she'd either cut off the man's blood flow or give away the extent of her nervousness to everyone. Instead, she returned the curtsy to the nobles in the hall and allowed herself to be led down the short flight of stairs to the dance floor. She tried to focus on not falling in the many-layered dress, and was again grateful for Evarl's steadying arm. Once safely on level ground again, she took a long moment to look around the hall.

The room was paneled in a dark mahogany with opulent and extravagant use of gilt work over every window and door. Ornate gilded frescoes decorated the edges of small balconies around the room, and carved, golden roses graced the frames of several large mirrors along the walls.

The room boasted ten sets of French windows, and above each pair was a smaller window bearing stained glass roses of varying colors and shapes. Framing the windows were dark red draperies, held back by golden cords. Most of the pairs were closed, but the one at the very end of the hall was ajar and seemed to lead out onto some sort of porch or veranda.

Between each set of doors were cleverly crafted sets of chimney lamps made to resemble torches, their blown glass shades emulating the shape and color of fire. Real flames flickered inside, safe from drafts should the evening be warm enough to leave the doors open. Glancing up, Deirdre noticed hanging from the ceiling one huge chandelier and the two smaller ones flanking it, all of which were made of tiered rows of prisms and decorated at the end with a huge faceted glass ball. Each one of these caught the lamplight and reflected it around the room in bars of color.

At the far end of the hall, near the open door, an enormous grand-father clock the same color mahogany as the walls chimed the hour sonorously. It reminded Deirdre of something she had read, but she could not quite put her finger on what it was. The clock seemed very much out of place in this world.

As Deirdre and Margret reached the bottom of the stairs, two of the lesser lords approached them and bowed.

"Greetings gentlemen," Lady Margret said. "Lady Deirdre, may I introduce you to the Lords Aster and Poll Feist, both of whom have holdings on Lady Judeth's lands."

The lords bowed to Deirdre, and she curtsied in return. She observed that their dress also matched the very Southern décor of Garey Manor, and she was amazed at how well the Garey family had done in duplicating the style.

Wearing an extravagantly belled skirt dripping with even more lace than Deirdre's, Lady Judeth swept across the room to where they stood, curtsied to them all, and exchanged pleasantries with the Feist brothers. She noticed Deirdre's scrutiny of the clothing that the men were wearing and smiled.

"The clothing here is a bit different, I know, but you will at least find the dancing to be familiar," she said.

The string quartet then began to play a lively piece. Aster bowed to Lady Judeth and partnered her out onto the dance floor. Poll turned to Deirdre and bowed to her, but Deirdre politely declined and watched as the young lord swung Lady Margret out to dance.

"You will have to dance eventually, my Lady," called Margret gaily as she danced away.

Deirdre smiled at her friend, but she sincerely hoped no one would ask her to dance. She was concerned about Tor, and she wondered how he was doing and if he was being treated well. She was worried about leaving that night, about the dragons, about everything. Dancing was the last thing she wanted to do.

More people were moving out onto the dance floor, and a flash of bright emerald green caught her attention. It was Lord Percy; he had spied her and was making his way over to where she stood. Stopping before her, he bowed deeply, and rose again.

"Lady Deirdre," he said, "has no one yet asked you to dance?"

"My Lord Percy, I am new to a lot of the customs of the court. I was not sure as to the etiquette here and have avoided dancing so as not to make a misstep, so to speak."

Lord Percy beamed at her with genuine amusement.

"You should dance with at least a few of the lords, my lady," he said. "May I have the pleasure of being the first to escort you?"

Charmed by his genuine courtesy, Deirdre could only laugh and accept.

———

Vexanious blew softly and poked his head over the door of his stall, looking for any signs of the grooms and stable boys. No one was in sight, and a soft snore came from the groom's loft, evidence that at least one of the servants had stayed behind. The others were having their own little party tonight on a nearby farm and probably wouldn't be back until dawn.

Using his teeth, he slid back the bolt on his stall door and gently opened it out into the main runway of the stable. Walking as softly as he could, Vexanious moved down the aisle, passing other drowsing horses, most of whom never even looked up as he passed.

By scent, he found the stall where the minotaur lay sleeping and opened the unbolted door, easing in like a dark shadow. Even the faint sound of the well-oiled hinges were enough to wake the creature, and he stood still as the minotaur slowly stood up, as if trying not to startle him.

"Minotaur," he said, softly, inclining his head in greeting.

The minotaur nodded a greeting back.

"I will need your help in the tack room," said Vexanious. "I assume that you know how to tack a horse?"

The minotaur hesitated, and then nodded again. Vexanious turned to leave, indicating for the creature to follow him. He felt a certain smugness at having a minotaur as a groom, and it occurred to him that very few Talking Folk could claim the distinction of working with a minotaur, even if the beast had claimed to be human once.

———

Tor followed Vexanious out of the stall, warily looking around for men-at-arms and grooms. Vexanious could do as he liked, being Talking Folk and all, but as a minotaur, he had to be more than careful. He couldn't afford to be sent to Coliseum. If that happened, he'd never have a chance to regain a human form, as he'd never be free again.

The tack room was only four doors down from the stall he had slept in and was lit dimly by a lantern turned down low. Tor adjusted the lantern's wick, providing more light, and they went inside to look at the bewildering array of saddles, bridles, and harnesses. Tor scanned the saddles and spotted Vexanious's where it hung on a rack. He and Vexanious reached it at the same time, and the horse looked at him a little oddly.

"You have a good eye," said the horse in a deceptively calm voice. Tor caught the tone in his old friend's comment and simply shrugged.

He picked up the tack and carried it back out to the main corridor. Vexanious craned his muscular neck around to watch, and Tor placed the saddle pad and saddle onto the horse's broad back, falling into familiar patterns of fastening buckles, testing the girth, and adjusting the bitless bridle so that it fit the stallion comfortably. Silently cursing his huge hands for their clumsiness, he nevertheless managed to tack Vexanious swiftly and surely.

The stallion looked at him for a moment with a strange, thoughtful look in his eye.

"I feel as if I ought to know you," said the horse, peering at him through his thick forelock. "Why do I feel this way? Did I know you before you were changed?"

Tor slowly nodded, and Vexanious lifted his head high and snorted. The horse's eyes rolled white for a moment, but then footsteps sounded softly in the corridor. Vexanious turned and bared his teeth, but Tor motioned for him to stop. It was Jan.

Lady Judeth's secretary bowed and pointed to the tack room. Tor nodded and motioned for Vexanious to move towards the door.

"What is going on?" hissed Vexanious.

Tor pointed to his mouth and then at Jan and shook his head. Vexanious nodded and relaxed slightly. Tor then pointed to Vexanious and then to himself.

"He is getting horses ready for you and the others?"

Tor nodded and watched Jan as he found and led out three mounts one at a time, readying each swiftly. They snorted at the smell of the minotaur but remained mostly steady under Jan's reassuring hand. One was a huge draft horse that looked as if it would easily carry a minotaur, and he hoped fervently that the animal was as easy to ride as it looked. He'd never ridden anything in this body. It had taken him days just to learn to properly walk in it. Riding a nervous horse was a skill he'd never had to master.

When he was finished getting the horses ready, Jan gestured for them to follow him and led the horses out into the silent night. No one stirred, and Tor, watching for the inevitable guardsmen, was surprised to find two slumped silently outside the door to the stable. He looked at Jan, and the man just winked and smiled.

Their journey was swift, crossing a small, darkened field not far from the building where the ball was occurring. It had gotten colder, and Tor could feel the chill of autumn more sharply than he had the night before. He looked through the darkness into the brightly lit hall and watched the dancers. He thought that he saw Deirdre once or twice, but he wasn't sure. A strange ache began to overtake him, and Tor found himself longing to be in the light, dancing amid the other lords and ladies. He cursed the shape he wore anew and found himself missing the bright lights, the sounds of laughter, the good parts about being human. His thoughts returned to Deirdre, and he wondered what it would be like to be the one dancing with her.

As he thought of her, a strange thing happened, and for a moment, he found himself seeing through her eyes as she danced with one of the younger Lords, Dean of Casing Hold, if he wasn't mistaken; he hadn't seen him in years. Dean was a solid warrior and excellent in a fight, as was the case with all of the lads from Casing Hold. More importantly, his family was loyal to the crown, something that lately had become more precious than gold or jewels.

The vision faded, and Tor rubbed his eyes, opening them to find both Jan and Vexanious looking at him oddly. Jan reached under his cloak to pull out a large parcel tied with twine. Tor eagerly cut the string and found several warm woolen shirts and trousers, hose, and a cloak that should fit him well enough. He removed his old cloak and stripped unself-consciously, shivering in the cold. He piled on two pairs of woolen hose, a pair of trousers, a tunic that had buttons in the front, and a new cloak lined with soft furs. He reveled in the feeling of warmth - it had been a while since he had been this warm - and looked back at Jan, hoping that the man would magically produce a pair of boots. When Jan shook his head sadly, he rewrapped his feet in their makeshift coverings, and rebuckled the sword at his waist. Already, he began to feel more human than he had felt in a long time. The warmth was delicious, and he gave a bow to Jan that caused the secretary's face to light up with pleasure.

Sighing, Tor walked slowly over to where the big draft horse waited. He needed to be able to ride the beast when it was time to leave, and now would come the true test. It acted predictably, throwing its head high and rolling its eyes until the whites showed.

The dray horse whickered nervously and danced at the end of its reins. Jan willingly relinquished the reins to Tor when he gestured for them and went to calm the other mounts. Tor half led, half dragged the horse a little ways away to try to calm him.

At first, all the beast did was raise its head and pull steadily backwards, but as Tor made slow, soothing motions and hissed air through his teeth in a poor approximation of a 'shhhing' sound, the gelding began to respond. Tor cursed his malefactors for removing even the calming ability a voice could have on an animal, and patiently, slowly moved towards the horse. After a short eternity, it allowed him to touch its neck, and a little after that, Tor was able to attempt to ride it. His earlier fears about being able to ride were mostly unfounded. Although his horns unbalanced him a little bit, he was able to sit in the saddle and, within a relatively short amount of time, had the horse under control.

During all of this, Vexanious's eyes never left him, and so intent was Tor in calming the gelding, that he missed the look of recognition and growing wonder that crept into the stallion's eyes.

———

The chimes sounded at eleven o' clock during a lull in the dancing, and several people paused and stood listening to the grandfather clock at the far end of the room sound the hour. In that moment, Deirdre remembered what story the clock had reminded her of and at once thought of Edgar Allan Poe. She also noted absently that the chime was that of Westminster and sounded so completely out of place that she didn't know if she would laugh or cry.

She settled on doing neither and, after finishing the dance with Lord Dean, bowed and made her way over to the punch bowl. As she waited for the liveried servant to pour her a glass, she mentally counted the chimes. At nine, he handed her the glass; at ten, she turned; and at eleven, looked up to find herself locking gazes with Lord Jasper some fifty feet across the room.

This wasn't the first time she had seen him that evening. He'd floated in and out of her peripheral vision since his arrival shortly after nine o' clock, but, much to her relief, he'd shown no interest in engaging her in conversation. She had slowly let her guard slip, getting drawn into conversations with the minor ladies, all of which ended up centering around Tor. Several had gone so far as to hint with curiosity about what it must be like to bed such a beast. Lord Jasper had hovered in the background of these conversations but had not come too close. Ever vigilant, Lady Judeth or one of the other major landed gentry would appear to rescue her from the conversation, and Lord Jasper would disappear again into the crowd.

Now, however, her self-proclaimed detractor was striding across the ballroom, weaving deftly between the couples dancing on the floor. Out of the corner of her eye, she noticed Lady Judeth doing a lively step with Lord Dean to the new piece the musicians had just struck up. Lady Margret was likewise engaged in dancing with one of the other lesser lords. It appeared she was on her own.

Lord Jasper maneuvered around one last pair of dancers and stopped directly in front of her with the same odd, uncomfortable expression she'd seen on his face through the peephole from above the dining room. He seemed at war with himself as he stared at her.

"My lady," he said tersely, bowing. "I realize that I said harsh words to you earlier. I would like to make amends. Would you dance with me?"

Deirdre stared at him in disbelief, and he swallowed and said almost pleadingly,

"Please…"

She considered this and set her untouched punch down on the refreshment table behind her. She curtsied stiffly to him and offered him her hand. At that moment, the music ended, only to be replaced with a slower waltz style, and Deirdre mentally rolled her eyes. With great reserve, she allowed him to steer her into an empty space on the still-crowded dance floor.

He was, she thought wryly, a wonderful dancer, able to skillfully guide her through some of the more complicated steps that Nerfal had only touched on once or twice. She watched him carefully for any sign of his intent, but throughout the whole waltz, he just simply danced with her. Only his deep brown eyes reflected his inner turmoil, and she watched them until the dance wound to a close. She curtsied and gave him what she hoped was a mostly genuine smile.

"You dance well, my lord. That was most enjoyable. Another tune is beginning; will you join me again?"

She kept her tone formal, but added just a touch of warmth so as to make him feel at ease. The dance that was beginning was another slow one, and several couples had left the floor, giving them more space to move...or talk. She hoped that he might open up to her if given the opportunity.

"My lady, if it pleases you," he said in an equally formal tone. Underneath, she detected a hint of uncertainty.

They stepped out again, and Jasper led her into the complicated pattern of another dance.

"My lady is very generous," said Lord Jasper softly, "and most forgiving after our encounter at dinner."

"I hold no grudges, my lord," said Deirdre. "I am new to Court, and I expected some to be a little skeptical of my origins."

"Lady, it is of your origins that we must speak," he said in a low voice. "Will you have a word with me alone? I am up to no tricks, I swear, but I must speak to you privately."

Deirdre bit her lip, glanced quickly at the clock, and then nodded as they swung towards the rear of the hall.

"After this dance, go out to the veranda," he said softly. "I will meet you there."

Deirdre nodded again; they finished out the dance and gave courtesy to each other before parting. Jasper vanished into the crowd, and Deirdre went to get a new cup of punch. As she stood sipping it, Lady Judeth appeared at her elbow.

"Was he awful?" asked Lady Judeth in a hushed tone.

"Oddly, no," said Deirdre. "He wants to speak with me on the veranda, alone."

Lady Judeth glanced over Deirdre's shoulder.

"There he goes, out the side door. I wonder what he wants to talk to you about," she mused. "I will follow closely, my lady, and tell the guards to be alert. Take care; he is a sly one."

Deirdre nodded, grateful that Judeth was willing to trust her to go and speak to Lord Jasper and savvy enough to understand that precautions had to be taken. She slowly made her way down the length of the hall towards the French doors that led to the veranda. Several times, courtiers moved to intercept her, but she managed to fend them off, claiming the need for air and refusing their persistent offers for company.

She stepped out onto the stone porch, feeling the chill of the night air enfold her. The veranda was definitely large enough to encompass dancers in the warmer weather but was now unoccupied due to the cold. Deirdre walked over to the sweeping stone balustrades that ran at waist height around the edge of the area and peered out into the night. The full moon shone down, occasionally occluded by the clouds above, tinting the white stone pillars that flanked the stairs a ghostly grey-blue and making them seem almost ethereal. The grass below was black in the shadow of the veranda but for the highlights of moonlight along its carefully groomed blades.

"Thank you for coming, my lady."

Lord Jasper's voice drifted up from the shadows below, and Deirdre watched as he appeared and began to climb the stone steps. He glanced furtively around and pointed to a stone bench outside the main glow of the ballroom lights. She accompanied him to the bench and sat down beside him, grateful for the layers of starched petticoats between the cold stone and herself. Lord Jasper turned slightly towards her, looking both young and unsure of himself. He seemed more like a nervous teenager than the confident man he had acted like at dinner. For the first time, Deirdre found herself wondering how old he actually was.

"My lady," he said and stopped. Deirdre could see the turmoil plain on his face. "My lady, can I trust you? Will you keep the secret that I am going to tell you?"

"It depends, my lord," said Deirdre. "Why are you telling me?"

"My lady, I lied earlier when I said my father was not involved. You were beset by Dark Wolves, and I denied it." Lord Jasper sighed, and looked off into the shadows beyond the building. "The others know me as I have presented myself, but in truth, it is only a charade. I only pretend to be such as they perceive me so as to keep my father from suspecting my true motives."

He stood and paced over to the carved rail, placing his hands on the cold stone and lowering his head. Deirdre watched him patiently.

"When my father told me to come, he instructed me that I was to tell everyone your real identity. He knows that you are not of our world, and he wants to destroy any chance you have to call the dragons in whatever way he is able. He believed that if the nobles knew your real identity, they would not accept you because your motives are not bound to the land. It is not your birthplace; therefore, how could you be willing to risk your life for it?

"That is what I was supposed to say, but I did not. When you entered the dining hall, and I saw the horns on your head, I knew that the last part was false. I could not bring myself to betray you, and I left the way I did because I needed time to figure out what to do."

He looked over at her and sighed again, turning his gaze back to the stars.

"You are the first person outside of Ganley Keep to know this next piece of information. I will keep your secret if you agree to never divulge mine. Are we in accord?"

"Yes," said Deirdre, "I agree."

Lord Jasper sat back down on the bench and hesitantly took her hands in his. Looking into her eyes, he began to speak.

"My ancestor, Gontral Ganley, was the original builder of Ganley Keep, and he did what he did to protect the family, or so our history is written. He worked heavy, dark magics and found a way to somehow control every evil thing, up to and including lesser demons, without aid. He wanted more, however, and he made a bargain with a very powerful entity so that, in exchange for complete control over the creatures of darkness while he was alive, he would give over his very soul upon his death. This was back when humans had first come to Keyralithsmus, and these beings posed a real threat to people.

"Power corrupts, however, and it has corrupted every one of my ancestors right down the line of succession, my father being no exception. The kings and queens have tolerated my family's presence through the ages as it is this magic that keeps the darkness at bay, and they have always upheld the peace...until now.

"I idolized my father. I grew up hearing the stories, listening to how power could benefit one and how all it cost was one's soul. Until I was thirteen, I was set to take over the reins when he died, eager for the benefits I would gain, and never thinking what I would be giving up. You cannot measure a soul in gold or pounds, so how can you know its real worth?

"Then something happened that changed my whole life. I had a dream, and in this dream, a great white beast came and spoke to me. It could have only been Tali, the great Tsavon. He said, 'This is not the way intended for you. Break the mold.' Then he showed me what had happened to my forefathers' souls. They had become the eternal playthings for the very demons that they had controlled. All of them were twisted or stunted into shriveled parodies of themselves, and they were tormented endlessly and would be for all eternity."

Lord Jasper shivered. He let go of Deirdre's hands, but continued his tale, still looking right at her.

"I woke, horrified, from this dream, and spent the rest of the night by my fireplace wrapped in my blankets, too terrified to sleep. I began the next day to feign ineptitude in my magical studies, pretending to be more interested in girls and gambling. By sixteen, I had a reputation of being tyrannical, and by twenty, a womanizer. I paid several women of ill-repute to keep my secrets and spread rumors. They took my money and did their tasks well. No royal lady wanted anything to do with me.

"My father tolerated my supposed excesses, giving me more money when I claimed to have gambled all of mine away and being patient with my magical 'blunders.' Lately, though, he has been pushing me to learn magic faster, and I fear his time is growing short. Both this ball and his errand to discredit you came as a blessing. I had no real intention of returning to Ganley Keep after the ball and had spent most of the last four hours trying to figure out what to do.

"Before I asked you to dance, I had actually packed my bags and crept down to the stables to get my horse. You can guess what I saw there."

Deirdre froze, and her eyes widened as she realized what Lord Jasper had seen. He nodded.

"I would like to come with you," he said. "We know each other's secrets, and I am going to leave tonight regardless. I would like to join your party."

"You don't even know where we are going," said Deirdre apprehensively.

"South, I would guess, to find the dragons," he said, standing up to pace over to the railing. "I do not blame you for not wanting to wait for the search party to return. I do not believe they were ever sent, and if they were sent, they may not have gotten very far."

"What?"

"I overheard my father talking to one of the councilors the day I left. He said that arrangements had been made to ensure that the dragons never came, and the Perstalians were allowed access to our country. He was planning something, but I never heard what. I left that afternoon."

"I should get word to my father," said Deirdre, rising.

"It would be intercepted. Someone at that castle has far too much influence and control, most likely someone very close to the crown. My money would be on Marshall Rialain." Lord Jasper shook his head, and said, "Lady Deirdre, may I come with you? I have nowhere else to go. I have no friends, no confidants, only paid servants. I would much rather try to help remedy the situation if I can."

Deirdre sighed, feeling even colder than she had been a moment before, and nodded. She was not certain of him, but the fact that he had come to talk to her rather than let slip her secret gave her pause. He sounded sincere, but she was not sure. Intently searching his face for a long moment, she finally nodded.

"Go to the entrance to the valley. I'm not one hundred percent certain when we'll get there, but it won't be long. I'll be leaving the ball in a few minutes. Meet us on the road."

"Thank you, my lady," said Lord Jasper, bowing. He slipped back into the shadows and was gone.

Deirdre fled back into the warmth of the building, feeling as if all of the benefits of the earlier bath were gone. She was frozen to the core, and she was not at all certain if what she had agreed to was good or not.

Lady Judeth pounced on her as she reentered the building.

"Is everything alright, my lady?" she asked, sounding worried. "You look pale."

"I'm fine," said Deirdre, "but I think it is time that we take our leave. I am very tired."

"Of course, my lady. Lady Margret has gone ahead to run you a bath and prepare your bed. I will accompany you back to your rooms."

They made to leave the ball, making a point to bid several of the major castle lords and ladies good night. Once outside, Deirdre relaxed and tried to prepare herself for the journey ahead.

"Is everything in readiness?" she asked softly.

"Yes. I have had word from Jan that Nersh has gone to make sure that your friend, the minotaur, is ready to go. She will meet us at the kitchen gate at half past midnight."

Lady Judeth paused for a long moment, then said.

"I have other tidings that are not so positive. Marshall Rialain is on the way here."

"Here?" asked Deirdre, alarmed.

She suddenly felt the weight of their imminent flight and tried to find the strength to deal with this new threat.

"After dinner, I received a message from the pigeon master that Marshall was coming to aid in the search for you," Lady Judeth continued. "We did send them a bird about your reappearance, but our birds must have crossed."

"It's a good thing we are leaving tonight," said Deirdre, with a shudder. "I don't trust him at all. Lord Jasper believes he is not what he appears to be."

"I am not sure that I trust Lord Jasper either," said Lady Judeth, "but in this case, I tend to agree."

"I am going to ask that you have a little faith in Lord Jasper," said Deirdre tiredly, looking at Lady Judeth.

"What?" said Lady Judeth. A sudden expression of disbelief crossed her face. "No... not...surely...? Is Lord Jasper...joining us?"

"I hate to say it," said Deirdre quietly, "but it was the only logical move. He presented a sensible argument for going. I am not saying I trust him completely - I don't - but I believe that most of what he told me tonight was the truth. That, plus some stuff that he knows about me...I'd rather have him with us."

"He did not attempt to blackmail you, did he?"

"No, but I just don't want to take any chances," said Deirdre, opening the side door into the corridor adjoining the grand staircase. Lady Judeth led the way through the door and into the main foyer. The house was so quiet as they proceeded that the clock in the foyer sounded as loud as a drumbeat. Quickly, they made their way up the stairs and along the brightly lit corridor to Deirdre's rooms.

They opened the door and stepped into clothing chaos. Pieces of winter wear including cloaks, stoles, and wraps were draped over chair backs and tables. Two packs stood open on a low table, and a third sat closed nearby. Lady Margret was already dressed in trousers and a heavy tunic, and she rushed about, rolling woolen hose and tunics as small as possible and stuffing them into the packs, muttering to herself as she went. She looked up as

Lady Judeth and Deirdre entered the room and breathed a sigh of relief.

"At last," she said. "Come, my ladies, let me help you out of your gowns. Jan brought your pack, Lady Judeth. Your travel wear is laid out on that settee. Lady Deirdre, yours is on that couch over there."

Deftly, Lady Margret unbuttoned their ball gowns and helped them out of their dresses. The two women then put on the warm woolen gear, and Deirdre helped Margret with rolling some of the hose. When she went to place them in the pack, her hand encountered a large, flat object, and she pulled it out to discover her mother's sketchbook. She stood looking at it for a few long moments, wondering how she could have forgotten something so dear.

"We found it in your pack when we pulled it from the wreckage," said Lady Margret. "It seemed important to you."

Deirdre felt tears begin to well, and she blinked them back, clearing her throat.

"Yeah," said she huskily. "Oh yeah."

She wiped away her tears and slipped the sketchbook back into the pack. Lady Margret handed her a few last items, and then they were ready to go. Lady Judeth shouldered her own bag, and the three of them silently left the room.

Lady Judeth led them down the servant's stair, which was oddly quiet and deserted at this hour.

"The servants not working have their own celebration tonight, and no one will be anywhere around to see us depart," she said. "Captain Evarl knows that some revelers will be departing the ball early and he has told his men not to be concerned with people leaving the estate. No one will stop us."

They exited the kitchen through the double Dutch-style door, and a familiar form awaited them outside. Lady Nersh stood draped in a dark saddle blanket, hiding her white fur from the moonlight, the panniers she had worn before the Dark Wolves' attack fastened over the fabric. The earlier clouds that Deirdre had seen from the veranda were moving swiftly across the sky, erasing the light coming from above. A low wind had started to blow, and Deirdre thought that she could just about smell a tinge of snow in the air.

Lady Nersh looked at them as they approached and said, "Are we ready to go? They are waiting for us at the far end of the orchard. The sooner we are off, the better."

Together, they slipped off into the darkness, leaving the bright lights of Garey Manor behind.

14

The hour had grown very late by the time they reached the edge of the valley. They had followed the road out but had still needed to be as cautious as they could so as not to draw undue attention to themselves. The moon was no longer giving them any light as it was now completely hidden behind heavy clouds. Stray flakes had begun to fall, and the flurries continued to strengthen as they made their way out through the pass.

"If this snow keeps up, it will delay Captain Rialain's arrival even more," said Lady Judeth absently. "It is a good thing that he already was underway by the time the pigeons were sent. He will not be able to hurry."

"That bodes well," said Lady Margret. "Your message might actually make it to the queen in one piece."

Vexanious shook himself, sending droplets of melting snow flying. He raised his head and stopped, sniffing the air. Tor and Nersh did also.

"Company," he said.

"It's Lord Jasper," said Deirdre. "He said he would meet us here."

"Are you sure that you trust him, Deirdre?" asked Vexanious.

"Mostly," sighed Deirdre. "I think we should at least give him a chance before we condemn him. I have some reservations as well."

They stopped at the edge of the woods and waited. From behind the thin curtain of snow, a vague figure emerged, revealing itself to be Lord Jasper atop a coal black stallion tacked in dark gear.

"Welcome, my lord," said Deirdre, blinking the snow out of her eyes. "I am glad that you could join us."

Lord Jasper glanced from Deirdre to Lady Judeth, then to the others that faced him. He looked at Tor for a long moment before shifting his gaze back to Deirdre.

"Thank you, my lady," he said simply. He looked at Judeth. "Lady Judeth, I ask that you accept my most sincere apologies concerning my actions at dinner. I realize that you did not witness all of them, but I assure you, no harm was meant. I was only trying to further distance myself from the others."

"We did witness a good bit, my Lord Jasper," said Lady Judeth, looking at him narrowly. "I will have you know that certain walls in my home have eyes and ears."

Lord Jasper's gaze narrowed, but he said nothing and nodded to himself.

"My lords, my ladies," said Nersh, "the hour is growing late, the night cold. Snow will soon make our trail visible to any and all who pass by. We should be away now, while the weather is still on our side, hiding instead of revealing us."

"Just so," said Lady Judeth and turned to Deirdre. "My Lady?"

"Yes," said Deirdre. "Let's be off."

Vexanious took the lead as they set off down the road, and the others followed. There was no overt hurrying, but a sense of urgency had set in, causing each of them to remain wide awake and tense with high-strung nerves. The road wove its way into the dark forest as the group slowly made its way southward.

Deirdre rode in silence, feeling both excited and scared by the whole adventure. They had done it; they were underway with no clear destination ahead of them on the most important and dangerous mission most of them had ever undertaken. For the first time, she felt that she was truly going to be able to do something that was not just an empty gesture.

The thought that followed closely on the heels of the first was the fervent hope that she wasn't going to get them all killed. It had occurred to her how Marshall Rialain might handle things if he caught them, and the words 'final and deadly' had accompanied that thought. She wondered if any of the others felt the same way given the fact that they knew him better than she did.

The fact that she couldn't shapeshift also troubled her. She never mentioned it to the others, but she thought that Nersh could tell. Often, Deirdre caught herself wondering how she was going to call the dragons if she couldn't even become a horse or an otter...or a bird. There was no one to train her in these skills, and it worried her considerably, making her regret that she and Nerfal had not had more time.

The last musing she pursued that early snowy morning crept in on the heels of the third one and had to do with Tor. She wondered briefly if the dragons would know a way to help Tor become human again, and in that moment her thoughts focused clearly on him, she had a vision.

She saw herself riding on Vexanious through the snow-filled night. The vision appeared to be through the eyes of someone behind her, and she could see along the sides of a muzzle and catch a glimpse of curved horns. It was Tor, watching her through half-lidded eyes, and she caught a whisper of what he was thinking and feeling through their bond. There was attraction, hope, affection, desire...all of these were present and directed towards her, but overlying all of these was a hopelessness regarding his shape and a deep sadness that he might never be human again.

The vision collapsed as she registered with surprise what she was sensing, and she glanced back at Tor to see if he had noticed her intrusion. He appeared to be glancing warily at the woods around them and did not seem to have felt anything out of the ordinary. She looked ahead again, through the ever-thickening snow and listened contemplatively to the muffled thud of Vexanious's footfalls. There was no evidence that what she had experienced had been real.

For a long while as they rode, she tried to figure out how she felt about him. Shape aside, he was decent, proud, caring, and even gentle at times, at least with her. His misfortune hadn't defeated him, and that said a lot. He was housed in the body of a monster, something that, had she truly been born into this world, would have frightened her more than anything else. He wasn't some slobbering beast, however; he had been human, and he held himself with dignity. She realized that there was no immediate answer to how she truly viewed him, and she regretfully put the thought aside until a time when she wasn't so tired.

Deirdre sighed and pulled the edges of her cloak tighter around her. The snow was finally tapering off, but the wind had picked up and made the air colder in exchange. Patches of moonlight filtered through some of the thinner cloud layers now, and as she watched the moon slip towards the horizon, Deirdre suddenly felt her lack of proper sleep catching up to her.

"Vex," she said wearily, "it's time to find a place to rest."

"There is a huntsman's cottage about a mile down the road," said Lady Judeth, riding a little closer up to join her. "It should be empty now with winter here and all. The gamekeeper migrates south with the herds and should be in Malepoer by now."

"We can rest there," said Nersh heavily. "I, for one, could use a good sleep by a warm fire."

"I do not think a fire will betray us tonight," said Lady Judeth, "but tomorrow, we are going to be hunted, once they find us to be gone. We should turn south off the track and travel across the country. With luck, it will take Marshall a day or two to reach the castle, and then another day to figure out which way we have gone."

The horses walked along the snow-covered track. No one spoke and a short while later, Lady Judeth led them off the road and down a narrow path that lay almost invisible amid the tall pines. Another five minutes and they were at the door of a small cottage with a little stable at its back.

All of them dismounted stiffly and preceded their mounts into the stable. There were only four stalls, but Vexanious stated that he would prefer being loose to aid them if the need arose. Tor, Jasper, and Margret pulled off the saddles and rubbed the horses down with some sacking they found in the small tack room at the end of the little shelter, while Deirdre, Nersh, and Judeth went into the cottage to air it and get a fire going.

The interior of the cottage was very dark and smelled strongly of pine and clean straw. Lady Judeth lit a small lantern from her pack with a deft application of flint and steel and led the way inside. Deirdre heard squeak and saw at least one little grey-furred body making a quick exit from the room. She shivered as she realized that they might be having company with them in the cabin. Wonderful. She hated mice.

"Cozy," said Nersh, eyeing their surroundings critically. "Well, it is clean and dry, and well-stocked with wood anyway. Let us hope that no one finds us today. I feel like I could sleep for about a month."

Judeth and Deirdre swiftly built a fire on the tiny hearth. When the others joined them, they spread the bedrolls out on the hard wooden floor and hung their cloaks on pegs near the fire to dry.

Two doors led off the main room. One led to a chamber in which they placed their packs, a second to a small, clean privy that smelled of lime, sweet rushes, and pinesap. Deirdre grimaced as she realized that this was as close as she would come to civilized facilities for a long while.

"I will take first watch," said Lady Judeth. "I have probably had the most sleep out of all of us lately. The rest of you try to sleep. Tor, would you take the second watch?"

Tor nodded.

"I will take the third," said Margret. "Nersh, you and Lady Deirdre get as much sleep as you can. Lord Jasper, you as well."

"You do not trust me to take a watch?" he said.

Margret looked at him sharply.

"No, I do not," she said. "I am not even sure why Lady Deirdre agreed to bring you along, but you are here on her word only. My trust only extends so far."

"Mine as well," said Judeth, and Tor snorted his agreement.

"So you would rather trust a minotaur to keep watch than a human?" said Jasper. At Lady Margret's nod, he laughed mirthlessly. "Fine. I probably deserve that. I will not take offense, my ladies. I will do what I can to earn your trust."

"Enough," said Deirdre. "We have to work together, or we will not make it even as far as Malepoer. Jasper knows the city, and Tor knows where to find Jack Parns. We can help Jasper escape his father's plans for him. Let's focus on what we have to do next and, for now, get some sleep."

There were a few more pointed looks between Margret and Judeth, but soon Deirdre curled up under her blankets and closed her eyes, listening to the others settling down around her. Rolling over to find a more comfortable position, she opened her eyes to see Tor where he lay by the entryway. For a long moment, their eyes locked, and Deirdre found herself thinking about her earlier vision through the bond. It had been very sudden, and she did not know what to make of her feelings or Tor's. In fact, she wasn't even sure anymore which of the emotions she felt were hers. She wondered tiredly if there would come a time when they actually were so close that they could read each other's thoughts. How weird would that be, she mused.

She rolled back over, intentionally breaking the gaze with Tor's dark brown eyes, and lay staring at the dim, fire-flickered ceiling for a few minutes until her eyes closed in sleep.

———

After waking midmorning and eating a rushed breakfast, they set out, taking care to leave as few traces as they could. Nersh led them on their way through the woods, picking out the safest route possible, and by early afternoon, they were all very tired from making their way through the rough underbrush.

"At least the snow is melting," said Lady Judeth. "It will be harder to pick up our trail. There is a southbound road that is heavily traveled not far to the west. Once we get onto that road, tracks will not matter."

They continued on for a long while, not talking much and being watchful of the woods around them. It was not long before they reached the road Lady Judeth had mentioned, and they gratefully left the woods behind them, picking up their pace to a steady trot.

Lady Judeth rode up next to Deirdre as the sun began to tip towards the horizon.

"It will still take Marshall at least another day to get to my home," she said. "We do need to make some haste, though. He will be able to make better time than we can right now. Nersh cannot run for long periods of time."

"No," said Nersh, "but I can leave you and hide if I have to. I know where we are going, so I could always meet you near Malepoer."

"Is there a place we can stay for the night near here?" asked Deirdre.

"There are several places on my map that we can use," said Judeth. "We have to turn off this road, though, to reach the nearest one. It is in the woods deep enough that we are unlikely to be seen, but it will not be safe to have a large fire, I am afraid."

They rode on a little way further with Judeth consulting her map at regular intervals for landmarks. Finally, she signaled them to turn off, and they rode down what looked like a game trail for a little while until they came to a small meadow. The remains of an old fire lay off to one side, but the area was otherwise undisturbed. Low, snow-covered grass carpeted most of the area, dotted here and there with the skeletons of wildflowers.

"We should be safe enough here," said Judeth. "This place is not known to many people. Most travelers on the road are heading to the village of Englebrook about a mile south of here. They have a warm inn and good food. In this weather, no one will be out."

They dismounted and loosely tethered the regular horses, allowing them enough room to graze. Finally untacked, Vexanious rolled in the grass, waving his long legs in the air and making everyone laugh. He stood back up again and shook, looking very pleased with himself. Deirdre grabbed his currycomb from the saddle bags and began to untangle the knots and burrs from his tail.

Lord Jasper and Tor went out to cut pine branches that they laid in a thick padding on the snowy ground. On top of them, everyone spread their blankets and soon sat quite comfortably in a tight circle.

"A fire would feel nice," sighed Lady Margret, settling herself down with her cloak wrapped tightly around her.

"It would," agreed Nersh, yawning hugely, "but for the sake of safety, we had better not until nightfall. We do not want any smoke to be seen over the trees."

Deirdre snuggled further into her cloak. The sun was almost on the horizon, but it would be several hours until full dark. She cleared her throat and waited until everyone had looked her way.

"I would like to put forth an idea," she said. "You don't have to agree, but I would be more comfortable if you did."

"Go on," said Lady Judeth

Tor nodded, and Lord Jasper looked at her intently, while Lady Margret, Vexanious, and Nersh exchanged glances.

Deirdre cleared her throat again nervously.

"We are all fugitives now, working for a common cause to save this land. If we fail, our homes will be taken from us, this land will be destroyed, and we may be imprisoned or even killed. I realized this fully after being attacked on the road to Garey Manor. All of you knew this too when you agreed to join me, correct?"

They all nodded, waiting for her to continue.

"I also think that we are more likely to get noticed if we keep using our titles. I would like to propose that we do away with titles and other such courtly gestures for now and call each other by our first names only. Lady Margret and I have done this in private, and I must admit, I am not used to being called 'lady' where I am from. My friends all call me Deirdre or Dee, and I would like it if you could all do the same."

Nersh nodded, and said, "I agree. It would make us all a lot less visible traveling through villages if we do not call each other lady or lord. Naturally, Tor and I will not be traveling with you into these places, but town folks would not expect nobles to abandon their titles."

"I have decided to renounce mine anyway," said Lord Jasper, shrugging. "I have no problems with this idea. I am done with being my father's cat's paw."

"I also have no problems with not using my title," said Lady Judeth, "although I am not going to renounce my lands just yet. I do not think that it needs to be that drastic. We may still come out on top of this"

"I am already in agreement," said Margret.

"I am as well," said Nersh.

"Then it is settled," said Deirdre. "I suggest that we start immediately, since we are going to have to practice."

"May I suggest a toast?" said Nersh. "A binding toast for our little company?"

"Yes," said Judeth, and walked over to her horse, retrieving a bottle of wine from the saddlebag. Deirdre arched an eyebrow at her, and Judeth just shrugged.

"Join us old friend," said Nersh to Vexanious, "You have been part of this as well."

"And not likely to stop now," said the horse, walking over to join them. He knelt down on the edge of their pine bough ring in the snow and watched his companions with interest.

Judeth uncorked the bottle and brought it and a silver goblet over to where they were sitting, handing both to Deirdre. Deirdre poured some of the wine into the cup and held it out in front of the wolf.

"A toast," said Nersh, "to newfound friendships and the salvation of our lands!"

"Hear, hear," said everyone.

The cup made it around the circle, the red wine sweet and summery to the taste. Deirdre held the cup for Nersh and Vexanious to have a taste of as the wine made its way to them. When everyone had had some, they all shared a few minutes of thoughtful silence, and then Jasper went to his packs and came back with some rolled maps. He was soon trying to find where they were in relation to the main roads to Malepoer.

"We have to be somewhere near the most southerly route. The Southern Trade Road would be the fastest"

"No," said Judeth, having retrieved a map of her own and unrolling it. She pointed violently at a marking on it. "We are three miles further east than you think. See?"

"According to *my* map, we have not yet made it to Chesterwood," said Jasper.

Margret joined them and pointed to the large, white tower on Jasper's map.

"We cannot go *there*," snorted Jasper. "Where do you think will be the first place they look?"

"I am not saying we go there. I am just pointing it out so you can see why we do not want to go so close to the Southern Trade Road just yet..."

Nersh shook her head and curled up to take a nap, and Vexanious rose to graze on some nearby grasses.

Deirdre looked over to Tor to find the minotaur watching her closely. He waved her over and picked up a stick, clearing a patch of dirt to write on in the dimming light.

"Jasper keeps staring at me," he wrote.

"I didn't actually notice, but I would guess he might," said Deirdre, glancing back at the others who were still arguing over the maps. "I'm sure he's never seen anything like you. I mean, most minotaurs aren't found in the company of lords and ladies."

"They have been very polite," he wrote.

"Would you rather they were otherwise?" she laughed. "I mean, they are accepting you at least. That's something."

Tor cleared the ground again, and wrote, "They are doing it for you."

"Partially," said Deirdre, looking at him. "Nersh and Vexanious already trust you. The others will soon get to know you better."

"Do you trust him?" he wrote and pointed to Jasper.

Deirdre glanced over at where Jasper was now laughing at something Judeth had said, and Margret was scowling at him. Judeth seemed to be fighting not to smile; the corners of her mouth were betraying her, though. The maps were still unrolled in their hands, but they seemed to be at least a little more at ease.

"I want to," said Deirdre. "He sounded so...I don't know, haunted, I guess. I want to believe he means what he says. I don't have the biases built in against him that you all do, so I have a different viewpoint. Same thing with you, right? I had no innate biases."

"Do not ever trust other minotaurs," wrote Tor. "Ever. They are all as bad as people think."

Deirdre nodded and looked up to where the stars had begun to flicker to life in the evening sky.

"It's hard to believe that it's only been three days since we left your home," said Deirdre. "I never expected our party to grow this large."

Tor snorted and glanced at her curiously.

"Well, it was originally just Margret, Nersh, Vex, and me," said Deirdre. "We've almost doubled in size since a week ago. My life here has been nothing but surprises. There's something else that's bothering me, something I hadn't mentioned before. I feel like the vision I had in the cave with Nerfal is part of all of this too. I keep mentally circling back to something that happened right before our group was attacked by the Dark Wolves. There was a bird that cried out, a falcon, and the scene looked so much like that from the vision that I keep wondering if they are connected. I've also had a dream, or what seemed like a dream, where part of the riddle from the vision was continued. There's more going on here than just a race to the South."

Tor hesitated for a moment and then wrote, "Have you had any other visions?"

Deirdre looked at him, startled.

"Ye-es," she said, slowly. "I had a vision about you. Last night."

Tor looked at her in surprise.

"I think I saw through your eyes," said Deirdre slowly. "Last night, on the road."

Tor pointed to her and wrote,

"Dancing."

"You saw me dancing? When? With whom?"

"Lord Dean," wrote Tor. "At the ball."

"So I was!" exclaimed Deirdre. "When I saw you, you seemed to be watching me while we were riding last night."

She saw Tor glance at her with surprise.

"I didn't mean to intrude on your thoughts," she said. "I suddenly found myself inside your head, seeing what you saw, feeling...what you felt, I guess."

Deirdre picked up a small stone and tossed it into the snow where it disappeared from sight.

"I don't know what to tell you, Tor," she said, looking up at him and meeting his eyes firmly. "I like you. I certainly feel indebted to you for saving me. We've only just met, though. Let's give it some time."

Something flickered in the minotaur's eyes, and he wrote,

"What of my shape?"

"That is another matter, though not so much as you would think," Deirdre said, pulling her knees up and wrapping her arms around them. "I don't find you ugly, if that is what you mean. Some creatures in my world's mythology had animal heads, and I always thought that they were fascinating, minotaurs included." She grinned suddenly and looked over at him. "My experience with them in reality is, admittedly, rather limited."

He snorted his approximation of a laugh.

"As to what the others think of you, I think they are trying to be fair at least. Nersh seems to know you, and Vexanious acts as if he has his suspicions..." She paused, then said quietly, "I really would like to know who you are."

"Soon," wrote Tor.

"Still not sure whether to trust me, huh? Fair enough. Tell me when you are ready," said Deirdre. "I won't force you to."

Tor nodded, and they sat together side by side. The sun had sunk behind the trees, leaving only clouds tinged with red and violet to color the sky. The stars had grown in brightness, and night was almost upon them. Deirdre stared at the darkening sky thoughtfully for a moment and finally looked over at Tor. He looked back at her and nodded.

"I have an idea," he wrote.

———

Nersh awoke and saw that it was full dark. She rose, stretched, and looked around at her companions. Vexanious was dozing with the other horses, Margret, Judeth, and Jasper were preparing a meal of dried meats and grains over a small fire, and Deirdre...

She snapped to sudden wakefulness and stared around herself in alarm, then caught a flash of metal at the edge of the meadow. She trotted swiftly towards the spot and had to stop short in wonder at what she saw.

Deirdre and Tor sat opposite each other, their right hands holding aloft the magic blade, and their left hands clasped together. Both of them had their eyes closed, and their heads were tipped back slightly, Deirdre's mouth set in a slight smile.

Nersh was barely conscious of footsteps behind her, but she smelled the man and didn't turn to look as Jasper knelt down beside her.

"Do not disturb them," he whispered. "They said that they were going to try an experiment with the sword. Do you have any idea what they are doing?'

"I am not sure," said Nersh. "They are in a trance of some sort, but I do not think it is anything bad."

"That is what we surmised," said Jasper. "I can tell by the way the sword feels, and the warmth that it radiates, it is magical. Outside of that, it is impossible to tell what is happening."

Nersh turned from the pair and nudged Jasper to rise.

"We wait," she said. "Keep an eye out for trouble, but let them finish what they have begun. Let us join the others for now and wait to see what happens."

———

Gone was the fall landscape and its colors of red, gray, and brown. Instead, a green expanse with one huge tree in the center met Deirdre's gaze as she looked around herself in amazement. The grass-lands were surrounded by tall mountains on all sides. Glancing up at the mountain peaks, she saw blue sky above them and no clouds. It was an almost unnaturally perfect day. It seemed a bit two-dimen-sional to Deirdre's art-trained eye. Everything looked flat, like a matte painting in an old movie. Set in the ground nearby, the point embedded into the earth, was Tor's sword, but there was no sign of Tor himself.

A gentle breeze blew from her left, causing her to turn, and when she looked back at the sword, there was Tor kneeling on one knee, his right hand still touching the hilt. His head was bowed, and as she walked towards him, he looked up.

"Where are we?" he asked in a low baritone voice.

"You spoke!" exclaimed Deirdre.

Tor opened his mouth in amazement, and Deirdre saw that here, at least, he had a tongue.

"I did! I spoke! Oh, it has been so long since I last heard my own voice. Wait...my own voice. This is not a minotaur's voice, this is my voice from when I was human. I am still a minotaur, correct?"

"You are," said Deirdre. "I think that we are in some sort of dream space. Maybe you could look human if you tried..."

Tor shook his head.

"I do not think that it is a good idea just yet," he said. "I think it would be too depressing to be human, even if it was in a dream, and then have to go back to looking like this."

Tor stood and looked up at the mountains. Neither of them spoke for a few minutes, but Deirdre observed that the landscape never changed, the leaves never moved in the light breeze, and no birds appeared in the sky. It was very unnerving.

"Odd place that we have come to," said Deirdre, finally over-whelmed by the silence.

"Yes. You called it a dream. I think you may be right," said Tor, bending to pluck a piece of grass and twirl it between his thick fingers. "This place is like a dream, only we, the dreamers, are awake."

"How do you suppose we get back?" asked Deirdre, glancing around.

"I think we have to remove the sword from the ground," said Tor. "The sword brought us here, so it should take us back."

"Maybe," said Deirdre, "but I'm in no rush to leave just yet. Being able to talk to you like this is much easier"

Tor nodded emphatically, saying fiercely, "I definitely agree."

"I do have a question about the sword, however," said Deirdre, sitting down next to the tree and touching the bark. "Has it ever shown any evidence of intelligence before? Any sort of ability?"

"That night you were attacked by the Dark Wolves, I felt an urging, a pull given off by the sword, to leave the temple. It was nothing specific, but it seemed to draw me in the direction of the attack. The urging stopped once you were safe," said Tor. "It led me either to the Dark Wolves or to you, I do not know which. It may be that it simply does not like evil creatures. I have to wonder what else it can do."

"True," agreed Deirdre. "Through the sword, we seem to have saved each other

"Well," said Tor, "saved or not, I curse the fact that I am trapped in this poor excuse for a body."

"At least you are still alive," said Deirdre. "That has to count for something."

"Perhaps," said Tor, looking at her in growing frustration, "but do you not see? It is not *me*. It is not *my* body. *My* body is rotting back at the capital somewhere, and I am stuck in this...this...thing! I have felt... well, I am sure you would know since you saw through my eyes and felt it last night. Angry! Frustrated! Betrayed! Alone! And..."

He stopped, cutting off his next words and turning away from her to stare into the distance.

"I am a prince of Keyralithsmus," he said, his head lowered. "My fiancé was murdered - by a minotaur no less. It was the final insult to place me in this body to destroy any chance of avenging her. I cannot avenge her. I cannot get back what was stolen from me."

Deirdre looked at the minotaur with a growing sense of awe and horror.

"You're Prince Benjamin," she said. "Everyone thinks you're dead!"

"I am as good as dead," he said sourly, looking back at her. "Do you think for one moment that I could walk into the capital and try to tell Brena what has happened to me? I would be shot with a crossbow bolt or run through with a sword for even coming near the castle. Add to that no tongue... No, it was safer for me to live at the temple and wait to see what fortune might dictate."

"I dreamed about you," said Deirdre, suddenly. "You were in the dragon's cave."

"Yes," he said. "In the dragon's cave, reading the riddle. I dreamed about you as well. I am beginning to think that there may be more going on here than just an oath sworn on a sword."

Deirdre nodded and looked at the minotaur thoughtfully.

"So they chanced leaving you alive for what, spite? Or is it that someone could have traced them somehow? Is that why they left you alive?"

"Yes. They had not killed me, so Tomille could not magically trace my death back to them," said Benjamin. "Since I was not in my body, he could also find no evidence of my death. I think they hoped I would be captured sooner or later by the hunting parties they sent out for me and sent to Coliseum to be placed in the games. Eventually, I would be killed, and they would get away with the murder without staining their own hands. It was a powerful spell, set by someone who controls very corrupt forces."

"Sounds like Jasper's father," mused Deirdre.

"Yes, it does," said Benjamin.

"We will have to be very careful," said Deirdre. "You must appear to be a regular minotaur."

"And you must keep calling me Tor," he said. "Do not even think of me as Benjamin or you may slip. I do not trust that Jasper is telling us the whole truth. Judeth and Margret we will tell in time."

Deirdre nodded.

"We should get back," she said. "Nersh and the others must be wondering what's happening with us."

"I would imagine that we present quite a sight," said Benjamin, walking over to the sword.

They placed their hands on the hilt and, together, pulled it from the earth.

———

Darkness had fallen when Deirdre opened her eyes and stretched her arms. Tor had stood and already re-sheathed the sword. A short distance away, a small fire burned and the rest of their group was sitting close beside it with the horses tethered nearby. The smell of cooked meat hung on the night air and made Deirdre's mouth water.

She looked at Tor and smiled.

"No dream, huh?" she asked.

Tor shook his head and picked up the writing stick.

"I miss talking," he wrote, and broke the stick in half.

"It will be interesting to see what happens now," she said. "I wonder what other tricks the sword has up its sleeve, so to speak."

Tor cocked his head at her curiously, and she laughed.

"It's a figure of speech," she said. "It means what other surprises the sword has for us."

Grinning rather frighteningly at her, Tor offered Deirdre a hand up.

She accepted, and let him assist her to her feet. He didn't immediately let go of her hand, looked at her imploringly, and seemed relieved when she smiled up at him.

"Your secret is safe," she said softly.

A chorus of voices hailed them from the small fire on the other side of the clearing. She and Tor turned and made their way over to the group. Only belatedly as they joined the others did Deirdre realize that she still was clutching Tor's hand in hers. What had once seemed so strange had become a comfort, and for the first time in a long time, she didn't miss home.

15

I t turned out that it had only been full dark for a short while when they returned to camp, and everything had been broken down in readiness to depart. A small fire had been lit for warmth, and a brace of plump rabbits were spitted and roasting, dripping sizzling juices into the flames. Nersh beamed proudly at her catch when Deirdre asked who had caught them, and they settled down to a finger-burning meal of tender coney.

There had been a lot of questioning glances when she and Tor had returned to camp, but no one had voiced what they all wanted to know. Deirdre, finally sated on the succulent meat and some of the wild grapes that Margret had found, told the group an edited version of their experience, leaving out Tor's identity.

A short time later, when the fire was extinguished and the ashes scattered, they started off silently and settled in for a long, cold night of riding. The moon had only just begun to rise, and Nersh led the way through the forest, navigating by instincts that unerringly led them southwest. Deirdre followed on Vexanious, talking to Judeth about the fastest way to Malepoer. Tor came next, followed by Margret, and finally, Jasper.

As they rode along, Deirdre quietly said,

"How do you think our latest party addition is holding up?"

Judeth smiled.

"Well, I think he was rather taken aback by Tor at first, but Nersh commented on the bond you have with him, and Jasper made a few assumptions, I believe."

"Oh?"

"Yes, well you two are bonded magically and that sort of thing tends to make those in the bond very protective of each other," said Judeth. "It also can lead to more physical aspects, so if he were to be aggressive towards Tor, you might be compelled to defend your partner. The longer it lasts, the stronger the bond becomes, and sometimes it is impossible to break if it exists long enough. Often the partners stay together for life, raise a family, and even die within a short time of each other."

"Oh," said Deirdre, faintly.

Judeth looked over at Deirdre.

"Does that worry you?" she asked.

"No, just makes me see the situation in a different light," said Deirdre. "I had no idea it could be that powerful."

"Well, most people know better than to swear on a magic sword," Judeth chuckled. "It is never that simple. Those swords often have something of a mind of their own."

Deirdre thought back to her conversation with Tor and how he had mentioned the sword drawing him out of the temple in time to fight off the Dark Wolves. She nodded absently, and said, "How do you know so much about magic?"

Judeth smiled and looked up at the sky overhead.

"When I was younger, I had every intention of learning magic. I read everything I could get my hands on." Judeth sighed and said, "Unfortunately, I was not very good at it, and when my father died, my attention had to be focused elsewhere."

"Ah," said Deirdre. She was silent for a moment, then asked, "In your readings, did you come across anything to do with shapeshifting?"

"Well, yes, actually, I did," said Judeth. "My forefathers were related to a family of horned Kin - visited on holidays, that sort of thing. Anyway, my great-grandmother was hornless Kin, but she was able to write a good bit about her experiences among her people. One of her cousins had described the process to her in detail, it seems, and she recorded it faithfully."

"Do you recall any of it?" asked Deirdre hopefully.

"A good deal of it, actually," said Judeth. "It was fascinating reading. Why?"

Deirdre sighed.

"Well, I might as well let you in on it, seeing as everyone else in our party knows. I am not from this world. I am the daughter of Nerfal's other-world union with my mother, and up until about five weeks ago, never had any idea as to who my father was. I've learned a lot of things during that five week span of time, but I am afraid that shape shifting was not one of them."

Judeth stared at Deirdre for a long moment, and then began to laugh.

"We are, without a doubt, the strangest band of adventurers ever to go on a quest," she chortled, "Two members of the Talking Folk, an off-worlder, a minotaur who cannot talk, and a bunch of denounced nobility."

Judeth wiped her eyes and got herself slowly under control.

"I will tell you what I remember," she said, "but I do not know how much of it will help you. It is mostly theories constructed by my great-grandmother, but there were a few passages here and there concerning actual discussions that she and her cousin had."

"What do you recall?" asked Deirdre eagerly.

"Well," Judeth paused and unfocused her eyes, becoming lost in thought, "there was a section that described the first time her cousin had shape changed. That one sticks out in my mind the most. I seem to recall that he said he was told to be the animal he would become as best as he could. To close his eyes and envision balancing on cloven hooves and to try to see the world as an elk would with split vision, odd perception, and fewer colors. He apparently felt great fear and for a moment, felt as if he was balanced on a great precipice, right on the edge, almost falling over but not quite. Then there was a jolt, much like falling, and he stood on all fours, feeling oddly wrong and right both at the same time. He opened his eyes as an elk."

"Wow," said Deirdre, "So concentration is the key, that and envisioning becoming the animal?"

"Apparently so," said Judeth. "My great-grandmother went on to theorize that the magic comes from the link with the land that the horned Kin have, and that only fear can keep you from changing."

"Therefore, it should be easy," said Deirdre, with mock sagacity.

"*Should* being the operative word. May I inquire what you will, in time, become?"

"A horse, for one, along with a falcon, and an otter," said Deirdre.

"I would save the bird for last, if I were you," said Judeth. "You are going to attempt this soon, I assume."

"Tomorrow when we stop," said Deirdre. "Probably after we've rested though. Will you help me?"

"Yes," said Judeth, "though what I can do is a mystery. I can make suggestions, and cheer you on maybe."

"That will do nicely," said Deirdre. "I believe that I can do this if I..."

"Hssst," hissed Jasper from the back of the line, "A rider approaches behind us!"

Nersh ran back to where Jasper sat on his stallion with a drawn sword in hand, and the others swiftly turned to join them. Tor drew his blade, and Deirdre reluctantly did the same, though she was in no mood for a fight. She could hear the sounds of hoof beats in the echoing forest, and the thrashing of brush as the horse crashed through, hurrying up their back-trail.

Judeth calmly pulled a small crossbow from a saddlebag, hauled the string back using a claw-like device, and loaded a bolt onto the taut cord, readying it. Deirdre looked at Nersh, noting her bared teeth and raised hackles. The wolf's ears lay plastered to her skull, and Deirdre had never seen her look so fierce. She tightened her grip on her sword and waited.

An exhausted grey mare suddenly broke from the darkness, breathing heavily and spraying bloodied foam everywhere. It was clear that the animal had been pushed far beyond its endurance limits and was in a bad way. Deirdre felt Vexanious tense beneath her at the sight of the tortured animal.

The form slumped over the mare's neck didn't look too good either, and as the pair approached the group, the mare saw them. It stumbled and plunged to its knees, screaming and spilling the rider in a heap upon the ground. The figure cried out as she fell, and then lay still.

Deirdre was off Vexanious in a flash, running to check on the rider with Judeth and Margret close behind her. Jasper and Tor went to where the mare lay gasping for breath. Tor touched Jasper's shoulder and pointed to the horse's left front leg where it hung at an odd angle. From the jagged bits of bone pushing through the skin of the foreleg, they could see that it had shattered, and Jasper drew his dagger. He looked quickly to Vexanious, who nodded his head in tacit agreement, before putting the animal out of its misery with a quick slash to the throat. The horse shuddered, kicked weakly, and lay still, its eyes already beginning to glaze over in the cold. The other horses whinnied at the smell of blood, and Nersh collected their reins, leading them a short distance away.

Deirdre meanwhile had realized that the slumped form lying on the ground seemed familiar, and when Judeth drew back the woman's hood, all three who had come to her aid gasped in recognition. It was Lady Alleen from Barrett Castle, looking haggard and pale in the moonlight.

"Get a fire going," said Jasper to Margret, as he took the woman into his arms. "We have to get her warm. Tor, get some blankets from the saddlebags."

Lady Alleen was barely conscious in Jasper's arms, and twisted feebly, moaning, her skin an odd pallid color in the moonlight. Her whole body trembled, and her skin felt clammy to the touch when Deirdre pushed the hair back from her forehead. Jasper set Alleen down, and Judeth sat on the ground, holding the woman in her arms.

"Tirana, make sure...Tirana...dried off," muttered Alleen. "Drove her too far...too hard. Tirana...."

"I don't see any obvious injuries. She looks like the fall stunned her," said Deirdre. "Get some blankets around her."

Tor brought over the blankets and gave them to Judeth who wrapped them around the semi-conscious form. Lady Alleen opened her eyes and saw Tor standing nearby. Her eyes suddenly seemed to focus, and she hitched in a breath to scream."

"Shh," crooned Judeth, rocking the woman, "Shh, it is just Tor, Deirdre's guardian. Remember? She came to us with him. He brought her back to us. Shh..."

Tor turned away and walked back to his horse, stroking its neck quietly to calm both it and himself. Deirdre felt his anguish sharply through their bond, and although this startled her so much she gasped, she pushed the feelings aside temporarily to stay with Alleen, even though she felt the pull of Tor's pain and wanted to go to him. She tried to send comfort to him and was pleased when he looked over at her with surprise and gratitude.

Margret found a small clearing a little way off the road and built a sheltered fire, using dead wood to avoid smoke. Jasper went to search for more wood, and Judeth and Deirdre helped Alleen over to the clearing, placing her blanket-wrapped form as close to the fire as they dared. They sat by her, and the rest of the party joined them, Nersh leading the regular horses, and Vexanious following behind them in case they gave her any trouble. Margret took the reins and tied them to a fallen tree, and then the party waited for a long while, letting the fire's warmth calm Alleen. Slowly, her shaking began to subside.

"Alleen," asked Deirdre, "can you tell us what happened? Why did you follow us? Is anyone else following us?"

"Not directly," whispered Alleen, "Not on your backtrail. They are coming by the road."

"Who?" asked Jasper. "What happened?"

"Marshal Rialain," rasped the lady. "He arrived the morning after the ball. He flew into a rage when he found you gone, and he killed..."

Her voice choked up at this point, and she had to swallow hard in order to go on.

"He killed Evarl first, Lady Judeth, proclaiming him a traitor. One of the lesser nobles was next, and then several of your household staff. Oh, Lady, he killed Jan!"

Judeth's face went pale in the moonlight, and she got up and walked over to her own horse. Tor went to her hesitantly, and she let him draw her into his arms as she began to weep.

"How did you get away?" asked Jasper.

"I was in the stables when they came in," said Alleen, "grooming Tirana."

She looked around wildly for the mare.

"She broke her leg, my Lady," said Margret, sorrowfully, putting her arm around Alleen. "I am sorry."

"Oh," said Lady Alleen, and she began to sob uncontrollably.

Deirdre got up and went over to where Tor and Judeth stood. Judeth was talking quietly to Tor, tears still streaming down her face, and she looked up as Deirdre approached. Judeth's face was an ashy grey color, and her eyes were puffy and shadowed in the moonlight.

"Poor Jan," said Judeth, trying to smile, and failing. "He was so good to me. We were best friends, he and I, and now..."

She gave a shuddering sigh and continued.

"We were lovers. Lovers, confidants. He was only twenty, and he was going to propose to me. 'Damn tradition,' he would write. I was going to accept."

Deirdre nodded and gave Judeth a hug. Judeth clung to her fiercely for a long moment, then pulled back, nodding that she was all right. Together, they returned to where Alleen sat. Kneeling down, Deirdre looked into the lady's eyes and caught her attention with a glance.

"Lady," she said, "what else happened?"

Lady Alleen sniffed and tried to compose herself. Valiantly, she pulled herself together enough to continue.

"We, Tirana and I, slipped out as soon as we were able and fled south. I came across the cottage last night and found scant traces of your passage into the forest. I destroyed the signs I found and made a false trail that led a mile into the woods in a westerly direction, and then stopped. I backed Tirana about a quarter mile and then went carefully North through the woods, making a wide circle around to connect with your southern trail."

Deirdre and Judeth looked at each other in amazement.

"How did you ever learn to do that?" asked Judeth.

"One of my cousins was a forester, and he taught me sometimes," said Lady Alleen tiredly. "We used to make a game of it. I never thought that it would come in useful, though."

"So you followed us, riding hard, for almost twenty-four hours?" asked Jasper.

"I wanted to warn you. I am almost certain he had me followed. I escaped too easily. Hopefully, this threw him off your trail."

"And perhaps not," mused Jasper. "We should put out the fire. Tor, can you and Vexanious please come give me a hand moving the mare's corpse off the road. We need to get out of here quickly."

The three of them went to deal with the body of the mare while Margret put out the fire, dousing it with water from her canteen, and covering the ashes with snow and leaves. Deirdre and Judeth helped Alleen to her feet and walked to the other horses. Alleen still looked ashen, but she no longer acted like she would collapse. Margret joined them and took the reins of her horse from Deirdre.

A short while later, the others returned from moving the mare. Jasper carried the mare's saddle and bridle with him. He pulled a cloth from his saddlebag, wrapped the tack, and tied the bundle to the back of his saddle. Deirdre walked over to Vexanious as he entered the clearing.

"Think you can handle two?" she asked the horse, nodding to Alleen.

"For a while, yes," said Vexanious. "She is right; Marshall would have had someone stationed by the stable, but possibly not someone good enough to follow her in the dark. We have been going too slowly, and we need to make better time from now on. We should go."

Deirdre nodded as Tor came over to stand next to her.

"If we get too heavy, I will get down and walk," said Deirdre. "You let me know, Vexanious. Don't overextend yourself."

Tor pointed to his horse, and she nodded in understanding.

"Or I'll ride with you," she agreed.

He walked back to his gelding, climbing into the saddle. The fire was out and Jasper was helping Alleen onto Vexanious's broad back. Deirdre swung up behind her and, as soon as everyone was ready, they were on their way again.

———

False dawn had just begun to tint the sky a pale grey when they found themselves coming out of the forest and facing a broad track that ran perpendicular to their course. The moon had set, and it was beyond dark in the forest. Nersh again led off, and they followed her dim shape as she went down the new road, heading south.

Deirdre held Alleen, now sound asleep, on Vexanious's back. The stallion had not uttered a hint of complaint even though Deirdre realized that they must have been wearing him out considerably, and she called Jasper to ride up next to her.

"I'm getting too tired to hold her any longer," she said. "Will you take her on your horse for a bit?"

"Certainly," said Jasper.

They stopped and carefully transferred the sleeping woman from one horse to the other. She never even stirred, and it wasn't long before they were underway again.

"Thank you," said Vexanious wearily, "I was getting a bit tired."

"Do you want me to walk for a little while?" asked Deirdre. "Or ride with Tor?"

"Would you mind?" he asked, sounding relieved that she had suggested it.

"Not at all," she said.

Vexanious trotted up to where Tor rode his horse behind Nersh. The minotaur's shape was undefined in the dim light that filtered through the trees, and he looked over at her as they came abreast.

"Do you mind if I ride with you for a little while?" asked Deirdre. "Vexanious is pretty tired."

Tor nodded and reined in his gelding. Nersh had heard them and paused. The others stopped while Deirdre climbed stiffly down from Vexanious's back and let Tor help her up in front of him to rest on the gelding's broad shoulders. The horse snorted softly, but made no other objection to the additional weight, and they started off again, Nersh an ever-present glimmer in the dark.

At first, Deirdre tried not to lean too much on the minotaur so as not to push him off balance, but after a while, fatigue began to get the better of her, and she relaxed, leaning back against his chest. He wrapped one arm around her to keep her from falling and guided the horse with his other hand. It was oddly very comforting, and she found herself drifting off to sleep. This was the closest she'd really been to him, she reflected drowsily, and found that being near him was not at all uncomfortable. She soon drifted off to sleep.

As they rode, Tor held her safely on the horse as they made their way through the waking world. It amazed him that she trusted him so much and could be so relaxed around him. He thought back on their talk the previous afternoon and went over the conversation again in his mind, feeling a slight thrill that they had been able to actually talk. The real shock was that she had been able to sense his emotions at Alleen's reaction to seeing him. That was unexpected, and he did not know how to feel about it. It indicated, however, that the bond was growing. Deirdre and Judeth's conversation about magic swords had not escaped his very sharp hearing earlier that night, and he realized that he needed to have a talk with Deirdre soon about their situation.

It wasn't, he thought, that he would mind being bonded to her. If he was ever able to become human again, she would be the logical choice for a consort, much as her sister had been. He let himself bask in the past for a long moment before shaking himself back down to reality with a tinge of sorrow and not a little guilt. He had loved Darlena very much and had been devastated by the news that she was dead. But...it had been years since he had last seen her, and he had given up all hope of recovering his human form, much less seeing his intended again. Darlena's death had hurt him at first, but he had already mourned for the loss of their relationship so many times over in the past that when the initial shock had faded, he found that a lot of the grief had vanished too. That was where his guilt came from, the speed at which the grief had vanished. Holding her half-sister asleep against his chest, a woman who believed him and accepted him for who he was, he wondered if Darlena ever could have done the same.

Not likely, he thought. Her fear of minotaurs had been deeply ingrained, like anyone who had grown up in Keyralithsmus. Darlena would never have been able to see past the specter of children's night-mares that he had become, and that was assuming he was even able to reach her. If he had rescued *her* from the Dark Wolves, she *still* would have tried to flee as soon as she knew what he was, savior or not. And he would have let her go, then fled himself to avoid the inevitable pursuit. That truth pained him as much as the recent turn of events had pleased him.

If Deirdre's acceptance of him had come as a complete surprise, being with this group a week later on the road to find the dragons was an even bigger one. When Jasper had asked him earlier to help move the mare, it was as an equal member of the team. When Deirdre had asked to ride with him, there was no hesitation in sitting in front of him on the horse. True, she had held herself stiffly at first, but when she relaxed against him, there was no sense of unease in her attitude.

Still, he owed it to her to make sure that she knew what their bond might be evolving into. If Judeth was correct, they might find them-selves never being able to separate once the bond took full effect. The part of him that was the old Benjamin, the noble and self-sacrificing idiot that he had been, he thought affectionately, would never have allowed Deirdre to be trapped in something she couldn't get out of if he could help it. That part of himself had not changed. Even if that meant having to flee back to the Nord-Ouest Temple when this was all over, he'd make sure he offered her the choice. He felt content with that decision.

An hour or so later, the sun crept above the horizon, and the light of the new day woke those sleeping and revived the spirits of the whole party. Nersh began to range off the track, looking for a place to stay, and finally found a spot a mile off the road. It was an old abandoned mill, complete with rotting windmill and cold, fresh water. They cleaned up their back trail as carefully as they could, asking Alleen's assistance and finding it invaluable. By the time she was done, there was virtually no trace that they had left the road at the tiny bend, and no hint that there was ever a trail that turned off towards the river.

The group was all too ready to get some rest, and there was a lot of good-natured, if tired, groaning as they dismounted and took care of the horses. Jasper made sure that each mount had a large measure of oats and grains along with some sweet feed for breakfast. The mill had a small paddock that was still sturdy enough to hold the horses, and they were untacked and let loose to rest. Vexanious stayed out in the mill yard, happy to be free of his saddle as well.

"One of us should stay awake and keep guard," said Deirdre tiredly.

"Sleep," said Vexanious. "We horses will hear anything that approaches. You need your rest. All of you."

He had looked pointedly at Tor, and Deirdre understood with dawning comprehension that Tor had been keeping watch more than anyone thought. He had not been taking any chances on the long night's ride.

Deirdre followed the others into the old mill. Overhead, small creatures rustled in the shadows, but otherwise, it was empty. The building was mostly sound and the roof whole. A cracked millstone still stood affixed to the gears, but the mill was long past the point when the sails would ever catch the wind again.

"How far is it to Malepoer?" Deirdre asked, unrolling her blankets on the old wooden floor.

"About three more nights," yawned Nersh, already half asleep. "Get some rest. We can eat when we get up."

Jasper led Lady Alleen over to his blankets and tucked her into them. He then sat back against the nearest wall, wrapping his cloak around himself. Deirdre watched, bemused and a little surprised to see him fussing about her like a mother hen. Jasper was proving very chivalrous, and she wondered if anyone else had ever seen that side of him. From what he had told her, she doubted anyone had, other than a few dubious ladies of the night, and it made her sad to think how lonely he must have been.

Tor unrolled his blankets by the door, glancing at Deirdre and smiling slightly. She smiled back and turned to Margret who bore a tired sadness on her face. On the other side of Margret sat Judeth, sobbing softly, her head resting on her knees and her arms wrapped around her legs, grieving at last for the people she had lost.

"Alleen's news hit us all hard," Margret said softly. "I wonder what state Remembrance is in if Marshall is able to pull off such a well-planned attack. This had to be his doing. Ramor follows directions, but he does not come up with ideas on his own."

"Marshall may be planning to use the royals to force Brena's hand," Deirdre said. "Somehow, I don't think he is on the country's side anymore, do you?"

"No. I think I can now also make some educated guesses about a few other issues. Such as why Darlena was killed so easily." Margret shuddered before continuing, her hands clutching her blankets until her knuckles turned white. "I had wondered about him, but I could not believe that he was that heartless. They were going to be wed."

"She was too much of a threat," said Deirdre. "After all, what if she had done something crazy, like, I dunno, going off by herself to find the dragons? No wonder he lobbied so hard for me to stay at the castle while his soldiers, the ones that according to Jasper were never sent, went to find them."

"And when you found a way to be out of his sight, he did not want to potentially risk you asking too many questions or going off to search on your own, so he had the Dark Wolves sent after you. That would mean that the Lord of Ganley Keep is in on this after all," Margret whispered.

She glanced over to where Jasper sat dozing, and said, "Do you think that he knows? Is he in on it?"

"I don't think he is," said Deirdre. "My instincts say to trust him."

"I think so too," said Judeth sadly, looking over at Jasper and Alleen with tears in her eyes. "He has been nothing if not helpful."

Margret hugged Judeth again, and Deirdre lay down on her blankets, pulling her cloak up over herself. For a long while, she watched the early sunlight stream through the windows and tried not to worry about what was to come. Without any warning, she fell asleep.

———

It was early afternoon when she woke and found herself to be the only one stirring. Judeth's bedroll was empty, however.

Quietly, she put her boots on and tiptoed outside, managing not to wake anyone in the process. The sun was lower now but still bright, and she quickly spotted Judeth's blonde hair and rose-colored shawl where her friend sat on the bank of the sluggishly flowing river.

Walking so that Judeth could easily hear her approach, she made her way down the bank and sat next to the Lady of Garey Manor. Neither of them spoke for a while; instead, they sat in quiet companionship on the river's edge, staring into the clear, cold water as it flowed by. Deirdre glanced back at the ruin of the mill, the blades of the sails rotted and the chute through which the water flowed now choked with weeds and water lilies. Around them, birds sang sporadic autumn songs and leaves drifted down from the trees in light cascades of gold and russet.

"I miss Jan," said Judeth quietly. "I wish that I had brought him with us."

"You couldn't have known what was going to happen," said Deirdre. "Marshall Rialain was a trusted captain in Queen Brena's army. Who would have thought that he'd do this?"

"I agree with what you and Margret were saying this morning," said Judeth, taking a deep breath. "The signs were all there. Why did we not see them?"

"I don't think that anyone wanted to believe that it could be possible," said Deirdre, brushing her hair out of her eyes. "How do you believe that the head of your own army, someone who has grown up with and is related to the royal family, is a traitor? No one would want to believe that."

Judeth looked over at her, seeming to see her for the first time.

"You are very different from the rest of us," she said. "Your outlook on things is unique. Are all people from your world like you?"

"I don't know," said Deirdre. "Our world is often very cold to strangers, and you learn how to fend for yourself after a fashion. I've been doing art in my studio and making a living from it for so long that I forget the outside world sometimes. I feel like a lot of people are not very kind to others. Maybe I am being unfair. I just don't know."

"I do not think you are," said Judeth, with a half smile. "You seem to be following an odd prophecy and that gives you an advantage. The rest of us, excepting maybe Tor and Jasper, are more or less along for the ride."

"I don't know if I like the idea of prophecy," said Deirdre. "Makes it seem so...out of my hands."

"You could choose to turn around and go home to your world right now if you wanted," said Judeth, "but you will not. You are too involved. Especially you and Tor."

"Yeah, especially," sighed Deirdre, looking at her feet. "I have no idea what to do about him. Swearing to protect someone who has saved your life really did seem like a good idea at the time."

"You did what you thought was honorable," said Judeth. "Do not be so hard on yourself. Your heart was in the right place."

Deirdre nodded and took a deep breath of the cool afternoon air.

"So, what can we do for the lords and ladies we left behind?" she said.

"The best thing that we can do is go on," said Judeth, firmly. "Any other action would be futile. We go on and find a way to call the dragons. I want to see Marshall pay for what he has done, and that is the only sure way to do it."

"When we get to Malepoer, we should send someone back to tell the Queen what has happened," said Deirdre. "Jasper and Alleen, maybe. I don't think Alleen will make it through that lies below the Southern Mountains. She seems somewhat fragile."

"I agree," said Judeth. "You might want to send two parties in case one is intercepted. I will go with Margret if you like and help draw attention away from you."

"We'll see what the day brings once we reach Malepoer," said Deirdre. "I don't want to endanger anyone if I can help it."

Judeth nodded.

"I just want to strike back somehow," she said. "I want to avenge Jan's death and clear Evarl's name. Traitor indeed! He was one of the most loyal men I have ever known."

"The time will come," said Deirdre. "This is why we are going. So this doesn't continue to happen."

Still lost in her anger, Judeth threw a stone into the river and stared at the ripples made by the current. Deirdre waited a moment, then decided to chance changing the subject.

"Judeth, I know the timing isn't great to ask this, but can I get your help for a few minutes? I want to try to shapeshift before everyone else gets up."

Judeth looked up with interest, and said, "I had forgotten about that. All right, I am ready. Shall we do it here?"

"Yes, while the others are still asleep. The less audience, the better," said Deirdre, standing and shivering with excitement.

Judeth also stood, and they walked to a flat grassy spot a little bit away from the river's edge. Deirdre took off her cloak and stood in the cool air, clad in her long tunic and woolen hose.

"Did your great-grandmother say anything about clothing?" she asked.

"Clothes did not matter, I guess. What you wore in one form did not translate over, but there was no mention of stripping naked either," said Judeth. "Did Count Nerfal say anything?"

"No, but I saw him change once, and he didn't take anything off first," said Deirdre. "That would have been way more embarrassing, and I would have remembered that."

"Shapers have always been very private folk," said Judeth. "They do not share these details with outsiders. Okay then, let us begin. Close your eyes and picture the horse you will become. Do you know what it looks like?"

Deirdre nodded and closed her eyes, bringing to her mind's eye the black and white mare she had seen in her vision.

"Try to think of things the way a horse does," continued Judeth. "Think of their vision, their movements. Feel the ground under your hooves, feel the wind through your mane. Be the horse."

Deirdre laughed at this statement and lost all of her focus. Judeth looked at her curiously.

"It's nothing," said Deirdre, chuckling and trying to regain her calm. "That sort of comment is something of a joke in my world. 'Be the ball' or "Be the tree.' I'm sorry, I'm sorry. I'll try to focus."

"Please do," said Judeth with an exasperated sigh, but she smiled.

Deirdre closed her eyes, focusing again, and sensed a hum of magic beginning to envelop her. As Judeth talked and she let the images flow through her brain, she felt more and more detached from herself. It did indeed feel as if she was at the edge of a cliff, and it encompassed her in a fever pitch of excitement and anticipation, as if her body was about to explode from the feeling.

She held firm to the picture of the rangy pinto mare she had seen in her vision seemingly ages ago and tried to feel the wind whispering in her cupped ears and flowing over her long, lean back. She reached the very edge of a mental cliff, no longer aware of anything but the precipice on which she stood. For a moment, fear held her back and made her tremble, but she cast it aside and leapt. There was no pain, no transition time, just a feeling of falling for a split second, as if on the edge of sleep, and then it was done.

Deirdre opened her eyes and was momentarily confused by her inability to see directly in front of her. More than anything, that confirmed the success of their attempt, and she opened her mouth to cheer only to have a thunderous neigh rend the silence of the early morning and startle both her and Judeth.

"You did it!" said Judeth. "Deirdre, you really did it!"

Deirdre canted her head a bit to watch Judeth jump excitedly around in an oddly sepia-toned world. Looking down, she saw her hooves where her hands and feet had been, and took a very tentative step forward, learning to balance in her new form. Succeeding, she took another, then tossed her head and whickered curiously at Judeth.

"Did Count Nerfal forget to mention that human speech is impossible in these forms?" Judeth asked. "Do not ask me why when there are talking horses around that have no problems with talking all day. Transformation was a gift from the dragons. Ask them."

Deirdre snorted and tried walking faster, finally breaking into a trot. She paced around the mill yard, neighing with excitement and raising her feet higher as she paced joyously in a circle. Vexanious trotted out of the woods where he had been grazing and stopped still to see the pinto mare moving freely over the ground. Tossing his head into the air, he moved to join her and matched her step for step around the yard.

"You have done it!" he said exuberantly and broke into a canter with Deirdre on his heels.

All of the commotion woke the others, and Nersh bounded into the yard, yipping with glee and leaping alongside the racing horses.

Judeth joined Jasper, Tor, and the others at the doorway to watch the spectacle occurring in the courtyard. It was Margret who came out and finally got everyone quieted down, reminding them that they were not going to hide very well if they kept up the level of sound they were making. Tor watched Deirdre with a mix of pride and affection. He had overheard Deirdre and Judeth the night before as his bovine ears never missed things said above a whisper, and he had wondered when they would try the shapeshift. Now he stood and watched Deirdre, feeling a whisper of her joy echo through the bond that they shared. It was infectious, and he tried his best to communicate his pride back to her. She glanced at him and whickered in recognition of his feelings.

Deirdre finally slowed and walked down to the river's edge to take a drink. She had only taken two gulps when she felt a hand pulling at her mane. It was Alleen, looking pale and still tired, but not so grief-stricken as she had the night before.

"No more while you are hot," she said, sternly. "Walk around with me until you are cooled down. You do not want to suffer from founder or colic of all things."

Deirdre let Alleen lead her up from the bank and walk her around in circles for a short time, cooling her down. Vexanious joined her, snorting and prancing in his excitement. Deirdre butted him with her head finally, and he calmed enough to simply walk next to her.

"You are subject to the laws that govern the body in which you inhabit," he said. "Count Nerfal told me that once. You have to remember that at all times, but he always said that the sacrifice was worth it."

Deirdre nodded her head and stopped still. Alleen seemed to know what she was going to do, for she stepped back and gave Deirdre space. Vexanious also backed off a step or two, and a blink of an eye later, Deirdre was human again. She felt tired and very, very hungry. She laughed and, suddenly, her legs gave way beneath her, and she found herself sitting on the ground feeling very dizzy. Tor and Jasper rushed over and helped her to stand and walk inside to her blankets.

"I believe that there was a passage concerning not transforming on an empty stomach," said Judeth, laughing and wrapping a blanket around Deirdre's shoulders. "We will cook up some food, Deirdre, and you should be fine. Then we should get underway."

"Yes," said Jasper, sighing. "We have another long night of travel ahead of us if we plan to get to Malepoer before Marshall Rialain."

They ate quickly and while they did, they filled Alleen in on where they were headed and why. They glossed over Deirdre's heritage - Alleen did not need to know that just yet - and did their best to make her feel welcome. As they got ready to leave, Alleen double checked their campsite and was key in making sure that there was nothing that pointed to their group directly. They packed up and were underway again before the sun had left the evening sky.

16

That night passed by uneventfully, aside from the bitter cold wind that came down from the north and caused them all to huddle miserably on their mounts. Alleen rode a great deal of the way with Jasper or Deirdre. Their only potential troubles came in the form of two villages, Efferdale and Chisentown, and these they skirted with no effort at all. Midway through the night, it began to snow, and the chill seemed to seep into their bones.

By the time dawn arrived, clothed in splendid oranges and pinks, everyone was half frozen and utterly exhausted. Shelter came in the form of a grove of pine trees a mile into the woods. Jasper and Tor cut small pines in half to make lean-to shelters, and they managed a small fire as they ate a tepid breakfast. There was no problem getting to sleep that day.

When they woke, the sun was high, and the air had warmed up to considerably well above freezing. They ate sparsely from the dwindling supplies brought from Judeth's manor, and after, Deirdre practiced her transformation several times, changing faster and faster. Judeth had told her that her great-grandmother had mentioned these changes happening in the blink of an eye, and Deirdre was determined to become proficient with transforming into one form before moving onto the next.

"You ought to try moving with a rider on your back," said Judeth. "Maybe Margret?"

Deirdre nodded and allowed Margret to climb up onto her back and ride her around a little, so as to learn how to balance with a rider. Margret slid on the slick hairs, having spent very little time on a bareback horse and tightened her grip on Deirdre's mane.

"You know," she said with a grin, "you might want to try wearing tack in case we get into a situation where we have to get out fast without me falling to the ground!"

"You can use Tirana's tack" offered Alleen.

Deirdre snorted and pawed the ground.

"We will take it off immediately if it bothers you," promised Margret.

As the sun began to set, she watched nervously while Alleen set the blanket and then the saddle onto her back, tightening the girth with practiced ease. When it came to accepting the bridle, however, she balked, and they agreed that the saddle was all they would really need for Margret to ride better anyway.

At Deirdre's nod, Margret climbed into the saddle, and Deirdre relaxed a little. It was much more comfortable as the saddle took the pressure off of her spine, and Margret was no longer sliding around. They practiced for about ten minutes before deciding that that was enough for one evening.

Unsaddled and back in human form, Deirdre had laughed about it.

"It's a totally different experience on the side of the horse," she told Margret as they went to pack their belongings in preparation to leave again.

"I can believe it," said Margret. "I do think you ought to try the bridle at some point in case we ever have to go into a city or town in disguise."

Deirdre agreed hesitantly, and they left the issue for a later date. A short time after, they were on the road again.

Midnight had come and gone without incident, and the party was travelling silently down the road, having skirted the town of Baederbron a short time before. This was the last obstacle they had to traverse before reaching Malepoer, and Nersh was walking besides Vexanious, chatting with Deirdre amiably.

"We should reach Malepoer by noon tomorrow if we go straight through," she said. "It would be best to rest a couple of hours outside the city and then go in. I know you will not like hearing this Deirdre, but you cannot go in alone."

"I was going to ask Jasper to accompany me," said Deirdre. "He mentioned that he'd been there a number of times."

"Yes, that should be all right," said Nersh. "He will have to be discrete, though. Malepoer is only two days' ride from his father's castle. We do not want to attract any unwanted attention."

She suddenly turned to look behind them, her ears at full listening height and she paused, frozen in midstep.

"Vexanious, do you hear something behind us?" she said.

The stallion stopped and perked up his own ears, listening carefully.

"A horse, I think, running full speed," he said, "and it is being pursued."

"I do not hear tack sounds," said Nersh. "Do you?"

"No."

Judeth rode up next to Deirdre.

"What is it?" she asked.

Jasper, Tor, and Margret also rode closer.

"A horse, no tack, running this way. Something is chasing it," said Nersh.

"Get off the path," said Judeth. "We should not be seen. Quickly!"

They rode into the thick bracken on the side of the road and stood alert, peering down the dark road and listening. The sound of hooves was clear to all of them now, and faintly, they could hear the sound of excited voices coming from further behind.

Deirdre strained to see down the path, trying to make out whatever it was that was following them. The hoofbeats crescendoed, and from out of the darkness came a frantically galloping figure. Deirdre gasped as the being passed them, for it was something straight out of her copy of Bulfinch's Mythology. A pinto centaur was running by them at top speed, or as close as he could come to it with two arrows quilling his rump. Nersh leapt from the group's hiding spot onto the road behind the creature.

"Stop!" she cried. "Centaur, stop! I am of the Talking Folk!"

The centaur slowed to a limping walk and wheeled around, stopping. His flanks heaved and his sides were sheened with sweat. Over his human-torso, he wore a woven tunic, and he had a long sword slung across his back.

"I cannot stop for long, lady wolf," he said, breathing hard. "The villagers are out to kill me."

"I have friends here, Centaur. Kin," said Nersh. "Deirdre, Judeth, come quickly!"

Deirdre nudged Vexanious out onto the road, and Judeth followed. The centaur tensed himself to run, but stopped himself. He took a few steps towards them.

"I am Lady Deirdre Ettar from the Mountain Reaches," Deirdre said. "This is Lady Judeth of Garey Manor."

"I must ask for sanctuary, my ladies," said the centaur, gravely. "I can run no further, truly."

"What is your name?" asked Judeth.

"M're Satal, my lady," said the centaur, bowing from his human waist.

Tor rode out of the trees, causing M're Satal to half bolt. Deirdre laid a calming hand on the centaur's shoulder.

"He's with us," she said.

Tor pointed back down the road to where the voices were getting louder.

"Deirdre," said Vexanious. "Dismount. I will lead them off and rejoin you. It is dark. They will not see me in the woods."

"Quite right," said Deirdre, sliding off and quickly unbuckling the girth to the saddle, pulling it from his back. "Let's go. Our friends are waiting and those voices are closer. Please join us, and we can get those arrows out."

They slipped back into the brush as carefully as they could, leaving very little trace. Vexanious thundered down the path, and the rest of them huddled in the woods, waiting until the angry band of villagers had stormed past. When the men were long gone, they all breathed easier, and in a very short amount of time, Vexanious returned. The stallion made virtually no noise coming back up the road, and once he was saddled again, they made their way deeper into the woods.

"We will have to travel through the countryside until we get closer to Malepoer," said Nersh, trotting forward to take the lead. "Not much farther anyway. Then we can rest and tend to those arrows."

They came out through the tree line about a mile or so later into a field brightly lit by the moon. Here, they set up camp, and Margret broke the shafts of the arrows off near the tip, and then gently tried to work out the barbed heads without damaging the centaur any further. M're Satal made a few pained faces during Margret's ministrations, but bore it stoically, and a short time later, the arrowheads were out, and the wounds were dressed with healing poultices. M're Satal then offered them a tarp from his packs, and Alleen and Jasper rigged it up, while Margret tended the small fire they had built. Tor gathered some more wood from around the clearing while Judeth cooked supper.

"We might as well stay here until tomorrow," said Nersh. "We can rest for a few hours and still get to Malepoer by early morning. Cross country will be faster."

Deirdre nodded absently and looked over at their new companion where he knelt on the ground with his legs tucked up under him, watching them curiously. He looked much as she had always pictured a centaur: horse body joined at the equine shoulder to a human waist. M're Satal's horse coloring was that of a black and white pinto, and the color pattern extended past the joining of horse and man, becoming multi-hued human flesh-tones where the pinto markings continued. Several patches of black skin appeared on his neck and arms, and one of the patches extended onto his right cheek until just past his bright brown eye. His left eye was a startling light blue.

His hair was more like a mane, running in a line down the back of his neck. Several hawk feathers were braided into it, and these gleamed brightly in the moonlight. To Deirdre, he seemed even more alien than Tor, for he appeared almost human until one of his pointed ears moved to catch a sound or one caught sight of his odd coloring.

M're Satal noticed her scrutiny, and he watched her without smiling.

"Have you never seen a centaur, my lady?" he asked.

"Well, actually, no. You are the first I have ever encountered," said Deirdre. "I'm not from around here."

"You are Kin?" he asked, eyeing her horns.

"Yes," she said and returned his stare. "From the Northern Reaches."

M're Satal shrugged.

"Perhaps you have lived a sheltered life," he said. "Nevertheless, I owe you all a favor for your kindness to me. How can I repay you?"

"When we leave Malepoer, we are going to need help crossing the desert below the Southern Mountains," said Jasper. "I have heard that the centaurs know a way?"

"We do, and I will see that you get there and try to get the help you need from my people, as I am headed home myself," said M're Satal. "I can make no promises, however, and the tribes down there have no love of minotaurs."

"Not many do," smiled Deirdre. "But he's my bodyguard, so he has to come."

M're Satal looked at her speculatively.

"And would you happen to be the same Deirdre Ettar that everyone is looking for? There is a bounty on your head. Some are saying that you are a traitor."

Tor snorted viciously and glared at M're Satal. The centaur shook his head.

"I did not say that I believed it," he said, "but I would keep a very low profile in Malepoer, my lady, if you plan to go in. The news is spreading quickly."

"What is your story?" asked Judeth. "Why the arrows and the angry villagers?"

"There is a new decree, supposedly sent out by the Queen herself, that bars admittance to villages for any magical beast or creature, excepting the shapers," said the centaur. "I did not happen to see the sign and helped myself to some water from the village well."

"They shot you?" asked Margret, horrified.

"Yes. They said that they did not want any 'filthy beasts' polluting their water," said M're Satal, his tail lashing from side to side, furiously. The anger was plain on his face. "I was heading home for a brief visit. Now mayhaps I will stay there."

"Marshall," said Deirdre. "This is Marshall's doing."

"So it would seem," said Judeth thoughtfully.

"But why?" asked Alleen. "What will it gain him?"

"It will further widen the chasm already forming between the humans and the magical beasts," said Nersh. "Marshall is aiming to do what could not be done three hundred years ago: drive all of the non-humans out of Keyralithsmus."

"He's doing a great job so far," said Deirdre angrily. "By the time we get back from the South, who knows how far he will have gotten!"

"That is where Jasper and Alleen can come in, if they are willing," said Judeth. "After we go to Malepoer, Deirdre would like you to go see Queen Brena, to warn her about Marshall's coup at the Garey Manor."

"That sounds like an excellent idea," said Jasper. "I may not have friends, but I have contacts that will make sure that we get through to Remembrance."

"Why me, though?" asked Alleen. "Why not Margret or Judeth?"

"Because you saw first-hand what Marshall Rialain has done," said Nersh. "You witnessed at least some of what happened."

Alleen nodded and pulled her cloak tighter around her shoulders. Jasper moved closer to her, adding his warmth to hers. Deirdre smiled and glanced over at Tor. He was looking at her, and she could feel that he was struggling with something internally. She got up and walked over to sit by him.

"What's wrong?" she said. "You've been jumpy for a couple of days, ever since we found Alleen."

Tor snorted and took a stick from the ground, writing in the fire-lit snow, "Can we talk?"

"Now?" asked Deirdre. "Can't it wait?"

Tor shook his head, and Deirdre could feel his discomfort and tension plainly. She caught Judeth's attention, figuring that her knowledge of magic might be good if something went wrong.

"Can you keep watch on us for a few minutes? Tor wants to talk, and I think it's important."

Judeth rose and waved them over to a dry space under a large spruce tree a little distance away from the others. Tor and Deirdre joined her, and they all sat on the needle-carpeted ground. Tor had already drawn the sword, and he pushed it as far as it would go in the frozen earth between them. He looked at Deirdre, and they touched the hilt together. The world vanished.

————

Deirdre once again found herself standing on the grassy expanse under the blue sky in the mountain valley. Tor stood by the tree, looking out at the mountains, and he turned when she approached. He still looked discomfited but also resigned.

"I needed to talk to you before we reached Malepoer, just in case something happens there, and we do not get a chance to talk later," he said. "You probably have noticed the bond growing stronger almost on a daily basis."

"You too?" asked Deirdre.

"Yes," he said. "I also overheard you talking with Judeth about magical connections the other night. What she said is the truth. The longer this bond continues to grow, the stronger it becomes, and the harder it is to break."

Deirdre looked at him in confusion for a moment.

"Are you worried you'll get stuck with me?" she asked.

"No!" he said, his frustration and surprise making him louder than he'd intended. "I am worried you will get stuck with me!"

He calmed himself and continued, pacing restlessly,

"There is no guarantee that I will ever be able to regain a human form. I could be a minotaur for the rest of my life. If the bond continues, you would eventually be bound to stay with me, as I am now."

"Would that be so bad?" asked Deirdre softly.

He turned and looked at her in surprise.

"I thought you wanted to go home someday," he said. "You could not do that if the bond continues. It would be too painful to be separated for long, and I could not go with you. Not like this."

"I have done a lot of thinking about going home," said Deirdre. "There's truly not much I'd miss. Only my grandfather, really, and I'd thought about getting him to come here...if he wanted to, I mean. Other than that, I've really given a great deal of thought to staying."

"There is also the obvious problem of me being a minotaur," said Tor, resuming his pacing. "If I never regain human form...I mean, I am basically a monster in the eyes of most of the populous here...would you want to face that stigma if we somehow do succeed in our quest?"

Deirdre looked at him thoughtfully.

"What are you *really* asking?" she said. "What is the real question that you keep dodging?"

Tor stopped pacing and looked at Deirdre, startled at her perception of his evasion. He'd thought about this for days now, and the real question was damn near terrifying for him to ask. He took a deep breath.

"I may never regain human form," he said slowly, "and if we do not break this bond soon, we will be bound together for the rest of our lives. If that happens, as Judeth said, most pairs do end up in a romantic relationship. They also get so closely tied to each other that if one dies, the other dies too soon after.

"I am this," he continued, gesturing to his body, "and I may never be other than this. Here is the question you want me to ask. Would you, knowing all of these complications, and the likelihood of me staying a minotaur, still want to stay in this bond with me?"

"Thank you," said Deirdre. "That is a real, honest question, and I'll give you a real, honest answer. Like you, I have been thinking about this a lot for the past few days, about going home, and about what Judeth had said the consequences might be. Like you, I have tried to sort out my own feelings on how this will impact me, and I appreciate you making sure that I knew the dangers of this choice.

"Here's what I believe -- you and I have already been connected for longer than we have been magically bound by this sword. About a month ago, I went into a cave to undertake a ritual that all shapers face. While I was there, I was given visions of what was to come, including your sword glowing blue during the Dark Wolves' attack. Then there was the dream we had of each other. Both of those happened before we met. I don't think we can blame all of this on a magical sword, do you?"

"No," said Tor, "I cannot. I did not realize that there was more to it, other than the dream."

"Well, there apparently is," said Deirdre. "Something, some-one...maybe the Land itself for all I know, wants us together. Maybe the sword is an agent of the Land. It sent you to find me, after all. Maybe we were brought together for me to help you and you to help me save the Land.

"So my answer to this is yes. Yes, I know the danger. Yes, I know there is a chance I will fall *madly* in love with you,"-- here she swooned dramatically, dashing her hand against her forehead and then grinning at him impishly -- "and never want to leave you. Yes, I know you might always remain a minotaur. Yes, I know the bond will become perma-nent if left too long."

She sobered, straightening, and looked him square in the eyes.

"Yes," she said seriously, *"we should not break this bond.* Something went to a lot of trouble to arrange our meeting, and I honestly think the consequences of breaking it would be very bad indeed."

He stood, stunned, not quite believing his ears.

"You are sure?" he asked.

"Positive," she replied. "Are you?"

"Yes," he said, managing not to shout for joy as relief washed over him. "I just wanted to make sure that you were fully aware of the consequences."

"Yeah," smiled Deirdre. "I got that. Are we settled on this? Can we go back now? If I don't get some sleep, they'll have to carry me to Malepoer in the morning."

Tor nodded and together they touched the handle of the sword, pulling it from the earth. Both of them were smiling as the bright world faded around them.

———

They came back to themselves to see Judeth watching them intently. She looked relieved that they had returned, and they filled her in quickly as to their conversation. She grinned at both of them, and when Deirdre yawned, ushered them back to the camp. Neither of them argued and, placing their bedrolls next to each other, were not long in falling asleep.

———

Morning came too soon, and they woke shortly before the dawn. Following a cold breakfast, they started out and, at length, they veered east until they paralleled the road. They made such good time that Nersh revised her estimate and figured that they would be within a mile of Malepoer fairly early. Jasper and Deirdre would then go in alone, and the rest of the party would bypass the city and find a place to the southeast to hole up for the day. There they would wait for

Jasper, Deirdre, and hopefully Jack, to join them and, with any luck, they would be able to find a place safe enough to use for a day or two to rest. From there, Jasper and Alleen would head back to the North, and the rest of the party would continue south.

The sun rose brilliantly, tinting the sky a pale, watery pink. Storm clouds were beginning to form on the horizon, and Deirdre groaned inwardly, not looking forward to the inclement weather. More snow seemed to be on the docket, and she was already getting sick of the cold.

They traveled on, twice having to hide as a farmer's wagon rolled slowly towards the city bearing a load of pumpkins and squash.

"At least harvest season is very nearly done," said Jasper. "We are lucky we did not come here several weeks earlier. This road would have been very full of people."

Nersh finally crossed with those not going to Malepoer to the other side of the road and bid Deirdre and Jasper a safe journey. They dismounted, and Jasper handed the reins of his stallion to Alleen.

"We will probably be no more than two miles past Malepoer down the Southern route," said the wolf. "May the blessings of Tali and Rathal go with you."

"Be safe, all of you," said Deirdre and walked over to where Tor sat astride the gelding.

"I'll be alright," she said, smiling up at him.

The minotaur nodded and took her right hand, giving it a brief squeeze. He let go and anxiously watched her walk off with the Lord of Ganley Keep's son by her side. He silently wished them both safe passage and yearned to be the one going with her. Cursing his form once again, he turned his horse and rode after the others as they made their way south.

———

Deirdre and Jasper walked silently for a little while, listening to the sparse calls of birds and feeling the sun on their backs. The early morning air was slowly warming, but the chill had not really left it. The road wound through the trees, slowly moving up the gentle rise of the land, and Deirdre could see a change beginning to happen to the leaves on the flora around her.

"Do you remember what Tor wrote?" asked Jasper, referring to two brief sentences written in the dirt the night before.

"Ask for either Randall Briarson or Merclay Tan at the Inn of the Firehorse, and mention Marshall's deception to Jack. I assume that there is no love lost between the captain of the guard and our elusive prey?"

"No," said Jasper. "No, I would have to say that you are correct there. Did Judeth give you the coin pouch?"

"Right here," said Deirdre, patting her side. "I threaded it on my belt and tucked it between my tunic and my hose."

"Wise of you not to wear skirts," said Jasper. "No one would expect a high-born lady in trousers."

"Easier to move in," said Deirdre, "and more comfortable in the cold. Where I come from, trousers are a mainstay for men and women. Skirts are just too much trouble."

They crested the little hill and stopped, looking down at the rambling city that lay before them. Smoke rose from numerous chimneys, and there was little sign of vegetation growing among the urban sprawl of houses or around the dark line of the river that bisected the city. As she looked further in from the visual chaos at its outer environs, however, the city developed a growing sense of order and structure, as if drawing itself up proudly towards its heritage. The center of the city was an ordered series of streets that were evident as being planned, even to Deirdre's untrained eye. It was the outer streets that made her cringe as she could only imagine what kind of vermin, human and otherwise, they might encounter there. She fervently hoped that Jack would not be living among the squalor, and they would not have to seek him there.

Jasper turned to look at her and grimaced, seeing consternation on her face.

"Welcome to Malepoer," said he, softly. "Have you nothing like this in your world?"

"We do," said Deirdre, pulling her hood up "and I don't like it any better there either. One of my favorite authors once described a city in his book as a sprawling monster and stated that it was too late to flee. I think I get what he means now."

Silently, they set off down the hill towards the city, heading for whatever awaited them. The smell that rose to greet them was rank, a mix of rotting foods, animal dung, tanneries, and a myriad of other smells that did not endear Deirdre to the idea of city life. They headed for the nearest gate, and then it really was too late to turn back. They passed through the guarded entryway and were within the environs of the city of Malepoer.

17

The little of Remembrance that Deirdre had seen in no way prepared her for the muck and muddy streets of Malepoer. The ground was cobbled in a reddish stone that was barely discernible under all of the filth that covered it. The stench of animal and human waste was appalling after the clean air of the woods, and Deirdre wondered how long it would take for her nose to adjust so that she could breathe without gagging. She desperately hoped it would be soon.

"How can they stand this?" she asked Jasper as they skirted a huge pile of horse manure that lay in the middle of the street. "Our cities back home are never like this."

"Not all sections are this bad," said Jasper. "Unfortunately, we may have to travel through more areas like this since we do not know where Jack is going to be or where the inn Tor mentioned is located."

"We could ask," said Deirdre, rubbing her nose.

"I intend to," said Jasper, "as soon as I see...ah, there! Boy!"

The last was addressed to a ragged street urchin who ran over to them looking like any of the thousand children Deirdre had read descriptions of in her books back home. This one happened to have the addition of several bruises and a black eye to improve his looks. His hair was wildly dirty, his face was covered in soot, and his clothes were held together with more patches than original cloth. He smiled at them as he ran over and looked at them expectantly.

"Yes, mi'lord?" he asked in a thin, reedy voice.

"Can you direct us to the Inn of the Fire-Horse?" asked Jasper.

"Certainly, mi'lord," he said brightly. "Go down this street here to Market, see? Then go straight ahead, an' turn left onto the Street of the Brass Doors, an' then right onto the Street of the Blue Shutters. The inn is halfway down that street. There is a big sign on it of a horse wi' big, fiery wings."

"Thank you, lad," said Jasper, and tossed the boy a small silver coin. The boy deftly caught it and vanished back into the crowd.

"So much for remaining inconspicuous," groaned Deirdre.

"Everyone asks urchins for directions," said Jasper absently, "and anyone overhearing us would not think twice about us inquiring about a particular inn."

"I hope you are right," muttered Deirdre.

They began to follow the street and noticed that gradually, after the space of several blocks, the area grew cleaner with less grime on the pavement. Ahead of them, they could see a large, clear area surrounded on all sides by buildings. There were many people there, and Deirdre caught a glimpse of what looked like tents. It could only have been the marketplace that the boy was referring to.

They came into Market and paused to get their bearings. To Deirdre, the whole thing looked like a massive sidewalk bazaar, with tents and vendors everywhere. Some sold things from the buildings that they were attached to, while others set up tents in spaces all around the center and carried on in an enormous din of sound and sight. Deirdre saw horse sellers and rug merchants, candle makers and metal smiths, saddlers and poultry men, all hawking their wares and all trying to out-shout their competitors. There was no one on horseback, and a number of signs around the square warned of the penalties of riding within Market.

Carefully, they crossed the plaza and started down the street on the other side. The cacophony slowly fell behind them, and they reached the first left hand turn. Looking down the street, they saw that the doors were of different colors, but the steps were all made of brick. Deirdre looked askance at Jasper.

"In Malepoer, the streets are defined by their unique signature. It is easy here in the center, but just be glad we do not have to search areas further out," he said. "Then we might well be told 'go to the street with the triple locks and the peach-colored shutters with the lavender trim.' Well, maybe not that bad, but you get the gist."

"So we need to find the Street of the Brass Doors," said Deirdre.

"Yes, and then the one with blue shutters. Come on."

Eventually, they found their way to the streets they were looking for. The Street of Brass Doors had gleaming brass front doors on every house. Easy enough. From there, they were able to locate the Inn of the Fire-Horse with little trouble. It was on a very well-maintained street, and all the houses did indeed have blue shutters, including their destination. The inn itself bore the marks of a well-run establishment, from the neat little stable yard in the back to the brightly colored front door. The sign out front had a carved winged horse on it, and the wings were painted in the colors of flame, with little streaks of gilding running along the veins of the individual flight feathers.

Jasper smiled triumphantly and led the way into the dim, fire-lit interior. The inn was large and had an enormous common area on the first floor with a stone fireplace warming the room on one side and a number of round tables scattered throughout. Several doors opened off from the back wall to what looked like the kitchen and two smaller private rooms, much like at the inn that Deirdre had stayed at the first night on the road to Garey Manor. A polished wooden staircase opposite the fireplace led up to a railed balcony that ran around three quarters of the building and off which doors to rooms could be seen. Leaning over the balcony were several pretty young women dressed in brightly colored outfits. They surveyed the room and its patrons with speculation, and one of them looked at

Deirdre and blew her a kiss. Deirdre felt her face flame and looked away.

At the far end of the common room, behind the bar, stood a tall, thin man who glanced up at them when they entered, then went back to finish what he was working on. The only other people there were a few wealthy-looking men who were sitting around one of the tables, enjoying a hearty breakfast that made Deirdre's mouth water. Jasper caught her eye, nodded at the bar, and they made their way over to it.

The barkeep looked up as they approached and smiled politely at them, sharp eyes taking in the details of their clothing and gear.

"Good morrow to ye," he said, "What can I do for ye?"

"We are looking for a friend of ours," said Jasper heartily. "He made us travel all this way and forgot to tell us where his house was, the lout! He did mention your inn, sir, and so we thought you might know where we might find him or his cousin, either of whom will do."

"And just who is this friend of yours, pray tell?" asked the barkeep, his voice becoming a slight bit more wary. The other men in the room paused in their conversation.

"My friend's name is Randall Briarson," said Jasper.

"Never heard of him," said the barkeep, now clearly ill at ease, "and his cousin?"

"Merclay Tan," said Jasper, smiling disarmingly.

"Now Merclay I know," said the barkeep, his smile returning. Deirdre noticed the other men returned to their meal and conversation. "Well, you visit with high class folks! Merclay Tan lives over on the Street of the Silver Lanterns. Keep going down this street, and turn right onto The Street of the Red Doors, then take your third left onto Silver Lanterns. His house is the third one on the right. Give him regards from Bernhard."

"Thank you, sir, we will do that," smiled Jasper again.

"Be sure you do, lad," said Berhard, winking. "Can I tempt ye with something to eat, ere you go?"

"No," said Jasper, "but thank you. Merclay was expecting us last night, and I would rather get there before it gets any later."

The barkeep waved them off cheerfully, and they left the inn. On their way out, Deirdre noticed that the table of men paid them no mind, and she sighed with relief. Back on the street, Deirdre looked at Jasper oddly as they continued on their way.

"You were mighty perky," she said skeptically.

"We were speaking in code," said Jasper softly. "If we had not known both of Jack's names, he would not have told me, and he might have sent word to Jack that there was someone looking for him. I was 'perky,' as you put it, because if we had skulked in and whispered, everyone would have suddenly developed a highly financial ear."

"Ah," said Deirdre, "and we have to use the barkeep's name, or we won't get in."

"Exactly. Not to mention that if anyone was around who knew me, they would never expect me to be cheerful," grinned Jasper and made a scowling face. "The Lord of Ganley Keep's son is taciturn and brooding, not open and happy."

"Jasper, no offense, but I think you were a little bit too happy."

Jasper snorted, and they made their way through the streets, following the innkeeper's directions. The houses became more and more ornate as they went on, no longer crowded closely together, and the streets were clean and tidy. They passed several members of the town watch who eyed their clothing with suspicion, but let them go on their way without harassment when they noticed the quality of Jasper's sword and the way he carried himself. Deirdre remained within her hood and tried to look unassuming. It seemed to work.

Turning onto the Street of the Silver Lanterns, they made their way to the third house on the right, a moderately-sized building with a small flower garden in the front. Like all of the houses on the street, it had a silver lantern of high quality hanging by the front door, and the estate itself was neat and well-kept. Jasper looked at Deirdre, and together they walked up the short flight of steps to the front door. Deirdre took a deep breath, and knocked.

A short minute later, the portal opened and revealed a huge, shirtless, bald-headed man who scowled down at them from what had to be a height of nearly seven feet. He folded his arms over his muscled torso and gave them a look that obviously challenged their reason for being on the steps.

"Yes?" he boomed.

"We would like to see Merclay Tan," said Jasper. "Bernhard sent us."

"Merclay is not home," growled the man.

"Well, then perhaps his cousin, Randall Briarson?" said Jasper politely.

"Yes. Randall is in. This way."

The man ushered them into a large, poorly-lit hallway, and Deirdre jumped as the door closed sharply behind them, making her uncomfortable at having their exit so swiftly cut off. The man walked past a collection of cloaks on pegs by the door and bade Deirdre and Jasper follow him down the passageway. He opened a door on the left hand side at the end of the hall and bowed them into what appeared to be a drawing room.

"Please wait here," he said and left, closing the door behind him.

The room was richly appointed in red velvet, and the mahogany wooden furniture had gleaming brass accents that shone in the light from the unshuttered windows. Several large armchairs flanked the brass-fronted fireplace, and a small fire danced behind an ornate brass screen decorated with cavorting dragons that blew spirals of flames.

The door behind them opened again a few minutes later, and a slight man looking to be in his mid-twenties strode inside. The giant filled the doorway behind him, making any exit, rapid or otherwise, nearly impossible. A sword now hung from the belt on his waist. The smaller man was good looking in a rakish way, clad in an open red robe over his bare torso and a pair of bloused gold silk pants, his dark blond hair disheveled as if he had just been woken from sleep. He stood staring at them, his blue eyes wide and with an expression of incredulity on his face, as if not quite understanding what he saw.

"Bernhard sent you?" he asked. "Where did you learn the passwords? Who told you? I certainly didn't give them to you."

"You are Jack Parns?" asked Jasper.

"Yes, damn it!" snarled the man, becoming more agitated by the second. "Now tell me! Who told you?"

"Jack Parns," said Deirdre, drawing back her hood, "I am Deirdre Ettar. An old drinking buddy of yours gave them to me."

"Fagh!" said Jack, "I know who *you* are. I suppose this "drinking buddy" has somehow come back from the dead?"

He sat down in one of the armchairs and motioned at Deirdre to take a seat in the one opposite. Jasper remained standing where he could watch the man in the doorway, his expression warily curious.

"I can see you are Kin, Lady, and because of that, I will speak with you. I don't know how you came by those passwords but telling me that the prince is still alive is outrageous to the very end of courtesy. He died. I saw his body, gored to death by a minotaur."

Jasper glanced sharply towards Deirdre at Jack's words, and Deirdre looked back at him, nodding curtly. She could read the smoldering questions in his eyes and raised a hand in a waiting gesture.

"O-ho!" said Jack, looking at Jasper. "You didn't know, Lord Jasper? Funny, that's a small detail I would think she might not omit in enlisting help from *you,* of all people."

Jasper turned his glare on Jack, his hands balling into fists. In the doorway, the giant placed his hand on the hilt of his sword.

"He is not dead," said Deirdre quickly, returning her attention to Jack. "He was changed by magic to become the very creature that slew his body. Their souls were swapped by dark magic, and he had to flee or perish. He wanted me to tell you that you were right about Marshall Rialain all along."

"What *about* Marshall?" asked Jack, still scowling skeptically.

"Marshall carried out a coup against the lords and ladies at Lady Judeth's ball," said Deirdre. "Our party crept away after midnight, needing to leave in secrecy. Lady Alleen of Barrett Castle caught up with us two nights later and told us that the other nobles were either killed or taken prisoner. Queen Brena has no idea what is going on, but we hope to get her a message in time."

"So, Marshall finally did it," said Jack, shaking his head. "I knew I couldn't trust him and to this day, I don't know why Brena did."

All of the anger seemed to run out of him, and he waved at the other empty chair.

"Be seated, Lord Jasper. Rontil, would you please get us all some of that excellent wine from Brakar? This may take a while to sort out."

The huge man left his place in the doorway, and Jasper took the other chair by the fire. Jack looked at both of them for a long moment and shook his head.

"You I don't get," he said to Jasper. "I can't fathom what you are doing with this lady if half I hear about you is true."

"It is not," said Jasper, "but it is nice to know that I get what I pay for."

Jack looked at Jasper narrowly, and then shook his head.

"I'll let that go for now," he said, turning to Deirdre. "So, you are acquainted with my old drinking companion. How did you end up meeting him?"

"He saved my life," said Deirdre simply. "My party was attacked by Dark Wolves on the way to Lady Judeth's estate, and he came out of hiding to save us."

Jack looked at Jasper, and the Lord of Ganley Keep's son nodded.

"It is true about the Wolves, though I do not know why," he said.

"Ah, but I think I do," said Jack. "Marshall has been to visit with your father here in Malepoer on numerous occasions of late. I have a lot of eyes in this city, Lord Jasper, and whispers have reached me that they met often and in secret. I would not be surprised if they were working together."

"But why?" asked Jasper, rising to pace around the room. "Even though he holds all of that power, Father has never broken the treaty before now. None of the Ganleys have."

"Who knows why men do what they do," said Jack, smiling bitterly. "You can never truly know another's heart."

He turned again to Deirdre.

"Why did he send you to me?" he asked.

"He is hoping that you would help us find the dragons," said Deirdre.

"Ah...the dragons. What makes him so sure that I will help you?" asked Jack, all of the cynicism returning to his voice as he sat back in his chair. "Why should I leave all of this? As you see, I live in opulent surroundings and am a wealthy merchant, well-known and well-loved for my generosity."

"Revenge," said Deirdre, "and a chance to save the woman you loved."

"Oh, ho, ho! You are forgetting one thing!" said Jack, sitting forward. "She tried to imprison me."

"After Marshall set you up, yes," said Deirdre, "but she still cares about you. I can tell from how she reacted to Lord Tomille almost mentioning your name. It hurt her, and it wouldn't if she didn't care."

Jack sat back, steepling his hands, and stared for a long moment into the fire. Rontil returned with four crystal wine glasses and a decanter. He proceeded to pour them all a glass of ruby red wine and then returned to his post by the door to sip his drink, his posture not so much blocking now as guarding.

Taking his glass, Jack played idly with the stem for a few minutes before speaking again.

"You need to find the dragons," he mused. "The lands to the south hold many dangers...and many rewards. It has been a long while since I have been south, and I should *very* much like to reacquaint myself with my old not-so-dead friend again. Mayhaps I can also find some trinkets there that would sell handsomely in these northern climes, ones that are a dime a dozen there, but are rarer than gold here. Rontil?"

The big man shrugged and drained the rest of his glass in one draught.

"City living is making us soft, Jack," he said, his deep voice thoughtful.

"Well then, it's settled," said Jack. He finished his own glass, setting it back on the tray. "Get the gear together and saddle a horse for yourself and Lord Jasper here. Sir, if you would accompany Rontil to settle our supplies, I will go in search of the items that your party will need for desert travel. Lady Deirdre, if you would like to accompany me to Market, I would be honored."

"I would rather stay with Deirdre," replied Jasper warily. "Why can we not stay here and wait for the supplies?"

Jack fixed Jasper with a hard stare.

"Your father must have gotten wind of your pending arrival," he said. "He's been in the city, watching or having his minions watch for days. *You* are better off out of the city."

"So why does Deirdre have to go with you?" asked Jasper, angrily.

"Because she is not known and will not be recognized as easily. Besides, I often travel in the company of a beautiful lady. I have a dress she can wear, and she can be my escort. I need to get information about what we need from one of you while we shop, and you are too well known."

"He's got you there," said Deirdre. "Your father's people won't know me, but you are a target waiting for a place to happen."

Jasper glanced at her unhappily.

"I want you to know that I am not comfortable with this," he said, "but you are not wrong in your assumptions. Very well. I will go with your man, Jack, but only because I believe our mutual friend would not send us to someone who would play us false."

"Good," said Jack. "That's settled, then. Rontil, will you please fetch Deirdre the red dress...you know which one. It should fit you, my lady. I apologize for the cut ahead of time, but it will definitely make you less recognizable. I am going to go get dressed and will return presently. My Lady. Sir."

Both of the men left, and Deirdre and Jasper were left alone.

"Deirdre, why did you not tell me about Tor?" Jasper hissed as soon as the door closed behind the others.

"Because he asked me not to. Only Nersh and Vexanious know, and that is because they knew him before the change," said Deirdre. "He says that it is too dangerous even to think of him by his real name, so don't."

She paced the room for a moment and then turned to him.

"How did your father know you were here?" she asked suspiciously.

"I do not know," grumbled Jasper, drinking the last of his wine and setting the glass down on a table nearby. "The only answer is that Marshall Rialain asked him to look for you and that you might be traveling with me. This is the only practical destination heading south after all is said and done."

Deirdre sighed and nodded.

"I hope that Tor was right about Jack," she said.

"I as well,' said Jasper. "Nersh mentioned that you and Tor have some sort of magical bond. Is there more to it than that?"

"Well...I don't know. We can feel each other's emotions a little," said Deirdre. "I know how minotaurs are viewed in this world, so..."

"Except that he is not a minotaur, now is he?" chided Jasper, gently. "We all knew he was once human, but honestly, that would not have made any difference because he saved your life. Minotaurs were not always thought of so poorly, you know. They have earned a reputation over the years by the actions of a few who broke the laws and have since been treated ill. We made them what they are. You obviously favor Tor, and so we would not have thought badly of you even if he was a true minotaur."

Deirdre drank the last of her wine to cover her embarrassment just as Jack reentered the room, followed by Rontil. The larger man handed her a red dress made out of satin, and Deirdre shook it out, staring at it critically.

"You've got to be kidding," she said.

"My dear, in that dress and a little make up, no one will recognize you," grinned Jack. "I will wait outside while you change. Jasper, if you would please go with Rontil, he could use your help."

Jasper stood and took Deirdre's hand, bowing over it.

"Take care," he said. "I will see you at the meeting place."

Nodding, Deirdre watched them all leave the room and changed into the red dress. The cut was tight, and the bodice was very low and revealing, not covering nearly enough. She stubbornly left her trousers on under the dress, trying to save some face, and bundled the rest into a small pile. When she opened the door, Jack stepped in, grinning, and held aloft a tray of various crèmes and powders.

"I have had to do this several occasions before. If you will allow me," he said and spent the next twenty minutes applying various things to her face.

When he was done, he held up a mirror, and she looked at herself in horror. She looked like a harlot, Deirdre thought, with enough makeup to paint a small ship. She turned to Jack, and for a moment felt like hitting him.

"I know, I know," he grinned impishly, "but believe me, I have walked through the center of Market several times with women on the run, and dressed like this, they have never gotten any more attention than for what they appeared to be."

"Small wonder," said Deirdre dryly.

"We'll get all of that stuff off again when we get back here later," he said, "I really need you to go with me, though. I need numbers, sizes, and information."

He produced a filmy red scarf that he wrapped loosely around her hair like a snood, effectively hiding her horns, then moved to leave the room. Seeing that she had not followed him, he said,

"Don't worry about your sweetheart. Rontil will return your lover safe and sound to you when we rendezvous with them later."

"He's not my lover," snapped Deirdre, glaring at Jack's amused and slightly arrogant expression. "Don't return him to *me*, just return him is all I ask."

"My Lady," bowed Jack with a hint of sarcasm in his voice and led the way down the hall. At the door, Jack took a bright red cloak from among those hanging there and handed it to her. Deirdre rolled her eyes but put it on, and Jack led the way outside.

Deirdre followed him down to the end of the street and then

turned left, back towards the Inn of the Fire-Horse. She was grateful that there were very few people on the street to see her in the disguise she was wearing, and she felt like sinking through the ground the closer towards Market they got.

"Put your arm in mine. There," said Jack, catching her arm and placing it over his own. "Try to put a little swing in your hips. If you don't act the part, no one will believe you."

"That was rather the point," muttered Deirdre under her breath.

"We are going to need some desert clothing," said Jack, ignoring her. "How many are there going to be in your party?"

"Two humans, one minotaur, and one wolf, besides you and your friend," said Deirdre dryly. "There are others, but they won't be coming with us."

"That wolf wouldn't happen to be Lady Nersh, would it?" asked Jack. "I haven't seen her in ages. She must be fairly old by now."

"She has more grey hairs than Carter has little liver pills," said Deirdre, smiling as they came near enough to Market to begin to hear the din of the ware sellers, "but she still has plenty of spring to her step."

Jack stopped and looked at her with wide eyes.

"What the...You!" he said in shock, and then laughed. "What gave me away?"

"It was the "dime a dozen" comment," said Deirdre. "That and you use contractions. Then again, I did refer to our friend as your old drinking buddy. You should have caught that. Fess up, how long have you been here?"

"About ten years," said Jack, resuming their walk and leaning towards her, lover-like. "You?"

"About six weeks, actually," said Deirdre. "Just long enough to turn an entire country on its collective ear."

"I guess!" said Jack, chuckling. "You've got me beat by, oh, about three weeks? Now is not the time to discuss this, however. We'll talk later. Follow my lead and don't forget to swing a little. Loosen up, have some fun. None of these people will ever see you again anyway, and even if they did, they wouldn't recognize you. Anyway, no one is looking at your face."

He paused and grinned at her as she turned beet red. She found him much more likeable when he genuinely smiled but no less aggravating.

"Now I *have* to come along. Your story sounds at least half as interesting as mine, and the natives here have no idea how naïve you must actually be!"

"Ha!" said Deirdre, indignantly. "I have been doing just fine, thank you!"

Jack laughed, and they entered the crowd at Market.

———

The next half hour was a flurry of activity and shopping that would have put an experienced mall-troller to shame. Jack seemed to know all the shopkeepers intimately, each one addressing him as Malkor the Trader and deferring to him as he shopped with seemingly endless care and bottomless purse. Deirdre watched as he noted each of the purchases in a small bound book. He glanced at her once and told her snidely that he was adding it to Brena's tab.

After the first shop, he told her that she needed to be a bit more demanding and to try to get him to buy things for her. Deirdre fell into the role, and Jack acted with exaggerated exasperation, rolling his eyes at the merchants, and indulgently buying her the occasional sweet or trinket. It became a game with them, and Deirdre actually began to have fun and forget how dangerous it was for her to be in the city. Jack's eyes glittered with amusement, and he sighed and coddled her appropriately.

The real purchases, however, were made with exact calculations and were all sent along by messengers to a small house near the gate through which they would leave. Tan cloaks, sandals, snowshoe-like contraptions, dried rations of meat and fruit, broad brimmed hats, and innumerable other items were sent off with a scurrying stream of servants, all tipped generously to deliver and forget. They even managed to find a wolf-sized pair of dog boots tucked away at the back of the leather smith's shop to protect Nersh's paws from the hot sands. They also found a large pair of fur-lined boots that Deirdre guessed would fit Tor, and these were also sent off to the storehouse, all without so much as an odd glance from the merchants, most of whom seemed more interested in Deirdre than in Jack's purchases.

"While you are a great distraction, I often deal in some strange items," said Jack. "Although," he added, eyes twinkling and glancing down with a grin, "the low cut of that dress doesn't hurt, either."

Deirdre blushed again and barely restrained herself from smacking him.

The last of the parcels were delivered, and a note was sent off to Rontil and Jasper to let them know to head out as soon as possible. Jack still had one last place he wanted to stop before they left the square.

"There's a little sweets shop over by the blacksmith's corner that makes candied rose and violet petals. I want to get some for the road. They are well worth the inflated price that the confectioner sells them for, and I am not going to see any for a long while where we are going," he said. "Might as well get some before we go. Please indulge me a few moments longer, lady."

They started across the square, weaving their way between the mass of servants, housewives, and peddlers when they suddenly noticed people parting to either side of the central road, and several market-goers gasped at what they had seen. Jack craned his neck around to see what the fuss was about and then ducked down into the crowd again. Deirdre saw a man on horseback riding around through the center of the square, and she looked over at Jack, who was glancing around himself for a clear way out of Market.

"I thought that they didn't allow riders in Market," said Deirdre.

"They don't," said Jack, ducking slightly and pulling her along with him as casually as he could. "That is no ordinary rider. That is your friend Jasper's father."

Deirdre looked back at the black-cloaked figure sitting astride his midnight steed as he rode around one side of the market. It would be only moments before they came fully into his view and, for whatever reason, Deirdre somehow knew that her disguise would not fool him.

"Quickly," hissed Jack in a tense voice. "Duck down and follow me."

He grabbed her hand and led her at a squirreling run through the throng of people in the square, dodging and weaving as best as he could while trying to stay unseen. Twice they bumped into someone, and the second of these yelled so loudly that every head in Market turned in their direction.

A scream of rage from the stallion penetrated the air. Jack glanced back and then stood up, running now at full tilt and dragging Deirdre with him through the crowd. Deirdre also managed to spare a glance back, and the sight that greeted her eyes imprinted itself on her memory.

Against the backdrop of the wooden buildings that framed the rapidly clearing Market reared the stallion, the rider sitting strong on its back, looking directly at them as they ran. The horse's head was thrown back, clipped black mane waving like a dull, dark shroud. Its reddened eyes stared wildly out of its gaunt, skull-like face, and its bared teeth gleamed horribly white. At its hooves were feathers the colors of blue flame that rippled and flickered as it pawed the air.

"Don't look back!" cried Jack. "Run! That's no ordinary horse!"

Deirdre grimly ran and dodged through the crowds, throwing herself one way and then skipping nimbly the other, half tripping, half racing through the crowds. She could hear the hooves of the rider's horse clattering like tumbled coconut hulls over the muddied cobblestones behind them and knew that he would catch them if they weren't quicker. People parted before the rider, not wanting to get in the way of the demonic steed and the furious being who rode him.

Jack pulled her down one of the streets that led out of Market, away from the crowds, and the way became easier for them to move. They released each other's hands and ran straight out as fast as they were able, taking rights and lefts with reckless abandon. Deirdre had hiked her skirts as high as she could in order to sprint, glad that she had kept her trousers on underneath. She had kicked off her shoes, no longer caring what she bolted through in her bare feet so long as she could run. The hoof beats followed them, and they mistakenly turned into a dead end alley blocked by a wall that seemed at least to Deirdre very high.

"Come on, climb!" shouted Jack. "It's only about twelve feet."

"I can't climb that!" exclaimed Deirdre. "I've never climbed a wall in my life!"

"Try!"

Deirdre hunted for handholds on the rough brick, but none seemed to give her enough purchase to hold onto. The hoof beats slowed but grew louder. Resolutely, they turned to fight, Deirdre realizing that she had left her sword back at Jack's house as Jack handed her one of his daggers.

A noise behind them made them turn back. From up above on the wall fell a knotted rope, and a man's face peered down from the top of the barricade.

"Up here," he called. "Hurry!"

Jack re-sheathed the weapons, and Deirdre grabbed the rope, climbing it as fast as her skirts would allow. The man reached a hand down to pull her up, and as soon as she was safely on the top of the wall, Jack swarmed up the rope like a monkey.

Within seconds, they had pulled up the rope and lowered it back down the other side. Deirdre went first, followed by Jack. Their benefactor dropped the end of the rope he had been holding and jumped down, landing as lightly as a cat. No sooner had he done this then from the other side of the wall came a scream of fury.

"Ye had best get out of here," said the stranger.

"Who are you?" asked Deirdre, looking at him fully for the first time.

He had chiseled features, bright blue eyes, dark hair...and an odd birthmark in the center of his forehead that almost looked like a spiraling star. The man smiled slightly, small crow's feet wrinkling the corners of his eyes. Deirdre gazed at him as comprehension dawned on her.

"Yes," he said, "Ye know who I am. Now hurry, before he finds his way around the wall."

"But..." Deirdre said, confused.

"Go," said their benefactor urgently. "I will talk with thee later."

Deirdre nodded and together, she and Jack fled.

"We have to get out of here fast," said Jack. "We can't stop back at the house, so I am sorry about your clothes. Rontil has the rest of our gear, and we will just have to meet him at the rendezvous sooner than we planned."

"Can we at least stop to wash my face off?" panted Deirdre.

"No time now," said Jack. "Once we are out of the city, I will find you a nice stream or pond or something. Move!"

They continued on running swiftly through the streets, and Deirdre finally had to stop to catch her breath. Jack glanced around them nervously as the gate was still a long way off. Finally, it dawned on Deirdre that there was a better solution.

"Look," she said, "how much further is it?"

"About a half a mile to the gate, and then a couple of miles further to the place we will meet Rontil."

"Ok," said Deirdre. "You are going to have to ride then. We can go faster that way."

"We don't have horses," said Jack. "Rontil has them."

"Yes, but you have me," said Deirdre and shifted her form into that of the pinto mare.

The transformation happened swiftly, and within seconds, she stood on all fours. The cobbles felt slick under her hooves, and she scraped one foot across them to get a feel for the footing.

"Aighh!" exclaimed Jack, stepping back and stumbling before catching his balance.

He stood there, one hand over his chest while he composed himself.

"Warn a guy, would you?" he said.

She tossed her head and motioned to him with her muzzle. He nodded and warily pulled himself up onto her back, grabbed handfuls of her parti-colored mane, and lightly kicked her in the sides. She jumped forward, and then it was her turn to glare at him. He shrugged apologetically, and they moved out.

There was some traffic on the streets where they passed, and the conditions of the road steadily declined until they were riding through refuse from both humans and animals. There was a strong smell of fish in the air, and Deirdre realized why the fish market was kept far away from the regular market crowds. The smell was hideous.

Jack guided her verbally through the streets, stopping once at a run-down stable to procure a dilapidated saddle and ancient bridle.

Deirdre initially balked when he came near her with the tack, raising her head as high as she could to avoid the bridle.

"Look," he hissed. "I know this is not your thing, but I can't just ride through the gate bareback. I promise to take them right off again once we are out of sight."

Deirdre reluctantly allowed him to place the saddle on her and let him put the bit in her mouth only after he had washed it in a rain barrel and wiped it clean with the corner of his cloak. It tasted as bad as Vexanious had described, and she stood unhappily as he tightened the straps and fastened the buckles of the bridle. He climbed into the saddle, and gingerly took up the reins.

"I won't pull on them," he said when she laid her ears back, "but I have to at least hold them."

She stomped a hoof in protest, but when he urged her that they had to hurry, she moved out vengefully in a jarring trot. He hung on grimly, and a short while later, they finally reached a small gate in the wall that seemed to be mainly trafficked by fish sellers and dung dealers. There had thankfully been no further sign of Lord Ganley and his terrifying horse by the time they reached the portal, and the guards waved them through with bored expressions. Deirdre broke into a canter once they were out of sight of the walls, and they made good their escape from the dangers of the Malepoer.

Once well outside the city, Deirdre finally slowed down, first to a trot, then to a walk, cooling herself out. Jack slid down from her back, keeping one hand on her shoulder to steady himself, and Deirdre could feel him trembling. She wasn't sure if it was from their flight or from her transformation, but she tried to walk smoothly and be as supportive as she could, staying in her horse shape long after she had cooled off.

They continued on in silence until they reached a cool, clear stream, and Jack removed the tack so Deirdre could change back. With Jack's help, she washed all traces of makeup from her face, and refreshed, they picked up the old saddle and bridle and continued on until they saw Jasper and Rontil waiting at the rendezvous point. The men were sitting astride horses and holding the reins of three pack mules loaded with the supplies for the journey.

"The rest of the group is down in the valley about three miles, waiting for us," said Jasper. "You two look done in."

"Trouble?" asked Rontil, looking at Jack with a raised eyebrow.

"We had a bit of a run in with Master Jasper's father this afternoon," Jack said lightly, swinging up into the saddle behind Rontil. "He gave us some exercise."

"My father?" asked Jasper as he turned his horse towards Deirdre and paused, momentarily struck by her attire.

"Oogle her later, Lord Jasper, we must go," said Jack sweetly. "Yes, your father. He definitely wasn't there to invite us to a picnic. He chased us across what felt like half of the city, I should think. He would have had us in a dead end alley if not for a man with a strange mark on his forehead who threw us a rope. Deirdre seemed to know him."

"I know *of* him, I think," said Deirdre, struggling up behind Jasper, the heavy ruffled skirts of the dress and the cloak making it almost impossible even with Jasper's help. She was again glad for her trousers, for the dress was not very warm, and she managed to tuck her feet under the edges of her cloak. "I've never met him officially.

This is definitely something we should discuss with the others, though."

They left the trail and trotted off into the woods, leaving behind very little trace of their passing. Deirdre wearily noticed that the sky was slowly becoming even more overcast, promising snow in the near future.

"M're Satal said that there is a cave often used by his people not far from here, at the foot of the Southern Mountains," said Jasper. "They headed there to wait for us, but Nersh said that she would remain behind to guide us in because she is the least conspicuous. We should be there before nightfall."

Jack looked up at the rapidly clouding sky and shivered.

"It can't be too soon, I think," he said. "We've got some weather coming in, fast."

"I plan on sleeping for a week," yawned Deirdre. "I am not used to all of this."

Jack laughed, and said, "Neither are we, Lady. Rontil and I have grown soft with all our easy living. Right, old friend?"

Rontil merely grunted and concentrated on steering his massive horse around rocks and fallen logs. The rhythm of the horse's gait was lulling, and Deirdre's eyelids became heavy in spite of her efforts to stay awake. Finally surrendering, she wrapped her arms firmly around Jasper's waist, closed her eyes, and rested her head on Jasper's back, falling into an exhausted doze.

Jack glanced over at her and smiled.

"That right there tells me more about you than anything that you could have said or done," he said softly to Jasper. "She obviously trusts you."

"I have worked hard to win that trust," said Jasper.

"But not hard enough?" asked Jack teasingly.

"Her heart is not tied to mine, no," said Jasper. "It is already given to another, I think."

"Ah," nodded Jack, sagely. "Competition."

Jasper laughed quietly and shook his head.

"There is no competition, friend. Neither I nor you could compete with bonds formed of magic," he said. "Your 'old drinking buddy' beat us both."

Jack groaned mockingly.

"Trust him to get the girl *again*," he said with exaggerated sorrow. "Even as a minotaur, he still wins."

Jasper snorted his amusement, and they rode on in silence under the leaden sky until a patch of white detached itself from the under-growth and resolved into the form of Lady Nersh. The first fat flakes of snow had begun to fall from the sky, and the wind was stirring in the treetops.

"Tali must be watching out for us," said Nersh as she trotted up to them. "It is good to see you again, Jack! Hurry now, let us get inside before the snow really falls. Come on, it is only a half a mile more."

She looked at Deirdre asleep in the scarlet dress in Jasper's care and felt her heart move at the sight of the brave woman so soundly asleep that the moisture of the snowflakes melting on her upturned cheek wasn't waking her.

"Come on then," she said gruffly and led the way back through the falling dark.

18

When they had arrived earlier in the day, the rest of the party had been exhausted and wanted nothing more than a hot meal and bed. The entrance was only high enough to allow one rider through at a time, but the cave to which M're Satal had led them was immense, easily large enough for the horses, all of their gear, and the comfortable fire that they had quickly built on the side of the cave opposite the horses. The rest of the floor was dirt, and M're had explained that the centaurs had brought soil in to help muffle the sounds of their hooves. He also mentioned that generations of centaurs had used the caves because of their dry climate and secure location. No one was likely to find them there.

The group waiting at the cave had purposely not discussed the deep-seated worry they all felt about Jasper and Deirdre's venture into Malepoer, but when, at last light, the group arrived safe and sound from the city, tension eased and everyone breathed a collective sigh of relief.

Tor had been the first out of the cave when the riders approached, his worry plain as he sought out Deirdre. Both Jasper and Rontil's horses had reacted very badly to his presence until he had backed off a sufficient distance. Rontil had gently assisted Deirdre from Jasper's horse and helped her to the mouth of the cave. Margret had immediately taken charge of her at the entrance, grimacing at the revealing red dress. Nersh followed Deirdre inside, and Jasper and Rontil brought the horses and mules in, leaving Tor and Jack outside in the thickening snow.

"It's good to see you again," said Jack pleasantly, giving his old friend a long look up and down. "Might want to shave at some point, maybe trim the hair back a little bit, though long hair is in this year. You do look a fright!"

Tor hesitantly reached out his hand to Jack, and the smaller man took it without pause, grasping it firmly.

"I can't tell you how relieved I am," said Jack, dropping the attitude he had cultivated all day with Deirdre and Jasper. "Seriously, I never thought to see you alive again. I'm sure there is a long tale that you, or someone, is going to have to tell me. Deirdre filled me in on what they did to you. I'm so sorry, man. That is the worst thing they could have done. And you've heard about Darlena?"

Tor nodded, and Jack grimaced for a moment, before waving a hand towards the cave.

"Well, you seem to have done something new and exciting by bonding to our otherworldly friend in there. Oh yeah, I know where she's from. Turns out we are from the same place. Funny how these things work out. Apparently there are a lot more ways in and out of this world than we thought. Man, it really *is* good to see you, even in this state. Well, come on, snow is not a good accessory for either of us. Let's go in."

They went inside and began to organize the supplies while Jasper and Rontil tended the horses. M're Satal had pulled a large pelt from somewhere in the back of the cave and was hanging it up on cleverly concealed pegs inside the door. The air in the room warmed instantly as the draft was cut off, and the fire no longer lost heat to the outside world.

After the equines were fed and settled, Rontil had pulled some of the dried rations from Jack's supplies and passed them around to everyone seated by the fire. Jack had noticed Vexanious standing a little way apart from the other horses and had gone over to talk to him, exchanging cheerful greetings as he ate. They got into a debate about which of the lords or ladies might turn when the Perstalians came through, and seemed very pleased to see each other again.

When everybody was done eating, Deirdre cleared her throat and made the official introductions.

"Jack Parns and Rontil..."

"Moullard," supplied Rontil.

"Moullard," continued Deirdre, "may I introduce you to Judeth of Garey Manor, Alleen of Barrett Castle, Nersh, whom I believe Jack knows, Margret..."

"Whom he also knows from days long past," said Margret. "And before you say it, Jack, I know it was not you."

"Thank goodness *someone* believes me," said Jack, dramatically.

"Lord Tomille does as well," said Margret. "The queen, however, is a little harder to convince."

Jack looked over at Tor, who nodded.

Deirdre yawned broadly. It was getting late. Jasper had already taken to his blankets and fallen asleep directly after they finished eating.

"We think we should hole up here for a couple of days," said Judeth. "M're says that this storm will wipe out any tracks, and we need to get our strength back after the last few days. Ramor will not find us here, and neither will Lord Ganley. We need the rest."

"I can't argue that," said Deirdre, yawning again. "I think that's a great idea."

Following a brief consultation, Rontil and M're Satal elected to take the first watch. Vexanious and Jack would take the second, and Tor and Judeth the third. Plans settled, those not on watch set up their sleeping arrangements with an eye to being in the cave for a few days.

Deirdre laid out her blankets on the ground behind the fire, putting the heat between herself and the door. Tor brought his bedding over and nodded to the space next to her, looking at her to see if it was all right.

"Sure, if you like," she said.

Tor laid his bedding on the floor and placed the sword between them. Deirdre looked at him for a moment and then realized why he had done it.

"So chivalrous!" she said, smiling. "I appreciate the gesture, though I don't feel it's necessary. We've been in the woods alone, and the Nord-ouest temple..."

Tor took his dagger from his belt and wrote, "I am trying. I need to get back to who I was."

"Okay," said Deirdre. "But please don't feel you have to impress anyone here, least of all me. You know I accept you as you are."

She yawned hugely and lay down, covered herself with her cloak, and fell asleep almost instantly. Tor lay down as well but stared at the ceiling for a long while before sleep came for him, thinking about what she'd said.

The night went by uneventfully for the first two watches, and near dawn, Judeth sat just inside the doorway, hands inside a fur muffler, watching the minotaur slowly sharpen his sword on a whetstone that Jack had loaned him earlier. She marveled at how skilled he was, and wondered, not for the first time, who he had been before. His reaction to Jack had been odd when the watch had changed. The two of them danced a cryptic spoken and written waltz of words until they somehow came to an accord, and Jack went to sleep.

Tor looked up, perhaps sensing Judeth's eyes upon him, and nodded to her before returning to his work of gently honing his blade to a fine edge.

"I do not want to intrude," she began softly.

He looked up again, brown eyes flashing in the firelight.

"I have spoken to Margret, Alleen, and Nersh," she said. "All of us want you to know that we have no problems with you or the bond you have with Deirdre. We all agree that you are more of a gentleman than many lords we have known of beautiful looks and high fortunes.

Telling her about the bond and offering to break it was a selfless move."

Tor smiled half-heartedly and picked up a stick.

"She does not want to break it," he wrote, looking over at her.

"Well, good," said Judeth emphatically. "Though, knowing her, I am not surprised. There is more between you than just a sword and a promise."

Tor snorted and gazed into the fire again for a long moment, then wrote in the dirt, "If you make it to Remembrance, promise me one thing."

"What is that?" asked Judeth.

"Tell Brena I am still alive."

Judeth's eyes widened, and she stared at him in disbelief.

"Does Deirdre know?"

He nodded, and Judeth looked at him, shaking her head.

"How is this possible, after more than two years?" she asked.

Tor wrote, "Deirdre can tell you. Too long. Marshall did this."

Judeth glared at the words he wrote, and when she looked up, her fury was plain.

"He has a lot to answer for," said Judeth through gritted teeth.

Jack rolled over from where he lay close by and leaned up on an elbow to face them. Tor wiped his writing area clean and looked at Jack curiously.

"How are you doing, Ben?" asked Jack.

Tor shrugged and indicated that Jack should join them. Jack sat up, his blanket still wrapped warmly about him.

"Did *everybody* know but me?" asked Judeth plaintively.

"Well, I mean, maybe not the people in Seaport or Remembrance, I don't think...oh, you mean in this group?"

Judeth made as if to hit him with the fur muffler, and Jack laughed quietly, moving to the side out of reach.

"Not everyone," wrote Tor. "Though I suppose we ought to tell Margret, M're, and Alleen."

"How did you know, Jack?" asked Judeth.

"Only two people knew those passwords, and I thought that both were dead. I was wrong with at least one," smiled Jack. "Our boy here has the luck of the oft-blessed."

Tor snorted and wrote,

"You call this blessed?"

"You're alive, aren't you?" asked Jack, "You are with trustworthy friends, and you have managed to win the affection of someone who can keep you from harm."

Tor started to object, and Jack cut him off.

"Oh yes, you have!" he exclaimed. "Do I not have eyes in my head? She likes you, at least a little. I call that blessed."

Tor leaned back, scowling and looking unconvinced.

"I agree with Jack," said Judeth, "and I think you like her too. The sword may have brought you two together, but I saw how you ran out when they got here and how you have been tiptoeing around her since then. You two have not really been apart since you met, but she was gone all day to an unsafe place without you. You had time to really think about it for the first time, did you not?"

Tor started to write something, but then stopped and erased it. He nodded slowly.

"What do I do?" he wrote.

"Be yourself," said Jack. "She likes you, so be you."

Tor looked at Jack.

"And you? What is your plan?" he wrote.

"I'm in on this to the end," said Jack. "Wouldn't miss it for the world! Just make sure to get Brena to reimburse me for our supplies, the loss of my home, all my money...oh, and accept me back into her favor."

"Once she has seen how Marshall really is," said Judeth, "I think there will be no problem with that."

The first hint of the dawn began to light the tops of the trees above them, and beyond the edge of the hide covering the door, the grey light that was filtering down showed that the snow from the night before had covered the forest with a deep blanket.

"We should be safe," said Jack, rising and walking out to stand peering out of the cave's mouth, "providing that only the centaurs know of this place."

"Go back to sleep, Jack," said Judeth kindly. "We will wake everyone at full light."

Jack shook his head, rising to walk over to the packs they'd brought.

"I have had a lot more rest than you have of late. I'm up now, and I don't expect that I'll be sleepy again for a little while. You said you need to find the dragons. Does it have to do with their prophecy?"

"What prophecy?" wrote Tor.

"The dragon told me a prophecy, and a lot of things in it have come true as far as I can tell. Including you, old friend," said Jack, pulling out a pipe and tobacco pouch from a nearby pile of supplies. He grinned suddenly and produced the boots he'd gotten for Tor at Market, handing them to his friend. Tor took them gratefully and began to unwrap the rags he'd been using on his feet.

"Almost forgot those," said Jack, walking over to the fire.

"What did it say?" asked Judeth, intrigued.

Jack filled the pipe, then lit it with a twig he'd pulled from the fire. He sat back down with them again and pulled his blanket around him, puffing on the pipe contentedly.

"I don't remember the exact wording," he said, "but I distinctly remember it mentioning transformed princes, the great betrayer, and a stranger who would set all things to right. Utter fantasy, of course, ridiculous even...until now."

"And the dragons have this prophecy?" asked Judeth.

"Well, I heard it from the one I met, but the real keepers are a tribe of shapers who live in the jungle beyond the desert."

"A lost tribe?" asked Judeth. "There are more shapers?"

"Yes. Apparently they broke off from the main group up here in the North and sailed south about three hundred years ago, right after Tali's sacrifice. There was some disagreement about allowing the humans to settle permanently in Keyralithsmus, but when Count Nerfal's family made the ruling call, this one group decided to leave.

"When Deirdre first came to my doorstep," he continued, "I knew who she was. I don't know how she and Jasper missed seeing the bounty notices all over the city, but I had seen them put up at the Merchant's Guild two days prior to their arrival. When she mentioned you, Tor, the form that she said you were in sparked a recollection of the prophecy, and when she mentioned Marshall's coup at my lady's castle, it all fell into place. The reference that I dropped from my home world cinched it. Yes, I am from her land originally, and when she caught my little intentional faux pas, it decided me once and for all. I had to help her. So, here I am, which is good because neither Rontil nor I can go back to Malepoer for a very long time."

"Who is he?" wrote Tor.

"Rontil?" asked Jack. "Rontil is my friend, my bodyguard, my assistant, my...take your pick. He's the only other surviving member of the doomed dragon hunting expedition I joined when I first got to this world, and it's from that little jaunt that I know of the shaper's prophecy. Most of the members of the party were backstabbing scum, but Rontil saved my life in a sandstorm, and I saved him from the dragon.

"You see, I was the one they sent to sneak in, and I was the one who struck a deal with the dragon after I overheard that the others planned to kill me when I was done poisoning his water supply. I told the dragon about the poison, and he gave me my life and some gold, quite enough to start my own smuggling business and keep me happy for a long time. I made Rontil hang back while the others rushed in to finish the 'dying' dragon, only to find that he was quite well indeed. They were cooked to a crisp. Not a nice way to go, but I wasn't too thrilled about their plans for me, so I didn't care.

"Rontil and I have been partners since. He watched over the operations in Malepoer while I was in Remembrance. We aren't rich enough to get noticed, but we can get something done fast and well when we need to. He heard the prophecy from the dragon as well, and when you told us, he also realized what was going on."

"Does he mind leaving home so suddenly?" asked Judeth.

"No, I don't think so. We wander so much that this isn't too much of a difference. We can always replace anything we lose on this venture, and we learned a long time ago to cut our losses if things got too risky. He says he is from a nomadic people, on his father's side at least, and he likes being on the move. Truth is, he's pretty closed-mouthed about his heritage."

He stood again and walked over to the pile of packs. Selecting one, he took it over to the fire and began to rifle through the supplies.

"I'm gonna start breakfast," he said. "I am starving, and I am sure the rest of the group is as well."

Judeth glanced over at Tor, but Tor's attention was focused on Deirdre's sleeping form, a thoughtful look on his face. Judeth smiled and went to help Jack make breakfast.

———

When Deirdre finally awoke, it was past noon, and all of her companions were awake and occupied with various tasks. She sat up, yawned, and stretched, looking about her in awe.

The cavern, which she had not seen well the previous night, was easily the size of a small house and had several smaller chambers leading off from it. The horses were staked along one side of the main cave with nosebags buckled to their halter straps. Vexanious was not among their number, but his tack lay in a pile nearby. Deirdre guessed that her friend was somewhere outside enjoying the bright sun.

She glanced up at the ceiling, marveling at the roof of the cave before looking at the rest of it. Smooth and dry, it was the best place for hiding, especially if the group was made of man-sized beings or larger. Looking around, she spied Jack sitting by the entrance cleaning up the ancient tack they had bought, and Rontil sitting nearby, smoking something in a small clay pipe. Judeth, Alleen, and Margret were moving supplies from one pack to several others, and Jasper sat with Nersh examining one of his maps.

In the bright patch of sun just inside the door knelt M're Satal, looking comfortable and half asleep in the warm sun. Deirdre watched him smile as he dozed and wondered what he might be thinking about. His ears moved to catch half-heard sounds on the air. She'd scarcely had the chance to see him in daylight before, and she thought anew at how alien he looked to her, even compared to Tor.

Thinking of Tor, she turned to look for him, but did not see him inside. Deirdre pulled herself to her feet and stretched again, feeling very stiff. She struggled into her boots and wrapped her cloak around her, intending to first take care of an urgent need outside.

Judeth waved her over, and Deirdre picked her way across the floor to where the other women sat busily sorting dried meats and vegetables into packets.

"We are resting here today," said Judeth. "Alleen and Jasper have decided to go north tomorrow morning when the rest of us head south."

"Where is Tor?" she asked.

"He is outside, getting some fresh air. It looks like we may get some more snow. Jasper and Alleen went for a walk earlier, but Tor said he wanted to do a little exploring. Vexanious is with him."

Deirdre's stomach growled, and Judeth smiled.

"There are some fish packets toasting by the fire," she said. "Jack and Rontil went fishing after our early breakfast. Have some."

"All right," said Deirdre. "I'll be back momentarily."

Stepping outside and breathing the cold, snow-laden air, Deirdre couldn't help thinking of her home in New Hampshire, and of her grandfather, Randolph. A pang of true homesickness went through her, and she suddenly wished with all her being to be home again. She wanted to sleep for days and forget the craziness that she had gone through for the past five and a half weeks. She nodded at M're Satal as she greeted him on the way out of the cave and reflected again on how truly alien this world was from her own. She sighed deeply and reminded herself that there was no way back until everything was taken care of here, and even then, she didn't think she'd go back for very long. Her homesickness subsided, but it was still there, a dull ache in her breast.

Climbing over some low rocks and boulders, she found herself a secluded niche screened by bracken where she felt she had some privacy. Emerging a few minutes later, she stood and watched the sun slowly fade behind more leaden snow clouds, and the bright, golden light fade from the air.

A sound caught her attention, soft at first, then growing louder and more insistent. It was someone singing, someone with an incredibly melodious voice that filled the air with a tone so pure that her heart thrilled with the tenor of it. She had heard that voice once before, and she followed the song, scrambling through the brush, determined to find its source. She glanced back once at M're Satal to see him still sleeping in the snow, and she wondered if he even heard the singing. She doubted it. This seemed to be for her alone.

Climbing to the top of a small rise, Deirdre looked down into a little hollow to see the unicorn standing a short distance away from her, eyes closed and mouth open in song. The sun passed back out from behind the clouds, bathing the little space in gold and causing rainbows of dappled brilliance to play across the unicorn's silken hide. Deirdre stood transfixed. The scene was magical, and the strength of it rendered her incapable of thought or action. At that moment, the only thing that existed for her was the unicorn and its song. All of the trials she had been through were temporarily forgotten, and all of the anger she harbored against those who had made her friends suffer faded away.

The song ended, and the unicorn opened his eyes. He turned to look at where Deirdre was standing and bowed his head. Deirdre curtsied in return, swallowing hard, and forced herself not to blink for fear that he would vanish again.

"My lady," he said, melodiously, "thou art well-come."

Deirdre was not surprised to recognize the voice as that of their rescuer from the day before. Even though she had guessed his identity, it made a difference to actually see him in his true form.

"You are Rathal, correct?" she asked, walking a step closer.

"I am," he said, "and thou art the Lady Deirdre Ettar nee' Hawes."

"Yes," said Deirdre, still astounded. She swallowed and managed to pull herself together a little more. "Thank you for saving us yesterday."

Rathal inclined his head in acknowledgement, and Deirdre watched the spiraled horn as it moved, amazed by its slender, fragile length.

"Thou art the first shaper I have allowed to see me in this form in over three hundred years," said the unicorn. "I could scarce not do the courtesy of helping thee, having seen thee this far."

"Why *are* you helping me?" asked Deirdre. "Not that I am not grateful –I am– but I was not expecting the grace of your assistance. Why are you risking yourself for me?"

The unicorn gazed at her for a long moment with his crystal blue eyes, and then walked closer until he stood a scant two feet from her.

"Thou art the last chance for this land to remain as it was meant to be. Once, a long time ago, there were no humans in this country. Then, three hundred years ago, we invited a wandering soldier of good heart to bring his family in, to be a sort of ambassador to humans that might follow. Follow they did, not a full half a year later, in the guise of a holy army whose purpose it was to stamp out the demons that overran this land." The unicorn snorted angrily. "Demons. Us. Thy family, mine, Tali's...In the battle that followed, many of us lost family and loved ones. It was only because of Tali's sacrifice that we were able to drive the army back over the mountains."

Rathal swished his tail agitatedly, but otherwise was still as stone.

"This time, there is no Tali to save the land. Only a mortal can sacrifice himself as Tali did, so I cannot offer myself up to the gods. Thou are not wholly of this land, so thy blood is unfit as well, but that same blood carries in it the ability to become a dragon. The dragons will rally to the call of any of Sheriados's get, and thy family doth come from her line. So, yes, I will help you if there is great need."

"Who was Sheriados?" asked Deirdre.

"Sheriados was the queen of the dragons in ages past. She lived and died long before I was born, but my grandfather knew her and described her as a bright shining star that burned for more than seven centuries before fading. During that time, she met and fell in love with a human named Durnor, and to him she bore a son, Crintock. He was the first of your kind.

"Early shapers could take any form they chose, but blood thinned with mating, until only the direct descendants of Crintock had more than one form. Most shapers never knew that it was a dragon that bred them, just as most dragons would never acknowledge the blood tie. Only one admits to it, Sheriados's granddaughter, Maricontrassor. It is she that thou must find across the desert below the Southern Mountains."

"So what kind of chance do I really have?" asked Deirdre.

"It all depends on thee," said Rathal, tossing his head so that his long mane rippled like foam on the sea. "Thou wilt only have one attempt to call the dragons. If thou dost fail, thou wilt die, and the country will fall."

"Not exactly fair, is it?" asked Deirdre.

"Thou can always turn back if thou dost wish," said Rathal softly. "No one would try to stop thee or condemn thee."

"You are forgetting these," she said, pointing to the small antlers on her forehead.

Rathal shook his head.

"In thy world, they would wither and fall off, leaving no trace," he said. "That is not really what is keeping thee here, though, is it?"

Thinking of Tor, Deirdre smiled and shook her head. Rathal backed up a step and turned to go.

"Thou art more capable of succeeding than thou knowest," said Rathal. "Have a little faith; it will take thee further than thou wouldst dare believe."

"Wait," said Deirdre. "Won't you come with us?"

"Deirdre Ettar, this is thy quest and thy honor," he said. "I will not be far off, but do not come looking for me unless there is great need, such as there was the other day. I cannot interfere overmuch. There are other forces at work in this land as well, and if I push too far, the balance will tip, and thou wilt no longer be safe."

With that, he leapt away, fleet as any deer, and was gone from sight within moments. Deirdre stared after him, and it wasn't until her neglected stomach rumbled gracelessly that she finally turned and went back to the cavern.

19

In the cave that night, the mood was one of festivity and of the comfort that comes with being safe, fed, and well-rested. Tor and Vexanious had returned with a yearling buck, and after a supper of roast venison, everyone had sat back, propped against packs or saddles, to relax. Margret and Alleen had been let into Tor's confidence, and after the uproar that followed, everyone had settled down to stare sleepily at the fire.

"What do you miss the most?" Jack asked Deirdre suddenly. "About our world, I mean?"

"Coffee," said Deirdre. "I miss real coffee."

"Oh," groaned Jack. "Oh, I do miss that. I also miss rock bands, radio stations, and cinema. And theater."

"Broadway musicals," grinned Deirdre. "I'm a sucker for a good show tune."

"*The Producers?*"

"Oh, I love that one! *Phantom of the Opera?*"

"Good choice, good choice!" said Jack, laughing. "*Les Mis?*"

"Too dark and depressing," said Deirdre. "*Godspell?*"

"Too religious! No Webber take on that either. *Avenue Q?*"

"Not my style, really, but *Wicked* was good."

"Does anyone have *any* idea what they are talking about?" asked Judeth, looking around at the others.

"Only from long exposure," said Rontil, shaking his head. "They are plays with songs in them. He sings while we are riding sometimes. It can get tedious."

"Don't forget chocolate," said Deirdre. "I really miss chocolate."

"It is so *good* to talk to someone about home," said Jack with a sigh. "I love chocolate, but those flowered petals are as close as I've come to satisfying my sweet tooth. We should import coffee and chocolate. They might be able to grow down south somewhere."

"Not to break in on the great reverie of food and song," said Margret, "but we might want to get some sleep. Tomorrow will be another long day."

"Spoilsport," said Jack teasingly and whispered loudly to Deirdre, "We'll talk later."

Deirdre laughed and rose to go get ready for some sleep. Tor followed her and again placed the sword between them. Deirdre looked at it for a moment and said nothing, but when she lay down, she placed her hand on the sword's hilt, glancing up at him. He looked at her in surprise and, laying on his own bedding, placed his hand over hers. She felt his emotions then - concern, affection, desire - and wondered what he got from her in return.

The words of the unicorn came back to her. *"That's really not what is keeping thee here,"* he had said, and he was right. She smiled at the memory and tried to express to Tor her own jumbled mess of feelings. They were hard enough for her to sort out, but there was affection, friendship, comfort, and yes, some attraction too. That last surprised her because it was new and had come seemingly out of nowhere. She looked back at Tor and saw him watching her intently, picking up on her confusion, if not its cause. She let go of the hilt and took his hand instead. He squeezed gently back, and Deirdre was still holding his hand when she fell asleep.

By a little after sunrise the next day, the group had eaten and was packed, ready to go. Deirdre sat in the saddle, Vexanious trembling beneath her, eager to be off. The mules had been loaded, and the cave was left as clean as they had found it. M're had checked the cave over and returned the hide to its niche once everything was in order.

Alleen and Jasper were on their mounts, getting ready to leave the rest of the group for their desperate ride north to Brena's court in Remembrance. Judeth had given Alleen her horse, agreeing that riding quickly would certainly be easier with two horses than with only one.

Deirdre nudged Vexanious over to where Jasper sat astride his stallion and smiled fondly at her fellow fugitive.

"You be careful," she said. "I wish you were going with us, but Brena..."

Jasper nodded. "Has to be warned," he finished. "We will be careful, never fear. Who knows? We might even get there in one piece."

Deirdre looked at him sharply at the joke, and he smiled sadly and shook his head.

"I know," he said. "Believe me when I tell you that I know how much danger we are in right now."

He took her hands in his and squeezed them, catching and holding her gaze.

"I will be careful, my Lady. Thank you for having so much faith in me. By this mission alone, I know that you trust me. Thank you for that. It means a great deal."

He released her hands and straightened up in the saddle. He then turned to Tor.

"It is good to know you are still in the world," he said to the minotaur. "Take good care of this lady, and good luck to you."

Alleen sat on her horse, looking pale but determined.

"I am glad we met, Deirdre Ettar," she said. "We will make sure that the others know you are not a traitor, and that you are doing your best for the land and all its people."

She waved to the rest of them, then looked at Jasper. He angled his horse's head to the north and smiled at Deirdre again.

"Good luck on your quest, my lady," he said. "May it be that we all meet again in Remembrance when this is over."

He clucked to the stallion, and together, he and Alleen rode off at a trot towards the distant capital, Alleen waving again from Judeth's little mare at the edge of the tree line. Deirdre watched them until they were out of sight, and then turned back to the group. She looked at them, an odd and rather unusual band, and felt a lump forming in her throat. These people, as strange and inhuman as some of them were, had been better friends to her in the short time she had been with them than most people she had known for her whole life. Their simple faith in her both humbled and uplifted her heart, and Rathal's words returned to her, making her realize that she could not let them down.

She cleared her throat and was a little uncomfortable with all of the eyes that suddenly focused on her.

Gathering her courage, Deirdre turned to the centaur.

"M're, will you lead the way?"

"Certainly, my Lady," he said.

He moved out with only a slight stiffness, glossy piebald hide shining in the sun. Vexanious followed after him, with Margret, Tor, Judeth riding double behind Jack, and Rontil bringing up the rear. Nersh loped ahead, ears alert for any danger. The sun shone in the cloudless blue sky, tinting the woods a pale grey. Trees cast shadows against the snowy backdrop and stood out as leafless skeletons against the sky.

The plan was to move as swiftly and as unobtrusively as possible. If Jasper and Alleen were caught, time would become priceless, and they needed to be through the mountain pass and into centaur lands by noon, effectively putting Keyralithsmus behind them. M're had told them the secluded pass was virtually unknown to humans. With luck, they would get through it without difficulties.

Deirdre thought back to M're's discussions with them the previous day. Centaur lands, it seemed, were also home to a growing population of satyrs, dryads, and other partly human creatures. None of them had anything good to say about Keyralithsmus as of late, and part of M're's travel had involved the gathering of information about rumors that had been circulating. He could not believe how wrong things had been going up north and was returning home with the news when they had met him on the road.

Vexanious stumbled, thumping a heavy hoof on a hidden root and cursing softly. Deirdre clutched at his mane, steadying herself, and looked ahead into the bright day. No more snow had fallen, despite the threatening clouds the day before, and the tracks that they were leaving would be ridiculously easy to follow. She glanced behind her, feeling an uneasiness, but there was nothing but her companions riding cheerfully along and discussing the weather as if on a picnic.

A thought struck her then, making her shiver, and she leaned forward to whisper in Vexanious's ear, "What's the date?"

"The date?" he muttered to himself. "Hmmm...we have been on the road for...I would guess that it would be around the end of La'arst, beginning of Firnow."

"It is the last day of La'arst, to be precise," said M're Satal from ahead of them, "by human reckoning."

Deirdre thought back to when her father had explained the seasons and how it had struck her as odd that the months in Keyralithsmus had lined up fairly close to those on her own world. She had given little thought to the time that had passed, other than to be aware of its passage, and she startled as she felt Vexanious trip over another root. Judeth rode up beside her and nodded.

"I feel it too," she said. "Tonight is the night that the spirits walk and the dead speak to those who can hear. It is the night when Lord Ganley is at his strongest, there in his black abode perched on the edge of the dark abyss."

"Halloween," said Deirdre softly. "No wonder I feel so creeped out."

"Not a good day for Jasper to be leaving us to go north," said Vexanious.

"Didn't Jasper realize that?" asked Deirdre.

"Of course he did," snorted Vexanious. "I overheard him talking to Alleen. She knew the danger of taking their leave now. They are planning to act as decoys so that we can escape. In fact, I would be amazed if he did not plan to leave today specifically to lead his father astray. I just never realized the date until now."

"Damn," whispered Deirdre. Tears built up in her eyes and began to roll unhindered down her cold cheeks. She wiped them fiercely away. None of them spoke, but all of them realized the sacrifice that had been made for their sakes.

———

The sun was high when they emerged from the shadows of the hidden pass into a fairly warm afternoon. The temperature had risen dramatically throughout the morning, though the winds that had followed them through the little canyon had chilled all of them to the bone. These same winds warped and stunted the few trees that grew at the edges of the large plain and made the landscape feel alien and desolate. All of them were still in high spirits, though cold, and the horses walked on in a doze as the sun began to crest. It had not snowed below the mountains, but there were puddles where it had obviously rained heavily the night before when the weather had gone south of their cave.

Deirdre peered out of her hood at the world around them, watching the sun touch the branches of the wind-twisted trees and highlight them in red and bronze. The puddles on the ground reflected the sun brightly, and Deirdre wished fervently for sunglasses.

"Not long now," said M're Satal. "We have to cross this small valley, and then we will be at my home. It is sheltered and will be warmer there. If you like, I will go on ahead and have some warm food and resting places waiting for you when you arrive. I also should give my Lead Dam and Head Stallion warning that Tor is coming. They have no love for minotaurs."

"That would be a good idea," said Nersh tiredly. "A rest would be most welcome."

M're Satal nodded.

"I will see what I can do," he said. "Just follow my tracks across the fields, and I will meet you there. Oh, and one other thing. I know that you have forsaken the use of your titles among yourselves, but I feel that they will be important for you to utilize among some of the beings that you meet. Most of them are still loyal to the crown, even though they feel betrayed right now. It may be to your advantage to remind them that not all nobles feel the way Marshall Rialain does."

Bowing to them flamboyantly, M're Satal turned and galloped off across the marshy expanse before them. They watched him race away, sending sprays of water into the air behind him, his white and brown tail held high like a flag.

Judeth, who was riding behind Rontil on his big, bay stallion, cried out in sudden alarm as the horse chose that moment to stumble and fall, spilling both riders into the muck. Jack rode over as Rontil stood and softly coaxed the stallion back to his feet as Judeth picked herself up, shaking muddy water from her woolen tunic and hose. Rontil walked the stallion for a couple of steps and shook his head at the limp that the horse had developed.

"He sprained it," said Rontil to Jack. "I will have to lead him from here."

"I am absolutely wet beyond belief," said Judeth. "Can we stop for a few minutes and let me change into something dry?"

Deirdre nodded, and Jack caught her eye, his glance mischievous.

"At least she's not hysterical," he said slyly, winking.

Deirdre snorted and laughed so hard, she started crying. Jack laughed along with her, and everyone else looked at them like they had completely lost their minds. This made them laugh even harder.

Meanwhile, Margret held up a cloak so Judeth would have something to change behind, and when Judeth was done, she balled up her wet clothes and tied them behind the horse's saddle. Rontil also stripped out of his sodden tunic and leggings, exchanging them for dry clothes while standing on the other side of his horse. Deirdre studiously looked the other way. Jack whistled.

"Can we double anyone up?" asked Margret. "Can you carry two, Vexanious?"

Vexanious snorted and pawed tiredly at the mucky ground. Deirdre managed to calm down and took pity on her horse, sliding off to land in the ankle-deep mud.

"Vex, do you mind taking Judeth? Here, Judeth, you ride. I'll see if Tor's gelding can handle a second passenger."

Judeth smiled gratefully at Deirdre and hoisted herself up onto Vexanious's back. Deirdre clapped the black horse on his shoulder and walked back to where Tor sat on his huge mount.

"How's your horse?" she asked the minotaur. "Think he's up to carrying two for a while?"

Tor eyed the gelding and nodded, reaching down a hand to pull Deirdre up into the saddle in front of him. The gelding grunted and sidestepped slightly, but settled easily enough as Tor nudged it up to the front of the party. They set off again, keeping a slow pace to make it easier for Rontil's stallion to keep up as he led it, and gradually, they made their way across the field. The horses puffed clouds of steam from their nostrils, and their hooves made sucking sounds in the mud as they walked.

Deirdre leaned slightly back against Tor and felt his warm chest at her back. She relaxed against him, enjoying the feel of the warm sunlight against her cheek as they rode along. From Tor, she sensed nothing but deep contentment. The calm peace of the cool afternoon was a vast relief, and she was determined to sustain the mood for as long as possible.

About a half an hour later, they rode up out of the little valley and found themselves entering a slightly more wooded expanse. M're Satal's hoof prints were easy to follow through the mud, and Deirdre listened with amusement as Jack and Rontil began a heated debate about the price of desert goods in Malepoer. This continued to escalate until suddenly, the trail led around the side of a huge rocky outcropping, and they were there.

The centaur village appeared as if by magic just beyond the rocks, a small city of brown and grey pavilions scattered down the hillside among the trees, looking for all the world like hillocks and boulders and blending in perfectly with their surroundings. There were dozens of tents - maybe over a hundred - and between them wandered beings straight out of myth. The group stopped, looking down the hill, and Deirdre watched in wonder. Here were the creatures she had been hoping to see all along: satyrs and fauns, dryads and centaurs. It was hard to comprehend seeing them all in the same place at once.

As they began to descend, M're Satal trotted up them and led them into the center of the tent city, a clearing where many creatures of all descriptions and types milled about. They made space for the riders, and all of them watched the newcomers with nervous anticipation. Two centaurs stood in front of the rest of the gathering, and it was to them that M're Satal led the party.

Deirdre dismounted stiffly and looked around at all of the eyes that had come to rest on them when they had arrived. While none of them seemed to view her with anything other than curiosity, there were some that stared at her human companions with slight discomfort and many who glared at Tor with out-and-out hatred. Deirdre was uncomfortably reminded that minotaurs were feared and hated by most other beings, and she worried for Tor's safety.

M're Satal bowed to the two foremost centaurs and made the introductions for both parties.

"My Lead Dam, my Head Stallion, these are the travelers I have spoken to you about. My Lady Deirdre Ettar, Shaper of the Northern Reaches, this is my Lead Dam, Cr'i Izra and my Head Stallion, T'la Farloth. Leaders, the others are Lady Nersh and Vexanious of the Talking Folk, Jack Parns and Rontil Moullard of Malepoer, Lady Judeth of Garey Manor, Lady Margret of Remembrance, and Tor the minotaur, formerly human and of high standing in the human realms."

The Lead Dam paced over to where Deirdre stood, the mare's chestnut hide glistening in the sunlight. She turned to eye Tor critically, lashing her flaxen tail across her haunches with a mix of displeasure and distaste.

"You may stake your non-talking beasts over by the well," she said finally. "M're assures me that this...*creature*... will not harm my people, but you must understand if I insist that his weapon be given up until you leave."

Tor snorted and laid his hand protectively on the hilt of his sword. Cr'i Izra's nostrils flared, and she stamped a hind foot angrily in the leaves. Other centaurs began to move forward, but T'la Farloth held up a restraining hand, and they stood impatiently, snorting and stomping in fear and anger.

"My Lady Cr'i Izra," began Deirdre.

"My title is Lead Dam, Shaper," said the centaur sharply. "Human titles have no meaning here with what the humans have done to us."

"Lead Dam, I am a lady to my people," said Deirdre, remembering M're Satal's words. "That title has honor. Tor will not harm you, but that sword must remain with one of us at all times as we are bound to it by magic. I will keep it if it may not stay with him."

"Shaper Lady," said Cr'i Izra haughtily. "I have little use for Keyralithsmus of late. My people and yours were here before the humans even dreamed this land existed, and yet now, our little village has become a refugee camp for any magical creature that needs sanctuary. Keyralithian laws and rules no longer have merit in our eyes."

"Lead Dam," said Deirdre, feeling anger building in her chest, "you yourself have named me. I am a Shaper first, and a lady of the court second. My allegiance is to the land, then the queen, but I will be the first to tell you that it isn't the queen who is making these decisions. One man is issuing these decrees without the queen's knowledge or consent. Our ultimate goal is to stop him."

Cr'i Izra eyed Deirdre narrowly.

"You are headed in the wrong direction if that is your goal," she said scornfully.

"Our quest is to call the dragons, Lead Dam," said Deirdre, "and they lie to the south. The man who has been lying to you has been lying to us all. He told us a group was sent to find the dragons and bring them back. That group was never sent, and so we are going to locate them ourselves."

The Lead Dam pawed at the earth for a moment and looked over at T'la Farloth. The stallion nodded, and Cr'i Izra breathed deeply.

"I am not pleased to allow that murderous beast into our midst, but I will till the morrow. You may keep his sword, and he must not go out of your sight. You or one of your group must be with him at all times. Go take care of your mounts and refresh yourselves. I will spread the news that you are all to be treated well, and I will speak with you again later."

Deirdre looked up at Tor where he sat on his gelding and saw that he was trembling with anger. He had not moved, however, and seemed to be in control of his emotions.

"Tor," said Deirdre softly.

He looked over at her, and the fire left his eyes almost at once.

"Let's get the horses taken care of and get some rest," said Deirdre.

Tor nodded and reluctantly unbuckled his sword belt, handing it to her. He then dismounted from the gelding, and they led the tired horses over to the watering trough. Deirdre slung the heavy belt over her shoulder and grinned at Tor.

"Well," she said, "at least I have a solid excuse to be near you now!"

Tor snorted but managed a small smile, and they went with their friends to find some food.

20

It was near dark when Deirdre woke to find Jack shaking her shoulder. She blinked at him blearily and sat up, rubbing her eyes. Nersh padded out from behind him while Deirdre tried to wake up fully, watching the inhuman shadows play beyond the pavilion's canvas sides, backlit by firelight. Glancing over at Tor, she saw he was still fast asleep.

"Don't try to wake him," said Jack with a sigh. "Cr'i Izra had her shaman place a spell on him. He won't wake until they release him."

Deirdre glared at Jack, who spread his hands wordlessly, "Hey, don't shoot the messenger!"

"There is a long standing hatred between centaurs and minotaurs," said Nersh. "To Cr'i Izra and T'la Farloth, the only safe minotaur is a dead one. They have to listen to their herd, and the consensus was that Tor had to be incapacitated. This is the kindest way."

"It's only until morning," said Jack. "We'll be moving out then, over the Lower Hills and down into the desert. Runners have been sent to contact some of the Alari tribesmen that the centaurs trade with. The Alari will see us safe across the desert."

Deirdre looked curiously at Jack.

"You're really excited to be going with us, aren't you?" she asked.

"Of course!" said Jack, smiling broadly. "How often does it happen that one finds oneself immersed in a page of history, especially history that may change the outcome of an entire land? I am in this until the end, my lovely lady."

He bowed to her with a wink. Deirdre felt her face going warm, and she coughed, glad of the dim light in the tent.

"So what now?" she asked. "Where are Judeth and the others?"

"Judeth, Margret, and Rontil have been asked to talk to a group of centaurs from the North, to update them on what has been going on there," said Jack. "Vex is with them, I believe."

"And we are to eat, and then sit down with Cr'i Izra and T'la Farloth afterwards in council," said Nersh. "The others are waiting by the main area fire."

Deirdre nodded and rose, taking Tor's sword with her.

"Will he be safe?" she asked, adjusting the belt over her shoulder.

"I will stay with him if you like," said Nersh. "I have already eaten and prefer to rest as much as I can before crossing the desert."

"Thank you," said Deirdre. "I'd appreciate that."

"He is my prince, too," said Nersh softly.

Deirdre nodded, and Jack led the way out of the pavilion and across the village nexus to where a huge fire burned. A giant wild boar had been spit-roasted and was being carved into generous portions by a satyr wielding an enormous knife. Deirdre had to force herself not to stare at the half goat man. He seemed even wilder than the centaurs and much more dangerous.

"Toto, we aren't in Kansas anymore," she said in an undertone to Jack.

"Great. Now I'm a dog," said Jack with a pinched smile. "Seriously, though, at least you can claim blood ties. I don't even have that much going for me."

The scene seemed to broaden, and Deirdre noticed more and more odd beings wandering around the fire-lit area. Some that she thought had to be dryads danced wispily across the sodden ground. Short, stocky, bearded men ate huge joints of meat and chatted with satyrs about caves and metallurgy. There were even a few giants sitting quietly among the spruce trees, eating haunches of deer daintily for beings their size. Amid all of these walked the centaurs, proud and noble, both males and females of all colors and patterns.

Deirdre watched a group of young, long-limbed centaur foals racing across the edge of the clearing. The one in front carried something that looked like a fox's tail in his hand and was waving it wildly around his head, giggling. His spindly-legged pursuers were shouting and laughing, racing recklessly over logs and stones. They burst into the clearing, and headed right for Deirdre, leaping aside at the last second to spring across the center and out the other side. Her perception of them in that moment was a sense of freedom and a knowledge of community that she had never had as a child. Her heart leapt as she watched the innocence of their play.

"All are here because they have nowhere else to go," came a gentle, unfamiliar voice from behind them.

They turned to find M're Satal and another, older centaur with many streaks of grey in his golden mane and tail. He carried a long staff carved with animals and arcane symbols. It was he who had spoken to them.

"This is K'ha Vrenil," said M're Satal. "He is our shaman and an elder of my tribe."

"Your pardon, Lady, for having to put your mate under a spell," said the centaur.

"He's not my mate," said Deirdre, startled at the thought, though warmed by it at the same time. She nodded at the sword across her back. "We're bound by this sword to protect each other, and he's my friend. Why did you put him under a spell? He hasn't done anything to your people."

"Cr'i Izra and T'la Farloth asked it of me for their own reasons, but I agreed to do it for a more sensible one. No one here has any love of minotaurs, for their race has a history of violence and uncontrolled rage. It would not take much for some of the younger stallions to take offense and attack him. He will be safer asleep, of that you can be sure, for there is no honor in attacking a sleeping enemy, and the stallions live for their honor."

He gestured towards the spitted boar, and Deirdre's stomach reminded her of how hungry she was. K'ha Vrenil chuckled, and they went towards the meat.

"M're Satal tells me that you may be the one whose arrival the shapers beyond the Alari Desert have foretold in their prophecies. I have met them in my youth when I traveled to their land in the south to learn from them. They are not like your tribe, Lady, for they live simply and in accord with the rhythms of their forest home. They do without a great many things and consider "civilized human ideals" to be a burden. Wealth, to them, is knowledge, not possessions."

The young satyr tending the spit grinned impishly at Deirdre, his gleaming eyes darting over her body, taking in her shape. He handed her a plate and winked at her lewdly, and Deirdre noticed that he was naked except for the fur on his legs. His interest was all too obvious.

"I hears that you likes it wild," he said, stepping closer to her, his eyes burning into hers like hot coals. "I can show you wilder things than that bull man ever could."

Deirdre stepped back hastily, bumping into Jack who put his arms around her protectively. She, in turn, grabbed his right arm and hung onto it for dear life. M're Satal snorted angrily, and K'ha Vrenil stepped forward and glared at the satyr.

"For shame, Marserius!" admonished K'ha Vrenil. "This woman should be treated better than that! She is our guest. Save your charms for the Maenads and their feckless ways."

"I beg pardon, mi lady," said the satyr, shrugging and still smiling at Deirdre hungrily. "No harm was truly meant. I just thought that you might be a bit different than most of those other human types, what seeing you been bedding a minotaur and all."

He handed them their portions, winked suggestively at Deirdre once more, and then turned to pass out food to some others who had arrived. Deirdre clutched Jack's arm tightly and didn't let go until they were well away from the satyr on the far side of the nexus. M're Satal stopped and looked at Deirdre with concern.

"Are you all right, my lady?" he asked, his voice worried.

"Yes," said Deirdre. "It's just that I am not used to being propositioned openly like that. And everyone assumes that I am "bedding" Tor. We're not even together - I mean, not really..."

She trailed off hesitantly, and K'ha Vrenil smiled at her, his manner reassuring.

"Satyrs have a certain outlook on women and sex," said the shaman, shaking his head. "They cannot help their natures but, unlike some, they do respect rejection if it is firmly given. They have also been one of the groups that have suffered most at the hands of the humans due to their ways. Rialain will have a lot to answer for when all is said and done.

"As for the other, it is assumed that when you are as tightly tied as you and Tor are, there is more to the relationship. The bond you have shines very brightly to any with magical abilities. To me, it looks like a ray of moonlight when the moon is at its most round, beaming through falling snow onto a forest floor."

"But we've only been bound to the sword for about two weeks!" said Deirdre. "How can it be that strong already?"

"Your bond is older than just two weeks," said K'ha Vrenil. "Is there another connection that you might have to him, one that was made earlier?"

Deirdre startled and looked at the shaman.

"He *was* part of my visions during my initiation ritual with the Land," she said. "And I dreamed of him once after that. He was human in both, and I didn't know who he was. The first time I saw him in person was when I was attacked on the road by Dark Wolves, and he came from where he was living nearby to rescue us. He said the sword had urged him to go."

K'ha Vrenil nodded to himself,

"This is a Land bond as well as a bond to the sword," he said. "The Land has been working through you both, I would believe, for some time. Ask Tor how he came to be living near where you were attacked. I would bet he had not been there too long."

"What does it all mean?" Deirdre asked.

"That I do not know," said K'ha Vrenil, his eyes twinkling. "But it will be fascinating to find out."

They continued on into the large clearing.

"So once we reach the jungle, then what?" asked Deirdre, detaching herself gently from Jack and sitting down on a log to eat.

"You must find the shapers and tell them who you are. They will hopefully help you ready yourself for the encounter with Maricontressor. She will then prepare you for your attempt to call the rest of her kind," said K'ha Vrenil.

Deirdre looked at the activity of the camp and marveled once again at the mythic diversity of the beings moving about.

"Why here?" asked Deirdre. "Why did they all come?"

M're Satal pawed the ground angrily, but K'ha Vrenil put out a hand to calm the younger centaur. Both of them settled themselves down onto the ground, and M're Satal spoke gravely.

"About six months ago, word reached us that satyrs near the Bearuegna Mountains were being driven from their homes. Then several of the centaur tribes were burned out of their territories below Remembrance. We all started gathering here and found that there was a common theme to what appears to be a plot to drive out of all the magical folk in Keyralithsmus. Since then, the line of animosity has been shifting southward. The notices I mentioned when we met are only the latest. All magical beings are being shoved out of Keyralithsmus. It will be the Talking Folk and the shapers next, mark my words."

Deirdre nodded, making a sudden connection.

"I remember that the stable master of the Carathusin Palace

mentioned the growing dislike of shapers and how the kin of stronger human blood were pulling away from those with the power to shapeshift. I think you're right. This is a planned attack."

"But why?" asked Jack, sharply. "And why would Lord Ganley be helping Marshall?"

"Jasper did say that he's overheard his father telling someone that he'd been promised something," said Deirdre thoughtfully. She paused to lick the pork juices from her fingers. "But he didn't know what it was."

"Whatever it is, it must be important enough to break centuries-old alliances. Lord Ganley is inviting attack by the Queen and most of the other nobles for these actions," said Jack.

"Except that with Marshall in charge of the Queen's forces, nothing would be done," said Deirdre, angrily putting her empty plate on the ground with a thump.

"Deirdre," said Jack sharply, "look at the sword!"

Deirdre grabbed the sword that hung across her back and moved it around to where she could see it. Pulling it partially free of its sheath, she saw that it burned in a cold, blue light along its entire length and cast an eerie glow on the faces of the people around her. They all stood up quickly; Deirdre slid the sword the rest of the way free from its scabbard, and Jack unsheathed his own sword as well. M're Satal snorted nervously and pulled an arrow from the quiver that hung at his hip, knocking it on the short compact bow that seemed to materialize in his hand. K'ha Vrenil held aloft his staff, and it gave off a yellow ambiance that seemed to closely resemble the light of the sun.

Deirdre froze at the sight that suddenly met her eyes. The far side of the village erupted in screams, and from that direction fled dozens of satyrs and centaurs, terror lining their faces. Dryads screamed shrilly, running past in their dresses of woven leaves, and the other, more warlike creatures ran for their weapons and armor. Behind them, driving them forward, came the Dark Wolves, silent in their attack and horrifying to behold. They swarmed rather than ran and drifted like smoke across the ground, leaving no impression of their passing.

"K'ha Vrenil!" cried Deirdre, breaking her momentary paralysis and holding the sword as high and as still as she could. "You have to free Tor from the spell! This blade is too heavy for me to hold for long!"

"Give it to me," cried Jack.

"No, the magic will only work for me and Tor. Hurry, K'ha Vrenil!" said Deirdre.

"I will free him," called the shaman. "Hold them off for a few minutes."

The centaur leapt agilely over and around the terrified refugees and disappeared at a gallop among the pavilions, away from the wolves.

Deirdre took a deep breath and cried at the top of her lungs, "Behind me, get behind me! They fear the sword!"

Startled satyrs heard her and hurried to comply. The group of centaur children ran in from the darkness, followed by several of the Wolves. The foals raced behind Deirdre, and she held the weapon as high as she could. Beside her, M're Satal loosed an arrow at the nearest Wolf, only to watch the shaft pass through the creature as if it wasn't there. He pulled a horn from his belt and blew it in a fanfare of several short, loud bursts.

"To me, all kith and kin!" he cried. "Rally the sword!"

The Dark Wolves snarled silently and advanced, staying just out of blade's reach. Deirdre held it aloft unsteadily at the ready, its weight already a burden. The Wolves feinted at her, running forward for a few steps, and then leaping back as she swung at them. They began to become bolder and stepped closer each time. It was clear they had noticed that the trembling of her arms was becoming more and more pronounced. They stepped into the firelight but remained in shadow as if the light was being absorbed or even destroyed.

No lightweight blade, the huge sword was tiring Deirdre out more than ever she could have imagined. Behind her crowded the frightened refugees who had no defense against the beasts held barely at bay. Jack stood bravely on her right, and M're Satal held his ground on her left.

One of the Dark Wolves suddenly leapt at her, judging correctly that her strength was almost gone. Deirdre swung with all of her might and felt the blade connect with the creature's body, slicing it cleanly in half as if through soft butter. The halves dissipated like smoke and were gone. The remaining Wolves backed up a pace and began their feints once again. Deirdre's arms shook with the effort to keep the sword held high.

A guttural roar came from the rear of the camp, and the throng behind Deirdre parted in new fear as Tor raced through them to where Deirdre stood. Behind him ran the centaur shaman, a determined look upon his face, and Nersh, her hackles raised and her teeth bared. Deirdre half-turned as Tor stormed to a halt beside her. She thrust the sword into his hands, noticing the way the hair on the back of his neck was standing up and the red cast that burned in his eyes. Tor took the sword and roared again, causing even K'ha Vrenil to back up a pace.

The Dark Wolves hesitated, milling about in confusion. They had faced Tor before, and the memories of that incident seemed clear in their minds. The smoky creatures slunk back and forth, seemingly made uncertain by Tor's appearance. One Dark Wolf crouched as if to leap on the minotaur and was destroyed by a clean swing of the blade before it had even left the ground. That seemed to decide the others. One by one, the Dark Wolves vanished. The last one stayed long enough to fix Tor with a baleful stare before fading away, the red glow of its eyes last to disappear.

Tor slowly lowered the sword, and the blue light along its length flickered and dimmed. Deirdre looked at the minotaur, and he turned toward her, his eyes still red. He snorted and held out his hand for the sheath and belt, and she gave it to him gladly. Then she turned to look at the assembled crowd of creatures as they watched the minotaur clean the sword and sheath it. Never mind that he had banished their attackers, thought Deirdre bitterly, they were still afraid of him.

Tor finished with the sword and handed it back to Deirdre, his eyes having resumed their normal brown coloring. He bowed to K'ha Vrenil who stood nearby, and the old shaman bowed back, smiling broadly at Tor. Turning, K'ha Vrenil addressed the multitudes before him.

"Fellow refugees," he said, "This minotaur has saved us with his bravery and show of strength. Are we going to repay him with fear? Are we not going to welcome him as we did his companions?"

There was a low grumbling from among the assembled beings, and Cr'i Izra stepped forward.

"Not I," said the Lead Dam. "The minotaur may have saved us, but I will never welcome him or any of his kind into my lands. He may retain his weapon, and he will not again be ensorcelled, but your company must be underway as soon as you can. The Dark Wolves followed you here, and who knows what else may be on your trail. We cannot help you further."

"Lead Dam," said K'ha Vrenil in a reproving tone, "you unseat yourself."

"Mayhaps," said Cr'i Izra, "but I do it without compromising my people. Can you say the same, Shaman?"

She turned and trotted off without another word, and the camp began to cautiously regain its rhythm. Several centaurs bearing litters arrived with those injured by the Dark Wolves, but most of the victim's wounds looked superficial. They would recover in time. Tor looked at them and snorted softly but whether in relief or regret, Deirdre could not say.

K'ha Vrenil led them back to the pavilion they were staying in, and they found that Rontil, Margret, and Judeth had returned safely amid the chaos. M're Satal introduced them to K'ha Vrenil and went to fetch food and drink for everyone. Nersh lay down in the pavilion and fell asleep almost immediately on the blankets, and the rest sat nearby, with K'ha Vrenil kneeling to join them much to Deirdre's delight.

"Tomorrow you will meet the Alari tribesmen," said the shaman peaceably. "They are a fair people and will treat you well. I will go with you to the desert to introduce you. They will be waiting there with horses for you all that are much better suited than yours to the desert climes. We are in luck. A caravan is leaving tomorrow for the jungle and, within two weeks, you will be across the sands, nearing the last stages of your quest."

"What will we do with our horses?" asked Jack. "Can we leave them with you?"

"We will watch your horses for you here," said K'ha Vrenil, smiling. "They will be well looked after."

"Deirdre," said Margret. "I have to tell you something. Vexanious and I have decided not to go with you. Your father needs to be warned as well."

Deirdre stood up, and opened the flap of the pavilion into the night.

"Vex!" she called. "Vexanious!"

The stallion walked over, chewing a mouthful of grass. Deirdre held open the tent flap, and he joined the group in the pavilion, still chewing placidly. He swallowed and said to Margret,

"You told them?"

Margret nodded and turned to Deirdre as she reseated herself on the blankets.

"I overheard one of the centaurs talking about having to look after horses that could not even talk, and another one commented on how unnerving it was to have one around who could," said Margret. "I went and told Vexanious, and this is what we decided to do. Count Nerfal does need to be warned, Deirdre. We want to go tell him."

Deirdre tried not to look hurt by the news of her friend leaving, and instead, pulled herself together and smiled at them.

"It's just that after all we've been through together, I thought that you two would always be with me," she said. "But you are right; my father does need to be warned."

K'ha Vrenil patted Margret's shoulder in a comforting way that somehow managed not to be condescending, and Margret looked at him gratefully.

"I will see to it that you are well-provisioned, both you and Vexanious," he said. "And you as well, M're Satal. You and Judeth also set off for the North tomorrow, to warn Queen Brena and let her hear it for herself how much in need her non-human allies have become. Make sure to tell that scamp Tomille as well, just in case other influences hold sway at the castle."

"You know Tomille?" asked Deirdre, surprised.

"Tomille and I go way back, my Lady," said the shaman, his eyes bright. "He is a lot older than he looks and a lot better at hiding his age than I have ever been or care to be. He is the most trustworthy of all of our allies, and we will need that gift before all things have come to pass."

M're Satal returned then with food and drink, and the party settled down to enjoy their last evening together.

———

Deirdre walked in a dream, the ground beneath her feet obscured by fog, and her movements limited by great stone walls. She came to the water's edge and climbed into the waiting boat, not questioning its sudden appearance in the slightest. The vessel launched itself and glided out onto the misty waters, moving so smoothly that the surface never even rippled.

The absence of sound made Deirdre's ears feel like they were going to pop continuously, and the boat glided on and on across the timeless lake. Finally, Deirdre saw a tiny flicker of light and, squinting through the darkness, she made out a thick white candle in a sturdy holder sitting on the shore of a small island. Something gleamed next to it, a dull iron glimmer that made her shiver and think of chains by another lake in another time.

Moments later, the boat grounded itself with a soft chuff of wood on sand, and Deirdre stepped out onto the island. The boat slipped back into the water as soon as she was on the shore, and it sailed away as silently as it had come, becoming swallowed by the darkness almost immediately. Alone and without means to leave, Deirdre looked at the candle and then at the iron chains bolted to a huge, rocky pedestal. She was back in the cave.

There were no hallucinations involved this time, and she wondered exactly what was expected of her. She shuddered at the memory of being locked in the manacles and of the sands rising and terrifying her. Was she meant to do it again, this time without drugs or ritual to give them meaning? There was no precedence, really. This was a dream.

She picked up the candle and looked around the tiny island. No shore was visible in any direction, and certainly, there was no easy way off. She walked around the whole of the shore in mere seconds, but when she came back to where she had begun, she was startled to find that the chains were gone and in their place was a book, the very same one that she had dreamed about only two weeks prior.

Startled, she picked it up and opened it, flipping through pages until she came to the poetic riddle she had seen before. The first two couplets were still there and had not changed.

Not-dragon fears the flame,
Not-dragon knows not its name.

Not-dragon from history back,
Not-dragon seeks out the track.

There was now a third couplet added, however, and it only increased the mystery by stating:

Not-dragon must fly high,
Not-dragon must feast the sky.

Deirdre stared at the new verse for a long time and was startled to hear voices whispering all around her, chanting the verses, first softly, but then louder and louder, echoing and reverberating off the cave walls like returning ripples in a pond, until she cried out in frustration and a touch of fear, "What does it all mean?"

Silence fell suddenly, returning the air to its deafening stillness, and as the last whispers faded, there was an echoing clang in the distance, as if a large, metallic object had been struck.

The dream was over.

21

Dawn found Deirdre once more bidding friends farewell.

It was a cold morning to be doing so, adding sunless misery to the mix and making her feel like she was being somehow abandoned. Margret sat astride Vexanious, looking pale and lovely in the grey morning light. The stallion stood proudly, head lifted high, pawing at the ground. Judeth sat calmly on a gelding the centaurs had found for her, stroking its shaggy neck. Next to her, M're Satal fiddled with his packs and swished his tail sharply from side to side, the only indication of his nervous energy that Deirdre could see.

"So," said Deirdre, "this is goodbye."

"Make it 'so long,' not goodbye," said Judeth looking up at Deirdre with teary eyes. "Goodbye implies that we will never see each other again. This is only temporary. We *will* meet again."

Vexanious snorted and nodded, his long mane fluttering.

"Indeed we will," he said, "but for the record, it has been an honor, my lady."

"It certainly has," said Margret, blotting her eyes with a dainty handkerchief. "Just think of how boring or even dangerous my life would be at the castle. Tali knows what Marshall is doing to the ladies who did not go to the ball, and those who did...I never would have gone on an adventure like this by myself. I plan to tell your father what has transpired. He has to hear that you are not a traitor."

"As does Queen Brena," said Judeth firmly.

M're Satal nodded and stomped a hind foot, saying, "I will tell the queen of how you rescued me from the villagers, and how you and Tor saved the refugees from the Dark Wolves."

"And I will give her your message, Tor," said Judeth smiling warmly at the minotaur.

"Go safely," said Nersh. "Do not take any chances and do not let Marshall's men get their hands on you. He already knows too much. We may be in luck, and they may not suspect any of us to return so soon. Take care."

Deirdre went over and hugged Vexanious tightly, breathing in the warm, sweet scent of him. He exhaled softly on her hair and nuzzled her cheek affectionately with his velvet muzzle.

"Do not take any guff from those desert horses," he said and turned to Tor. "Look after this lady, old friend. You two belong together. Let no one tell you differently."

They made the rest of their goodbyes quickly, and Judeth nudged the gelding with her knees, turning its head to the north. M're Satal and Margret on Vexanious fell in behind, but all of them looked back once to wave at their friends before they rode up and around the rocky outcropping. The forest quickly swallowed them, and then they were gone.

Deirdre, Nersh, Jack, Rontil, and Tor looked at each other. Their number had almost halved itself, and they drew closer together in that instant for comfort. K'ha Vrenil gave them a few moments to collect themselves, then cleared his throat from where he stood nearby. When he had their attention, he spoke.

"We have to go as well," he said. "The caravan is leaving at dusk. We need to get there in time to go with it."

"We?" asked Jack, curiously, raising one eyebrow in what Deirdre noted was a passable Spock impression. "Are you saying that you are coming with us?"

"If you will have me," said the shaman. "I have several skilled apprentices here that can take over my job for a time, and one journeyman who can guide them. I fear I have also made my own opinions too clear of late to Cr'i Izra. She does not appreciate being corrected, so some distance would not be amiss before tempers flare. Lady Deirdre is going to require a tutor in magic, for she will need every ounce of expertise when she arrives at the jungle home of Maricontressor. Also, I wish to see the beauty of the place once more before I die. Nowhere in this world is there more beauty...or danger."

"You are more than welcome to join us, K'ha Vrenil," said Deirdre, gratefully. "It would be an honor to learn from you. If it's okay with everyone else, that is."

The others in the group nodded in agreement.

"Excellent! I had my packs readied in case you were amenable. Our supplies are waiting with your remaining horses. Two of our young stallions have volunteered to carry any without mounts. I think that you, Master Rontil, should go with one of the lads instead as your gelding is still lame."

Rontil nodded, and they continued towards the horses.

"It is a pity that my people are not more tolerant, but minotaurs are not well-loved by any of the woodland folk," said K'ha Vrenil, falling into step with Deirdre.

"Or by most people in general, it would seem," said Deirdre, lifting her pack to her shoulder.

"Ah, but the Alari tribesmen are different, you will see," said K'ha Vrenil. "They judge someone by his worth, not by his race. They wait to judge, unlike so many of us who judge first and then recant later. They are an odd race, but they are very loyal to friends and allies."

"And very dashing if what Brena told me is true," said Jack

K'ha Vrenil smiled as they arrived at their mounts and began to get them packed for the ride.

"The queen made a huge impression on the Alari prince, Al-

Basheem," said the shaman, "but that was over ten years ago. He already had three wives and over twenty ladies of the court, not to mention six sons and nine daughters. He offered to make her his head wife, but she refused, thinking that he was joking, though he was not. Regardless, they have remained friends over the years."

"I remember that she told me a little about that," said Jack, chuckling to himself. "I always wondered if there might be more to it than she had said."

"Well, it is Al-Basheem's oldest son, Al-Kadir, who is leading this caravan. He is just now nineteen and already has two wives and five concubines. The wives are not with him on this trip, I believe, so only the concubines will be present." K'ha Vrenil looked at Deirdre with a half smile. "Make sure that he knows that you are promised to Tor, or he may make a play for your hand."

"But we..." Deirdre stopped and looked over at Tor where he was saddling the big gelding. Tor glanced over at her as she paused.

"Tor? Are we officially...together?" she asked him hesitantly.

Tor looked visibly startled. He handed the reins of his horse to Rontil, walked over to where she stood, and picked up a stick from the ground. Kneeling on the cold earth, he wrote, "We never agreed on it, and I was not sure how to ask."

"It does seem a little bit awkward, doesn't it?" said Deirdre. "I do like you a lot. I know we haven't known each other very long, and we will have to have some very serious talks about what we both expect before anything is officially settled, preferably sometime far, far in the future. I don't fit the mold of the meek, retiring lady, minding what her lord husband tells her to do, as I am sure you might have guessed. I also apparently steal the blankets when I sleep."

He snorted his amusement, hesitated a moment, and wrote, "We can have all the conversations you desire. I do not expect you to be retiring or meek. I do not think you could be. It is not who you are."

He paused, his hand trembling, then wrote,

"All that aside, this will make it easier on both of us. Will you let me be your consort, Deirdre Ettar?"

He glanced back up at her, and Deirdre saw that his human skin had gone ashen. She found that she had to steady herself suddenly on Jack's shoulder, and he grinned and slid an arm around her waist to support her. Deirdre was very thankful for this as her knees were solidly threatening mutiny. Tor rose and helped Jack guide her to a fallen log, and Deirdre sat down on it gratefully, all of the blood drained from her face. Tor sat down next to her and took her hands in his. Nersh looked on with a grin.

"I guess the answer would be yes," Deirdre said, looking at their joined hands, then up to his face. "I am just a little...overwhelmed... I think is a good word for it. I really was not expecting this, but...yes. I will take you as my consort, Tor."

Tor pulled Deirdre into a hug, and Deirdre laughed as his joy resonated through their bond. As she rested her face against the rough spun fabric of his tunic, she felt an air of contentment wash over her, and she could feel Tor's sense of amazement that she had accepted him. As they embraced, something tightened magically between them with an almost audible "snap," and she looked up at him to see if he'd felt it too.

At his nod, Deirdre looked over at K'ha Vrenil questioningly.

"Ah," he said. "You felt it then? That was your bond. Pledging your-selves to one another has strengthened it further. That feeling was it settling into place, and it is even brighter now than it was when I spoke to you yesterday. Did you tell your young prince of our discussion?"

Deirdre nodded, and Tor knelt down to write once more. Jack just stared at the shaman.

"You knew?" Jack asked him.

"About Tor's history? Yes, the spirits are very good at giving me the information that I need at times," the centaur said, and grinned. "That, and I had a chat with my lady Nersh here this afternoon when I asked her opinion about joining the group. She felt it prudent that I know, especially after the Dark Wolves attacked last night. I am sure that whoever is ultimately controlling those things now knows that Tor is still alive and is with your party. Leaving today is wise."

They watched Tor and Deirdre write and talk back and forth for a few moments, and then the shaman sighed and said to Jack,

"It is a good thing that he asked her. He can begin to heal his heart by doing this."

"Do you think he will ever be human again?" asked Nersh.

"His soul has been wrenched from his body, and his body lies slain," said K'ha Vrenil. "Had he simply been transformed, it might have been reversible, but with only a corpse to return to, I cannot see how it is possible. Not without greater magics, anyway, and those are far beyond what most mortal beings know."

"Does anyone know them?" asked Jack curiously, climbing onto his horse's back.

"Only the dragons," said K'ha Vrenil, shouldering his own packs and lifting his staff. "And the gods."

Deirdre rose from where she and Tor had been conversing and lifted her pack to go. The centaur stallions eyed Tor uneasily, but the chestnut held her pack for her so that she could climb onto his broad back, and without further comment, they headed off through the woodlands.

Glancing back at Tor, Deirdre tried to process what had just happened. She could feel Tor strongly through their bond now and was much more aware of him than before. His feelings felt jumbled and complex, very similar to her own. For all intents and purposes, she had just agreed to marry him, to spend the rest of her life in Keyralithsmus as his partner...and his mate. It was not something she had expected to happen, at least not so soon.

She turned around and looked ahead, watching the light slant down through the leafless trees. In a few hours, they would reach the edge of the Alari desert and thus begin the third phase of their journey south to find the dragons. In less than two months, she had met her father, become a member of a shaper tribe, been named a lady of Keyralithsmus, fought for her life against evil creatures, bonded with

Tor, and fled south as a fugitive. It was a lot to take in, all things considered. She listened to Jack and Rontil banter back and forth from where they rode behind Tor, and the lightness of their manner made her smile. It *is* a lot to take in, she thought, but I wouldn't trade it for anything.

K'ha Vrenil came up alongside her, and they rode in easy companionship for a little while, neither of them saying anything.

"It is nothing like you expected, is it?" he asked finally.

She thought of their friends who had gone to warn the queen and her father, of the people who had died at Garey Manor, and of the individuals, human and non, whose futures were dependent on the success of their trip to below the Southern Mountains. A movement caught her eye, and Deirdre looked over to see Nersh make a leap for a late orange and red butterfly that was finally migrating south, making its slow way to warmer climates. She reflected back on Nerfal's words, way back at her grandfather's house in a time that seemed so long ago - *I would give almost anything* - and promised herself she would not fail.

"No," said Deirdre. "It's nothing like I expected. But it's more amazing than I ever dreamed it could be."

EXCERPT FROM THE IVORY QUEEN

"My lord, they went this way!"

Prince Benjamin wheeled his white gelding around and urged it into a canter, riding over to where the rest of the hunting party had gathered around a man on one knee. He reined in his mount and stared down at the fresh prints, which stood out black and stark in the damp earth.

"Is it the minotaurs, Marshall?" Benjamin asked.

The man on one knee by the tracks looked up, the new captain's bars on the shoulders glinting as he moved. Benjamin noted with satisfaction that they suited his friend well; Marshall had earned them on hunts such as these.

"There is no doubt, my lord," said Marshall. "They passed through here not an hour ago. Shall we go on?"

Benjamin looked at the sky to where the sun sat well past its zenith, casting the land into deepening shadows. There was still enough daylight left to deal with the beasts, he thought, and the horses were fresh enough to go on. He nodded his answer. Marshall stood, swung back up into the saddle of his roan stallion, and they were off again in pursuit.

They raced through the woods, riding parallel to the line of tracks. Marshall brought his horse abreast of the prince's, and Benjamin flashed a brief grin at his companion while they galloped through the darkening day. The shouts of the other hunters echoed behind them. The forest grew thinner as they crested the rise of a small hill and found before them a broad expanse of tree-speckled fields. At the far edge, they spied their quarry. Benjamin cried his excitement into the wind, and the horses fairly flew over the ground, eyes rolling and flecks of froth dripping from their jaws.

The minotaurs heard them coming and turned, drawing their weapons. There were four snowbulls, massive shaggy creatures with dingy white fur, and three smaller bulls of varying colors. The leader, a pure black bull with a white star on his forehead, stood defiantly facing the men that had pursued them and did not flinch as the hunters drew near. He stood sword extended, a mad look of rage in his reddening eyes.

The riders slowed their horses and dismounted some distance from the bull-headed creatures. Leaving the mounts in charge of the youngest guard, they stepped forward, ready to meet them.

"Evenly matched," called out the prince. "Surrender now, and we will let you live."

The creatures all laughed and snorted loudly. The horses danced in the young man's grip, rolling their eyes and pulling wildly to get away. The black bull stepped forward, his sword still held out before him.

"Surrender?" he asked softly, his eyes never leaving those of the prince. "And be sent to live on Coliseum? I think not."

There was a flash of movement on the edge of Benjamin's vision, and he suddenly found himself grabbed by his own men, his sword wrenched from his grip. His hands were roughly tied behind him, and he looked around to see all of the guards pointing crossbows at him. He looked around frantically, searching for his friend.

"Marshall!" he cried. "What are they doing? Help me!"

The captain of the guard walked slowly around to face the prince, his back now towards the minotaurs. He smiled at Benjamin, an unpleasant, calculating smile that chilled Benjamin's blood to the core. The black minotaur came up to stand beside Marshall, his own look of triumph adding to the prince's dread.

"My dear Benjamin, what an awful place to have to learn about trust and desire. You have known me as your friend since childhood, one who was always the little cousin to the prince. I have always been your trusted companion. However, I desire both your fiancée and your fortune. These two notions are mutually exclusive, but, fortunately, a good solution recently presented itself."

He nodded slightly, and the black minotaur thrust his sword forward through Benjamin's chest. For a long moment, the agony was so unbearable that Benjamin could not breathe, but the pain almost instantly receded. He found himself facing his own body, which was pierced through with the weapon he held in his own hand...only it wasn't his hand anymore. It was the minotaur's. He looked into his body's own eyes and saw his confusion echoed there before it faded, and his corpse slumped heavily on the blade. In a moment of sheer terror, Benjamin felt his new hand drop the sword, and he watched as his human body crumpled to the ground in a pool of spreading red.

The sound of crossbow bolts hissed, and there were bellows of pain from behind him. The guards dropped their weapons, and took hold of his hands, once more binding them behind him. Numbly, he watched Marshall walk over to the body and kneel down to check it for a pulse. Then the captain rose, pulled the blade from the corpse, and turned to face Benjamin, now watching through the eyes of the minotaur. Blood ran down the length of the sword and dripped steadily onto the snow.

"You see this? It is called NightBringer. Used properly, it will draw the soul from one being and transpose it into the body of another. The essence of the one who uses it, however, is pulled into the weapon and stays there."

Marshall smiled cruelly and continued, "It was easy to trick the black minotaur into killing you. I believe he did get to see through your eyes for a moment until your body died, and the sword claimed him. A fitting end for a filthy beast."

He cleaned the weapon on the snow and returned it to its sheath. Before addressing Benjamin again, he pulled a knife from his belt and then walked towards the bound captive. Struggling to be free, Benjamin found his center of balance thrown off by the much larger proportions of his new body, and he fell heavily to his knees. He looked up to see Marshall peering down at him with an uneven mix of compassion and disdain.

"I could not bear to kill you outright, Ben. We have known each other too long for that. But I know how clever you are. If I leave you as you are now, you will find some way of getting word to your sister by convincing someone that you are indeed Benjamin."

Benjamin struggled to speak; his mouth felt unfit to form words, and the bull's tongue was thick and stupid.

"Marshall," he gasped out at last, " You can't do this! We are cousins!"

"My dear Benjamin," said Marshall. "I will spare your life, but I am going to remove from you the one thing you might use to betray yourself, and therefore me, with."

He nodded to the guards, who once again overpowered the prince and tied him hand and foot as securely as they could. Dazed as he was, Benjamin found it hard to put up a struggle. The men pried his long-muzzled maw open, and Marshall grabbed his tongue and sliced it from the minotaur's mouth without hesitation. The fresh pain was sharp and bright. His mind reeling, Benjamin felt his tenuous grasp on the world dissolve as he slid into unconsciousness.

———

When Benjamin awoke many hours later, the moon rode high in the sky. He was freezing, disoriented, and his mouth was filled with gummy, coagulated blood. He sat up slowly, feeling the heavy unfamiliarity of the minotaur whose body he wore. It was very cold, and he wrapped the cloak that had covered him around him. Night had descended, and the world was pitch black. His eyesight was pitiful, especially in the dim light, but he made out the shapes of the dead minotaurs and rose to walk unsteadily in their direction, spitting and drooling blood. The taste was foul, and he tried not to move his mouth too much for fear of starting the bleeding full force again.

The other minotaurs lay cold and still in the moonlight. No one had touched them save for lopping the head off of one of them and stripping it of its cloak. He clutched the thick wool more tightly around himself. Marshall must have done that, he mused, but why? His old friend had not wanted to kill him, but to trap him as a tongueless minotaur was almost as bad if not worse.

Benjamin went to work searching the bodies of the minotaurs and snowbulls. He found flint and steel, several more cloaks, several knives, loaves of coarse, grainy bread, and a few tough, leathery apples. None of the food seemed appealing at the moment, but he knew he would need the supplies in the near future when his appetite returned. His fingers felt clumsy and huge; walking was particularly difficult due to the addition of the tail that swung about as if it had a mind of its own. The more he fretted about it, the worse it got. It threw him off his balance so badly that he finally was reduced to tying it to one of the rope belts that the snowbulls used to keep their loincloths in place and wrapping the belt around his waist several times.

It was the deep of night when he finally finished retrieving what he could from the dead minotaurs and turned reluctantly to look at his own body where it dangled from the tree. He moaned and went to see what he might retrieve from the corpse. There was only one thing he wanted if Marshall had left it, and he found it still around his body's neck where it had hung almost all of his life. He removed the sapphire heart from where it lay around his neck, snapping the chain in order to get it off as he could not bear to linger near the stiffening body for long.

Putting the pendant in a scavenged belt pouch, Benjamin slowly made his way across the snow field and towards the shelter of the woods. He had to go south and get word to Brena in spite of Marshall's plan. He'd find someplace to hole up and heal first, but then he'd try to get in touch with Brena. He had to.

At the edge of the woods, he turned back just once to look at the battle scene, and then trudged slowly into the woods, swallowed swiftly by its shadows.

Chapter 1

From her vantage point where the scrub brush lined the narrow path at the base of the low foothills, Deirdre Hawes looked out over the Alari Desert. The air had become drier and warmer throughout the course of the day, and now the hot sun beat down on the baked earth as it crept towards the West. Sitting on the centaur's back, Deirdre could see a long way out into the desert, and the heat was palpable. Her stomach churned as she considered the enormity of the journey that still lay ahead of her, and she resolved to only think of the next step. It made her quest much more palatable.

She sighed deeply. After the long weeks of travel from the Mountain Reaches in the North to below the Southern Mountains, she had hoped that they would be able to stop for at least part of an ever-shortening day, but according to K'ha Vrenil, the only caravan across the desert in the next few weeks was due to leave that evening, and they needed to join it if they were going to cross safely. There would be no rest just yet.

Following a well-traveled path from the centaur camp through the mountains, the group had made it to the edge of the foothills by early afternoon. After weeks of cold, the heat was a shock to the system that quickly became smothering. Packed away were the warm furs and woolens, replaced by the tan and white flowing robes preferred by the desert nomads that they would be traveling with.

Only the shaman, K'ha Vrenil, and the other centaurs were unaffected by the sudden change in temperature. They trotted along almost exuberantly, smiling and chatting with each other, seeming excited by what lay ahead. Beyond them, out on the sands, a bevy of colorful tents were clustered by the foot of the trail. The sight of the camp in the afternoon sun seemed to invigorate the younger centaurs, and they picked up their pace to a trot as they neared the camp.

Afternoon shadows rippled across the stone-strewn ground as the travelers made their way to the edge of the desert. The path itself was relatively smooth, however, and the centaurs and horses had no problem crossing the last quarter mile to where the stony ground gave way to sand. The hard clop of their hooves became a soft chuff as they stepped onto the shifting surface, and there they stopped.

Ahead, the small city of tents was arrayed against the skyline only a short distance away, and robed figures moved briskly to and fro between them. A light breeze caused the canvas to billow slightly and tug against the ropes anchored securely to long stakes set in the sand. Deirdre watched as the fabric rippled and found herself wondering what the inside was like. Her last camping expedition had been over five years ago, and tents were something she had thought to leave behind.

A man emerged from the nearest structure and waved when he saw their group. His voice rang out young and strong as he walked towards them, arms open in welcome. He was dressed in a long grey and white striped robe of what looked to be finely woven wool, and his head was wrapped turban-style in a long flowing scarf of bright saffron. A small creature moved on his fist and cried shrilly, marking itself as some sort of bird of prey. Deirdre could hear the bells on its jesses ring as it shifted its feet.

"Hail, K'ha Vrenil!" he cried, his voice joyous. "You are well come to our camp!"

Hail, K'ha Vrenil!" he cried, his voice joyous. "You are well come to our camp!"

"Hail, Bo-Denair!" called K'ha Vrenil, trotting forward to clasp the man by the forearm not bearing a bird. "It has been too long! How is it that you are traveling with this bold company? Last I saw you, you were with the eastern caravan."

"Ah!" grinned the man. "Therein lies the tale of an unfortunate comment to the wrong man, a young lady who could not keep a secret, and an irate prince. I was "encouraged" to make a prolonged visit to

Al-Basheem who then sent me forth with his son to learn some sense. But come! Introduce me to your friends!"

"My dear Bo-Denair, may I present Lady Deirdre Hawes of Keyralithsmus and her companions Tor, Jack Parns, Rontil Moullard, and the Lady Nersh. The two lads here are C'he Verise and T'ri Narvil, children of my sister, B'ri Renai."

The man bowed to them with a flourish.

"You are all welcome to our camp," he said. "A minotaur and a member of the Talking Folk! I never thought to see the like and certainly not together! You must have quite the story to tell! I cannot wait to hear it! And my lady, your loveliness is a welcome gift among the desert peoples. Fine gentlemen, welcome to you too!"

Deirdre blushed, and Nersh grinned, showing all of her teeth. Tor looked at K'ha Vrenil, who smiled reassuringly at the prince and then turned to Bo-Denair.

"I was under the impression, my friend, that the caravan was leaving tonight, but I see no preparations to break camp. Were we misinformed?"

"Indeed, we were originally planning to leave tonight, but Al-Kadir's favorite mare went into labor early, and he is with the mother and her newborn now," said Bo-Denair. "The foal may not survive, sadly, but he will not break camp until it is strong enough to travel - if it lives. Either way, we will be here for a day or so more before we leave, so permit me get you settled into your resting places, and we will go see Al-Kadir. Will your nephews be staying with us the night?"

K'ha Vrenil glanced at the two young stallions, both of whom shook their heads.

"We wish to be off home again, Uncle," said T'ri Narvil, pawing the ground impatiently. C'he Verise nodded.

Deirdre took the hint and slid from his back; he reached over to steady her and hand her the bag he had carried. She thanked him and accepted the pack, watching as the others also dismounted and shouldered their gear. K'ha Vrenil accompanied the younger centaurs and their other mounts a short way down the path, spoke to them in low tones, and watched them as they trotted around one of the low hills and disappeared. K'ha Vrenil turned and walked back to the group, shaking his head.

"I am afraid my nephews have little love for humans," he said as he reached them. "They will stay no longer."

Bo-Denair shrugged and waved for them to follow him among the maze of tents. People were moving around the encampment, preparing for the coming evening, and they paused in whatever they were doing to watch the strange procession go by. Most of them took no notice of Deirdre, which suited her just fine, but she could feel Tor's growing tension at the eyes that lingered on him. There appeared to be no animosity in the glances the Alari were giving him, however, so she tried to be as reassuring as she could through their bond. reaching out to take his hand as they walked. He didn't glance down at her, though he did squeeze her hand in thanks.

After a short walk, they came to a large tent of light rose-colored canvas, and Bo-Denair held the tent flap back for them, bowing them inside. He somehow managed to do this without upsetting the falcon on his fist - no mean feat - and Deirdre followed K'ha Vrenil into the tent. It was bare of furnishings save for a ground covering of woolen rugs and a lantern that was suspended from the ceiling, giving off bright light from its mirrored interior.

"This will be your tent during the journey. You may leave your belongings here, and they will be transported each night when we travel. During the day, all of these tents will be set up in a great circle with a covered common area in the middle. We Alari do not do a great deal with magics outside those that allow us to live comfortably amid the desert sands, but you shall see...yes, yes, you shall see!...that our magicians are the best at keeping the heat of the sun at bay. Now come! We shall go to see Al-Kadir. He has been waiting anxiously for you to arrive."

BOOKS IN THE KEYRALITHIAN CHRONICLES

The Crystal Pawn (March 2020)

Deirdre Hawes had never thought of her life as extraordinary until one day she met the father she never knew and thus began the adventure of a lifetime. Armed only with the knowledge that she is heir to magical gifts that would allow her to call on the aid of the long-vanished dragons, she finds herself drawn into a web of intrigue and murder where the powers behind the throne are aligning to make sure she doesn't succeed, no matter the cost. Deirdre soon finds her life in the hands of those she's been told not to trust, but trust them she must if she is to have any hope of not only completing her quest but surviving to make the journey home.

Together with several loyal friends, she makes her way south. As they travel further, she discovers that not everyone is as they seem and that preconceived notions of what is good and what is evil are often mere simplifications of a much more complex truth. When forces long-aligned with the crown begin to show their true intentions, it is up to Deirdre and her companions to safely make their way below the Southern Mountains and across the desert to the jungle where the dragons are said to reside.

BOOKS IN THE KEYRALITHIAN CHRONICLES

The Ivory Queen (April 2022)

On the run from the forces attempting to take over the country, Deirdre and her companions must cross the desert and enter the jungles to find a lost tribe of her kinsmen who hold the key to her being able to call the dragons and end the war. She also has to master her burgeoning powers and find a way to succeed with ever increasing forces allying against her as she races the clock to save what has become her home.

The Ebon King (Forthcoming)

Cut off from the people she loves the most, Deirdre must devise a plan to rescue her love and find a way to bring the Ebon King to the southern lands as only he can unite the country against the invading forces threatening their homeland from within and without. Only with the help of a some unexpected friends will she accomplish her goals to finally save Keyralithsmus and restore peace to all in habitants human and magical.

ALSO BY DEBORAH JARVIS

Wolves Running

The secret is out about the shapeshifters of the world, and as they face the wildly disparate reactions from all parts of the globe, the local groups of Shifters are trying to adapt to being out in the public mind. For some, like Sasha Wellington, the revelation of her status as a wolf shifter is not something she can reveal just yet in her role as a biology teacher at a Colorado High School. As a matter of fact, that is probably the last thing she should consider.

Things begin to change when one of her friends from student-teaching days suddenly discovers he is a shifter, and she has to find a way to get him trained so that he will be able to keep his identity hidden. Bringing the younger wolf home to her family's house for New Year's, Sasha discovers that there is more to her young protégé than she originally thought and finds herself at a crossroads between the world she has built for herself in Boulder and the life that has always been hers amid the snow-capped mountains of Wyoming. In order to make these two parts of her life work, she will have to risk not only her livelihood as a teacher, but possibly the safety of her family and her friends in order to help achieve the lasting peace all of the shifters desire.

SOON TO BE RELEASED

Forever Demond (Forthcoming)

For Marcy Collins, being at a dig in a previously undiscovered catacomb in Rome should have been the highlight of her career, and it was until late one night, when an uninvited figure enters the dig site. When the man disappears right in front of her, Marcy finds herself on the edge of unravelling an ancient story, one that is connected to the very catacombs she is helping to excavate.

When she meets the man again within the Hall of the Animals at the Musei Vaticani, Marcy realizes that there is much more at stake than a mere chance encounter and begins to research the mysterious Francis De Mond. As she uncovers more of his background, she begins to realize that De Mond and a tragic figure within the archives of the monastery may just be one and the same. As others begin to make the same connections, Marcy becomes the one person De Mond can turn to for help, and when his enemies finally reveal their true intentions, she may be the only person who can save him.

ABOUT THE AUTHOR

Deborah Jarvis has been writing for a long while and has been an advocate for all things greyhound for slightly less time than that. She teaches high school and college literature and writing, and lives in New Hampshire with her husband Rob, her son Will, two greyhounds, a fluffy lab, and four cats. Her daughter Rosalynde lives nearby.

The Crystal Pawn is the first book in *The Keyralithian Chronicles*. The second book, *The Ivory Queen*, is also available, as is *Wolves Running*, the first in an urban fantasy series. She is also working on the third book of *The Keyralithian Chronicles* and another interesting project that will be illuminated soon.

For more information, including social media, email, and the author's website, visit:

www.linktr.ee/the_rael_coyote

Made in the USA
Columbia, SC
01 September 2024

40929655R00205